# STRANGERS

# SHE

# KNOWS

# CHRISTINA DODD

HQN

Recycling programs for this product may not exist in your area.

ISBN-13: 978-1-335-08127-8

Strangers She Knows

This edition published by arrangement with Harlequin Books S.A.

For questions and comments about the quality of this book, please contact us at CustomerService@Harlequin.com.

HQN
22 Adelaide St. West, 40th Floor
Toronto, Ontario M5H 4E3, Canada
www.Harlequin.com

**Printed in U.S.A.**

# Praise for
## *New York Times* bestselling author
## Christina Dodd's Cape Charade series

"Christina Dodd reinvents the romantic thriller. Her signature style—edgy, intense, twisty, emotional—leaves you breathless from first page to last. Readers who enjoy Nora Roberts will devour Dodd's electrifying novels."
—Jayne Ann Krentz, *New York Times* bestselling author

"Featuring an unforgettable protagonist, who makes Jack Reacher look like a slacker, Dodd's latest superior suspense novel builds on the well-deserved success of *Dead Girl Running*."
—*Booklist* (starred review) on *What Doesn't Kill Her*

"Action-packed, littered with dead bodies, and brimming with heartfelt emotion, this edgy thriller keeps the tension high."
—*Library Journal* (starred review) on *What Doesn't Kill Her*

"Dodd's gripping voice will appeal to fans of Sandra Brown, Nora Roberts, Linda Howard & Jayne Ann Krentz."
—*Mystery Tribune* on *What Doesn't Kill Her*

"No one does high-stakes, high-voltage suspense quite like Dodd, and [*Dead Girl Running*] is another guaranteed keep-the-lights-on-late read. Dodd is at her most wildly entertaining, wickedly witty best."
—*Booklist* (starred review)

"Complex, intense, and engrossing, this riveting romantic thriller has a chilling gothic touch and just enough red herrings and twists to keep readers on edge."
—*Library Journal* (starred review) on *Dead Girl Running*

"You can always count on the ingenious mind of Christina Dodd to deliver fascinating, unusual and highly intriguing stories. Dodd is truly a masterful storyteller!"
—*RT Book Reviews* on *Dead Girl Running* (Top Pick)

For Tom and Scott Ham

Thank you for helping me rebuild the Ford F100.

I couldn't have done it without you.

# STRANGERS
# SHE
# KNOWS

# CHAPTER ONE

*Cape Charade*
*Washington's Pacific Coast*
*This Spring*

THE CAPE CHARADE UNDERTAKER, Arthur Earthman, never wanted to hear noises in the casket display room, especially after midnight.

But this had been a week of interesting firsts.

On Tuesday, a beautiful young woman, a grieving widow, had come into his office carrying a marriage certificate and a State of Washington Certificate of Exhumation. He hadn't even known Washington state required a Certificate of Exhumation, since he'd never exhumed a body before.

Through its entire existence, Cape Charade had been merely a wide spot on Highway 101, a place where summer tourists stopped for gas and lunch. The tiny cemetery, founded in 1879 by Arthur's ancestor as part of his mortuary business, had never contained more than 5,300 dear dead souls.

The widow, Miranda Nyugen, had been so sorrowful, so grief-stricken, so respectful of her Vietnamese husband's traditions, that Arthur ached for her. It didn't hurt that she was a beautiful woman—medium height, curvaceous, with shoulder-length, dark, shining hair, fair skin and piercing blue eyes. She had whispered her story in a voice shattered with heartbreak.

She had met Mitch in California, two weeks before he was due to go overseas with the Army. He convinced her to wed, and they had driven to Las Vegas and married. They spent the next two weeks in bed, and he had left her alone, grieving, waiting for his emails and calls. The longer he was gone, the more and more infrequently she heard from him. At last, when she heard nothing for too many months, she scraped together all of her money and went to visit Mitch's parents.

In their shame, they could hardly look at her. Mitch had left the Army, gone to work at Yearning Sands Resort in Washington, and been killed while committing criminal acts. His immigrant family was deeply ashamed of him and the shadow his perfidy had cast upon them. Rather than bring his body home to them for burial, they had allowed him to be interred in the Cape Charade Cemetery where no one would visit him, no one would grieve for him.

Miranda said she didn't believe Mitch had committed any crimes—Arthur knew better, but he didn't tell the young widow that—and she couldn't bear for him to remain in the ground here, unmourned and unloved. She would take him back with her to Wyoming to her family burial plot.

When Arthur asked why she would go through so much trouble for the husband she hardly knew, tears welled in her eyes.

Miranda and Mitch were the parents of twins, a boy

and a girl. The children deserved to be able to mourn at their father's grave.

So today they had exhumed the casket with its body from its corner of the cemetery, making sure not to desecrate any of the surrounding graves, and now Arthur sat in his kitchen and told the whole story to his wife, Cynthia, as she cooked his dinner. When he was done talking, she turned away from the stovetop and asked, "You believe all that? About the wedding and the family and the kids? When did you become the world's biggest sucker?"

"I haven't!" *Had he?*

The scent of garlic and oregano wafted from the pot. "It's because she's pretty, isn't it?"

He prided himself on saying the right thing in delicate circumstances. "Not as pretty as you, honey."

"There's no fool like an old fool," she retorted.

"I'm not old!" Better to protest age than whether or not he'd been unwise.

She laughed, opened a can of stewed tomatoes and dumped it into the pot. "Did this woman pay for the excavator?"

"Yes. I have the check for that and the cost of my services." He pulled it out of his shirt pocket and placed it on the table.

"She wrote a check?" Cynthia left the stove, came to the table and examined it. "Hmm. Did you give her a discount?"

"No!" He had.

"Did you pay for flowers?"

"Yes. But we get a reduced rate from the florist."

"Arthur." Cynthia tapped her foot. "*Where* is the casket?"

"Mrs. Nyugen is grief-stricken and she wanted to pray for his soul in the proper surroundings—"

"You put him in the chapel? Why would you do that?" Cynthia threw her arms into the air in exaggerated exasperation. "That body's been in the cold, heavy, damp ground for four years, and now it's in the warm chapel? You know what could happen." She stomped back to the stove and very, very vigorously whisked the marinara.

"It's a magnificent casket, top of the line. You know, when the Nyugen family purchased it, we wondered if they felt guilty about leaving him here or if that kind of coffin was Vietnamese tradition."

Cynthia slammed a lid on the sauce.

"Anyway, I cleaned the exterior and did repairs on the seals before I would let him in there."

"Arthur William Earthman, you didn't *let* him in there. He's dead. You *placed* him in there. You could have *placed* him in the casket viewing room where the carpet isn't new!"

When she called him by his full name, it was time to distract her. "It's only for one night," he said in his most soothing voice.

"Don't use that undertaker tone with me!" She stirred pasta into the now boiling water.

He got up from the table, strolled over close behind her and rubbed her bottom. "Nothing excites me as much as watching you cook."

"Yeah, well. Nothing excites me as much as watching you vacuum."

"After dinner, I'll vacuum the living room."

"You must be feeling guilty." Her voice was still sharp. "Anything else you want to confess?"

"No. I swear. That's everything. Isn't that enough?"

"Plenty. Here." She handed him a full bowl of greens and a bottle of dressing. "Toss the salad." She watched him toss, and she sounded more like his Cynthia when she said, "After dinner, when you vacuum—wear a frilly apron and I'll make you the happiest man on earth."

So the distraction worked, as did the frilly apron, and when those disturbing noises from the mortuary woke Arthur out of a sound and well-deserved sleep, he tried to convince himself those sounds were his imagination. Finally he got up, murmured reassurance to Cynthia's sleepy questions, pulled on his boxers, cursed his ancestor for attaching the family's personal home to a funeral home, called 911 and went to investigate.

The noises were definitely coming from the casket display room where Mitch Nyugen had been placed prior to his transportation to Wyoming. Arthur wasn't a superstitious man—his business precluded fearing vampires, zombies or any form of the human body after the soul had departed—so he kept the lights off as he crept through the funeral home, intending to catch the intruders by surprise. He figured it had to be a couple of teenagers on a dare, and he intended to give them a good scare.

As he got closer to the chapel, it didn't do his nerves any good to see a faint light coming from under the closed door—it had been open earlier—and hear a low hum, like an electrical appliance.

Reaching the casket display room, he slammed open the door, flipped on all the lights and yelled, "Hey!" And reeled back in horror.

The coffin was open.

A dark-haired, young and slender woman stood over it, doing something inside—*to the body*.

"What are you doing?" Arthur shouted.

Right away, he realized something was off. She hadn't jumped, and he hadn't frightened her; it was almost as if she'd been waiting for him. She looked up at him through her veil of hair. Her blue eyes glowed with a mad obsession.

Miranda Nyugen. It was Miranda Nyugen. "Arthur," she crooned.

He started forward.

She lifted one finger, then pointed it at the object on the top step. "Don't step on that."

He stopped. He looked. "Is that part of the body? His hand? My God, woman, that was your husband."

She laughed wildly, her head thrown back, her enjoyment rich and intense. "Arthur, you vain and silly man. Don't you know when you've been played?" She started toward him. She held a small circular saw in one hand. She held her other hand behind her back.

"You've been cutting up the body? Miranda, you need help."

"It's my own interesting little obsession. We all get to have our obsessions, don't we?"

*"No."* He turned to leave, to get back to Cynthia

and make his report to the sheriff who was on her way, but couldn't get there fast enough.

"You don't imagine you can leave?" Miranda grabbed his arm in a surprisingly strong grip and spun him around—onto the point of the arterial tube she'd stolen from his embalming set. A moment of resistance, then the six-inch-long needle pierced the skin and sank between his ribs in a long, upward motion. He had one moment of stupid hope: that she had grabbed a clean and unused arterial tube.

Then he realized it didn't matter. He knew anatomy as well as any physician; either through skill or blind luck, she had penetrated his heart.

He looked into her avid blue eyes.

Skill.

In his ears, he could hear each beat of his heart, and with each beat, he knew the powerful muscle contracted, pushing blood into his chest cavity.

*Beat.*

He writhed. He fell.

*Beat.*

Miranda Nyugen picked up the gruesome souvenir on the step.

*Beat.*

She placed it lovingly into her backpack.

*Beat.*

She leaned into the coffin, extracted something, dropped it into her backpack.

*Beat.*

She used one of the brass candlesticks to shatter one of their prized stained glass windows. Dark rushed in, misting his eyes with night.

She dragged a chair over, got ready to climb out.

Someone screamed. Cynthia screamed.

*Beat. Beat. Beat.*

Miranda turned back, and all he could see was the porcelain gleam of her teeth as she smiled that terrible smile.

*No, Cynthia. Run away!*

He waited for the next beat.

It never came.

He never knew it. Not in this world.

## CHAPTER TWO

IF THERE'S ONE thing that's worse than not waking up after brain surgery, it's waking up after brain surgery. No matter how brilliant the surgeon, having someone poke around in your brain results in bruising and swelling and disconnected nerves.

For the surgeon, success equates a patient who comes to consciousness and is not in a vegetative state.

For the bruised and swollen brain patient, success equates sitting up and not falling over, learning to hold a spoon and use it (FYI, sticking it in your eye hurts), and being able to complete a sentence without forgetting half the words. Let's not even talk about potty training for adults.

Oh! And may I say, the medical staff gets agitated when a person (me) gets confused about her first name.

My husband, Max, told them not to worry.

That's because he knows the truth. I was born Cecilia, got married too young, was the victim of an abusive husband who had murder/suicided my cousin Kellen Rae Adams and then himself when she had come to rescue me. Being dumb, young and scared (I know, excuses! But I'm trying to give you the whole picture), I took her identification and ran with it. I made every bad decision, had been as cowardly as it was possible for a person to be, but then…then I grew. I made the decision to truly be Kellen, to live for my cousin, to make myself worthy of my new name.

A six-year stint in the US Army had helped with that.

Except apparently after brain surgery, when I had flashbacks.

I know. I should be glad that I opened my eyes and once again saw my daughter and my husband, knew who they were, had their support and their love.

I am.

I am!

Any woman who caught a bullet with her head and was lucky enough to wake up afterward, and then, years later, successfully survive the surgery to remove said bullet, is glad for all the good things in life.

But while I was spending five hours a day with a physical therapist, my daughter was growing up without me, and my husband, Max, wouldn't talk to me about anything that might worry me, and that means anything of substance. Honestly, everything was about me—*I heard you took your first step today. Your manual dexterity is improving by leaps and bounds…on the left hand. Your hair is growing out and you don't look like a cracked Chia Pet troll anymore!*

Okay, that last one was me. No one said I looked like a Chia Pet troll, cracked or otherwise. But when they shave your head and slice through the skull, and the swelling extends over half your face, it's not a pretty sight. Not that I'm vain, but…

Okay, I guess I am.

As I recovered, my hair grew in white, so I dyed the

tips a brilliant green. My mother-in-law said I looked like a healthy lawn. Now I change the color seasonally, and not merely to irk Verona, although that is an added benefit. At Christmas, I dye my hair stained-glass-window red, in the autumn, pumpkin-spice orange, in February, purple because…why not? I had to re-dye the springtime daffodil yellow. I love daffodils, but the yellow turned my complexion sallow.

After a mere month in the hospital, two months in a rehab home, another two weeks in the hospital to fix a cracked hip (I got impatient and tried to get up on my own), a return to the rehab home, working, working, working, and finally discovering I had problems that would never be fixed and memory quirks that were downright scary… I got to go home, to Yearning Sands Resort.

Meanwhile, my Aunt Cora had died in a memory care center, I'd missed so much of my little girl's life she was barely a little girl anymore and my married life had faltered at the altar.

Turns out, that was the least of my worries. Our worries.

I'm Kellen Adams, and the fun had barely begun.

## CHAPTER THREE

*Yearning Sands Resort*
*Washington's Pacific Coast*
*This Spring*

RAE DI LUCA stacked up her Level Three lesson books, opened the piano bench and put them away. She got out the Adult Course Level 1A book, opened it to "Silver Bells," and put it on the music rack. "Mom, you have to practice."

Kellen didn't look up from her book. "I know."

"When?"

"When what?"

"When are you going to do it?"

"I'm at the good part. Let me finish this chapter."

"No, you have to practice *now*. You know it helps with your finger dexterity."

When had their roles reversed, Kellen wondered? When had ten-year-old Rae become the sensible adult and Kellen become the balky child?

Oh yeah. When she had the brain surgery, her right hand refused to regain its former abilities, and the physical therapist suggested learning the piano. But there was a reason Kellen hadn't learned to play the piano earlier in her life. She loved music—and she had no musical talent. That, added to the terrible atrophy that afflicted her fingers, made her lessons and practices an unsurpassed agony…for everyone.

She looked up, saw Rae standing, poised between coaxing and impatience, and the Rolodex in Kellen's punctured, operated-on and much-abused brain clicked in:

**RAE DI LUCA:**
FEMALE, 10YO, 5'0", 95LBS. KELLEN'S DAUGHTER. HER MIRA-CLE. IN TRANSITION: GIRL TO WOMAN, BLOND HAIR TO BROWN, BROWN EYES LIGHTENING TO HAZEL. LONG LEGS; GAWKY. SKIN A COMBINATION OF HER ITALIAN HERITAGE FROM HER FATHER AND THE NATIVE AMERICAN BLOOD FROM KELLEN; FIRST PIMPLE ON HER CHIN. NEVER TEMPERAMENTAL. KIND, STRONG, INDEPENDENT.

Kellen loved this kid. The feeling was more than human. It was feral, too, and Kellen would do anything to protect Rae from threat—and had. "I know. I'm coming. It's so much more fun to listen to you play than practice myself. You're good and I'm…awful."

"I'm not *good*. I'm just better than *you*." Rae came over and wrapped her arms around Kellen's neck, hugged her and laughed. "But Luna is better than you."

"Don't talk to me about that dog. She howls every time I sit down at the piano. Sometimes she doesn't even wait until I start playing. The traitor." Kellen glared at the dog, and once again her brain—which had developed this ability after that shot to the head—sorted through the files of identity cards to read:

**LUNA:**
FEMALE, FULL-SIZE POODLE/AUSTRALIAN CATTLE DOG/AT
LEAST ONE OTHER BREED, 50LBS, RED COAT, BROWN EYES,
STRONGLY MUSCLED. RESCUED BY RAE AND MAX WHILE KEL-
LEN RECOVERED FROM SURGERY. FAMILY MEMBER. RAE'S
FRIEND, COMPANION, PROTECTOR. MUSIC LOVER.

Luna watched Kellen in return, head resting on her paws, waiting for her chance to sing a solo protest to Kellen's inept rendition of "Silver Bells."

"Everybody's a critic." Rae set the timer. "Come on. Ten minutes of scales, then you only have to practice for thirty minutes."

"Why do I have to practice 'Silver Bells'? Christmas isn't for seven months."

"So you'll have mastered it by the time the season rolls around."

"I used to like that song."

"We all used to like that song." Rae took Kellen's left hand and tugged. "Mom, *come on*. You know you feel better afterward."

Kellen allowed herself to be brought to her feet. "I'm going to do something wild and crazy. I'm going to start learning 'When the Saints Go Marching In.' It's the next song in the book, and I like it."

"You can learn anything you want after you practice your scales and work on 'Silver Bells' for fifteen minutes."

No one wanted to be inside today—certainly not Rae Di Luca, certainly not Kellen Adams Di Luca, and they certainly did not want to be upstairs in their private quarters in the Yearning Sands Resort. Not when spring had come to the Washington state Pacific Coast. April and May's drenching rains turned the world a soggy brown. Then, on the first of June, one day of blazing sunshine created green that spread across the coastal plain.

Kellen made her way through the ten minutes of scales—the dog remained quiescent for those—then began plunking out "Silver Bells."

As she struggled with the same passage, her right hand fingers responding only sporadically, Luna started with a slight whine that grew in intensity. At the first high howl, Kellen turned to the dog. "Look, this isn't easy for me, either."

Luna sat, head cocked, one ear up, one ear down, brown eyes pleading with her.

"I would love to stop," Kellen told her and turned back to the piano. "How about a different tune? Let's try 'When the Saints Go Marching In.'"

She played the first few notes and out of the corner of her eye, she saw the dog subside. Then, as she worked on a tricky passage, made the same mistake, time after time, the dog sat up again, lifted her nose and howled in mourning for the slaughter of the song.

Rae giggled, and when her mother glowered, the child controlled herself. "Come on, Luna, I'll take you outside."

The dog didn't budge.

"She thinks she's helping you," Rae explained. "Come on, Luna. Come on!" She coaxed her out the door, turned back to Kellen and said sternly, "Twenty more minutes!"

"Yeah, yeah." Kellen struggled on, trying to make her recalcitrant fingers do her bidding. Even when she finally got the notes right, it wasn't a piano tune so much as jack-in-the-box music. When at last the timer went off, she slumped over the keyboard and stared at the fingers of her right hand.

They were trying to atrophy, to curl in and refuse to do her bidding ever again. But the physical therapists assured her she could combat this. She had to create new nerve ways, train another part of her brain to handle the work, and since two hands were better than one and her right hand was her dominant hand, the battle was worth fighting. But every day, the forty minutes at the keyboard left her drained and discouraged.

Behind her, Max said, "Turn around and let me rub your hands."

She noticed he did not say, *That was good*. Or even, *That was better*.

Max didn't tell lies.

Kellen sighed and swiveled on the piano bench. Again that Rolodex in her brain clicked in:

**MAX DI LUCA:**
MALE, 38YO, 6'5", 220LBS, ITALIAN-AMERICAN, FORMER FOOT-BALL PLAYER. HANDSOME, TANNED, CURLY BLACK HAIR, BROWN EYES SURROUNDED BY LONG BLACK LASHES. ONCE HIGH UP IN THE DI LUCA FAMILY CORPORATION, STEPPED DOWN TO RAISE HIS DAUGHTER, NOW DIRECTOR OF THE FAMILY'S YEARNING SANDS RESORT ON THE WASHINGTON COAST. KIND, GENEROUS, RESPONSIBLE, LOVING. A STICKLER FOR DUTY. FAR TOO MUCH WILLPOWER, WHICH IS IRRITATING TO KELLEN IN MATTERS RELATING TO THEIR MARITAL STATE.

He took her right hand gently in both of his and, starting at the wrist, he massaged her palm, her thumb, her fingers. He used a lavender-scented oil, and stretched and worked the muscles and bones while she moaned with pleasure.

He listened with a slight smile, and when she looked into his face, she realized his lips looked fuller, he had a dark flush over his cheekbones and his nostrils flared as he breathed. She looked down at his jeans, leaned close and whispered, "Max, I'm done with practice. Why don't we wander up to our bedroom and I'll rub your…hand, too."

He met her eyes. He stopped his massage. Except for the rise and fall of his chest, he was frozen in that pose of incipient passion.

Then he sat back and sighed. "Doctor says no."

"Doctor said be careful."

"Woman, if I could be careful, I would. As it is, nothing is best."

"I am torn between being flattered and frustrated." She thought about it. "Mostly frustrated."

"*I'm* just fine." Max didn't usually resort to sarcasm, so that told her a lot. Married almost two years and no sex. He was a good man, but he was coming to the end of his patience.

"If we're refraining because we're worried I'm going to pop a blood vessel while in the throes of passion, I'd like to point out there are solutions that *you* might enjoy."

"That isn't fair to you."

"You're massaging my hand. That's pretty wonderful."

"Not the same." Again he took her tired hand and went to work.

Bitterly she said, "*Kellen's Brain*. It's like a bad sci-fi fantasy."

He laughed. "It's improving all the time." When he had made her hand relax and Kellen relax with it, he said, "I've been thinking—the Di Luca family owns Isla Paraíso off the coast of Northern California. The family bought the island seventy years ago with the idea of placing a resort on the island, but now that doesn't seem likely. Someone needs to go there, look things over, make decisions about its fate."

Kellen nodded. "You want to go there? See what you think?"

"Actually, I thought we should all go there."

He was still working her hand, but with a little too much forcefulness and concentration.

"Ouch," she said softly.

He pulled away, horrified. "Did I hurt you?"

"Not at all. Except that you're treating me like a child."

"What do you mean?"

"You're not telling me what's really going on. Why do you want to go to this island?"

"I told you—"

"I don't doubt that what you told me is the truth. But it's not all the truth. Max, what's wrong?"

Max sighed, an understatement of a sigh, as if he dreaded what he was about to say. "You're not going to like it."

"I gathered that."

"Mitch Nyugen."

"What about him? He's dead." She remembered she couldn't always trust *Kellen's Brain*. "Isn't he?"

"Yes. He was buried in the Cape Charade Cemetery."

"*Was* buried?" Unease stirred in her belly.

"This week, his widow arrived from Wyoming."

"He wasn't married." That brain thing. "Was he?"

"No." Max was as sure as Kellen was not. "Yet the woman who claimed to be his widow had all the necessary paperwork to have his body exhumed."

"Oh, no."

"She had the coffin placed in the chapel. Last night, the undertaker, Arthur Earthman, found her there, with the coffin open. She murdered him, and almost killed his wife, Cynthia. The widow escaped ahead of the sheriff, and she left her calling card."

Kellen knew. She knew what Max was going to say. "She cut off Mitch's hands."

"And took them." Max looked up at her, his brown eyes wretched with fear. "Mara Philippi is back. And she's here."

# CHAPTER FOUR

KELLEN FELT THE same terror that shone in Max's eyes.

Mara Philippi. My God. That nightmare had been put away once. All the terror, all the horror that was Mara Philippi had been in federal prison in solitary confinement. "I knew I'd seen her. At our wedding, talking to Rae."

"Yes."

"Tell me again how she escaped the prison?"

"She is a master at manipulating people, giving them what they want and getting a favor in return. You know how her people feel about her."

"Fanatical dedication. Until she kills them and takes their hands for her grisly souvenirs."

"You killed Mitch. She never got his hands."

"Until now." Kellen took a few breaths, gave herself some time to ease that feeling of claustrophobic fear, before replying. "You think if we went to this island, we would be safe."

"I would like to hope so. If we went quietly, quickly, without fuss."

"How soon?"

"Right away."

"Who's going to catch Mara?"

"Not you, my darling. You are still recovering." He cupped her atrophied hand again.

"I've been recovering for more than two years!"

"Recovering from having a bullet removed from your brain!" Max could be forceful when he wished. "You're not going to track Mara down. We've got every kind of law enforcement on the case. Local police, state police, Coast Guard, FBI, Interpol. Law enforcement hates when civilians try to handle crimes by themselves, mostly because people end up dead."

"I know."

"Plus they want Mara back behind bars. Do you know how foolish they look that she escaped and they didn't even know it?"

"I suspect. But we live at Yearning Sands Resort." Kellen waved a hand around at their luxurious manager quarters. "We're protected by a great security team."

"We are. But Mara worked here. She knows this place far too well for comfort, so let's not put our people in the line of fire."

"Of course, you're right. But we can't leave right away. Rae has a week of school left."

"She's homeschooled. By my mother. With five other children. I've already hired extra protection for the children. It won't be hard to convince the parents to be careful. Cape Charade is abuzz with horror since last night's murder. Killing the undertaker…cutting off the hands of a corpse…" Max looked pale and sweaty. "Do you know why Cynthia Earthman is alive? Because Mara gave her a message for you."

"For me? Not you?"

"For you," he repeated. "She told Cynthia, 'Tell Kellen I'll take everything from her, the way she took everything from me. I'll make her sorry she betrayed me.'"

"I didn't betray her!" Silly to care, but a knee-jerk reaction.

"And you're not the one who brought her down. I did." Max had tackled Mara before she fired a fatal shot into Kellen. "But the message was specifically for you."

"At one time, she considered me a friend." Once, when Kellen had received a threatening gift, Mara had been kind. She had offered help. "She thinks she knows me."

"She's a serial killer with issues we can't imagine."

Kellen could imagine a few of them. "When she was handcuffed, and we were waiting for law enforcement to pick her up, she said, 'I chose you as my opponent because I thought we were alike, that you were worthy.'"

"Alike in strength, she meant, and worthy of a good fight. She still sees you as her opponent."

"And as a false friend. You know what else she said? She said, 'You think I'm done? I'll never be done.'" Kellen balled her hands into fists, then stretched them as far as she was able. "She'll never quit."

"She's insane."

"Absolutely psycho. We have to tell Rae."

"What? No. Rae is a child!" Max could not have been more appalled.

"She's ten, and she's a brave, savvy child. Remember when she went with me into the Olympic Mountains?" If he didn't recall, Kellen did, and all too well. "Killers on our trail, bullets flying, and that kid—

she was seven, Max—kept up, bandaged my wounds, found help when I would have died."

"I know. She was wonderful!" Max's eyes went dark with old terrors. "And I was petrified. No, Kellen, we can protect Rae. Let her be a kid along for the ride."

"She's not going to forgive us when she finds out we pulled the wool over her eyes."

"If we play this right, she'll never know."

He was just so hopeful, so scared, so concerned about his baby girl, Kellen had to yield. "All right, but we'll revisit this decision as needed."

He obviously didn't mean it, but he said, "Sure. Sure."

Kellen wanted to ask if there were any leads, but without warning, her words had vanished and she was mute, her throat constricting with terror and the desperate need to take the world back to where it had been five minutes ago, before she knew Mara had returned to deal death once more.

She had exercises for this. Breathing exercises. Relaxation exercises. She fought panic to get that first, long breath.

Max didn't recognize Kellen's struggle. "Taking Rae out of school a week early isn't going to affect her in terms of what she learns. Even my mother lets the kids enjoy the last week of school with the minimum of work."

Kellen breathed slowly, deliberately, the way her therapist advised.

Max continued, "All they do is have pool parties, cupcake parties, field trips. I haven't spoken to my mother yet, but—"

From the door a furious voice said, "You want to take me out of school for the last week? Why? Why would you do that to me?" Rae stood there, her cheeks bright red, her eyes blazing.

Max jumped guiltily, and turned to face their daughter. "Honey, it's no big deal——"

*No, Max. Wrong answer, Max. It's a big deal to her.* But even as Kellen fought to speak, the constriction in her chest and throat grew, strangling her.

*Breathe!*

Rae's voice rose. "No big deal? For you! What about me? You want to take me away from Chloe? And from Maverick and Rayleigh? We're in class together. We play Dragon Spit together. We go everywhere together. They're my *best friends*."

"I know, sweetheart." Max probably thought he was being conciliatory. But he was doing it wrong. "This is an emergency——"

"Emergency!" Rae's voice calmed. "What kind of emergency?"

Good. Max was going to explain the situation to Rae.

"We have to go to Italy to visit the relatives and this is the only time they can all get together." He sounded patient.

Kellen stared in surprise at Max. He had not only lied, he'd thought out his lie ahead of time. He was serious about not letting anyone know where they were going. But he hadn't thought out how to handle their daughter... Or maybe he had, in his own ham-handed way.

"I don't care about relatives! I want to stay here and

go to camp! Girl Scout camp. Weather camp. Robotics camp." Rae's voice hit a high note that had Max viewing her in alarm. "I want to stay here and have fun. With my friends!"

"If you go to camp, you won't be here having fun with your friends." Max's logic was impeccable.

Kellen clapped her hand to her forehead.

Max glanced at her as if confused. "Please. If you have something to say, say it."

*Stop talking.* She shook her head, frantic to make him stop talking, frantic at herself for being unable to take command of her voice.

He took her head shake as a sign she didn't want to speak, and turned back to Rae. "You'll have the chance to see your friends, I hope really soon, but we've got to do this as a family."

*Great, Max. Throw some blame on me.* Even if she could speak, Kellen wouldn't have said that out loud. Kellen had come into Rae's life when the child was almost seven. Before that, Max and his mother, Verona Di Luca, had raised her. Now, three years later, because of the time Kellen had spent in the hospital and in physical therapy, she still hadn't assumed the complete role as Rae's mother.

In a voice rife with tragedy, Rae declared, "You don't love me anymore."

Max rose and started toward Rae. "Of course we love you."

Rae shot Kellen an accusing look. "I notice *Mother* has nothing to say." She pointed a finger at Max. "Don't come near me!" She stomped her foot, whirled and ran up the stairs, wailing loud, dramatic tears.

Max stared after their usually cheerful, loving daughter. "What the hell?" He turned to Kellen and spread his fingers. "What the hell?"

*Breathe. Relax. Breathe.*

Verona stepped into the doorway.

**VERONA DI LUCA:**
FEMALE, 67YO, 5'10", 130LBS, HANDSOME RATHER THAN BEAU-TIFUL. A MATRIARCH OF THE DI LUCA FAMILY, MOTHER TO MAX AND HIS SISTER IRENE, GRANDMOTHER TO ANNABELLA AND TO RAE. AMERICAN WITH ROOTS DUG DEEP INTO ITALIAN TRA-DITION. IMPRESSIVE AND AUTHORITATIVE.

"Here we go," Verona said.

"Here we go—where?" Max asked.

"Puberty has begun."

"Puberty?" Max almost shouted. "She's only ten." He turned to Kellen. "She's only ten, right?"

Kellen nodded—and *breathed*.

"She'll be eleven next year," Verona said. "Don't you remember your sister at eleven?"

Max froze, transfixed with alarm.

Verona said to Kellen, "She was exactly like that. A lovely child one moment, the next a temperamental, shrieking virago."

In desperation, Max said, "But Rae is so mature. So calm. So capable. So kind. So—"

"So flooded with hormones." Verona was enjoying herself. "When she was motherless, she was forced to mature early. Did you think you would never pay for all that maturity? Now she has a mother, everyone is well—" she nodded at Kellen "—and she can regress. She'll be by turns rude, cruel, secretive—"

"Were you like that, Kellen?" Max asked.

Kellen shrugged her shoulders. Yes, the exercises had helped, the constriction had eased, but she still didn't trust herself to speak.

"I certainly was." Verona smiled like the wicked queen in *Sleeping Beauty.* "Ah, Maximilian, how I will enjoy this."

"Maybe not close up," Kellen whispered. She could speak. Not loudly, but she could speak.

Max pointed up the stairs, then pointed at Kellen. "And you want to tell that demon the truth of what's happening?"

He did have a point.

Verona was a smart woman; she caught his comment and pounced on it. "What is happening?"

"Mom, you heard about last night's crime in Cape Charade's mortuary." Max wasn't asking a question.

Verona sobered. "Of course. So awful. Is it...that woman who...?"

"There can be no doubt." Max rose, went to his mother's side, and put his arm around her. "Kellen and I are taking Rae now, today, and going away."

"Now?" Verona sounded as incredulous as Kellen felt.

"There's no time to waste," Max said.

"Rae was screaming because she has to leave during the last week of school?" Verona looked up as if truly comprehending Rae's tantrum. "She's going to miss all the fun!"

"Mom, this woman, this Mara Philippi, is a psychopath, a serial killer." Max's voice got stronger, then quieter. "She cuts off people's hands when they disappoint or betray her."

Verona breathed deeply, as if she was fighting an asthma attack brought on by shock and fear. "What about Luna? Rae won't leave without Luna."

"I'm sending Luna on ahead to our eventual destination with our cook."

Kellen's eyes grew wide. *They had a cook?*

"You have a cook?" Verona echoed Kellen's thoughts.

"Olympia Paolergio."

"Olympia Paolergio? From the village? From Cape Charade?" Verona sounded incredulous. "She's not even one of our staff!"

"Kellen can't cook. She can't handle a knife or use fire. I can cook, but no one wants to eat what I prepare. Rae's too young to do more than grate cheese and pour milk—and she grates her fingers and slops milk all over the kitchen. Olympia has agreed to go with us, do light cleaning and prepare our meals." Max patted Kellen's shoulder as if comforting her.

And why? Kellen didn't remember an Olympia Paolergio. Who was this woman?

Verona gave her a clue. "Long ago, Olympia worked here and she can be…"

"Difficult? I know," Max said. "But she also…"

"…will do much for money." Verona's brown eyes grew sharp behind her glasses. "My God, Max, how much are you paying her?"

"Enough to get her to agree to the terms. To sign a contract."

"A hefty amount, then."

"As long as she sticks it out."

"She will." Verona rubbed her fingertips together. *Money.*

He leaned into his mother's gaze. "You have to go, too."

"What? Now?" Verona strode toward him, grasped his shoulders. "We've got a week of school left. I'm the teacher!"

"I've called in a substitute." Max really had made all the arrangements. "With Mara Philippi in the neighborhood, we can't take a chance of her using any of us in a hostage situation."

"I'm just the grandmother!"

Kellen knew what to say, and at last, she had the breath to say it. "You're a matriarch of the Di Luca family. If Mara took you, she would bring us all to our knees."

Verona stared at her daughter-in-law. They had not always gotten along. They still sometimes rubbed each other raw. But Kellen never doubted Verona's loyalty to the woman who had given her a much beloved granddaughter. Verona nodded. "I understand." She turned to Max. "Next week, I was going to visit your sister and Annabella—"

He answered, "You should go visit the family in Italy right now."

"It will cost a fortune to change the tickets." The Di Luca family had money, but they had never forgotten their thrifty Italian peasant background.

"I've already done it," Max said. "I've arranged

for Irene and Annabella to meet you there. Go pack. You're leaving tonight."

My God. Max was really scared, and that made Kellen really scared.

Verona was a sensible woman. She understood fear. "Law enforcement?"

"I'll clue them in…but not yet." Max wasn't happy about his decision, but he had no doubts. "I want to move swiftly and without notice, and while I have the greatest respect for law enforcement, they're not known for quick, seamless action. For now, we'll handle this ourselves."

"I have a friend who served with me in the military," Kellen said. "Diana. She's a mercenary now. Do you want me to contact her?"

Max nodded slowly. "That's a good idea. If we asked her to track Mara, we could cut this hunt short."

Kellen smiled. She loved having the *cool* friends.

Verona was not comforted. In a trembling voice, she asked, "Max…what about Rae and Kellen?"

"I'll keep them safe," he said.

"We'll keep you safe, too." Kellen needed to make that promise to them as much as she did to herself.

He transferred his attention to her. "I'll be with you, and we have each other's backs."

Kellen relaxed. He knew the right thing to say to give her back her warrior pride. "I would kill for you," she promised.

"I know."

Verona said tartly, "Make sure it doesn't come to that."

# *CHAPTER FIVE*

MAX PILOTED THE HELICOPTER, a Robinson R44 Raven II, his hands sure on the controls. The morning sun shone behind them. The Pacific Ocean off the California coast stretched on and on, the swells glittering in the sunlight. As they left it behind and headed over the water, the blades chopped at the sky, tossing bits of blue like confetti…

Maybe that was Kellen's brain having a fanciful moment.

"Where are we?" Rae's cantankerous voice sounded in Kellen's headphones. "This isn't Italy."

Kellen exchanged wide-eyed glances with Max.

He pointed at the controls as if to indicate he was busy and didn't have the time to explain this to their daughter.

"Coward," Kellen said, and turned to Rae huddled into the back seat, wrapped in her bedtime quilted blanket. "We're going to Isla Paraíso off the California coast."

"California? You said—"

"Actually, it was your father who said we were going to Italy." Kellen cheerfully threw him under the bus. "We're coming here for some private time together as a family."

"We've been around the world to end up in California?" Rae used the word *California* the way the Old Testament used the phrase *Sodom and Gomorrah*.

"We did take the long way around," Kellen acknowledged. As they traveled away from Yearning Sands Resort, they left clues that would draw Mara after them. Then when they turned back to the States, they traveled with as much stealth as possible, using private transportation that whisked them from point to point quickly and quietly.

The Di Luca family's money and connections had their advantages.

"Are we there yet?" Rae asked so sharply, Kellen heard the echo of Verona in her tone.

"Yes! There it is!" Max pointed.

A smudge on the ocean became a golden shadow that swiftly took shape.

Isla Paraíso: a wedge-shaped island covered in golden grasses that rippled in the eternal west wind. The wide end of the wedge lay to the east, where a series of pocket beaches glowed with soft sands and gentle waves. From there the island rose, a strong slope ascending to the west side where high cliffs dropped into the aggressive ocean. The surf there ripped and roared in constant fury, trying to bring down the rock that dared challenge it.

Rae scooted forward as far as her seat belt would let her to gaze out the window.

Max dipped down as they got closer and took a wide circuit that offered a bird's-eye view. "The geologists tell us that this massive hunk of rock separated from the coast and drifted out to sea." His voice was warm and instructive. "But they don't know why."

Listening to him, Kellen smiled and relaxed. He was such a nerd. He knew a lot about the things he loved, and he loved geology, loved the earth's movements and earthquakes and volcanoes that had created his family's Mediterranean homeland and America's West Coast.

He began a wide circle around the island. "See there? The caves dug into the cliffs, facing west? Those are the World War II military installations that watched for a Japanese invasion. The military burrowed into the cliffs with dynamite and concrete. Some of the caves have collapsed, but I've heard some are still there and you can still go down and sit in the watch rooms and scan for submarines and planes."

"Wasn't World War II like a thousand years ago?" Rae asked.

"A thousand years ago, like when Grandma was born," Max said with a straight face.

"Max," Kellen said.

"That's what I thought." Rae believed him.

"Max!" Kellen said.

He grinned at her, then faced forward again.

As the helicopter flew over a stand of redwoods, a herd of deer fled the sanctuary of the branches and galloped through the grasses.

Their beauty made Kellen's breath catch.

Max said, "The environmentalists want the Di Lucas to turn this island into a wildlife sanctuary. Isla Paraíso is twenty-four square miles of unique plants, birds and mammals. There are species on the island that exist nowhere else in the world. Every year we have an intern come from UC San Diego to catalog the birds, animals and marine life." He hovered above a cluster of rocks near one of the eastern beaches. "He camps there, in Paradise Cove. It puts him close to his work and it's protected from the worst of the winds."

"I assume he's got a tent to keep off the rains?" Kellen asked.

"Yes, but it's California in the summer. It doesn't rain very often. That's one of the main challenges." Max followed the coast north. "There's no water on the island, no wells or springs. The main house and the caretaker's cottage both have cisterns that collect rainfall, and filtration systems that make it drinkable. Usually the winter brings enough water to fill those cisterns, but in the drought years we've had to bring water over from the coast. The island drops right off into the ocean. There's no harbor. The water around it is deep. Hiring someone who can maneuver in close enough to offload *anything* is a challenge. You can imagine what it all costs."

Actually, Kellen couldn't imagine a number that high.

Max continued, "Turning this into a resort, even one that specializes in guests who care about rare wildlife and birds, is a risky proposition."

Rae asked, "Is that why we're here? To check out the island and make a decision?"

"That's one reason," Max acknowledged. "The Di Luca family believes a wildlife sanctuary is a strong possibility, for practical as well as ecological reasons."

"So you *didn't* bring me here just to pick on me?" Rae asked.

Kellen turned and grinned at her. "That's the other reason."

Rae grinned back.

Ever since her meltdown, Rae had *mostly* been her usual lovely, funny, charming self. They'd left Yearning Sands Resort and traveled to Bella Terra, California, to the Di Luca Winery in Pennsylvania, to Italy, Morocco, Spain, Mongolia—all in the space of three weeks, assuming Kellen had figured the time zones right—and then zoomed straight to Eureka, California, where they had picked up one of the Di Luca helicopters and flown to the island. Rae had clearly considered that her parents had lost their minds for creating such an agenda, but she'd treated them with warmth. It was as if the surge of hormones had retreated, leaving her sensible again.

At the same time, Kellen was constantly braced for the next outburst.

Max confessed he thought Rae had realized how absurd her tantrum was, and wouldn't repeat it.

Kellen did not snort. Not out loud. But privately she thought Max was the master of wishful thinking.

"We'll hang you by your thumbs every evening," Max promised.

"Daddy, stop it!" Rae said with humor.

"The caretakers live there." He dipped down again, toward the bottom end of the island, toward a cottage built sometime after World War II.

Its small size wasn't an illusion of distance; it was tiny, one or two bedrooms, with a porch that faced east, a garden plot, a greenhouse and wide live oaks in the side yard. A woman came out of the house and looked up, shading her eyes.

Max waved.

She didn't wave back, but continued to watch them.

"That's Jamie Conkle. She and her husband live here year-round. They watch and let us know when someone tries to drop anchor and cause trouble."

In the rush of travel and worry, Kellen hadn't thought about it. "I suppose you do need caretakers."

"Jamie Conkle is a brilliant gardener. Since the Conkles moved here, she has made them self-sufficient in their food supply. With her greenhouse and her garden and her fledgling orchard, she now grows all her own fruits and vegetables. And raises chickens. She's got crab pots and fishing lines, so they've got everything they need. Because of her providing us with food and Olympia's cooking, we're able to stay on the island and be self-sufficient, too."

"Awesome. I'll go down and meet her!" Rae's eyes were shining.

Max grimaced. "Um…maybe not."

Rae sat up straight and indignant. "Why not?"

He glanced back at her. "It's no reflection on you. I've visited the island before, and I've met Jamie Conkle. She's…different."

"That's okay. Right?" Rae looked vaguely anxious, a girl verging on adolescence. "You told me it was okay to be different."

"It is okay, but she's different—and difficult. She doesn't do well in conversation. She doesn't entertain other people's opinions. She likes to be right. She can be razor sharp, and we should respect her desire to be alone. Right?"

"I guess." The constantly social Rae sounded uncertain.

The beach to the east was a long sweep of pale sand and frothing waves, and on the sand was a narrow, eight-foot-long white shape. From above, Kellen couldn't figure out what it was…

Max pointed. "Rae. Look there."

Rae fought her seat belt to half rise off her seat. "Daddy! Is that a SkinnySail?"

"Might be," Max acknowledged.

"What's a skinny sale?" Then light dawned for Kellen. "Wait—you didn't buy one of those boats Rae's been asking for?"

He looked sideways out of the corner of his eye. "Might have."

Exasperated, Kellen said, "Max, you spoil that child!"

"Mommy, you sound like Grandma."

Kellen snapped around and glared.

Rae subsided in her seat. But she couldn't stop the grin on her face. "A SkinnySail. Mommy, don't be mad. Daddy and I will take you sailing on the ocean."

"Be still, my heart," Kellen muttered.

"You can't be afraid of boating *and* of biking!" Rae protested. Once upon a time, a couple of years ago, she had thought her mother was a superhero.

The kid was over that now.

"I'm not *afraid*. But if I wanted to boat, I'd have joined the US Navy, and if I wanted to bike, I'd have joined the…" Kellen racked her brain for an apt analogy.

"The Wicked Wheelies?" Rae suggested.

"The Out Spoken?" Max offered.

"Wheels…of… Fortune!" Rae was having fun now.

"We don't have bikes on the island," Kellen said loftily.

"Yes, we do." Max sounded surprised. "I ordered them and had them sent here. How else are we going to get around?"

*It's a mostly deserted island. Why do we have to get around?* But even Kellen knew that was a foolish question; they couldn't stay in cooped up and wait for the moment Mara Philippi was apprehended—or, as Kellen feared, descended on them. She said, "Riding bikes on this island won't be like biking in the mountains. Right?"

From her first moment on a bike, Rae had craved speed and loved the abrupt descents and jumps involved with mountain biking, and she wasn't even teasing when she said, "From what I've seen of the island, starting at the house and cycling downhill to the other end will probably involve speeds up to—"

This time Max whipped around and glared.

"Probably not more than thirty miles per hour." Rae obviously thought she was offering encouragement to her mother.

Kellen couldn't imagine traveling the rugged, bumpy paths of the island on a bike at thirty miles an hour. Or rather—she could. And it scared her to death.

Max faced forward. "We'll take you out on the boat. Kellen, you'll love it!"

"Isn't that a two-man boat?" Kellen was almost sure it was.

"If we leave off the motor, it's a three-man boat," Max answered.

"Three very small men," Kellen said.

"I'm the only man." He puffed out his chest. "You two are itty-bitty feminine bits of fluff."

"Daddy, you're a misogynist." Rae sounded disgusted.

"Maybe so. But I bought the boat." Max changed course and headed west, toward the peak of the island.

There a tall house rose. Built in the 1920s, ornate, painted in firm tones of blue and brown with scarlet accents, it was the epitome of a rich man's ostentatious home, a sprawling French chateau with a mansard roof, iron lace trim and a madness of windows and doors and shrubs. A widow's walk, surrounded by all that black iron trim, rose at the highest point.

The land around the house was an emerald blanket of shorn lawn and well-watered shrubs. A dozen massive live oaks spread their protective branches over the property. Abruptly, where the irrigation stopped, green ended and native yellow grasses took over the land. A few outbuildings, garages or sheds, stood off to one side with their foundations straddling the green/gold line. An incongruous bank of solar panels covered the roof of the largest building.

"I like it." Rae's voice sounded bemused. "It's so… lonely."

"It's not too bad," Max said. "Not too lonely. We've got each other."

The size of the place floored Kellen. "I wasn't expecting a mansion. Not out here. Who lived there?"

"The house is named Morgade Hall after the fam-

ily who lived in it," Max told them. "Gerard Morgade
was a newspaperman in the early part of the twentieth
century. He made a fortune in the business—"

"As a writer?" Kellen could hardly believe that.

"Owner. Probably insider trading. Blackmail. He
had a reputation as a ruthless businessman, univer-
sally loathed. He bought the island, hired a contractor
who built the house using a fleet of boats and scores of
workers, and moved his family here. The lack of an-
chorage kept them isolated while he traveled between
the island and the mainland on his yacht. In the fifties,
he died here, the last of his family."

"His wife?"

"Died in 1948."

"He had no children?"

"Four or five kids. None survived the forties. I
know the oldest daughter got murdered by her husband in, I think, 1949."

Kellen glared at him. Rae knew about Kellen's first
husband, about the abuse she'd suffered, and because
of that, Rae worried about her mother and women in
general.

He must have realized what he'd said, for he quickly
continued, "People died earlier in those days. There's
a cemetery not far from the house." He flew them
west and showed them the small fenced and overgrown
graveyard. "Living on this island, they might not have
gotten the medical attention they needed when they
were hurt or ill. Or maybe it was the war."

"Why couldn't they fly to the mainland?" Rae
asked.

"Helicopters came into their own in the 1950s, so if

there was a storm and their yacht couldn't put to sea, they had to stay put." Max glanced back at Rae. "In fact, that's still a problem. Northern California has its share of big storms, mostly in the winter, but we *could* get stuck here."

Rae confounded Kellen with her response. "In a storm? Cool."

"I know you're not afraid of storms, but you want to be stuck here?" Kellen asked.

"If I have to be stuck here anyway, I might as well have a good reason." That sounded reasonable and only a little surly.

"If you've seen everything you want, I'll land now." Max didn't wait for an answer, but brought the helicopter down fast enough to make Rae squeal and Kellen put her hand on her stomach. At the last moment, he pulled up and gently set the helicopter on the edge of the yard. He turned to her and grinned. "Like a roller coaster, isn't it?"

Kellen grinned back. He hadn't worried about whether the swift descent would cause her brain to hemorrhage or rattle in her skull or any of the things he had worried about and the doctors had assured him wouldn't happen. He was like a mischievous man-boy, a husband who enjoyed teasing his wife, and she liked that. She liked it a lot. Maybe the run of *Kellen's Brain* was almost over.

"There we have it." Max gestured across the well-tended lawn. "Morgade Hall."

# CHAPTER SIX

SEEN FROM ON the ground, the mansion was a madness of cupolas and patios and windows and painted wood and white stone and gray slate roof tiles.

Max took off his headset and waited until they had removed theirs before he told them, "It's anywhere from three to six stories, and is rumored to have over one hundred rooms." He unbuckled and helped them get down and onto Mother Earth again.

"Wait until I tell Chloe about this place!" Rae put her backpack on the ground and dug around for her phone.

Kellen looked at Max, shook her head and gestured to him. *This is your problem.*

He went on one knee beside his daughter and caught her hand. "Honey, you don't have your phone with you."

Rae stilled, her hand in her backpack, her eyes wild and fixed on Max. "What? Of course I do. I put it in here. What do you mean? *Why?*"

"There's no way to connect here on the island," Max said. "It's an internet-free zone."

In an overly-cheerful tone, Kellen said, "Your dad and I thought it would be great for *all* of us to disconnect."

Actually, Max and Kellen thought it would be great to make sure Mara didn't trace them using their phones' GPS locators.

On their travels, Max and Kellen had carried burn phones. After discussion, they'd allowed Rae to keep her phone—they thought it would make the trip less stressful for Rae—but Max had hired his teenage cousin, Wendy, to hack and disable the GPS. But Wendy had warned them there was always someone out there who was better, and that someone would be Mara. The woman had been illiterate. During her incarceration she had demanded, and received, specialized reading classes. That, added to her brilliance with technology and numbers, meant their burn phones, and Rae's phone, ultimately had to go.

Rae's mouth hung open. She looked from Max to Kellen to Max to Kellen, as if trying to comprehend people who had sprouted antennae from their foreheads. Then her mouth snapped shut, and she said, "That's the stupidest thing I've ever heard!"

Ah. Verona's granddaughter. Plainspoken and impatient. "Your dad and I are stupid people."

Rae didn't care whether Kellen smiled and at the same time, stared with pointed intensity. As far as Rae was concerned, she had been robbed. "When did you seize my phone?"

"We put it on a train to Russia," Kellen confessed. "Mine went to South America. Dad's went to Newfoundland."

"We have no *phones*?" Rae's voice rose, not even questioning the strangeness of what Kellen had said.

In the distance, they heard a bark.

Her shout had summoned a friend.

From the direction of the house, they saw a blond-ish-red streak bounding toward them.

Rae forgot her grievance, dropped to her knees and extended her arms. "Luna! Bella Luna, my darling doggie!"

Luna leaped and slammed into Rae, and they rolled in the grass, child and dog ecstatic with joy.

Kellen and Max watched affectionately. Then Kellen moved closer to Max and said quietly, "We do have one form of communication, right?" She nodded at the helicopter, with its powerful radio.

"Yes, I've got a special frequency for my law enforcement contact. I'll be checking in once a week and hoping to hell the first report states they have Mara in custody."

"What do you think the chances of that is?"

"They've had three weeks to narrow the lead."

Which was a non-answer, but what could he say?

"I don't think Rae will think of the helicopter when she thinks of communications, and if she does—well, I'll lock the door."

A green golf cart, slightly battered, careened across the lawn toward them.

"Dylan Conkle," Max said in Kellen's ear, and when Dylan stopped and got out, Max strode forward to shake his hand.

Kellen observed and cataloged.

**DYLAN CONKLE:**
MALE, 30YO, CAUCASIAN ANCESTRY, 6'2", 150LBS, HAIR THE SAME BLONDISH-RED AS LUNA, PALE SKIN, RED FRECKLES

ON FACE, NECK, HANDS. BLACK-RIMMED GLASSES. GENUINE
SMILE AT DOG AND CHILD. PLEASANT SMILE TOWARD KEL-
LEN AND MAX.

"Welcome to Isla Paraíso," Dylan said to the general area. He didn't meet Kellen's eyes. He pretended he hadn't seen her outstretched hand. Because he didn't shake hands with women? Or he didn't want her to notice the low-level tremor in his fingers?

More surprising to Kellen was how he reacted to Rae's sunny smile and cheerful, "Hi!"

He startled as if Luna herself had spoken, then grinned sheepishly and touched his forehead, like an English peasant to his lady.

Even Rae looked at him as if she didn't know how to react to such weirdness.

Max climbed into the helicopter and handed their luggage down to Dylan.

While Dylan stashed it in the golf cart he said to Kellen, "My wife is sorry she couldn't be here to greet you."

"I'd love to meet her," Kellen told him.

Dylan's pale blue eyes grew wide behind the thick lens of his glasses, and he stood very still as if to avoid detection. "I'll let Jamie know."

Translation: *I said the proper thing, but the truth is, she doesn't want to meet you.*

So Max was right—Jamie Conkle really didn't want anybody intruding on her privacy. Interesting.

"If you'd like to walk," Dylan said, "I'll transport your bags to the house."

"Yes. Thank you." Max inclined his head, but his gaze never left Dylan.

Dylan headed across the lawn at full speed.

Kellen waited until they had walked a little way before asking, "What's wrong with him?"

Max glanced at Rae and Luna, romping along beside them, apparently oblivious. "Coming to the island was Jamie's idea, I'm sure of it, and Dylan hasn't managed the isolation nearly as well as she has."

Kellen did not like the sound of that. "What do you mean? About him?"

"He drinks too much—makes his own moonshine. He grows his own weed—Jamie won't do it for him—and he spends entire weeks bombed out of his mind."

"Marijuana is a drug. So is alcohol," Rae said indignantly. "He shouldn't do that to himself and his family!"

So much for her not paying attention to their conversation.

"You're right," Max told her. "But he does, and he barely manages to do what little we ask of him—watch over the house, mow and water—and if it weren't for Jamie, we'd get rid of him. But she wants to stay and when she needs to, she drives him to do the work."

"He's a nice-enough-looking guy," Kellen said.

"*She's* a beautiful woman. Tall, slender, short dark hair, dark eyes with sweeping lashes, long legs and a walk that from the back looks like dancing."

Kellen was amused. "Are you in love, Max?"

"No, dear, I only love you. But when I look at her, I remember why I love all women so very, very much."

Kellen laughed, low and warm. "That's one of the

reasons you are so personable, Max Di Luca. You love women. You even like them."

"What's not to like?"

"Trust me. I was in the military. There are a lot of men who don't like women, who consider them no more than cattle. Who make a woman want to come out punching."

"How many of those guys did you take down?"

"Never enough. One falls, three more take his place." Kellen wasn't bitter, but man, it did grow old.

"Dylan and Jamie—don't they love each other?" Rae's voice quavered. Her pal, Maverick, had this year lived through the horrors of her parents' acrimonious divorce, and Rae had been scarred by the duties she had assumed as best friend.

"I don't know. Maybe they did once, but it's a love that's dissipated in the sunshine and solitude of Isla Paraíso. With only each other to talk to, their differences have rubbed each other raw. I don't know how much longer that troubled marriage can go on." Max shrugged, a man amazed at the vagaries of human nature. "But then, I was saying that three years ago."

Rae stood stock still in the lawn. "I want married people to love each other!"

Kellen took advantage of the moment to put her arm around Max's waist. "We love each other, Rae. Does that help?"

"Yes. I suppose so." Rae didn't sound so much sulky as uncertain. "But if their love wasn't forever, will yours be?"

## CHAPTER SEVEN

MANLIKE, MAX GOT a panicked expression, so Kellen answered, "I think so. I served in the military, a tough environment, for six years. I learned what I want from life. Your father's been in charge of two different Di Luca wineries and our Yearning Sands Resort. He's seen a lot, he's got experience in lots of human relationships. Plus, he raised you by himself, with Grandma's help, for six years, and being a single parent is no easy deal. We're both smart and competent. Plus, we have that special bond that drew us together in the first place."

"What's that?" Rae asked.

"I don't know what it is for him, but for me, it was knowing from the first moment that he's a strong man who would lay down his life for love and family. He's the kind of guy a woman would be a fool not to love."

Max hooted and started for the house again, towing Kellen with his arm around her shoulder. "Then there have been a lot of foolish women."

"Daddy, that's not true. I think you're so involved with Mommy, you don't notice how the women watch you."

Kellen smirked at Rae, at her smart, observant kid.

Max, being Max, didn't believe them, and chuckled.

For an intelligent man with a great deal of understanding about himself, he was an idiot. Which was fine with Kellen. She didn't need him to know how many women were willing to fling themselves at his feet.

"You don't touch each other very often," Rae muttered.

Kellen and Max froze midstep.

It was true. They didn't touch often. At the time of their wedding, they had been groping (ha) toward sexual familiarity. Then Kellen fell into a coma and went into surgery, and all their needs had been brushed aside. Touching each other had become something forbidden, a torture of desire, a thing to be avoided.

Max turned them to face Rae, and Kellen figured he was going to hand Rae some acceptable excuse the child could swallow about obvious affection being ill-mannered.

But he said, "That's true. I don't touch Mommy nearly enough. Why don't I fix that right now?" Before Kellen could react, he bent her over his arm like a silent movie star and, while her head was whirling, he kissed her.

Um, with their mouths open. His was open because he was making all the moves. Hers was open because she was gaping like a fish.

Rae screamed with laughter and delight.

Max lifted his head and stared into Kellen's face. "Close your eyes," he said, and moved in again.

The kiss became less a comedy and more… Just more. Slow and sweet. Then slow and hot. When Max lifted his head again, Kellen had to blink the faint sheen of tears from her eyes. Not that she was crying, just that the heat had been so intense her body had to act like a sprinkler system to cool her off.

It hadn't worked very well. She was still very, very warm.

She stared into his eyes, his warm, beautiful brown eyes, and thought…nothing much at all. Except that as hard as he was breathing, he might come in for another pass. She would like that. She licked her bottom lip—

Rae said, "That's enough, please. I guess you are married pretty good."

Max and Kellen both flinched, a reaction to the interruption, and predictably Max found his focus first. Carefully he stood Kellen on her feet. In a mellow tone, he said, "Right, Rae. We are married pretty good. We, um, should go in and meet our cook, Olympia. She's been here for two weeks, using the Conkles as a cleaning crew and preparing for our arrival. Let's hope that she especially got the kitchen ready to go. Rae's hungry."

"And you?"

"*So* hungry." As he slid his hands away from Kellen, it was clear he wasn't talking about food.

They walked together, not touching, the rest of the way toward the house, and when Kellen slid a glance toward him, he wore a smug, lopsided smile.

She looked hastily away. If Rae wasn't right there with them, she'd demand to know what he thought he was doing. What happened to his self-restraint? What happened to being all worried about the effects of unbridled passion on *Kellen's Brain*? She had been frankly irked at his restraint, but now, after so long…

The story in the military was that six months without sex made you a virgin again. Maybe true. She rubbed her palms on her jeans. Her hands were sweating.

At the house, Dylan had unloaded the bags, then carried them inside.

Kellen turned to Max. "What did you do with the, um, special bag?"

It had been the middle of the night when they picked up the helicopter from Max's cousin, Jason Di Luca. He stashed their luggage inside, helped Max get a half-asleep Rae on board, and indicated the long canvas bag behind the seats. In a low voice, he had told them, "Firearms. A bolt-action 30-06 and a Remington 308 with scope. A Ruger 9 mil semiautomatic and a couple of compact handguns. Probably overkill, but better prepared for anything than not." He shook hands with them both, pressed a kiss on Rae's forehead, and sent them on their way.

The bag hadn't come out with the rest of the luggage, and now Max said, "The bag's in the helicopter. I don't want Rae to see it and think…anything, so I'll bring it in when no one's around to ask questions."

"Where are you going to store them?"

"Gerard Morgade seems like the kind of guy to be a big game hunter. I'll bet a big, important guy like him had a gun safe."

"A gun safe would be good."

The housekeeper must have heard the helicopter, or Dylan warned her that they had arrived, for the front door slammed open and she stepped out onto the wide veranda.

**OLYMPIA PAOLERGIO:**
FEMALE, CAUCASIAN ANCESTRY (RUSSIAN? GERMANIC?
SLAVIC?) LATE 40s, 5'5", 130LBS, BUILT STRONG AND TOUGH.
COOL BROWN EYES, WELL-CUT HAIR, SUSPICIOUSLY AUBURN
WITH HIGHLIGHTS, WELL-APPLIED COSMETICS, CRISP, IRONED
CLOTHING, IMMACULATE, POLISHED NAILS. PROOF POSITIVE
THAT ALL GOOD GROOMING IS NULL WHEN CANCELED BY THE
APPEARANCE OF A FAINT, DARK MUSTACHE ACROSS THE
UPPER LIP.

"Welcome to Morgade Hall." Olympia's gaze swept the little group, and lingered on Luna. "I'm glad the dog managed to find someone to pet it. I was tired of her importuning me. Come in. The house is large and difficult to navigate. I'll perform a tour." She held the door for them.

"Not necessary," Max said. "I've been here before."

Olympia swept him a freezing glance, then began the tour anyway. "The house is a magnificent reimagining of a French chateau, with a wide, sweeping stairway that leads up to a gallery above. There old-world paintings line the walls. Carvings enliven the woodwork and antique furniture creates a classic environment."

Kellen followed Olympia and agreed with all her assessments, but she also noted that a closer look showed the wear of many years. The carpets were shabby, and rectangles of brighter paint gave testimony that long-vanished paintings had once hung on the walls.

Olympia guided them briskly through the first floor. "The main ballroom is here."

"The main ballroom? How many are there?" Rae asked.

"Several," Olympia answered. "This is the largest. One imagines it alive with light and music."

Kellen was surprised to hear Olympia had an imagination. "Oh, look. There's a piano. Goodie."

Rae giggled.

Olympia was oblivious to their teasing. "The piano has been tuned. Follow me. The library is here. There's a door onto the porch, a fireplace which you will seldom use, and I believe the chairs to be comfortable."

"Look at all the books!" Rae wandered in and stared in awe at the walls of shelves lined with leather-bound books, pieces of glowing art glass, framed paintings and photographs. "So many stories. It's like in *Beauty and the Beast.*"

"Very dusty to my mind." Olympia sounded vaguely disapproving. "Those books shouldn't be disturbed."

"Grandma says if a book isn't read, it cries in its soul." Rae sounded stiff and disapproving.

"I don't know what that means." Olympia wheeled around and across the hall. She waited until the Di Lucas had joined her and threw open another door. "The dining room is here. I'll be serving breakfast at seven—or if you wish, later." Her glare indicated she would not approve of a different hour.

"We can try seven for a while. See if that works." Max sounded mild.

Olympia's outrage made Kellen hide her grin. No wonder Verona had expressed doubts about Olympia Paolergio. She was a gorgon.

Olympia's heels struck each step sharply as she led them upstairs. "I put the child in this bedroom, obviously designed for a Morgade daughter." She opened the door close to the top of the stairs and gestured Rae in.

Rae eyeballed Olympia as she walked in; she wasn't used to being called "the child." But once she entered, she forgot her chagrin in a breath of awe.

The room was gloriously pink. The bed had floaty curtains and a canopy. All the furniture was painted white with flecks of gold. An oriental rug in subdued tones of blue and gold covered the oak floor. Although faded by time, this was the room for a princess. "This is…" Rae's voice faded. She went to the bed and sat on the old-fashioned bedspread, then slowly reclined and stared up at the gauzy canopy.

"Okay. That settles that. Where do we sleep?" Max clearly had no doubt Olympia had made the decision for them.

"I put you in the master bedroom." Olympia led them down the long corridor toward the double doors at the end, and flung them open. "It has an attached bathroom."

Kellen stepped in.

Max followed.

Kellen stopped cold.

Max bumped into her.

"Holy cow," she said in awe and horror.

The room was easily the size of the downstairs ball-room and featured the bed as a centerpiece. Placed on a raised platform, the four broad, polished oak posts reached toward the tent-shaped, robin's-egg-blue ceiling where, dangling from the highest point, was a large—no, wait, extra-large—Moroccan metal lamp.

Kellen cleared her throat. "This looks like a combination of Arabian Nights and primitive phallic art."

Max choked on a cough. Or was it a laugh? "So, dear, not this room?"

Kellen cast him a disgusted look and turned to Olympia Paolergio. "Is there somewhere else we can rest our weary heads?"

Olympia looked offended and astonished. "I was told to prepare the master bedroom."

"With one hundred rooms, there must be something less…suggestive." Kellen started back down the corridor, throwing open doors.

Olympia hurried ahead of her. "That's not necessary, Mrs. Di Luca, I've been organizing the house ever since I arrived and I have several suggestions. If you're sure you don't want—" She gestured back at the master bedroom.

"I am so sure."

"I can certainly see who wears the pants in this family." Olympia huffed her way to a wide door next to the master bedroom. "This was Mrs. Morgade's bedroom. It also has an attached bathroom. If you wish to seek further, I must tell you—most bedrooms do not."

The Morgades hadn't slept together. How interesting. Kellen walked into a room decorated sparsely with chests and tables and a few well-chosen sculptures of Japanese origin. The queen-size bed hugged the interior wall and faced the windows where every morning they could watch the sun rise. "This will do." Actually, Kellen quite liked it.

"Yes, dear," Max said meekly.

"You can sleep in the master if you prefer." Kellen looked daggers at him.

"No, dear."

Kellen turned to Olympia. "Will you ask Dylan to bring our bags up here to our room?"

Olympia huffed again. "When you're ready, come to the dining room. I've prepared a snack." She departed.

Kellen turned on Max. "The pants in this family?"

He laughed out loud.

"Who says that? Who even thinks it?"

He kept laughing, the crinkles around his eyes deepening, inviting her to laugh, too.

So she did. "You didn't help a bit!"

He made a lunge for her, toppled her onto the bed, rolled on top of her, all warmth and weight and rocketing blood pressure. He looked down into her face. "Are you kidding? You should have seen your expression. It was priceless! And—"

The door slammed back against the wall.

They both jumped guiltily.

Rae stood there, glaring as if the wrathful face of puberty had taken form. "I don't know what you think is so funny."

Max turned to Kellen. "*This* is who wears the pants in the family."

He picked one hell of a time to be witty. Kellen ignored him and asked Rae, "What's wrong? I thought you liked your room."

"It's too far away!" She stalked in.

"From us?" Kellen considered that. "I'll bet we can round up a small lamp for your room and one to light the corridor so you can find us at night."

"Why would I want to find you at night?" Rae asked belligerently.

"Sometimes you have nightmares," Max said.

"I'm too old for that now." Rae had chosen to forget that after being torn from her home, and during the days of chaotic travel, she had twice crept into her parents' bedroom, crawled in next to Kellen, and shivered until she forgot her dream and went back to sleep.

Those nightmares were one reason Kellen had agreed to continue their silence about the threat that had sent them fleeing. They weighed the chances of Mara immediately tracking and attacking them against Rae's psychological turmoil, and decided that, by all indications, they'd made a clean getaway and they could wait.

At Max's request, Kellen had hired a tracker, a friend from her Army days, and set her on Mara's trail. According to Diana's latest report, so far their plan was successful. Right now, Mara was far, far away and with Diana's help, would soon be apprehended.

That would make Kellen happy. Because she was a coward. She didn't want to explain the truth of the situation to her newly sharp-tongued daughter. Max really wanted Rae to remain an innocent child as long as she could, while Rae would not appreciate the deception.

Whoever said parenting was easy had never been a parent. She looked at Max. Especially when the parents had differing opinions.

Now Kellen backtracked and used a different angle to speak to Rae's anxiety. "Still, I like the idea. Sometimes I like to come and check on you."

Rae mulled that over. "That's all right, I guess."

Luna ran in, a big, strong dog with her nose to the floor. She stopped and smiled at Kellen—she held no grudge about the piano music—then dropped her nose again and sniffed around the room, following a trail only she could discern.

Rae flung herself onto a low-slung chair. "No phone. No apps. No online. What are we going to *do* here?"

"Tomorrow we're going to explore the island," Kellen said.

"The whole island? Really, Mother?"

Rae used that snotty tone that made Kellen think she was about to go off like a Roman candle. Putting her arm around Rae's shoulders, she said, "Olympia has a snack for us in the dining room."

At the word *snack*, Luna alerted and sat up.

Rae didn't budge.

Kellen got her up with a little gentle pressure. "Not the whole island. Not in one day. But don't forget, your dad ordered new bikes for us."

"See? I'm a good guy," Max said.

"A guy without pants," Kellen answered.

"Pantless Max," he agreed, and came around to Rae's other side. He helped Kellen maneuver her out of the bedroom and down the hallway. "Tomorrow, we can take a picnic lunch and find out what we've got here. I can't wait to explore the beach. It's going to be different here than in Washington."

"This is all cliffs. We can't jump off the cliffs." Rae was displeased and unwilling to have her mood changed.

"It's not all cliffs. You saw that." Max may have

sounded exasperated. "There are all kinds of beaches, and while it's quite a climb, about a half mile from here there's a stairway down and we can sit in the warm sand, wade in the cold Pacific—"

"Until our legs turn blue." Rae had been to Northern California before.

Luna trotted beside them, all lolling tongue and smiling teeth.

"We'll throw a stick in the waves and listen to Luna bark until it comes back. She's going to love it so much!" Even before Kellen finished speaking, it was obvious she had hit the right note.

Rae put her hand on her dog's head. "Okay. We can do that."

## CHAPTER EIGHT

WHICH MEANT, OF COURSE, an unexpected storm blew in with a midnight clap of thunder and after an hour of pouring rain the weather settled into a constant drizzle that lasted through morning wake-up and into breakfast in the massive dining room.

As the promised bike ride and picnic disappeared, the expression on Rae's face made last night's thunder and lightning seem like kittens and flowers.

Max cleared his throat, but before he could say anything about entertaining them, Kellen said, "Rae, let's investigate the house."

Rae's face began to turn tantrum red.

"It's like a Gothic mansion, big and old and—"

Rae took a deep breath.

Inspired by panic, Kellen added, "—has an attic!"

Rae paused in midbreath. Slowly she let it out.

"Imagine," Kellen coaxed. "Old trunks with funny clothes and hats."

"We can dress up." *The Castle in the Attic* was one of Rae's favorite books.

"Yep!" Kellen passed her the plate of toast, the butter and the shaker. "Cinnamon sugar?"

Rae piranhaed her way through two slices of cinnamon toast, two soft-boiled eggs, two pieces of bacon, a plain piece of toast, watermelon, blueberries and half a peach, and when she finished, she leaped to her feet, cheery and impatient. "Are you ready to go?" she asked her mother.

"Almost. I thought we'd pack a snack."

"I'll find a picnic blanket." Rae ran out of the room.

"Never let her get hungry," Max murmured.

"What do you suppose she's going to use for a picnic blanket?" Kellen asked.

Olympia stepped into the doorway. "What's Rae want with an antique linen tablecloth?"

"Oh," Max and Kellen said in unison.

While Olympia created a lunch basket for Kellen and Rae to carry with them, Kellen exchanged the linen tablecloth for an old khaki-colored wool Army blanket and Rae took Luna outside to use the facilities. While she was gone, Max said, "I found the gun safe in Gerard Morgade's study, with the key in the lock. I'll bring the weapons inside and stow them. Mara might be far away, but I don't trust her to stay there."

"Always prepare for the worst," Kellen said. "I learned that in the Army."

"I learned it in the wine business."

They grinned at each other.

Rae and Luna came back through the door at a run. "Come on, Mom!"

Kellen, Rae and Luna looked for the stairs to the attic.

It proved a greater challenge than either of them expected. A Gothic mansion? More like a Gothic maze: long corridors of windows and paintings, stairs that got progressively narrower as they went up and, now and then, large ballrooms and small bathrooms. They kept getting lost and having to turn back, and one time they went around in circles along a dim corridor lit only by windows along the top of the wall. Doors opened only into murky closets stacked with linens and cleaning supplies. The floorboards creaked as they walked, and Kellen experienced a terrifying sense of claustrophobia. When Rae finally spotted the narrow doorway that had led them into this loop, and they at last returned to a more traveled part of the house, Kellen had to stop and breathe slowly and deeply. She couldn't speak; her throat was constricted and her chest tight.

Rae waited patiently, looking more than a little unsettled herself. "It feels like Hogwarts," she said. "The stairways and doors change when you're not looking."

Kellen nodded, and when she could speak, she said, "If you don't have a nightmare about that, I will!"

"That's okay, Mommy." Rae put her hand in Kellen's and smiled up at her. "You can come to my bed and sleep."

Kellen smiled back. "I might. Now let's pay attention to where we go. We have to get back from this adventure."

The last flight was steep and constricted, and ended in a narrow attic door that had once been painted white. It was now a sort of yellowish color, and creaked like the ominous warning in a scary old movie.

"Mommy, you go first." Rae stayed close to Kellen's back.

But nothing ominous lurked behind the door. Here they found a large, airy, white-painted room with casement dormer windows set into the sloped ceiling. Spacious window seats loaded with squishy cushions, two couches upholstered in faded maroon flowered material popular in the fifties, and a worn maroon easy chair with an ottoman. A large bookshelf held well-read paperbacks and hardcovers.

Rae lost her trepidation, gave a delighted gasp, dropped the picnic basket, and ran to one of the west-facing window seats. She crawled in and pulled a throw over her legs.

Luna ran with her and wagged her tail.

"Can she come up?" Rae begged. "Can she? It's not really furniture."

Because Luna wasn't supposed to get on the furniture, except on Rae's bed when Rae was in it, and not even then…but that was a battle Max and Kellen had chosen to ignore. "Invite her up."

Rae patted the seat next to her.

Luna leaped and looked out the window, wagging her tail, then turned to face the room. She curled up at Rae's side, and kept an interested eye on Kellen as she explored.

Luna's innate loyalty was one of the reasons Max and Kellen elected to let the dog on Rae's bed; they had not a doubt Luna would protect Rae with her life.

The problem was—with Mara Philippi on the loose, they knew there was a chance Luna would be called on to do her duty.

When Kellen and Rae had together gone on their perilous adventure into the Olympic Mountains, Rae had proved to be stalwart and loyal. Should Kellen now ignore Max's wishes, take matters in her own hands, and tell her about Mara? Should she warn her

of the need to be always vigilant, to be suspicious…
to be afraid?

For Mara was a thing to fear. When Kellen first
met her at Yearning Sands Resort, Mara had been the
spa manager, a pretty, shallow, fit young woman who
seemed committed to nothing more than winning the
International Ninja Challenge. The image she'd created
for herself convinced Kellen, and the whole staff, of
her superficiality. Mara had set herself up as rival and
friend to Kellen, but when the winter turned dark and
storms isolated the resort, Kellen discovered the hor-
rifying truths, and those truths had almost killed her.

She remembered the threat Mara had sent her. *I'll
take everything from her, the way she took everything
from me. I'll make her sorry she betrayed me.*

Mara was still far away, so whether or not Max
agreed, perhaps this was the moment to set Rae on
her guard. As Kellen searched for the words, Rae said
in a dreamy voice, "I can hear the rain on the roof."

Kellen looked at her daughter staring out at the
showery sky and sea and clouds. With a pang, she realized Rae the child was becoming an adult, a painful
process of confusion and wildness, that would someday result in a poised, beautiful young woman who
didn't need her anymore.

But not yet. Right now, Rae did need her mother,
and Kellen didn't have the heart to destroy Rae's delight in this moment and this place. So Kellen dismissed her dark memories, and looked around for
something to entertain them.

Unframed paintings covered the far wall, colorful
works of crashing waves, soaring gulls, stands of red-

woods and one rather sad portrait of a young man in a World War II US naval uniform, gazing out to sea. "Someone lived up here," she decided, "and not just one of the servants."

Rae rested her forehead on the windowpane. "I'd like to live here. It's a wonderful place."

Kellen ran her finger along the shelf's edge. When it came away barely dusted, she said, "I never thought the housekeepers would get this far. They did a really good job. You could live up here."

Rae turned. "Really?"

Seeing Rae's hopeful face, Kellen cursed herself. "No. You'd be too far away, and it's dark up here."

"I wouldn't mind."

"Even when you have a nightmare?"

Yesterday's belligerent denial was gone. Rae grimaced. "I guess not."

"Besides, no bathroom that I can see." Although perhaps it was through the next door.

Rae picked up a pair of binoculars from a shelf in the alcove and pointed them outside the window. "Look! A bird nest in the top of one of the oaks." Her voice brightened. "There are babies!"

"Let me see!" Kellen grabbed another set of binoculars and crawled into the window seat. These binoculars were heavy, and with her uncooperative hand, it took her a few minutes to gain control and focus on the tree. She found the nest, then the gawping mouths of the infant birds, and then she focused on the mother, tearing bits of meat into shreds to feed them. "Is that an eagle?"

"I don't know. We could look it up online—"

"There are books on the bookshelves!" Kellen slid out of the window seat, grabbed the first book on bird watching she could find, and shoved it at Rae. "Look it up!"

Rae was interested enough not to grumble, and used the binoculars and the book, back and forth, until she could shout, "It's a peregrine falcon!"

"Wow. I don't think I've ever seen one before." Kellen wandered over to a wall of cupboards. "That's wonderful!"

"They're a fully protected raptor."

"It's a beautiful bird. I'm glad it's protected." Kellen opened one door and found a closet filled with art supplies. "Someone painted up here!"

"Yes, Mother, it looks very well painted." Rae was dreaming; she didn't want to be interrupted with prosaic matters.

"I meant art."

Rae didn't react, so Kellen closed the door and snooped further. The other doors revealed old Christmas decorations, stacks of notebooks and pens, a well-stocked linen closet, and finally a recessed door that looked as if it went into the other part of the attic.

Luna slipped off the cushions and came to Kellen's side, sat in front of the door and wagged her tail as if expecting Kellen to open it.

Kellen turned the cut glass knob.

The door was locked.

Luna looked up at her as if to say, *Come on!*

"I'll see if I can find a key," Kellen told her.

Rae had followed Luna, and when the door failed

them, she went to the desk and rifled through the drawers. "Somebody up here wrote a lot of letters."

Kellen hurried over and took the pile Rae held. "Three-cent stamps! Postmarked in the 1930s and '40s." She wanted to open them, but it seemed vaguely rude.

"Look!" Rae held up a small blue leather-bound book. "It's a diary!" She felt no qualms; she opened it to the first page. "'September 1, 1938. Ruby Evelyn Morgade, my book.'" She turned the page and read, "'I turn fifteen years old today and my sister sent me this journal as a gift. Bessie says to keep it hidden from Father or he'll read it, and all my secret beliefs and deep emotions will be revealed. He doesn't deem his wife or children should be allowed private thoughts, and he is the head of this household so he controls us all.'" Rae looked up, frowning thunderously. "I don't like her father."

"What a jerk," Kellen agreed.

"Who does he think he is?"

"He was the rich newspaperman who owned the house. In those days, men did pretty much what they wanted with their families. And to their families."

"The olden days?"

"Yes." Kellen hesitated, then reminded her, "Now, too. My first husband abused me. I was lucky to escape alive."

"I know, Mommy. I'm sorry." Rae hugged her, and leaned her head against Kellen's shoulder.

When had she grown tall enough to reach Kellen's shoulder? "So consider your partners carefully," Kellen said. "No one's perfect, but no one has the right to hurt you."

"You told me before. I believe you. Let's sit down and read Ruby's diary!" Rae led her toward the couch.

"She wanted her thoughts to be private," Kellen reminded her.

"From her mean old father. Not from us! She would have liked us!"

"I think she would have." This was the entertainment Kellen had been looking for: a journal from long ago, and a gentle recalling of growing up in a former time.

Rae thrust the diary at Kellen. "You read it." She snuggled against Kellen's side.

"The handwriting is awfully small." But beautifully formed and clear. Kellen clicked on the floor lamp beside the couch. "I'll read for a while, then you."

The world receded as they read:

Father found out that Miss Harriman allowed me to study the business section of the newspaper, and after he raged at her, she lost her temper and told him I had a fine mind and I should be allowed to leave this island and go to school and I deserved to know more than how to make some rich man a pretty wife. He fired her, of course. I cried and begged, but he is adamant. I even asked Mother to intercede, but she refused. She told me Father always knows the right thing to do and we should obey him unconditionally. Then she went out in the garden to putter. Father doesn't want her to do servants' work; he dislikes her with dirt under her fingernails, so she wears gardening gloves and never kneels while she plants and weeds. That's as close to defiance as she ever gets. He has crushed her spirit, if she ever had any. He really is the dreadful beast Bessie calls him. He's gone off to the mainland to find another tutor. I hope someone runs over him or shoots him. I hope he dies. I hate this house with its empty, echoing rooms, its cowed servants, its secret passages.

"Secret passages!" Rae exclaimed. She looked around at the walls as if her x-ray vision could pierce their interior and reveal their mysteries.

*That is not good.* Hastily, Kellen read on.

I want to see the world, and I'll never get off this island until I wed the man he forces on me.

I am doomed.

Kellen stopped reading. She looked at Rae.
Rae looked back.
They were both appalled.
"Poor Ruby. Did she ever get off the island?" Rae asked.
"I don't know."

"We can look her up online."

Kellen waited for Rae to remember…

"No, we can't." Rae clutched her hair. "We don't have service! How am I supposed to talk to Chloe every day?"

"You could do like Ruby. You could write Chloe a letter."

Rae looked at Kellen as if she'd fallen into madness.

"Yes, you could," Kellen insisted. "If your daddy ever has to take the helicopter to the mainland—"

"Will he?"

"I don't know. I don't think so."

"Then why are you talking about it?"

*Because I want you to feel happy. Because I don't want you to feel cut off. Because I want you to have a confidante.* "If for some reason he does go, he could mail the letter for you."

"Like with an envelope and stamp?" Rae made it sound so primitive.

"Exactly." Kellen knew Max probably wouldn't be happy about her making such a promise, but she hoped, she really hoped, their sojourn here would be brief.

Rae mulled it over. "You know what would be great to tell Chloe? That we found *secret passages* in the house!"

"That would be exciting." Kellen considered all the angles, and decided she'd rather be close when Rae discovered her first secret passage, and said, "Shall we look right now?"

"Yes!" Rae jumped to her feet, ran to the wall by the door and started knocking on it.

Kellen examined all the walls, realized the window seat was inset in an inner wall set back three feet from the outer wall, and deduced the passage must be there. "Here, Rae." Kellen felt around the window trim, found a notch at the bottom, and when Rae had joined her, she pressed it…and with a click, the wall swiveled open and musty air rushed out.

"The secret passage." Kellen gestured Rae in. "After you."

Rae stood, wide-eyed, and stared inside.

Dust rested deep on the unfinished boards of the floor. The wall studs were gray with age. Cobwebs draped the entrance, and a spider dropped down to hang as if interested in the new world that had opened to it.

Rae took a breath. "It's dark."

"It really is. You first."

"No." Rae took a step back, ran into Kellen, jumped. "I'll wait until I've got a, um, flashlight."

"That's probably a good idea." Kellen breathed easier. Rae would not be wandering into the secret passages on her own. "Do you want to read some more of Ruby's diary?"

Rae looked at the window where rain still washed the glass with gray, and sighed dramatically. "There's nothing else to do." She grinned. "Unless you want to go down and practice piano."

"Right. We'll eat lunch."

"Yes. Lunch…"

"And read another entry." While Rae opened the picnic basket, Kellen opened Ruby's diary again.

Father decided I didn't need a governess anymore. He said too much education in a woman is
a terrible thing. So he brought me a companion.
Hermione Jasper is twenty, an orphan with no
resources and only a public school education. Of
course he would pick someone like her. She has
no family to fall back on, ergo no choice but to
obey him in all things. She is to report to him
all my activities, keep me on a strict sched-
ule of riding, embroidery, elocution, piano, drawing and—because he doesn't want me to run to
fat—swimming in the pool.

Considering his girth, I find this to be most
amusing.

I long for Miss Harriman, with her intelligent insights and constant wit, and I distrust
this Hermione.

Father won't let me read the financial pages,
but he wants me to keep up on current events
so I can converse with the man he chooses to
be my husband. So I know all about Germany and
the horrors they are inflicting on Europe. Father
approves of their tyranny. He says to the victor
go the spoils, and Germany is strong and white,
and the Jews and Gypsies deserve whatever
Hitler hands out to them. Sometimes, when he
doesn't notice, Mother looks at him as if he is
a particularly disgusting form of slug. She isn't
white. Not even he with all his power could

*make the world proclaim her white. Or me, either. I'm half hers. She has begun to speak to me in Japanese again, as she used to before he forbade her. I remember quite a lot, and am getting better all the time...*

"Ruby's mother was Japanese?" The mere idea mentally knocked Kellen off her feet.

"Is that weird?" Rae had very little experience with prejudice.

Kellen opened the basket and unpacked the sandwiches. "Yes! He seems like the kind of guy who would want a submissive woman of his own race. At the same time, some men find American women, with their education and their free speech, to be too challenging."

Rae spread the blanket on the floor.

Luna joined them, sitting at the edge of the blanket and watching eagerly.

"I guess he could have gone to Japan and bought a girl." Kellen loaded Rae's plate, then her own, and they dug in.

"Bought her? That's gross." Rae stuck her finger down her throat and made a gagging noise.

"Disgusting." Kellen took Rae's dill pickle spear off her plate.

Rae took it back, polished off her lunch, gave some cheese to Luna (Kellen pretended not to notice) and said, "I wonder if there's a picture of the lady downstairs."

"Ruby's mom? There's got to be."

Rae jumped to her feet. "Do you think she's dead? His wife?"

"Yes. Long ago. Remember? Daddy's told us."

"Yes, but I didn't *know* them then."

Kellen loaded the remains of lunch into their lunch basket. "We need the family Bible for the dates. Come on. Let's find Gerard Morgade's wife."

"And Ruby's mother."

Picnic basket in hand, Kellen and Rae left the attic and clattered down the stairs. In their hurry, they failed to firmly shut the door behind them.

INSIDE THE ATTIC, the inner door opened.

The outer door opened.

A soft laugh followed them down the stairs.

They didn't notice.

## CHAPTER NINE

KELLEN AND RAE rifled through the library, looking for Morgade family photos, and found a picture of the newlywed couple.

Gerard Morgade was tall, overweight, in a beige suit with a waistcoat, a stiff collar and wide cravat. He was probably forty—and without expression. He showed no pleasure in the occasion or his young wife.

The bride had a pale painted face with red lips, wore a Japanese kimono that gave her shape, yet beneath that she was obviously nothing more than a malnourished girl.

Rae pointed. "That's them!"

"That's vile." Kellen was more upset than she supposed she should be, but the idea of that cold, cruel man taking possession of a teenager to use for breeding and as hostess…

Max stepped into the door of the library. "The sun is out. Do you want to—?" He focused on Kellen. "What's wrong?"

"Mommy's remembering her first husband." Rae sounded too wise and very kind.

Kellen's mouth twisted. How odd to have her daughter read her so well. But sometimes, she looked at Rae and thought that was what she would have been like, if her parents had lived or Aunt Cora had been loving or…

*Or.* She'd made choices in her life, not all of them good. That Cecilia/Kellen thing, for instance.

Now she was proud of the person she'd become, and she believed Cousin Kellen would be, too. She had a daughter and a husband, and the bullet was gone from her brain. Except for the pesky matters of Mara Philippi, vicious murderer, and a fight to save her hand from atrophy, how much better could life be?

Max engulfed Kellen and Rae in his arms. The three of them stood together, warmed and united, and Kellen thought she could stand like this forever.

But after half a minute, Rae wiggled free. "Daddy, we found Ruby Morgade's diary!"

"Did you? In the attic? I didn't think you'd find anything but cobwebs."

"It's actually clean up there," Kellen said.

"Did you know Mrs. Morgade was Japanese?" Rae showed Max the photo.

Max took the framed portrait. "That must have been a scandal in its time."

Kellen eased the photo out of the frame, turned it over and found their names carefully written in faded ink. "She is Reika. I wonder what happened to her and the kids during the war."

"Why?" Rae had seen a few of Max's old war movies, but other than that, she hadn't a clue.

"The Japanese were the enemy, so the government moved all Japanese Americans off the coast and into the interior." And into internment camps. But Kellen wasn't going to try to explain that.

"Why?" Rae said again.

"The government was afraid the Japanese-Americans would try to help Japan invade the US." Max didn't bring up the internment camps, either.

Rae persisted, "I thought Germany was the enemy."

"Germany was the enemy, too." Kellen could see where this was going.

Max met Kellen's eyes. "And Italy."

Rae's eyes narrowed. "Did our family have to move off the coast?"

"No," Max said.

"Did the German-Americans have to move off the coast?"

"No," Kellen said. "Not the people from Europe. Only the people from Japan."

"That's not fair!" Rae's indignation blazed hot. She turned. "I want to go read Ruby's diary and find out what happened."

"We can do that." Kellen put her hand on Rae's shoulder. "But not now. The sun's shining. Let's go to the beach!"

Rae wavered.

"Ruby's diary will be there tomorrow. Olympia's making another picnic basket. I've got on my swim trunks and my flip-flops." Max showed his feet. "Come on, kid. Time's a-wastin'!"

Luna barked in agreement.

"All right, Luna. Anyway, I'm starving!"

"Still?" Kellen questioned. "We just ate a picnic upstairs."

"Just a little one!" Rae tore out of the room and headed upstairs to change.

Luna bounded after her.

"I swear that dog speaks English." Kellen started toward the stairway, too.

Max followed. "I can't believe Gerard Morgade would have allowed the government to take his wife and child."

"How could he stop them?"

"Money. Influence."

"Yes. Of course. Money and influence." She glanced back at him. "What are you doing? Where are you going?"

"I'm coming with you."

She paused, her foot on the first step, her fingers wrapped around the banister. "Why?"

"With the hand and everything, I thought you might need help pulling on your bathing suit."

A bubble of amusement rose in her throat. "You're going to help me…get dressed?"

He wore his smile cocked sideways. "Whatever help you need."

"What makes you think the pleasure of your touch won't blow up my brain?" She mocked him and his previous restraint.

He was completely serious. "I've been thinking about what you said about you making me happy. Maybe I could make you happy, too, sort of gently, building up to the big event, and if there's any doubt about your health, I could back away and—"

Kellen stood on the first step, faced Max straight on, put her arms around his shoulders (he was still taller), and said, "You want to control my orgasm?

Really, darling, there's no need. I've already tested it. Please remember, I don't need *you* to have an orgasm."

His mouth dropped open. He flushed from T-shirt to hairline. His eyes turned a brilliant brownish-gold. He took a long, hard breath, leaned down, put his shoulder to her belly, picked her up and ran up the stairs.

His shoulder slammed into her midriff.

She moaned and laughed at his eagerness.

At the top of the stairs, he skidded to a halt.

Kellen craned her neck, trying to see around him.

Rae's forceful, scornful voice said, "Daddy, *put her down.* We're going to the beach!"

Max slid Kellen off his shoulder, stood her on her feet, and balanced her with a hand on her arm. "Of course, I'm just helping Mommy up the stairs."

Holding a plastic bucket and wearing a pink-and-blue bathing suit, Rae swept them the kind of knowing glance Professor McGonagall would give a Hogwarts student. She stomped down the stairs.

Kellen cupped Max's jaw in her hand. "We'll take up this matter tonight. In the meantime… I'd better put on my own bathing suit." She sauntered toward their bedroom, and before she entered, she turned back toward Max.

He stood, rooted to the spot.

It was gratifying to wonder which of them was the hungriest.

She whispered, "Tonight."

# CHAPTER TEN

KELLEN WORE HER modest one-piece bathing suit and an ankle-length, long-sleeved dress as a cover-up, and as they walked across the green lawn toward the cliffs, she could feel Max scrutinizing her. "Stop it," she said out of the corner of her mouth.

"I can't help it. That bathing suit fits you like—"

"You can't see my bathing suit."

"I know what it looks like."

"It's new. You've never seen this bathing suit."

"Describe it to me."

Kellen glanced at Rae and Luna, running ahead and shrieking. "Imagine I'm wearing a suit from 1900, with a black knee-length skirt, a black ruffly shirt and long white underwear down to my ankles."

"Sexy." His voice contained a low, prowling growl.

"How could that be sexy?"

"Because you're naked underneath."

He was incorrigible. "I'll tell you a secret. I'm always naked beneath my clothes." She guessed he wasn't the only one who was incorrigible.

"I know." He sighed loudly. "I never forget it."

If not for Mara, Kellen would be thoroughly enjoying this retreat.

*I'll take everything from her, the way she took everything from me. I'll make her sorry she betrayed me.*

Max put his arm around Kellen and stopped. "What's wrong?"

"Just thinking."

"If it's going to put that look on your face—stop." He leaned closer and said softly, "You know what Diana said. She's closing in on Mara, and when she does, she'll call in Interpol and that will be the end of our wicked villain."

"We'll be free to go home."

"Or stay, if we want." Max hadn't changed the way he stood, yet Kellen felt that sweet, enveloping heat of sexual desire.

"We need to dunk you into the icy waters of the Pacific Ocean," she told him.

"What?" He pretended innocence.

"Come on!" Rae ran back toward them. "Hurry up! We've got to go to the *beach*."

"It's been there for a billion years. It won't go away," he assured her.

"Number one hundred and three on the endless list of things parents say to annoy their children," Kellen said.

"No kidding!" In one of those lightning switches, Rae suddenly sounded mature and exasperated.

"Since I've already annoyed you anyway, Rae, let's check out the old garage." He didn't wait for an answer, but headed for the dilapidated structure set in the grass beyond the end of the lawn. This was the building with the solar panels.

"Why? Because we haven't seen rodent droppings lately?" Kellen grinned at his back.

Rae ran after him. "Daddy! We're going to the *beach*!"

"This won't take a minute." Max flipped back the bar on one of the old-fashioned carriage house–style doors. It creaked and sagged as he opened it and walked in.

Kellen showed Rae her wide-spread hands.

Rae looked up at the sky as if seeking guidance.

They followed Max into the shadowy interior.

The smells of a garage hit Kellen first: oil, paint, tires, gasoline. And dust. So much dust Luna sneezed twice.

At first she could see nothing but the two grimy double-hung windows set into the back wall, and two more in each of the side walls. Then her eyes began to adjust to the dim light, and she saw a cluttered wooden workbench that stopped short of the back door. Motor oil spotted the cracked concrete floor. Gray vintage gas cans lined one side wall and a blue plastic kerosene can sat between them. At the end of the line, an Incredible Hulk of a battery charger kept the cans in line.

On the other wall, a slope-shouldered 1930s refrigerator, no longer working, sat surrounded by stacked red-and-yellow wooden boxes marked Coca-Cola, and filled with six-ounce bottles. A wooden ladder leaned against the wall. Brooms, rakes and shovels hung on nails along with…a horse collar?

Ah. At some point in the far distant past, this must have been the stable. That would account for the more-than-double garage size.

In the middle of the wide concrete floor, a large tarp covered a roughly pickup-sized shape. A mattress, a single with all the markings and colors of the sixties, leaned against the bulbous front of the tarp. Max pulled the mattress away, dragged it over to the wall and leaned it between the studs. He returned, reached up and pulled the chain to turn on the single light bulb that hung from the ceiling. Lovingly he rolled back the tarp to reveal...

**PICKUP:**
FORD F-100, 1955, INLINE 6 AS INDICATED BY THE GRILLE, ORIGINAL PAINT: GOLDENROD YELLOW. DUSTY, WELL-CARED-FOR. ONE LOW TIRE.

"My God. The rumors are true," he said in awe.

Rae wailed, "Daddy, I don't want to look at a crummy old pickup. We're going to the *beach*."

"It's not a crummy old pickup." He sounded shocked.

"It's the holy grail of vehicle fixer-uppers," Kellen told Rae.

"I don't care. I don't *want* to fix it up." Rae hesitated, because she loved robotics and anything mechanical. So she added, "Not *now*. Let's go to the *beach*."

Kellen held up one finger, asking Rae to be patient. "Max, you knew this was here?"

Rae sighed loudly.

Luna sat and thumped the floor with her tail.

"I had heard rumors." He walked over and ran his

palm over the bumper as lovingly as he had run his hand over Kellen's bottom. "It's in pretty good shape."

"For a truck that's been in a marine environment for...its whole life?" Kellen guessed. "Yes, it is."

"The Di Lucas bought it new and used it for island transportation until a few years ago. Then we replaced it with the electric golf cart. Our first caretaker was reputedly dedicated to the truck and kept it waxed and running." As he spoke, Max opened doors, rolled down windows, rolled up windows, kicked the tires, and generally acted like a man in the act of buying a car.

"How many caretakers have there been?" Kellen glanced out the back window and saw the waving grasses trampled by the remnants of a path. To the house, she guessed.

"Olof Humphreys was the first one. He came here as a young man and remained for umpteen years until he had a stroke and had to be transported to the mainland. He lingered for too long, poor guy, hating every minute of being there. Then we hired the Conkles. I wonder if the key's in the ignition." He leaned in the driver's side, and sagged in disappointment. "Nope." He looked around. "I wonder where the key is."

Rae sighed in drama and despair.

"Probably somewhere in here." Kellen skirted the truck, the workbench, and ran into a spiderweb. Automatically, she ducked, brushed frantically at her face and hair, and glared when Rae said, "Mommy just did the spider dance." And laughed.

"Smart kid." Kellen spotted the keys on the workbench, made her decision, and took his arm. "But the battery has to be dead and once we get the battery charged, before we can try to start it, we'll have to prime the carburetor."

"Right. Because there's no fuel in the line." Max's eyes shone with excitement.

Kellen guided him toward the open door. "So I'll help you look for the keys later. Right now, we really do need to go to the beach."

He made a whimpering sound much like Rae's.

Kellen waved Rae ahead and said to Max, "You know, I'm quite a good mechanic. I could help you get that truck running."

He flinched away from her. "No!"

She covered her grin with her palm, and when she thought she had control, she asked, "Did I threaten your manhood?"

She must not have completely hid her amusement, because he said, "You dented it."

"You want to repair the truck yourself?"

"Yes."

"Okay, but you have to include Rae."

"Of course!"

He had always intended to include his little girl in his project. That was only one of the reasons she loved him.

"Daddy! Mommy! C'mon. Let's go to the *beach*!" Rae dragged out the last word as if that would bring them along.

"Okay! We'll go to the *beach*!" Max imitated Rae's tone and volume. In a softer tone, he said to Kellen, "Dibs on putting sunscreen on your...shoulders."

Kellen got goose bumps that lasted until she got into bed that night...and beyond.

## CHAPTER ELEVEN

"MOMMY."

The whisper at midnight, right above Kellen's face, brought her out of a dead sleep and into wide-eyed terror. She jumped so hard she snapped her mouth closed and made her teeth ring. When she processed the voice and her role, she calmed herself and whispered, "Rae, what's wrong?"

"Mommy, I had a nightmare."

Kellen had been afraid of this; too much change and excitement, and a sudden separation from her beloved grandmother, and Rae's subconscious was rolling out the nightmares. "I know, sweetheart. Hang on." She rolled over and pushed gently at the inert form beside her. "Max, move over."

Some deep-voiced mumbling occurred while Max crawled to his edge of the mattress.

Kellen had worn him out. Poor guy. Thank God she'd managed to put on a nightgown, bully him into some night shorts, and unlock the door before she fell into a beach-exhausted, sex-saturated sleep.

Kellen lifted the covers.

Rae scooted in. The child was shivering, clutching her tattered blankie and stuffed llama, in the grips of some shadowy dread.

Kellen pulled her close, trying to warm her.

Rae whispered, "Can Luna come up, too?" Which the dog wasn't supposed to do, not on the family bed. Max didn't approve.

But… "Sure." Why not? What was a queen-size bed for, but to accommodate parents, child and animals, stuffed and real? Kellen patted the bottom of the bed.

Luna leaped up and stretched out on their feet.

Not exactly what Kellen had planned, but bonus points to the dog for bringing Rae through the shadowy corridor and into their bedroom. "Did the nightlight in your room help?"

"No. That's why I saw the lady!"

"What lady?"

"An old lady with silver hair. I dreamed someone was standing over me—"

"I know that feeling."

"—and I was scared. But I remembered what you said about facing my nightmares and I opened my eyes to look at her. She was supposed to disappear, and she was still there! She put her finger to her lips for me to be quiet, then she touched my forehead, then she went into the wall and vanished!"

"She touched your forehead? Like how?"

"Like you do when you kiss me goodnight."

"So it was a nice touch."

"Yes. But she was real." Rae curled into a tighter ball, still shivering.

"That sounds like a pretty good dream to me."

"She disappeared into the *wall*."

"That's kind of spooky," Kellen acknowledged. "What did Luna do?"

"Nothing."

"She didn't bark? She didn't growl?"

"No, she lifted her head and stared at the lady."

"You know if Luna thought you were threatened, she would protect you. That's her job, and she takes it seriously."

"I know," Rae said in a small voice.

"You've had a lot of nightmares since we left Yearning Sands."

"Because of the dead man with no hands."

Kellen went on alert. "How did you hear about that?"

"From Chloe, and Maverick and Rayleigh." In a return to her snotty tone, Rae said, "Before you took my phone away."

Kellen chose to ignore the snottiness. "Pretty awful story, isn't it?"

Rae whispered, "Yes."

"Scary."

"Yes."

"But that's in Cape Charade, and we're safe on Isla Paraíso, so right now, let's say your lady was a dream, too."

"She wasn't!" Rae was all rigid indignation.

"Shh. You'll wake your daddy."

Rae subsided.

"Tomorrow we'll look around your room and see if we can figure out where the lady came from."

"Ruby said there were secret passages, and we found one!"

"That's right." *Which is probably why you dreamed about them.* "Tomorrow we'll find out if one of them opens into your room. Okay?"

"Okay."

"No matter what we find, we're going to move you to the bedroom right across the hall. You need to be close to your daddy and me."

"Yes, please." In a very small voice, Rae asked, "Do you think Grandma is okay?"

Until Kellen came into their lives, Verona had been Rae's primary maternal influence. They had had time apart, of course, but not like this; not where Rae couldn't speak with her every day.

"I'm sure she is. She's going to Italy with Aunt Irene and Cousin Annabella, and you know how much she enjoys visiting the relatives."

"She'll be safe there?"

So no matter how hard Max and Kellen had tried to keep the truth from Rae, she had caught the echoes of their fears. "Your grandma describes your relatives in Northern Italy as tough, smart, mean, suspicious and with the kindest hearts…once they know you. She absolutely will be safe there."

"Okay."

"Can we go to sleep now?"

"Okay."

Kellen held Rae until the child went limp in slumber, then slowly she pulled her arm out from under Rae's neck and massaged her numb hand.

Max scooted up behind her. "Is your arm asleep?" He sounded alert. So he'd heard the whole thing.

"Rae's not a lightweight anymore. She's getting to be a young woman, and Max, she knows there's something wrong."

"I know."

Kellen rolled tightly against him. "I think we should tell her the whole truth."

"I don't think it would help. Here she can run around and still be safe. I don't want her to be afraid."

"She's already afraid. She heard about the murder at the mortuary."

"I understand that, but what good would it do to tell her about Mara? Kellen." Max wrapped his arm around her. "She worries about you. If we tell her what Mara said—"

"Yeah. Right. It would blow all her circuits." Which was true. "But I still feel guilty for not bringing Rae into the operation." Which was also true.

"You have to stop thinking of Rae as a soldier. She's not. She's a child."

Kellen remembered the children she had seen in Afghanistan, holding rifles, fighting in wars so old their distant great-grandparents had started them. She didn't want that for Rae. "Right. You're right. But Max, no matter how much we try to protect Rae, this disruption to her routine has really sent her into a tailspin."

"This mansion and Ruby's story are fuel for her imagination."

"She knows about Mara's grisly visit to the mortuary."

"I wish we'd taken her phone sooner." Max sounded savage.

"No, Max. She has to know what her friends know. But while this trip might be fraught, it's not all bad." Kellen cuddled with him. "Do you know what happened before dinner?"

"I cannot imagine."

Kellen smiled into the darkness. "Rae wanted to know more about World War II. So I said, 'The library,' and we went there. You'll never guess what we found."

"A book on World War II?"

"The *Encyclopedia Britannica*, 1953 edition."

His shoulder twitched under her head. "The *Encyclopedia*. Sure. Why didn't I think of that? Did you show her how to look stuff up?"

"I did. She read about World War II, then she asked if I realized there'd been a world war before that, then she read about worms…"

He chuckled, warm and deep. "I used to do that. Look one thing up, then keep going. Living here is like being forced to return to, I don't know, 1953."

"I suppose that's not bad except—" she hated to break the mood, but she had to ask " do you suppose we've permanently lost Mara?"

"The report your Diana sent says she's closing in on her."

"She thought that last week, too. Is Mara playing her?"

Max helplessly lifted his hands. "I wish I knew. But what I do know is—if Mara dares come back to the US, she'll be arrested and returned to prison. If she stays in Europe, she'll be arrested by Interpol, returned to the US and returned to prison. We're as safe here as it's possible to be, so let's hope for the best, expect the worst, and stick close to each other."

Luna crawled a few inches closer to the head of the bed.

Kellen said ruefully, "I don't know that we have much choice."

# CHAPTER TWELVE

*Five weeks later...*

A THOROUGH SEARCH had found no secret passage in Rae's pink bedroom, but Max and Kellen moved her into a smaller room—pale yellow, closer to them—amid reassurances Rae was welcome in their bedroom anytime.

That wasn't strictly true, but like all parents they were very careful when and where they celebrated their union, and the need to be vigilant and discreet made them all the more frantic when they came together.

A locked bathroom door and a shared steamy shower proved to be a good solution.

Max did express frustration about the constant need for speed, and promised that when this was over and they left Isla Paraíso, they would go on their long-delayed honeymoon and spend long, slow, heated hours in bed...

The same day Max made his promise, Kellen began a regular program of running and kickboxing. Not only did she need a way to redirect her sudden thirsty desire for leisurely sex, but as she worked out, she rediscovered the pure pleasure of movement. She jogged, sprinted, punched and kicked. Something nagged in the back of her mind, some instinct burned in her gut. She needed to prepare, to train. The five weeks had been paradise in so many ways. Yet if Mara continued to slip past Kellen's Army friend and all the law enforcement agencies…

Impossible! Yet Mara's threat cast a long shadow, and being fit gave Kellen confidence in her ability to handle…anything.

Also, it beat practicing the piano—which Rae insisted she do every day. The dog still howled, but Kellen *was* getting better, more in control of her dexterity.

Rae romped with Luna in the house and on the lawn, devoured every book in the library—the encyclopedia had been a special pleasure—and with her dad, she worked on the truck. For the most part, she was the wonderful child she had always been.

But once she had thrown a tantrum about missing her grandmother—totally justified, for in her life, they'd never been separated before for more than two weeks—and once because someone had stolen her favorite drinking glass…which she'd left on a table in the library.

Puberty was difficult, Kellen told Max.

Patience, Kellen told Max.

And, with a grin, Kellen told Max, "She reminds me of my cousin Kellen Rae. My cousin was smart, confident, impatient and brave. Celebrate the fact Rae takes after her. She's always going to be a leader."

The Di Lucas discovered that Luna, who could run forever, had a weakness. The grasses and thistles stuck in her tender paws. So much to the dog's distress, she was frequently sidelined, locked in the house, while

Rae bicycled far and wide across the island. Luna made her displeasure at being left behind clear; she hid in the closets or the corners, in unused rooms and the far reaches of the house. They had to find her, coax her, show her their love until she deigned to come out and be her usual cheerful self.

Interestingly enough, Max seemed to be having more trouble adjusting to life on Isla Paraíso than either Kellen or Rae. He had been in charge of so much of the Di Luca businesses for so long, the lack of responsibility made him twitchy. He had even been known to sit at night in the library and listen to Kellen read Ruby's diary. Luckily, the Ford F-100 did *not* run, and somehow, somewhere in his past, he'd wanted an old pickup to fix up. As a distraction, Kellen judged the F-100 to be a godsend.

All in all, Kellen believed that, as a family, they were doing pretty well. Having all the time in the world had had an odd effect; without structure they constructed their lives along their needs and preferences.

*I'll take everything from her, the way she took everything from me. I'll make her sorry she betrayed me.*

Yet the memory of Mara's threat cut into Kellen like a wound that threatened to turn gangrenous.

Today, as the sun rose, she ran the narrow path south and downhill, through the waving grasses, east on the winding track through the deeply shaded redwoods. The massive trees muffled the sounds of the waves, and the silence here was old and watchful, as if a soul lived in each redwood, and each soul had seen too much of change and sorrow. She was glad to turn east into the bright sunlight toward the Conkles' cottage, but when she saw Jamie working in the yard, she veered off.

**JAMIE CONKLE:**
FEMALE OF COLOR, 32YO, 5'7", 125 LBS. BEAUTIFUL, BUT—BLACK HAIR AND DARK, RESENTFUL EYES BEHIND NARROW BLACK-FRAMED GLASSES. PERPETUAL WARDROBE: LONG SLEEVELESS DRESS THAT SHOWS OFF ARMS SCULPTED BY DAILY SHOVEL AND HAMMER LABOR, AND SNEAKERS WITH SOCKS. LIVING HER DREAM, BUT NEVER HAPPY, AS IF REALITY COULD NEVER COMPETE WITH THE SHANGRI-LA OF HER IDEAL WORLD.

In the first week on the island, Rae had begged to visit Jamie. She didn't believe Jamie wouldn't like her. So Kellen and Rae had biked to the small house carrying the gift of one of Olympia's pound cakes wrapped in a bow.

Jamie had met them at the door, pointed out that baking such a frivolous cake used precious energy better preserved for future generations. When she saw Luna, she informed them the dog might kill the rare fowl in the area and should be kept penned.

Kellen and Rae had retreated.

Five weeks later, Kellen had occasionally seen Jamie bringing the food basket to Olympia, and once she'd caught a glimpse of someone who looked like her on the second floor of the mansion. But when Kellen called her, Jamie had rounded a corner and vanished. Into a secret passage, Kellen supposed. But why would Jamie be inside and upstairs? When she visited to ask, Jamie explained in contemptuous tones that with so many people now living in the mansion, *someone* had to check the condition of the water tower on the roof. She managed to make it sound as if Kellen had deliberately made work for her, and when Kellen offered to take over that duty, Jamie had brusquely dismissed her.

Odd. The woman was just odd.

Dylan, when intoxicated, was far too friendly. And he was always intoxicated.

At the low end of the island, Kellen passed the dock where the SkinnySail was moored. She slowed, then stopped. Arm raised, she held her hat firmly on her head, protecting it from the constant breeze, and smiled at the memories.

*Max wrapped his arms around Kellen's shoulders and pointed at the SkinnySail, waiting at the waterline. "Isn't she a beauty? Want to go out with me? I can teach you to sail."*

*Kellen knew nothing about boats or boating; she left that for Max and other enthused family members. To her eyes, this boat was small, sleek, with a mast and a motor. What the motor said to her was,* Sailing doesn't always work and sometimes you have to be saved. *"No, that's fine. You teach Rae. I'll stay on the beach and read."*

*"It's big enough for the three of us."*

*"If one of us wasn't a former football player, maybe. You weigh a ton! Add me and Rae and the whole thing will founder."*

*"Maybe. Then it's time for swimming lessons." He laughed at Kellen's expression, kissed her on the mouth and then yelled, "Come on, Rae, let's sail!"*

*Before he finished speaking, Rae prepared the sail*

*to be raised and together, she and Max pushed the boat into the waves.*

*Kellen watched Max haul out the oars and gesture Rae to her place by the motor. She was going to steer them out beyond the breakers and into open water.*

*Living at Yearning Sands Resort had taught the child all the things they had hoped when they moved there: she biked, she sailed, she could survive in the wilderness. She had taught adults how to make a fire and tie a rope. Her confidence was as blinding as her smile.*

*Max cast off.*

*The waves came into this beach at an angle; Max said that meant it was easier to get out beyond the surf. Easier might not be the correct term, because Max and Rae struggled mightily, using oars and the motor. Then they were out into the ocean and sailing out of sight...*

That *out of sight* thing worried Kellen, so next time, she decided to go along. Max removed the motor to save the weight. They all hopped in and sailed away...

Max and Rae had a fabulous time, and returned drenched. Kellen simply returned drenched.

She was, she realized, the official Isla Paraíso party pooper.

On the other hand, she knew how to do enough stuff: rappel out of a helicopter, aim and shoot a weapon and, now, speak Italian well enough to find a bathroom and order a meal. She had even learned to crochet an afghan, which Verona triumphantly pointed out was great physical therapy for her hands.

Kellen would rather play piano.

She determined that her other accomplishments

voided the need to join Max and Rae on the briny deep out of some misguided sense of adventure.

Turning away, she followed the ocean cliffs around toward the mansion. As her feet pounded out the miles, she breathed hard, exalting in the isolation, the wildness, the waves. As birds soared above her, her soul rose to meet them...

The mansion came into view and she dropped into a walk. She should go into the kitchen, converse with Olympia about lunch and dinner, but during the weeks they had lived here, that woman hadn't warmed to the island or their family.

Kellen did the cowardly thing; she dodged a meeting with Olympia, went around to the front door, and ran up to the shower. When she was clean and dressed in shorts and a T-shirt, she stopped by the library, picked up Ruby Morgade's diary and headed for the garage.

The carriage house doors and the door against the back wall stood wide to let the breeze sweep through. She paused outside in the shadows to watch Max and Rae together, and she smiled.

Her husband and daughter were working on the truck, deep under the hood, fiercely discussing whether electrical tape would repair the worn radiator hose, and having a marvelous time. Something must have alerted them to her presence, because Rae looked up and said, "Mommy, *you* know. Can we use electrical tape to repair the radiator hose?"

"If you use enough of it." Kellen strolled in.

"That's the problem." Max held up a partial roll. "This is all we've got."

It wasn't.

Kellen had been slowly cataloging all the equipment in the metal drawers under the tool bench. That first caretaker had kept tools and spare parts to fix the wells, generators, vehicles, toilets—you name it, it was there, including black electrical tape.

Kellen exchanged a look with Luna, who sprawled on a wool blanket close to the back door.

A good mechanic always looked through the toolboxes before she started working on a vehicle.

Max was an amateur, but he was having such a good time figuring it out on his own, Kellen bit her tongue, keeping her advice to herself, unless he asked.

And he did everything in his power not to ask.

"I wonder if there's a roll of electrical tape in the house," Max muttered. "Seems like there should be." He looked at the roll in his hand, decided to go for it, and leaned in to wrap the hose. F-100s operated with six-cylinder engines in an eight-cylinder engine compartment, and enough room to stand inside if he needed. Kellen guessed, at the rate he was going, pretty soon he was going to need to.

Rae sat on the fender of the F-100 in an old, oversize pair of mechanic's coveralls with well-rolled cuffs, and sent a dark frown at Kellen. "It's the Fourth of July, and Daddy says we can't have fireworks."

"Didn't bring any." Max bobbed up from under the hood.

"It's too dry for fireworks." Kellen cleared herself a spot on the tool bench, boosted herself up, picked up her stress ball and squeezed it in her right hand. Not because she was stressed, but because it strengthened her grip. "It hasn't rained since the first day we got here. The grass is like tinder. If we set off any kind of spark, we'd be surrounded by the smoking remains of the whole island…if we weren't burned to a crisp with it."

The lack of rain was a worry. The cisterns were low; Max figured they had about two weeks' worth of water left before they either had to call for some to be brought across the ocean or leave the island. As Max said privately to Kellen, if only there was a break in the Mara case.

But Interpol had lost her. The FBI insisted she wasn't on United States soil. Most worrisome, when Max checked the radio for reports, Diana, Kellen's tracker friend, had disappeared.

"It's the Fourth of July. We should celebrate. We could shoot off fireworks at the beach. The sparks would go over the ocean." Rae beamed. "Problem solved!"

Kellen looked out the back windows. She could see the green lawn where the sprinklers regularly nourished the carefully cut grass, and the dividing line where the sprinklers stopped, and the wild grasses took over in a dry, golden profusion. "Luna would not be impressed."

At the sound of her name, Luna left her blanket and came to stand at Kellen's feet and stare. Regardless of her inability to climb, she wanted up, onto the workbench.

"If you can get up here, you're welcome," Kellen told her.

Luna gave a lovely doggie sneer of contempt, backed up and took a running leap. She landed on the bench, skidded along the wood, took out a pile of tools and stopped when she slammed against the window frame. The thump and clatter brought all movement in the garage to a halt, and everyone stared at Luna, who with elaborate casualness stretched out beside Kellen and smiled at her audience.

"Luna was our rescue dog," Max said. "But I've often wondered what her job was before she came to us."

"Burglar?" Kellen suggested.

Rae chided, "Mommy, Luna's not a thief. She simply likes to be comfortable with us."

"Right." Luna bumped Kellen's hand with her nose and on demand, Kellen scratched her neck.

"Luna would like fireworks," Rae said.

With awesome patience, Max said, "We don't have any fireworks."

"Could we shoot off guns?" Rae asked.

Kellen put down the stress ball. "Guns?"

"Isn't that why we shoot off fireworks? Because it's like the Revolutionary War, all shooting and stuff?" Rae was pretty glib for a kid who'd never fired a weapon.

Kellen was glad she was honestly able to say, "There were no firearms in Morgade Hall when we arrived. Right, Max?"

Max straightened up. "No. No firearms here when we arrived. Which is weird, because a big tough guy like Morgade should have firearms all over his house. And animal heads mounted on his walls."

"Daddy, that's gross!"

"Yeah, it is. Anyway, no firearms when we got

here." He gestured to Kellen. "Would you try to start the truck?"

"Sure." Kellen jumped down—Luna remained comfortably relaxed on the bench—climbed into the driver's side, turned the key in the ignition, then pushed the starter button.

The starter moaned, but the engine didn't turn over.

"Are you sure you're doing it right?" Max asked.

Kellen got out, walked around to the front of the truck and looked at Max. Just looked at him.

"Yeah. I guess that was stupid." Max wiped his greasy hands on a rag. "I feel like I'm not getting anywhere with this thing. The damned truck should start!"

Kellen affectionately watched him scratch his head and smear grease on his forehead. The first time they'd come out to work on the truck, Max had aired up the low tire.

Since then, like his optimism, it had slowly been deflating.

Rae frowned darkly into the depths of the engine compartment. "Daddy, the spark plugs are groaty. What would happen if you took them out and cleaned them?"

Kellen gave Rae a nod of approval.

Max viewed his little girl with suspicion. "It's worth a try." He glared at Kellen.

She shrugged. She hadn't told her. Rae had thought of that on her own.

"Okay. Smart kid." He beamed, and asked Kellen, "Will it work?"

"Good chance."

"Rae, hand me a spark plug socket wrench." He started removing the spark plugs.

Rae leaned on his shoulder and watched. "Be careful getting those out. We don't have any wires if you break them."

*Right in that drawer, wires and new spark plugs, too.*

*Keep your mouth shut, Kellen.*

She hadn't yet investigated the contents of the old white refrigerator. She suspected it hadn't run for a long time, and she rather feared she'd find the first caretaker's lunch in an advanced state of petrification.

She opened the door.

Petrified food wasn't what she found.

It was worse than that.

Hastily she shut the door.

*Holy smokes. How long had all that been in there?*

She must have squeaked, because Max pulled his head out of the engine compartment. "What's wrong?"

"Nothing." She caught sight of a movement just inside the door.

*Mara.*

No. Not Mara.

Dylan Conkle, grinning guiltily.

"Dylan. What are you doing?" She rested her cool gaze on him. It wasn't the first time she'd caught him sneaking around to listen to their conversations.

"I, um, came up to mow the lawn and I brought the food basket." He put it down in the corner and sidled farther into the garage. "What're you doing? Trying to get the old truck running?"

Rae answered. "We're not trying. We're going to do it."

"Right. Sure." Dylan's voice had that patronizing tone people got when talking to kids. "You're daddy's little helper, aren't you?"

He got close enough to the truck that Max, who had been watching him, asked, "What have you been drinking? Have you been making your own liquor?"

Dylan reversed his path, backing slowly away. "Not really. I mean…yeah, maybe. It's like a craft beer thing only with grains. Very respectable."

"Don't drink that stuff until after you've delivered the basket." Max looked him right in the eyes. "You don't have a tough job. You might want to keep it."

Dylan's smile faded. He turned and scurried away, and his departure left a profound silence in the garage.

Max grimaced. "He's going to kill himself or get fired, and I don't know which will come first."

One thing Dylan's sudden appearance had shown Kellen—although Mara had not been a continuous, sentient fear, her subconscious had been on the lookout all the time they'd been here. She looked at the refrigerator, then at the empty doorway where Dylan had stood. Picking up Ruby's diary, she asked brightly, "Want me to continue with Ruby's story?"

"Yes!" Rae said.

"Go for it," Max said.

Kellen read, "'My brother is dead.'"

"Oh, no. Poor Ruby!" Rae sounded sad for the woman she had never met.

"Poor brother," Max said.

Kellen started again…

# CHAPTER THIRTEEN

---

*My brother is dead. With his bullying and his demands for perfection, Father drove Alexander away. Alexander joined the Navy and Father cut him off without a dime. He has been writing me and my dear Hermione has been gathering the letters before Father could confiscate them.*

---

KELLEN STOPPED READING.

Rae craned her neck around to look at her mother.

"What?" Max asked.

"Ruby didn't like Hermione," Rae told her father.

"Something must have happened." Kellen hooked her finger in the diary. "We can be sure no one likes Mr. Morgade, so Hermione wouldn't, either. Ruby sounds charming, and she and Hermione are close to the same age and the only young women on the island—"

"There had to be staff," Max pointed out. "Maids to do the cleaning and stuff."

"Yes, but they would be working all the time. *All* the time. I'd guess Ruby and Hermione bonded, and

I mean, really—if Mr. Morgade is gone most of the time, how would he know whether all his instructions are obeyed?"

Rae grinned at Kellen. "I like Hermione!"

"Me, too." Kellen sobered. "Although she's taking a terrific chance. If Morgade finds out, he'll toss her aside the way he did Miss Harriman. She might never work again. A single woman on her own could starve."

Rae took a long, frightened breath. "Read more. Read faster!"

Alexander went through training and he was happy. He shipped out to Hawaii, and he was happy.

Three days ago, the Japanese attacked Pearl Harbor. We heard many brave men were killed. President Roosevelt declared war on Japan. Mother is devastated. She cried because her people murdered so many. Then this morning she got the news about Alexander.

He was in a hangar preparing a plane to take off when a Japanese fighter dropped a bomb and demolished the building. He was my next oldest sibling, twenty-one years old, and he's dead. My heart is bleeding.

Father said he deserved what he got for disobeying him.

I hate Father so much. Now there is only Bessie, married and living on the east coast, and Larry in Britain, at Oxford, where it is not at all safe. The Blitz targets all historical buildings, and I fear for him.

Then there's me, here on this horrible island, learning the correct way to pour tea and direct servants while the world goes up in flames.

---

Father went to the mainland to deal with the news stories. I sent him a message, begging him to return. Mother isn't well. She isn't crying now. She sits and stares.

He hasn't come.

He won't.

He doesn't care. We're Japanese. We're liabilities now.

---

Father is incensed. The Navy has come to Morgade Island. They arrived without warning, presented Mother with papers and began construction on a structure that looks to the west.

Men are swarming everywhere.

All the time, dynamite blasts shake the ground. Ships are bringing materials.

Men everywhere. Handsome men. In uniform!

Father is nowhere close to here. He has written Mother and told her to tell the Navy to get off. Which is laughable. Then he wrote to explain he had no choice because if he hadn't yielded to the military's demands they would have moved Mother and me off the coast and into an internment camp.

The nasty old man made this occupation our

fault. Even Mother is rousing from her sorrow about my brother... We got his body back, and buried him here on the island.

---

Father came. He's in a cold rage, seeing the men on his island. Morgade Island. The Navy calls it Isla Paraíso, which is what it was called before Father bought it. That makes him angrier. He hates seeing men here who are young and handsome, who use slang and don't care who he is or whether he's important. He hates having no power.

He tells me to speak only to the officers. But they're old. Most of them are over twenty-five. I met one private first class named Beaufort Rash. He has a southern accent, he's cute, and he's twenty. He worked for the Southern Pacific Railroad before he joined up. He joined on D-Day, but he promises he doesn't blame me for what the Japs did. I looked him in the eyes. I told him my brother died that day, because my brother joined before it was glamorous. I was proud of myself; I didn't ask Beaufort if he'd yet lost any relatives, and he shut up.

Hermione laughed when I told her, then told me not to take it to heart. She said most men like that have been spoiled by their mothers and sisters, and don't realize they should be careful what they say. She says I taught him a lesson, and good for me.

Today I got a letter from my sister. Bessie heard about the Naval occupation of the island and writes to warn me to take care, for all these soldiers and sailors wanted only one thing from me, and that was my virtue. I wrote back and told her I had so concluded. I am not as stupid as everyone seems to think.

But there is one boy...

"What? A boy?" Rae's eyes were shining.

The spark plugs were laid out on the workbench, cleaned and polished. The wires were straightened and inspected. Luna rested her head against Kellen's thigh. Rae was sitting on the F-100's fender. Max leaned against the grille. They were both listening raptly.

"Is this boy going to rescue Ruby from her wicked father?" Rae asked.

"Listening to Ruby's story, I think she's going to rescue herself." Max gathered the spark plugs, muttering, "I've got to re-gap these."

"Yes!" Rae pumped her arm. She wasn't talking about the thrills of re-gapping.

Kellen rustled the pages of the diary. "I think we'd better stop here, or we'll be here until evening and Olympia will be furious. Also—" She rocked on her bottom, numb from sitting, and winced. "Rae? Would you take this basket to Olympia?"

"Sure." Rae was not enthused.

Kellen suggested, "Maybe you can help her make sandwiches for lunch."

"She doesn't like my help." Rae took the basket and dragged her feet toward the back door.

"I wish you would help her. I'm *starving*." It was true, Kellen realized. All that running…she *was* starving.

As if Kellen's words reminded Rae of food, her eyes got round and her step got enthusiastic. "Me, too." She raced out the door.

"That kid. When she's hungry, we're all in trouble. She's enough to make a bull elephant tremble." Max extricated himself from the engine compartment. "Is Rae unhappy here?"

"I don't think so. Not exactly. But she only has us. Olympia doesn't like kids. Jamie doesn't like anybody."

"Then why did you send her away?" Max was darned observant…for a guy.

She placed her hand on the old refrigerator. "Max, you've got to look at this."

"What is it?" He walked over and opened the door.

Stacked inside were explosives: military dynamite and rolls of cable.

Max shut the refrigerator door. Fast. "Holy shit."

"Yes. Exactly."

He opened the door again. "These are leftovers from…?"

"I guess from World War II when the Navy occupied the island."

He shut the door again as if shutting it could make it disappear. "Do they still work?"

"I don't know!"

"You were in the military."

"We had current munitions!" She took a breath. "The Army fed us rations packaged in the Vietnam War, but the artillery was up to date!"

"Right." He leaned a hand against the refrigerator, then hastily pulled it away. "Dynamite shouldn't have an expiration date, should it? It's a chemical compound set off with a blasting cap."

"The blasting caps are in the vegetable crisper."

"Of course they are." He was trying to reason his way through this. "As long as the chemicals are kept dry and in a stable environment, as they have been, then we have really good explosives."

"I believe you're right."

"What do you do with dynamite?"

"You blow things to kingdom come. I currently haven't got a reason to do that. Do you?"

"Not currently." His brown eyes glowed as he got an idea. "Hey, if Mara shows up, we could run one up her ass and light the fuse."

"Max!" Shocked and unwillingly amused, Kellen laughed.

"You have a problem with that?"

"No."

"Anything else good in here?" He opened the door and looked into the tiny freezer compartment at the foot-long metal cylinders. Gingerly, he picked one up and read the label. "Flares. We've got flares. Military flares."

"Flares, illumination, hand held, star cluster, white, green and multi-color."

"I always wanted to shoot one off. In the Army, did you shoot one off?"

He didn't very often look at her with a reverential gaze, and she could not lie—she liked it. "In Afghanistan. You bet. For illumination. Parachute flares, too." She took the flare out of his hand and examined it. "This is vintage. It's different than the ones I used. This flare opens like a sardine can. But after that, the theory is the same. Remove the firing cap, place it on the bottom of the tube, align it correctly, aim and strike it sharply on a hard surface. Your palm, if you're steady, but there's a recoil, so I prefer to use the ground. They go up as high as seven hundred and fifty feet before the star cluster ignites. The star cluster lasts six to ten seconds. At least…the flares I used did." She handed it back to him. "I don't know about the old ones."

"And what could we do with them?"

"Well, we could…" Kellen shook her head. "No, we couldn't."

"What? Shoot them off tonight to celebrate the Fourth of July?"

Great. They thought alike. One of them had to be mature. Didn't they? "The grasslands are a tinderbox out here. A flare would set the whole island on fire."

"Come on, honey." He wrapped his arm around Kellen. "Rae deserves a treat."

"Don't try to blackmail me with my daughter. Although…"

"Although?"

She experienced the same feeling she had known those times in the military when her platoon waited and waited and waited for an attack, and finally got wild and rowdy in their need to blow off some steam. "Rae's right. We *could* shoot them off over the ocean. We'd set nothing on fire." Really, it wouldn't hurt.

"Right! And look." He pointed toward the corner of the garage. "Big old washtubs, right there. We'd take the washtubs down to the beach with us. If anything happened, like some sparks blowing back at us—"

"—or the flare failing altogether?"

"—we'd be ready to put out the fires."

"Max, you're crazy. I'm crazy. That would be wrong. What if we didn't succeed and the whole island went up in flames?"

"There is nothing you and I can't do when we try."

THAT NIGHT A flare lifted off the beach at Isla Paraíso and lit the sky over the Pacific with a blast of multicolored lights.

Just over the horizon, Mara Philippi stood on the deck of a yacht, and caught her breath in surprise and pleasure. "Look, Owen." She spoke toward the chair at the stern. "They're welcoming us to Isla Paraíso! How unexpected—and charming."

# *CHAPTER FOURTEEN*

OLYMPIA DELIVERED HER usual English country house breakfast to the dining room: bacon, sausages, eggs prepared two ways, wheat toast, white toast, French toast, a bowl of oranges from Jamie's orchard. Kellen thought how lovely it felt to be waited on in such palatial splendor.

Unfortunately, after she placed the dishes on the table, Olympia didn't leave. Instead she stood, stern and sour-faced, hands wrapped in her apron.

Max was reading his backlog of wine studies and paying no attention. Rae was eating a little of everything. Which left Kellen to ask, "What's up, Olympia?"

"There are rodents in the kitchen."

That got Max's attention. He lifted his head and stared, transfixed, at their cook.

"Some large thing has been in the pantry, moving things around, polishing off the leftovers of yesterday's cake." Olympia looked sternly at Rae, who was still eating French toast and bacon with total concentration.

"You don't think… You're not saying that she…" Kellen was shocked.

"I'm not saying anything." Olympia changed her attention to Max. "Men are notorious for thinking they can barge in and grab anything they want."

Max's expression didn't change—which showed a lot of control on his part.

"I assure you, I sleep with Max and he does not get up in the middle of the night and disappear to eat cake." Kellen's tone was gentle; her expression was as forbidding as Olympia's.

"Of course not. I meant that Dylan person. He has the keys to the house. He always smells as if he's been smoking marijuana." Olympia pronounced each syllable. "And the list of goods Mrs. Conkle compiles never matches what's in the basket. I assume he's been eating all the way up here. I wouldn't be surprised to find a raw chicken gone someday."

It was sort of funny, but not.

Rae was paying attention now, watching the scene with her brow furrowed.

Max said, "We're not in any position to change locks out here."

"Send to the mainland," Olympia said.

"I told you when we came here we wouldn't be making contact except in the matter of life and death." Which was not strictly true, considering Max's weekly radio call to get a report on Mara, but Olympia didn't know that and Max sounded implacable. "I'll look for a bicycle lock in the garage. If I find one, I'll attach it to the pantry door. In the meantime, why don't you secret anything attractive like cake or cookies in a cupboard known only to you?"

"Humph!" Olympia banged her way back into the kitchen.

Kellen looked at Max and mouthed, "What a bitch."

He said, "It's not easy getting someone on short notice to cook and do light cleaning on a deserted island with none of the usual amenities."

Kellen noted Max hadn't disagreed.

"What's happening?" Rae asked.

"Someone ate the cake last night from the pantry," Max told her.

Rae wrinkled her nose. "It had coconut. I didn't like it. Hey, would you tell Olympia to stop playing her music at night? It creeps me out."

"She does have retro taste in music," Kellen said.

Max looked at them both.

"I went to Rae's room to check up on her after the fireworks. I thought she might…" Kellen gave Max the look that meant, *have nightmares*. "Music was wafting up the stairs. Old songs from years ago."

"Like Ruby would have played!" Rae said.

Kellen hadn't thought about that. "That's exactly right."

Rae slid off her chair. "Can I be excused? Can Luna and I go for a bike ride?"

"May I?" Kellen corrected her, then thought, *Geez, I'm channeling my aunt.* "Yes, you may be excused. And yes, you and Luna may go for a bike ride. First brush your teeth. Put on your sunscreen. Don't take Luna too far and when you turn back, check her pads for thorns. We don't want her limping again."

"I'll be careful!" Rae tore out of the dining room.

Max and Kellen looked at each other.

"Getting away has been good for her," Max marveled.

"I was thinking the same thing. She's strong and I'd swear she's grown at least an inch while we've been here." Kellen took a breath. "Except… I wonder if Rae is sleepwalking."

"What? Why?"

"Olympia wouldn't lie about stuff disappearing from the kitchen."

"Rae wouldn't lie, either. Or steal!"

"She tells the occasional fib." Kellen lifted one finger to stop his protest. "We all do. Not the point. We tore her from all that was familiar and dragged her halfway across the world. She's still suffering from nightmares. With all those hormones raging through her, sleepwalking is a possibility."

"And sleep-eating?"

"Yes. Unless it's me and you're not telling me."

"You think you're sleepwalking?"

"No, I think I still have a brain that's healing and I could be blacking out. How would I know?" She said that as if she was calm about the possibility.

She wasn't. Of all the conditions that her medical team had told her could happen, the possibility of blackouts terrified her most.

"I'd tell you. I'd take a chance with Mara and return you to the mainland for treatment." Max scooted his chair close to hers and kissed her, soft and comforting, with a warm undercurrent of passion that tugged at Kellen's senses. "Trust me. Ask me next time. Don't wonder and worry."

"I do trust you." She kissed him, too, and looked into his eyes. "I love you."

"I know," he said smugly. "This wasn't what I intended for our honeymoon. It's a couple of years late. I planned a sailing trip on the Mediterranean. I thought the sun would shine all day and the moon would shine all night and we'd make love wherever and whenever we wanted."

"This is a great honeymoon." She had never meant anything so much.

"Except for the wherever and whenever part."

She giggled. "I like making love as fast as we can while hushing each other so Rae doesn't hear."

He laughed, too. "Yes, it's great. Just great." He drew back. "I do wish the police would intercept Mara so we could get off this island. I thought they'd have her by now."

"Do they have any idea…?"

"Where she is? Not the last time I talked to them. But I'm keeping contact to the bare minimum. I'm not taking any chances."

Kellen nodded, then turned her head to listen. "What's Luna barking about?"

Olympia walked in. "That dog is scratching at the back door. It's going to ruin the paint!"

Max and Kellen got to their feet and hurried into the kitchen.

Kellen opened the door.

Luna jumped at her, barking, then ran outside and to the foot of the stairs. She turned and barked again. *Come on!*

Kellen leaped off the porch and sprinted across the yard.

Max raced ahead.

Luna outpaced them both.

They met Rae pushing her bike, dust-covered, limping and crying.

Luna circled her until Max and Kellen got there.

Max gently took the bike from her.

"Mommy…" Rae's lip trembled and her eyes welled. "I hurt myself."

"I see that, sweetheart." Kellen slid her arm around Rae to support her. "Broken bones?"

"No."

"You're sure?" Max asked.

Kellen shot him a look. "She'd know."

"But would she tell us?"

"Of course I would," Rae snarled. "I'm not stupid!"

Max looked startled.

Kellen had been assessing her as they walked. "You've got contusions on your cheek and forehead."

Rae held out her hands.

"On your palms." Bits of dirt and rock were embedded in the skin. "I'll bet that hurts."

Rae nodded, and the tears started again.

"Your left knee and calf are ripped up and it looks like you scraped off a toenail. Nothing serious, but nothing fun. What were you doing?" She really expected to hear something about riding fast downhill.

"I just… I was trying to…"

"Trying to what?" Kellen asked.

"I built a jump."

Max made a noise deep in his throat.

Kellen looked back at him in bewilderment.

Proudly, he tapped his chest and mouthed, *My kid.*

Kellen turned back to Rae. "You built a jump? For your bike?"

"Out of the boards in the garage." Rae sounded less

sniffy and more enthusiastic. "It was working great!"
She sagged. "Then one of them broke."

Max held the screen door for them. "Those boards
are so old, honey, they're rotten."

"You're telling me!"

Kellen helped Rae inside. "Let's get you in a bathtub, clean you up and see what exactly we're dealing
with."

Max slammed the screen and said, "I'll see if I
can find something to make a jump out of that won't
break." He didn't even notice the blistering glare Kellen gave his retreating back.

# CHAPTER FIFTEEN

"YOU KNOW, OWEN, if you'd been smart, you might have entertained doubts as to why I wanted to learn how to handle your yacht." Mara Philippi glanced at Owen Kenoyer, seated at the back of the…at the stern, strapped in and trolling for some game fish to mount and stick on his wall. "But you thought it was cute that a beautiful, saucy woman wanted to handle such a massive vessel. I made you feel indulgent." She shot a grin at the back of his head. "Like most men, you're easily led with the stroke of a finger. So to speak." She checked the rudder to make sure it was cranked to the left, allowing the yacht to make lazy circles in the water. "Probably all this knowledge I've gained will be useless in the future, unless I decide to buy my own yacht, and if I do, I promise never, ever to take on a young lover I pick up in church. When your wife finds out, what will she say?"

Predictably, Owen didn't answer.

"Probably nothing, or maybe she'll want to thank me. I imagine she's used to your philandering, and with the money you've got and the nasty little fetishes you enjoy, she'll be relieved to have you out of her hair." Mara laughed. "So to speak again… Have you noticed when you talk about sex, almost everything you say becomes a metaphor, and humorous? Stay there, I've got to go below to open the bilge pumps." When she returned, she leaned on the rail and gazed at the faint smudge on the horizon that was Isla Paraíso. "It's sort of a shame to scuttle this vessel when I was really getting the hang of it. I could get used to living like this." She looked around affectionately.

This beast must have cost two hundred thousand or more.

She focused on Isla Paraíso again. Her humor faded, and she began to breathe deeply, like a woman on the verge of orgasm. "I hate to leave you here, but I have an appointment with Kellen Adams and her family. Her husband, Maximilian. Her darling little girl, Rae. I think in the past few years, while I was in prison, Kellen has grown quite fond of them. The best part is—they're afraid that I'm coming. They think they've outsmarted me…and they did for a while. I followed them to Italy before I realized I was on a wild goose chase. That *I* was being followed. That was a mistake. The woman they hired was tough, but not as tough as me. Burns are such painful wounds, the little pieces of agony that make up successful torture. When I was done with her, she told me where they had gone. I removed her hands—my signature, as you now have discovered—and left her to die." She swallowed in chagrin. "I should have known. I should have *known*. I went to Morocco and almost got killed before I found out she hadn't known where they were!"

She thought she heard a whisper on the wind, whipped her head around and glared at Owen. "I can hear you laughing. Don't think I can't. Don't think this doesn't add another hour to Kellen's torment. I'll see to it myself."

The yacht was riding low in the water now, starting to flounder.

She loaded her supplies and weapons into the dinghy. "I wondered—where will they end up? Where will they think themselves safe? Somewhere in the States, of course, on one of the Di Luca family properties. Someplace safe. That narrowed it down considerably. They weren't going to a busy winery where every guest is welcome. No. It had to be isolated, easily guarded. I admit, Isla Paraíso wasn't my first guess. I didn't even know they owned an island off California. I mean, who does that? The family's got money, I'll say. After I got it narrowed down, all I had to do was check their spreadsheets." She turned to face Owen. "Did I mention I spent the time in prison learning how to read? I demanded they teach me to overcome my dyslexia, and they *had* to. A judge made them, and I didn't even have to sleep with her. I was condemned to life in prison, and the government *still* had to give me a chance for employment. God, these laws! You know what I mean. I hear you carrying on about exactly this. So wasteful!"

The yacht shuddered and tilted toward the port bow.

She stumbled and clutched the railing. "I'd better be careful. I'd hate to end up floating on a door in freezing water."

Again he didn't reply.

"It's a scene from *Titanic*, Owen. You don't know a thing about historical pop cinema, do you?"

Nothing.

"I watched a lot of movies in prison. I'm a film expert now. An expert in a lot of things… Anyway, once I had the rudiments of reading, I researched the really good parts of computer hacking. It was all part of my evil plan." She performed a good approximation of Maleficent's laugh then, pleased with herself, she said, "I admit, I'm not good enough to do a *lot* of harm, but I am good at breaking and entering without leaving a trace, and hacking a specific computer, and reading a spreadsheet and seeing a single glitch in the shipments to Isla Paraíso. That was it. Once I checked the contents, I knew. A few extra pounds of meat, a few extra vegetables, enough miscellaneous cooking supplies…and three bicycles." Mara put her hand over her pounding heart. "Three bicycles. Whatever could that mean?"

Owen still didn't answer.

Mara glanced over. "Honey, look at that. You've got your fish." She pointed. "It's on your line. It's leaping. A giant swordfish. How cool is that?" She pulled the long-bladed knife from her belt and used it to cut the line. She turned to Owen. "Sorry. You probably didn't want to see me use that knife again. It slipped so easily between your ribs."

Owen sat, his head bowed over his bloody chest, his hands severed and resting in his lap.

"The yacht's really sinking now. You don't mind me leaving you here, do you?" Mara was amusing herself now, reciting all her cleverness. "I'm headed for Isla Paraíso. It is isolated, all right, it's just not easily guarded. All that coastline! What were they thinking?" She tapped her lips, swollen from Owen's bites.

"Probably that they didn't want to alarm the child. If that was the idea, good plan. Better for me if she hasn't been warned." She watched the Pacific Ocean swells swamp the yacht. "This looks like a deep spot to sink a vessel. I doubt if anyone ever recovers it, Owen, or you. So sleep in peace. Sorry to take you by surprise like that. But at least your last moments were strapped in a fishing stool getting your rocks off and never suspecting you'd been a fool. So you died happy." Mara lowered the dinghy into the water and climbed over the rail and aboard. She started the engine and when it was running smoothly, she pulled away. "Goodbye, Owen. Goodbye!" Mara directed the dinghy toward the island and pushed the engine to its full speed.

She smiled.

She had been looking forward to this for a long, long time.

## CHAPTER SIXTEEN

WITH SCABS FORMING on her knees and her hands wrapped in gauze, Rae was miserable. She didn't want to read. She didn't want to watch movies. She wanted to mope, and she was doing a fine job of it until Kellen suggested they read more of Ruby's diary.

Rae brightened. "Yes! Let's go to the attic. I love Ruby. I feel closer to her there. She's so smart and brave and her father is so mean!"

---

Today, the commander of the island fortifications came to the house. Father invited him to dinner; I think he had illusions that General Tempe would make me a good suitor. At the table, Mother asked him if he was married. He said he had been. His wife had left him to become an actress and their three young sons lived with her parents. He looked at me sideways as if he knew what Father wanted. I asked him if he would like more candied oranges. We grow oranges in a protected orchard and they are very tasty. I also asked about a party for his men. I said I thought the boys of my age would appreciate a chance to drink, dance, talk about their homes and families. The general looked at me differently then. He understood me very well.

When he had gone, Father shouted at me. He said these days, no man of power would have a half—Jap girl, regardless of her father's influence, and I had better learn to beg for scraps. I told him I didn't want an old man like him who cared only for power and nothing for love, a man who everyone loathed.

He hit me. He knocked me down. Mother cried out. Hermione dragged me away before he could trample me under his feet.

I didn't know he cared whether I insulted him, told him that he is an ogre and that we all hate him. But apparently he does. So I succeeded in some small way to hurt that giant cruel ego, and I'm glad. I'm glad, and I wear my bruises proudly.

Father was gone by morning.

We'll have our party.

---

His name is Patrick. Patrick Sullivan. And he's white, he's white, he's white! Not Father's kind of white, nor even Beaufort's. Poor white. Irish Catholic white. Father would call him trash. He's 19. His parents immigrated from Ireland. He graduated from high school, the first in his family. The day after, he left home and traveled hundreds of miles on a bus to go to trade school to learn to be a printer. He joined the Navy the day after Pearl Harbor, and the Navy sent him to school to learn mechanics. Now he's here because he can fix machinery and he can write reports. See, he really wanted to be a reporter, but he spells funny. He puts the letters backward. He admitted he writes stories, too, but he was ashamed to show me until I promised not to laugh. As if I would.

The story was wonderful! Yes, he needs help with his grammar and spelling, but it was about preparing for war: unpolished, rough, full of the contrasts of terror and courage, homesickness and purpose. He doesn't know it, but I typed up the story, corrected the errors, and sent it to the Armed Forces Magazine.

Now I wait to see if they accept it, and while I wait, I see him every day.

Mother knows. She says nothing.

Hermione knows. She packs us a lunch.

Dear diary, I'm in love.

---

Patrick sold his story! I told him and he didn't believe it until I showed him the acceptance letter and the check. Then he still didn't believe it. He tried to say my father had done it as a favor. I laughed until I cried. Then Patrick asked about my father, and I told everything. His father is hard-working, loud-laughing, loving, so Patrick didn't believe me at first. Then he realized I was telling the truth, and he held me while I cried. I didn't even realize I wanted to cry. It was very freeing, like a burden had been lifted I didn't know I carried. We were out in the redwood grove; there we could be private. He kissed me, so sweet and gentle. He told me he loves me, and I admitted I love him, too. I went home, my feet barely touching the earth. I've done a good thing. I've given a man confidence in himself. He returned the favor by offering his love. I don't think I've truly ever been loved before.

Mother was waiting on the porch. She didn't speak or look at me.

---

Mother must have told Father, for he is home and furious. He told me I could never see Patrick again, that he's going to speak to General Tempe and have him transferred into the thick of the fighting.

While he was shouting at me, a telegram came. My brother, Larry, hadn't told us, but he had joined the British Air Corps. On his first bombing raid, his plane went down into the English Channel. He is lost to us. He is lost to the world.

Larry was father's heir. Larry was intelligent, distant, dignified, thoughtful... He was so much older, 24 years old. I didn't really like him, but I think Father's expectations weighed on him. Now he's free, if such a thing is possible. Before Father went into his study, he looked around and said bitterly, "Now I have only daughters, and Bessie is barren." (She isn't barren; Father picked out her husband, and her husband cares *nothing for her.*) But what a thing to say on the news of his son's death!

Mother collapsed, sobbing. Larry was always her favorite, and she is devastated. Hermione and I put her to bed with a hot water bottle, and Hermione keeps a vigil at her side.

I'm going out to wait for Patrick. I now need him more than ever.

———————

Dear diary, that which all have warned me about has come to pass. I have given myself to my darling Patrick. In the midst of grief and despair, we met in the redwood grove and he comforted me. I am now a woman, scarred by sorrow and warmed by love. I hope to see him again tomorrow.

Amid the ruins of my family, I am guiltily happy.

———————

Kellen knew what this meant.

Did Rae?

Kellen peered at her daughter. Should she talk to Rae about what had happened between Ruby and Patrick? Was this the right moment to talk about sex?

Rae forgot her bruises and bounced happily on the couch cushion—and winced. "Yay for Ruby! Everything will be okay for her now. Right?"

Kellen *could* dodge the issue. But should she? Someone had to talk to Rae. She was The Mother. The full weight of tradition and responsibility landed this right on her shoulders. She swallowed, more nervous than she would have thought possible. "Do you understand what Ruby was trying to say? In her diary? About giving herself to Patrick?"

"They had sex, right?"

Rae was so casual, Kellen had to catch her breath. "Yes. How do you know that? What do you know?"

"Just the stuff Grandma taught us in school. Ejaculation, condoms, STDs, orgasm, sexual responsibility, same-sex relationships, ministration—stuff like that."

"Ministration?" Kellen asked faintly.

"Yes, like when you have your period." Rae frowned, deeply concerned. "Do you suppose Ruby and Patrick used a condom?"

*Eep!* "Unless he was prepared—no. And I think it's highly unlikely he thought he would ever get the chance to..." Kellen hesitated over the term to use: *Get lucky? Get laid?* Being in the military had ruined all her delicacy of phrasing.

"...have intercourse with Ruby?"

"Right." Kellen would have to thank her mother-in-law when next she saw her for taking charge of Rae's sex education. Verona had made this conversation so much easier... Kellen guessed. So why was she so uncomfortable?

Probably the knowledge that Rae knew what was happening between her parents, really understood it, made Kellen feel (ahem) awkward.

But she plowed on, saying what had to be said. "Having intercourse, especially for the first time, is a big deal *now*. In those days, it was best to be married first. There was a lot of bad talk about women who..."

"Had intercourse? Well, sure!" Rae was still frowning. "Now I'm worried about Ruby. She could be pregnant!"

"Yes, she could be."

"With her father, that would be difficult." Rae slid a sideways glance at the diary. "We could read more."

Kellen flipped through the pages they had read, then flipped through the pages left to read. They were a little more than halfway done, and what would they do when they finished Ruby's story? The diary bound the family together, kept them entertained in their down moments, gave them a connection to the island. "I think we'd better stop, because kiddo, we need to go practice the piano."

Rae frowned at her bandaged hands, and wiggled her fingers. "I don't think I can." She grinned at her mother. "I guess you'll have to practice for us both."

## CHAPTER SEVENTEEN

MARA WALKED UP to the Conkles' cottage and lifted her hand to rap on the door—and listened. The couple inside—Dylan and Jamie, she reminded herself—were shouting. About the garden, the environment, the Di Lucas, the child. It wasn't a friendly fight. Not even. Oh, so much opportunity for a canny opportunist.

She rapped firmly on the door.

The shouting stopped.

A pause.

Jamie Conkle opened the door.

Mara recognized her from her picture, and thought that in person, Jamie looked like a preppie East Coast environmental bully, all narrow black glasses and squinty-eyed suspicion. She reeked political correctness; even the dirt under her fingernails had been properly composted. Without saying a word, she irritated the shit out of Mara.

"Hello!" Mara flashed a smile she knew would be just as irritating to Jamie. "I'm Miranda Phillips, this year's Isla Paraíso intern and botanist."

"Last year we had a biologist," Jamie said.

"I'm to do all the work, regardless of the science." The job description had made that clear. No wonder no one wanted the position. "I was instructed to introduce myself here—"

Obviously Dylan didn't find her smile irritating, because he pushed Jamie aside, took Mara's hand and pulled her into the cottage. "Hi! I'm Dylan Conkle, and I didn't know you were coming."

"Um, the university sent a message…" Mara shot a sideways glance around, looking for some way to communicate with the outside world. "They said they were going to, anyway."

"The mail is delayed these days." Dylan shrugged and sneered.

Jamie shoved back at Dylan.

Dylan pushed his glasses up on his nose.

"Right. Old technology." Mara openly looked around.

The place was a dump: one tiny room that included the living space and kitchen, and an open door into the even smaller bedroom and, Mara supposed, a bath. The cottage smelled the way old houses do when they're close to the sea—of salt, fish and mold. Nothing was that old: furniture, appliances, the gas fireplace. But everything looked worn and sad.

"Sorry about the mess," Jamie said.

"Sorry I dropped by and caught you unaware." Mara cut a glance toward Dylan. God forbid he should do anything to help his wife.

"What happened to Bill Miller, last year's intern?" Jamie asked.

"I don't know about Bill Miller. I suppose he got a job." He had, with Mara's help, and when she removed him from the rotation for this position, she inserted Miranda's name and waited to see what would happen. Nothing, that's what. No one fought for this job—which told her a lot. "I'm a graduate student. They don't tell me all the good stuff. Um, they did say I could buy fresh produce from you, you'd keep an account and charge it to the university at the end of every month."

Jamie nodded frigidly. "That's the way we've done it before."

"With the new folks living up at the big house, we're going to be hopping!" Dylan said.

"Shut up, Dylan," Jamie answered.

"You know you're worried about the old—"

"Shut up, Dylan!" Jamie put all her power into her voice.

"Yeah. Shh." In an elaborate pantomime of shushing, Dylan put his finger to his lips. He stared meaningfully at Mara. "It's a secret."

Jamie looked as though she was going to plant her fist in his throat, so Mara said, "The university also said if I had any problems to let you know and you'd help."

"Of course we will. Right, Jamie?" Dylan elbowed his wife and grinned with lopsided good cheer. He pointed at the sagging plaid couch. "Sit down, Miranda."

Mara sat rather gingerly.

He flung himself down beside her and sprawled with his arms over the back of the couch. He smelled like sweat and liquor. Strong liquor like something out of a still, which made sense since out here, liquor stores didn't exist.

Okay. He was drunk, and how much easier did that make Mara's job?

"The other interns have been self-sufficient." Jamie was so pissed at Dylan, she wasn't really paying attention to Mara.

Perfect. "I've got everything I need. Tent, supplies—you name it, the university had it for me." After a single glance at her fake ID, they'd blithely handed everything over. "I think they meant in case of a storm or something."

"It's California in the summer," Jamie said. "We don't have storms."

"Remember that freak storm the year we got here? Some kind of late-season front came out of Siberia. A tree fell on our generator and the whole damned garden washed away. That's when I knew that I—" Dylan stopped himself, as if even in his drunken stupor, he didn't dare say how much he hated this place.

Yes, Jamie had him cornered here, and the only way he could slip away was to waste his life with drugs and alcohol.

"I'm set up in Paradise Cove." At the far end of the island from *the folks up at the big house*. "I think I found Bill's spot from last year. Protected from the weather, if there is any, by the boulders and that overhang?" She looked at Dylan for confirmation.

He nodded sagely. "Been there. Used to visit Bill there."

She placed her hand briefly on his knee and stood. "That's all, then. I'll be off. I've got seaweed to inventory and peregrine eggs to count." She needed to look like she was doing the work, and besides, with nothing else on the agenda, she might just do it.

Jamie followed her to the door. "Be careful. Three years ago, we had an intern get too close to the nest. The mother dove, talons out, and slashed him across the cheek. Just missed his eye. He got an infection and had to be medevaced out."

Mara faced Jamie. "You can't blame her. A mother will fight to the death for her chick."

"You can depend on that," Jamie said.

"Oh, I am."

JAMIE SURVEYED HER HUSBAND, sprawled on the couch, smiling at his boner like it was a thing of beauty. When they met, he was all charm and ambition, telling her what she wanted to hear.

Liar. And loser. He was both of those, and a drunkard and wastrel to boot.

Yet if she wanted to stay here, she was stuck with him. The Di Lucas demanded a couple to care for the island, and justifiably. One person couldn't handle the maintenance, although she did the majority of the work, and if one of them got hurt, the other would have to deal until help arrived.

She *hoped* if anything happened to her, Dylan would be sober enough to do just that.

"Are you going to tell the folks up at the big house that the intern has arrived?" She waited, hoping he wouldn't say exactly what she anticipated.

"Why tell them anything?"

He never changed.

"Honey, come on over here." He patted his lap. "Let's…talk."

Like she needed him pawing at her because Miranda had turned him on. Jamie didn't budge. "We tell the big house folks because that's the rules, and the Di Lucas make the rules. This is the only job we've got. I'm not getting fired over that woman."

"She's a nice girl." He was still smiling at Jamie, trying to cajole her.

So drunk he couldn't stand up and chase her around, not even for sex. "If she's a graduate student, she's got to be around twenty-six. She's no girl. Look, Dylan, you want to tell them or shall I?"

"Tell who about what?"

The bad part was—he wasn't faking confusion. "Did you take the food basket up to the house yet?"

His eyes shifted to the side. "I don't remember."

"I'll take it up and tell them."

"You hate to go up there."

"You didn't do it, so I have to."

He put his head on the back of the couch and watched her out of slitted eyes. "I don't know why you loathe them so much."

"Then you haven't been paying attention!"

He groaned. "Sorry I mentioned it."

"Rich people! They're scum, a drain on the environment. Here we're trying to save one tiny spot on the earth and keep it pristine, and they arrive and use up the resources—for a *vacation*." Jamie did loathe them, all the rich people, the ones who treated the earth as if it was an endless resource for their pleasure. "They're here to see about turning Isla Paraíso into a resort. People tromping all over the island, littering the beaches, shooting at the native birds—"

"Um, they said something about a restricted place for some people to, um, view the untouched land and resources to properly appreciate—"

"Bullshit! Those people don't care anything about anything except making a profit." She paced to the window and looked out at the golden grasses, the ancient green of the oaks and, in the distance, the silver glimmer of the Pacific. "If they can make money off Isla Paraíso, they will, and this place will be ruined, like all the other beautiful places of the earth."

Dylan let out a snore.

Jamie turned. He was deeply asleep, mouth hanging open, head lolling to the side.

He didn't care about Isla Paraíso. No one cared like she did. No matter what, she had to remain here, and that meant serving the folks up at the big house whatever they wanted whenever they wanted.

She went out to the root cellar and found the food basket exactly where she'd left it. Picking it up, she started up toward the big house, walking rather than using the electric cart, using her own energy rather than wasting the earth's energy.

Yes, she would follow the Di Lucas' rules. In fact, in the case of Miranda Phillips, it would be a pleasure to tell them the intern had arrived.

Jamie thought of Miranda's hand on Dylan's knee.

She didn't trust that woman. She didn't trust her at all.

# CHAPTER EIGHTEEN

RUNNING…AGAIN. Kellen liked it. She ran close to the collapsed caverns where, in World War II, men had watched for a Japanese invasion. She ran through the redwood grove, absorbing the peace of two thousand years of growth. She avoided the Conkles' home, told herself she was giving them privacy. Tiring early, she turned toward Morgade Hall and slowed as she ran up the expanse of lawn. That gave her time to get her breathing under control. Determined to do her duty to her family—to keep Rae fed and cheerful—she climbed the steps of the back porch and stuck her head into the kitchen. "Olympia, has Dylan delivered today's produce?"

Olympia jumped and put her hand to her heart. She breathed deeply, turned, put her hand on her hip, and glared as if Kellen had deliberately sneaked up on her. Max confessed that when he hired Olympia, he thought her so without imagination she would be impervious to the big old creaky house and the windswept isolation of the island. But while her cooking remained exemplary, her attitude, never marvelous, had disintegrated, and the previously well-groomed woman was letting herself go. Her T-shirt and denim skirt were wrinkled, as if she'd picked them up off the floor. Her overgrown bangs dangled in her eyes and gray roots were showing. Over the weeks, she had slowly ceased to wear cosmetics and was down to a smear of lipstick. Yet her mustache was in full bloom.

In forbidding tones, Olympia said, "I haven't seen either one of the Conkles today."

"Max will speak to Dylan again." Moving fast, Kellen ducked out. Max, Rae and Kellen had worn a path to the garage, and as she fled, she wondered—how could an island that contained only six people—she and Max, Rae and Olympia, Dylan and Jamie—make half of them crazy?

Kellen supposed she should wonder if the half she considered crazy also considered her half-insane. But no. As an adolescent, Rae had her moments, but they were sane, united, a family. Out of loneliness, desolation and self-loathing, Olympia, Dylan and Jamie were splintering into thousands of pieces.

She walked into the garage to find Max, arms outstretched, bellowing at the truck. "Why won't you work?"

Kellen skidded to a stop.

So much for her assurances about the Di Lucas' sanity.

Rae was stretched across the fender, head stuck down as far as she could under the hood. "Daddy, what's a carburetor?"

"What?"

She came up out of the depths and clearly articulated, "What...is...a...carburetor? Because there's a carburetor kit on the workbench and I think we could rebuild it."

Kellen slowed backed toward the door.

Too late. Max had pinned her under his gaze. "A carburetor kit? Rae found a carburetor kit conveniently placed on the workbench?"

Well, hell. It seemed Kellen had arrived at exactly the wrong time. "Rae's a smart kid. Rebuilding the carburetor might get the truck running." She honestly thought Max was going to have steam coming out his ears. "Look. All I did was find the carburetor kit in one of the drawers. Anyway, carburetor kit or not, it's not easy to rebuild a carburetor. If you're lucky, there'll be instructions."

He still looked irked.

Which made Kellen lose what was left of her patience. "*And* if *you'd* looked in the drawers—"

Max swung away, took a breath, smoothed his hair back from his forehead. "All right. You're right. I could have looked." He swung back toward Kellen. "Anything else I should know about in those drawers?"

Kellen lifted one shoulder. "Maybe. Why don't you look?"

Rae had dug herself out of the depths of the F-100 and stood, head cocked, listening to them. "You two don't fight very often."

"No, but honey, it doesn't mean we don't love each other," Max said.

"It's okay," Rae said. "It makes you seem almost normal."

*Almost normal?* Max mouthed to Kellen.

Kellen smiled, but a little tightly. Rae was right, she and Max didn't often fight; maybe the tension on the island was getting to them, too.

On the other hand, maybe she was angry because he had been a jerk.

Rae skipped back to the box that held the kit. "Can I open it? Can I?"

That got Max's attention. "Wait! Rae! That's got a lot of little parts and we need them all."

"I'm not going to spill it." Rae sounded irritable, too.

Kellen walked over to the wall where the mattress stood, looked at it, garish with roses, stained and dirty—and kicked the hell out of it. Front kick, side kick, left foot, right foot, turning kick, backward kick.

Dust flew.

She couldn't keep it up; her legs trembled from the effort of running and kicking.

So she started punching, palms out, clenched fists, boom, boom, boom, knocking the stuffing out of the old mattress, and loving it.

"What's Mommy doing?" Rae asked.

"Getting out her aggressions," Max said.

"Practicing my fighting skills," Kellen corrected him without a trace of a smile.

A female figure, silhouetted by the sun, stepped into the wide open doorway. "What are you people doing in here? In this garage? Why aren't you at the house?"

Kellen recognized her by her figure, tall and curvaceous, and her attitude, hostile and all-knowing.

Rae looked up from the spark plug Max had placed in her hand. "Hi, Mrs. Conkle." She didn't use her usual cheerful Rae voice; in one visit, Jamie Conkle had convinced Rae to step carefully around her.

Kellen stopped pounding the mattress and walked toward Jamie. "Max and Rae are rebuilding the pickup." She did *not* say, *None of your business*, although that was what she thought.

"Why?" Jamie held their basket of the day's produce over her arm. "Why would you rebuild that…thing?"

"We can't all have the talent for gardening." Max sounded like he had his jaw clenched.

"It's a petroleum-burning engine, the only one on the island. We don't need that kind of environmental smog-maker here. We have the electric golf cart." Jamie radiated indignation like a halo.

Deliberately Kellen turned the subject. "What did you bring us today?"

Jamie would not be diverted. "Really, you shouldn't try to bring that thing back to life. The internal combustion engine is to blame for all of today's problems."

"That's a sweeping statement." Kellen put her hand on the basket's handle.

Jamie resisted for a moment, then released and stepped back. "Rethink the truck. On Isla Paraíso, we're saving the environment, not destroying it."

Kellen leaned forward so she was face to face with Jamie. "We'll worry about that when he gets it running."

Jamie leaned back, then flounced away.

Kellen watched her go. Amazing how Jamie made her feel inferior, privileged and resentful, all at the same time.

Jamie stopped, looked up, pointed.

At the same time, Kellen heard a helicopter coming in fast and low.

Her heart started pounding. *Why were they here? Was it good news at last?* "Coast Guard," she called to Max.

He extricated himself from the truck, and sounded as hopeful as she felt when he said, "My God. Do you suppose…?" He ran out.

Kellen and Rae followed. As the helicopter descended on a blast of air, Kellen absentmindedly began doing her finger exercises.

Like a hummingbird alighting on a limb, the helicopter settled on the edge of the lawn. The engine throttled back, the roar diminished, and the door opened to allow one of the Coasties to jump down. He surveyed Max, Kellen and Rae and as if he had every right, he asked, "Who are you?"

"We're the Di Lucas. We're living on the island for the summer," Max said. "My family owns it."

"Sure, I recognize you. I served with a couple of Di Lucas in San Diego." He offered his hand. "Chief Petty Officer Juan Deung. Call me Juan."

"Yes, we Di Lucas are a prolific and similar bunch." Max shook hands with him.

As Max introduced Kellen and Rae, Juan offered his hand to them, too, and kept talking a mile a minute. "The Conkles used to have a radio for emergency use, but Dylan got loaded, called in and claimed there were pirates raiding the island. We arrived full force. That cost your family a bunch of money, and Jamie Conkle smashed the radio and refuses to get it fixed. So when we're in the area, we come by to check on them, make sure they're okay."

"You just missed Jamie." Kellen gestured down the hill.

"That's fine," Juan said in heartfelt relief. "She always lectures us about wasting the earth's resources flying the helicopter. And because the helicopter blades might harm rare birds. It's not like we're out for a joy ride, you know? Some guy and his yacht have disappeared in this area. No sign of him yet, and there's a storm out there in the Pacific churning away. Have you heard about the storm?"

"We don't hear about much here," Max said.

"Big storm, a typhoon right now, and some forecast models are predicting the steering currents could send it our way. No one's getting excited yet. Except the TV weather people, because they love possible disasters. But it's California. July storms are unlikely."

"El Niño. Or La Niña," Max said. "I can never can remember which is which."

Kellen looked around at the golden landscape. "A storm wouldn't be all bad. It's been a dry year. We sure could use the rain."

"I don't suppose you've heard, but we've had some massive fires all over California." Abruptly, Juan got to the point. "So…spending the summer here, huh? Why's that?"

Max turned to Rae. "Why don't you go talk to the pilot? I'll bet he's an interesting guy."

"She," Juan said.

Max stared hard into the helicopter, at the tinted windows that reflected the sun. "I see! Erroneous assumption. I'll bet *she's* even a more interesting *woman*."

"Really, Dad." Rae ran over to the helicopter's open door and within a few moments of hard talking, she had been invited inside.

"While on duty, we're not supposed to let kids in, so please keep that quiet. Now, what did you want to tell me you didn't want her to know?" Juan was one observant guy.

Max and Kellen exchanged glances.

Kellen took a step back.

Max would do the talking. "We're on the island because we're having trouble with a stalker."

"Must be quite a stalker for you to come out this far."

"She's an escaped convict, a serial killer."

Juan's eyes narrowed. "Female serial killer? Not too many of those. Is this the one we're supposed to keep an eye out for?"

"Mara Philippi. One and the same."

"Bad news. Did you know she's killed people all over the US? When she does, she cuts off their hands and collects them as souvenirs?" Juan looked right at Kellen. "She dehydrates them."

"We did know," Max said. "We knew her before she went to prison."

"Lucky you." Juan was impressed. "Did you know after she escaped from federal prison, she had one guy exhumed so she could cut off his hands? Some kind of revenge thing." Juan made a choking sound.

It wasn't as if any of this was news to Kellen, but— she tried not to think about it. Now, in the face of Juan's incredulous recitation, she began to feel frightened.

Max glanced at her. "We really do know all about

Mara Philippi. We were instrumental in her capture the first time."

"Scary, scary woman." Juan looked toward the Coast Guard helicopter where Rae had hopped down, still talking to the pilot. "Is this Philippi person after the kid, too?"

"Mostly after my wife." Kellen must have looked panicky, because Max reached back, wrapped his arm around her waist, and gave her his support. "But yes. Given the chance, she would kill us all."

Kellen leaned against him and wished Juan would stop talking.

Max said, "When you landed that Coast Guard helicopter, I was really hoping—"

Kellen corrected him. "*We* were really hoping—"

Max nodded. "We were really hoping you were here to tell us she'd been caught."

"I'm sorry." Juan looked like he meant it. "I didn't know anything about you being out here or that that female killer was in the area."

"*Possibly* in the area," Max said.

"I assume Commander is aware, and everyone else is on a need-to-know basis."

"That's right."

"I'll talk to my pilot, tell her we never saw you."

"That would be much appreciated."

"You do have a way to defend yourselves?" Juan asked.

"We do," Max said.

*The guns in the gun safe.* Remembering them made the constriction in Kellen's throat ease.

"You do have a method of communication? In the

R44? In case there's trouble?" Juan indicated their helicopter on the other end of the lawn. "That radio works, right?"

"I check in with my law enforcement contacts once a week," Max told him.

As Rae ran up, Juan said, "Here she is! Rae, did Carmen convince you to join the Coast Guard?"

"It's a great job for a woman," Rae said. "Being a Coast Guard pilot is one of the coolest jobs around."

Juan laughed. "I knew she would sell you. Carmen would be fantastic in a recruiting office—but she won't leave the pilot's seat. Hey, next time we come, I hope we have better news for you all."

"From your mouth to God's ears," Max looked around at Kellen and Rae, and at the island grasses waving in the salty breeze.

Kellen spoke up. "Yes, family is a blessing, and lately we have been very blessed."

"I hear you." Juan headed for the helicopter. "I grew up with five brothers. That's how I learned to dance—waiting for the bathroom."

# CHAPTER NINETEEN

KELLEN STARTED HER half hour of piano practice. Her musical ability hadn't improved, but the way her hands responded to her command was better, especially her right hand. Really, measurably better.

Yet Luna didn't seem to notice any improvement. Ten minutes into the practice, the dog began to moan, and then to howl. She was obviously in pain with the awfulness of Kellen's music, and she wanted the world to know.

Kellen paused. "I'm doing my best!"

Rae jumped up. "Mom! I'm going to ride my bike. I'll take Luna."

Luna hopped up, too, and wagged her tail.

Kellen's hands stilled on the piano keys. She looked at her daughter, fresh-faced and excited—and taller. Visibly taller. The scabs on her face hadn't healed yet, and she had a pimple on her nose and one on her forehead. She was growing up too fast—yet she was still a child, all unknowing of the dangers out there lying in wait. Of Mara.

This morning Juan, with his awed and horrified narration of Mara's heinous crimes, had brought Kellen's fears surging back. "Where are you going?"

Rae looked startled. "I dunno. Just riding."

"I don't think you should ride by yourself."

"I'm not. I'm going with Luna. Anyway, what difference does it make?" She got a petulant tone in her voice. "There's no place *to* go."

"You could get hurt."

"How?"

"You could fall again."

"Big deal. I've fallen before."

"And it was a big deal!" Maybe Kellen was a little too sharp.

Because Rae was sharp back. "Dad made me promise not to perform jumps unless he's there."

"There are cliffs." Kellen was groping now, fighting panic and the desire to say, *There's a maniac killer out there.*

"Do you mean I'm so dumb I'm going to ride my bike off a cliff? Come on." Rae's eyes flashed with hurt and anger. "Give me some credit!"

Luna lay back down, put her head on her paws, and watched as if she was following a particularly tense tennis game.

"I don't mean that. I just mean…" Kellen couldn't say what she meant. She couldn't say she was afraid Mara Philippi would come to get Rae. Kellen couldn't say she felt incompetent, so lousy at piano the dog had to howl, and carrying a load of guilt that her daughter was stuck on this island without friends or family.

What was it that Max had told Juan? *Mara's mostly after my wife.* In a twisted, terrible way, this exile was her fault.

"Look. I'll ride down to the Conkles' and pick up some more lettuce for dinner. Olympia said she didn't get quite enough this morning. Is that safe enough?" Rae had her hand on her nonexistent hip.

"I… I guess. But it's five miles. Luna can't run that far."

"No, I suppose not." Rae knelt beside Luna. "Can you stay here with Mom? I know the music is awful, but she's halfway done."

That wasn't what Kellen intended at all. "Rae, no, don't—" *Please take the dog. She'll protect you!*

But suddenly, Kellen couldn't speak. Tension froze her throat, her vocal chords.

"Mom?" Rae ran over. "What's wrong?"

Kellen couldn't breathe.

"Mom?"

That was the last thing Kellen heard until she opened her eyes. She was stretched out on the living room floor on the antique rug…that had a red stain on the ivory background. She put her hand to her cheek and pulled it away, smeared with blood.

Max knelt beside her. "Kellen? Kellen? What happened?"

"I… I couldn't breathe. I guess I passed out." Kellen kept staring at the smear on her palm. "What did I do?"

"You hit the coffee table with your face." Max helped her sit up. "Thank God, it's just a little cut. Rae, would you get us a damp towel?"

Rae stomped out of the living room.

"Is this the same as the aphasia?" Max asked Kellen.

"No, I'm not forgetting the words. Everything freezes: my chest, my throat, my vocal chords. I can't breathe."

Rae returned with a towel so wet it dripped all the way across the floor.

"Rae! We want to wipe off Mommy's face, not give her a bath." Max sounded exasperated. "Go wring it out."

Rae sighed violently and stomped out again.

Max returned his attention to Kellen. "It's happened before?"

"Yes, but never like that, where I black out."

He was on his feet in an instant. "I've got to call the doctor."

"No." Kellen lunged, grabbed his leg. "You can't. Literally, you can't."

"I can call from the helicopter. I can take you to the hospital. I will! You could die."

"What I really need right now is an ice bag and that damp dish towel to wipe my face."

"Rae!" Max yelled. "Hurry up!" Then he couldn't wait, and headed into the kitchen himself.

Kellen heard him scolding Rae, and he was back in less than a minute with an ice bag wrapped in a dish towel and another damp dish towel.

As he knelt beside her to clean her face, she looked him in the eyes. "After all I've been through, I'm not going to die from this. I spoke to the doctor."

"Why didn't you tell me?"

"Because there's no reason to worry. She said it's not surprising, given the stresses of relearning so much, that the most valuable asset I have, my words, should sometimes choke me." Kellen took the ice bag and gingerly pressed it on her face. "She gave me relaxation exercises to do."

"You should do them!"

"I am!"

"I haven't seen you!"

Kellen took a long, calming breath. "There. You just saw me do one."

Max stared as if he didn't understand.

Patiently she explained, "Relaxation exercises aren't like punching a bag. They're mostly just breathing. Meditation. You've seen me meditate."

"It's not working!"

"It's like the piano. I'm not good at them yet, but as long as I practice every day, I will get better—am getting better. I know that Rae and Luna don't think so, but—"

In the kitchen, the back door slammed.

Kellen looked around. Luna wandered in looking desolate. "Where's Rae?" she asked the dog.

Max strode to the front window and looked out. "She's going for a bike ride."

Kellen pushed herself to her feet. "She's not supposed to. That's what we were fighting about."

"Why? Where's she going?"

"She wanted to ride down to the Conkles' to pick up the vegetables for tonight's dinner." Kellen joined him at the window and watched her little girl ride out of sight.

"Nothing wrong with that."

"But what if—?"

"What if what? What if Mara is here? No! While we're safe here, she's gone on a wild goose chase, seeking us all over the world."

"And maybe looking up her former murderous colleagues?"

"According to the report I got from Diana...before she disappeared...there's nothing to indicate that. You know Mara better than anyone. Would she do that? When she's at the bottom and has nothing to offer?"

Kellen didn't take offense at his assumption she knew Mara better than anyone. The friendship between them had been fraught with rivalry, and in the end Mara had been willing and eager to kill her. But when Kellen looked back on the time she'd spent with Mara, when she added in all the facts that had surfaced, Kellen had come to know more about her twisted, devious mind, and understand the way she had fooled everyone so completely. "Mara has to be in charge. Mara has to be on top. She loves a challenge, but only as a chance to sharpen her teeth in the battle to win again. And—" Kellen was thinking out loud "—when she focuses on one single problem, she focuses completely. If she's after us, after me, and we're sure she is, right?"

"According to all reports."

"She won't look left or right. In a way that's an advantage. If she managed to bring in any of her old criminal network, that could cause us real trouble. But she wants to bring me down by herself. That's important, that she does it alone." Kellen leaned back, satisfied with her analysis of the situation. "That's it. But that doesn't fix anything. It doesn't make our conundrum better. How did she escape from a top security prison? How could she be so smart she outwits us and the authorities?" Kellen was asking for reassurance, for him to tell her everything would be all right.

Max was patient with her, and he obliged. "This island is isolated. Most people don't even know Isla Paraíso is here, or that the Di Lucas have anything to do with it. And you heard Juan Deung. He was surprised to see us and understood the need for silence. If Mara figures out she lost us, how could she pick up our track and follow us here?"

"That woman—"

"—is wildly intelligent in a horrible twisted way. I agree." He took Kellen's damaged hand and massaged it. "But if she could find us, how would she arrive? The island doesn't have a harbor. It's darned hard to get any kind of vessel even close. We'd notice an aircraft."

"Yes." They would.

"If she figured out a way onto Isla Paraíso, how will she hide herself? Unless she's planning a quick slaughter, and you know that's not how our girl works, to scope out our circumstances would take time. She'd have to bring all her food and water, and sooner or later—probably sooner—the Conkles will see her, or we will, and then we have her in our grasp." He showed Kellen his other hand, then clenched his fist.

Kellen watched Rae disappear over the horizon. "All that's true, but if she somehow found Rae here, she could do terrible things to her."

"We both agree it's you Mara wants."

*I'll take everything from her, the way she took everything from me. I'll make her sorry she betrayed me.*

"Mara sneaked into our wedding. She could have confiscated a butcher knife, used the turmoil to stab me to death. She disappeared after I lost consciousness, and only reappeared when I was healthy again. The incident in Cape Charade at the funeral home... that was a warning. A horrible, gruesome omen she crafted to frighten us. It worked." Kellen turned away from the window and gripped the back of the chair so tightly the wooden finials bruised her palms. "I'm frightened, because I know Mara doesn't merely want me dead—she wants me to suffer."

"Rae's a pretty smart kid. She's not going to talk to a stranger."

"No? No. It's just that she's so…"

"Friendly? Outgoing?"

*"Mad at me."*

Max looked toward the kitchen, noted the trail of water, realized what he hadn't realized before Rae hadn't expressed concern about her mother's fall. Sweet little Rae had been exasperated and angered. "Why you in particular?"

"Because I'm her mother. Because she's ten years old. Her world is upside down. Her hormones have started on their rampage. She needs all the attention and all the love."

He got it. "And you just got all the attention."

"Because somehow she suspects it's my fault that we're here."

"Now, that's impossible. I told her it was my fault."

"You're her daddy. You've always been there for her. It *can't* be your fault." She turned and looked out the window again. "Mothers and daughters—we're either best angel friends or hell's demons incarnate, and there's nothing in between."

"As my mother always says, 'Craziness is inherited—you get it from your children.'"

"We need to tell Rae."

"No. Right now, Rae's just so volatile. So vulnerable. She's having so much fun here!"

"Max…"

"Kellen, let's give it a little more time." He leaned in, all big brown eyes and warm persuasion. "Let's wait until we get a report that Mara's coming for us."

"What if we don't get the report in time?"

"We have to trust that Diana will surface to send us a warning. We have to trust law enforcement. They have a lot at stake."

"Not as much as we do!"

"Just a few more days," Max pleaded. "Let Rae be an innocent a little longer."

Kellen surrendered, not to the logic, but to the appeal. "When she finds out, she is going to be angry."

"If everything goes as planned, she will never find out."

## CHAPTER TWENTY

RAE RODE HER bike as hard and as fast as she could, away from her father and mother and that creepy house where it was all boring with nothing to do and weird music played and a white lady came into her bedroom and no one believed her, and she had to escape like a prisoner whenever she wanted to go somewhere. Like there was even somewhere to go.

She pointed the bike at the Conkles' house. It was five miles downhill all the way, so that was easy riding, and she conveniently forgot she'd have to ride uphill all the way back.

In this distance, Jamie Conkle's greenhouse glinted in the sun, and as Rae got closer, she could see swathes of plants inside. The Di Lucas had installed a greenhouse at Yearning Sands Resort, but the gardener was strict about humidity and grow lights, and she wasn't allowed inside. This place was unguarded, and the Di Lucas owned the island. They owned everything on the island, so surely she could go into the greenhouse. She parked her bike, set the kickstand. It fell over. She left it and opened the glass door, and tip-toed inside.

It was warm, sunny, really warm, really sunny. Long rows of raised beds boasted feathery carrot fronds and tall tomato plants loaded with red and yellow fruit. The greenhouse smelled of rose and thyme, basil and parsley. Rae loved plants. She loved vegetables. She loved this place. She crept along the rows, brushing her hands over the—the cucumber plants had prickly leaves. "Ow!"

"What are you doing in here?"

Rae jumped and spun.

Jamie Conkle advanced down the aisle toward Rae. She was tall and full-bosomed, with dark eyes and dark hair, and she glared like a witch on Halloween. She seemed not to care that Rae was a Di Luca and the Di Lucas owned the island. Jamie was mad, and she acted like she owned *everything*. "You can't be in here."

"I wanted to see… I like the plants and…"

"I don't care. I don't care! This is my place. My island. I keep it. I protect it. I made my man come here. I made him live here. He complains. He wants to go back to the life on the mainland, with those Californians and the bacon-eaters and the, the people who eat apples that have been sprayed with—" Jamie acted as if Rae's life in Washington made her a pariah, some creature who carried disease to infect the greenhouse and the island.

Rae turned and ran. Up one aisle, down another aisle. She found a door, opened it and ran out into the fresh air. She was crying. She didn't want to be crying. Everyone liked her. Why didn't this lady?

She glanced back. Jamie was still after her, moving swiftly.

With seconds to spare, Rae grabbed her bike, mounted and rode as fast as she could down the road. Toward the beach. She glanced over her shoulder and saw Jamie come out of the greenhouse and stare balefully after her.

She hated today. She hated everything about it. As soon as she was out of sight, she slowed down. Through that pile of boulders was a path down to a beach, and that's where she wanted to be. There she could throw herself down, and cry and scream, and no one would care. Not like anyone cared anyway...

She dropped her bike onto its side in the grass and ran through the boulders, down the cliff and onto the hot white sands. She stared at the waves.

Her life *sucked*.

She was stuck on this island with her *parents*.

She had no friends.

She missed her grandma.

She had pimples on her nose.

She needed a bra.

She hated everyone.

"Hello."

Rae jumped and turned to see a woman who was about her mom's size, medium-tall, black hair and blue eyes, dressed in knee-length khaki shorts, sleeveless shirt and hiking boots. She looked fit: bare arms and legs tanned and well muscled. She held a clipboard and had a pencil behind her ear.

"Wh...who?" Rae stammered. "Who are you?"

"I'm Miranda Phillips, the botanist assigned to Isla Paraíso for the summer." Miranda gestured widely. "Did you know a botanist is here every summer?"

"Yes, but I didn't know there was one this summer." Embarrassed by her tears, Rae wiped at her face.

"Who are you?" Miranda asked.

"I'm Rae Di Luca." This woman, whoever she was, looked familiar. "My parents own this island."

"Oh. Oh! Hey." The botanist stuck out her hand. "Didn't we meet a couple of years ago at your parents' wedding?"

Rae immediately felt relieved. "Yes! I knew I remembered you!" She wiped her palm on her shorts and shook hands.

"Nice wedding. I enjoyed it. Your mom's dress—wow! Italian designer, of course, but still—wow! If only she hadn't collapsed. That was a tragedy."

Everything Miranda said assured Rae she had really been there.

Miranda's bright smile lost a few watts. "I don't think your mom was happy to see me, though. We used to work together. We were friends. Things went bad… When I went, I was hoping to get things back to normal between us. But she wouldn't even talk to me."

Rae immediately felt an empathy with this woman. "She makes me so mad."

"You, too?" Miranda offered a fist bump.

Rae bumped, and admired the way Miranda moved and talked, without any glitches. She didn't have a crippled hand. She didn't freeze up and stop talking, like something was choking her. She wasn't feeble…

*No.* Rae's innate sense of fairness stopped her before she went too far—and that made her mad, too. She wanted to be mean. She felt mean. But she knew her mom wasn't feeble. She was merely damaged, and fighting back. Rae knew she should cheer about that. But she was tired of being the cheerleader for her mother.

When was someone going to be the cheerleader for her?

Miranda was still talking. "I like your dad, but he's all hers, so maybe don't tell that it's me who's doing the botany study this year? In fact, maybe don't tell them you met me at all."

Rae's inherent caution and good sense took possession of her. "I… I don't know. I usually—"

Miranda smiled and made a gesture that meant, *Pass.* "No problem. I completely understand. I mean, your dad did give the okay about me being here, but you don't want to keep things from your parents. You're to be commended. I just thought—" she glanced around the solitude "—I might get lonely while I was here, and it would be nice to talk to someone."

No pressure. Miranda had her reasons for wanting to avoid Rae's mother, and they made sense. "I know. Me, too! I mean, there's no one here, and no Wi-Fi or phone. Just the wind and the waves and the grass and the trees. It's so *boring.* No TV! Just DVDs and my parents. And Dylan Conkle, who is some kind of space case, and Jamie Conkle, who acts like I have a disease."

Miranda sat down in the sand. "I thought it was just me. When I went up to the house to check in, Jamie treated me like I was some kind of mass murderer. I mean, me! I was assigned to this island to do the annual survey, and you'd think she owned it and I was stomping on the coral reef."

"There no coral reef here. The water's too deep."

"It's a figurative coral reef."

"Oh." Rae felt stupid. "I knew that." She sat, too. "My dad knows you're here? On the island? He okayed it?"

"Huh." Miranda scratched her head. "I thought it was him, but maybe it was a different Di Luca. Somebody did, though."

"He never said anything, so maybe it *was* him and he doesn't want my mom to know." For a moment, the idea made Rae brighten. Then she sighed, because at rock bottom, she liked having her folks behave like they enjoyed being married, and keeping secrets didn't fit. "Where are you staying?"

"My equipment's up there in the rocks." Miranda pointed toward the top of the cliff.

"I came through there. I didn't see anything."

"I keep it all stashed pretty tightly under the overhang. If I don't, the wind kicks up off the ocean and my stuff goes flying!" Miranda bent her leg and rested her arm on her knee.

Her shorts slid up, and on her thigh, Rae saw a scar. It looked like the bite of a big dog. She wanted to ask what had happened.

But Miranda saw her looking, pulled her shorts over it, and kept talking. "Which is okay if it's just a pan or something, but—" she showed Rae the clipboard "—all this data has to be recorded on a certain time and in a certain place, and that's work I can't redo."

"Do you like being a botanist?" Rae was really curious. The island was so different from the Washington coast; same ocean, but the plants, the sea birds, the predators, the field mice and the marine life entertained and amazed her.

"You know, I do. I didn't know if I would, but it's pretty jazz." Miranda sounded reflective, then she straightened. "You should go now. If we see each other, we'll wave from a distance."

Rae didn't want to leave. "You know, if my dad okayed you being here, I don't know what difference it makes if I talk to you."

"Your mother—"

"She's such a drama queen!"

Miranda gave a surprised laugh. "She is, isn't she? What's she done now?"

"Her brain surgery was two years ago. At least. Today she pretended to black out. Then she pretended she couldn't speak. All to make me stay inside and to get my dad's attention." Rae knew she was wrong. She didn't care. "I am so tired of her being first!" She felt surprised that had burst from her. Then she realized— it was true.

"Brain surgery is a big deal." Sensible adult reasoning.

"I know. But the doctor says she's fine. That's why we came here, now that she's better. For bonding time."

"You need to bond with your parents?" Mara asked, clearly incredulous.

"No! I mean, no! And what about me? What about my friends?"

"It's almost like they don't want you to have friends."

"Right!" Loneliness caught at Rae's throat, and she gave a quick, hiccupping sob.

"It's not fair. Like you said—drama queen."

After her outburst, Rae felt better, and she really felt better knowing she wasn't the only one who thought her mother was faking it. With that, her decision was made. "What exactly are you doing? What are you putting on the paper?" Because if she was going to keep this friendship a secret, she should at least learn something. It would keep her from feeling the teeny, tiniest bit guilty. Although she would have to work on not imagining what her grandmother would say.

"I'm finding the particular tidal pools that were studied before and counting the anemones and other living creatures in the pool. See?" She showed Rae the charts. "The state of California wants to know how rising water levels are affecting the plants and animals on the island. I'm counting birds, too, taking notes of the species and the number of nests."

"I thought you said that you're a botanist."

"So?"

"Botanists study plants."

Miranda's bright blue eyes narrowed and got a hot spark that made Rae draw back.

Then Miranda smiled, that warm, interested, sympathetic smile. "Aren't you a smarty? The Di Lucas only allow one scientist on the island every year, so it has to be someone who knows a little bit about all the 'ologies." She twinkled her fingers. "Botany, marine biology, zoology, ornithology... I even know a little archeology in case I come on the ruins of a prehistoric human settlement."

"Oh. That makes sense. Except—why do we only allow one scientist a year?"

"You know how it is with rich people."

"I'll talk to my father, explain we need to allow more scientists to—"

"No! No, it's okay. The island is so pristine, we

don't want a bunch of people tramping around ruining the, um, grasses."

"But if we allowed people who specialized in one science, isn't there a better chance they'll discover something wonderful?" That made sense to Rae.

"Yes, and there's a chance they'll accidently stomp on something else they don't recognize. Really, don't ask your father. This job is important to me. Promise you won't tell."

"I promise." But Rae was disappointed—and for the first time, she had second thoughts. As paranoid as her mom was, Rae knew it was because she loved her. Maybe she shouldn't have promised not to tell about Miranda.

Before she could ask if she could cancel her promise, Miranda teased, "Besides, we're not really seeing each other, are we?" and smiled so brightly her teeth glinted.

"I said I wouldn't say anything." Rae glanced at her watch and gasped. "I have to get home."

"Sure, you'd better hurry. What are you doing tonight?"

"Mama and I are reading more of Ruby Morgade's diary. I'll see you tomorrow!"

MARA WATCHED RAE ride away, peddling hard up the hill, and smiled. She'd been hoping to catch the kid and have a little talk, gather some information and sow some dissension. That couldn't have gone any better.

Now if only sweet little Rae could keep her mouth shut...

Probably not, so Mara had to work quickly.

## *CHAPTER TWENTY-ONE*

THAT EVENING, Rae was affectionate and Kellen was apologetic. The breach was healed and, except for the F-100, all was once again right with the world.

Then, after breakfast the next morning, Olympia followed Max out of the dining room and into his office.

Max was cheerful when he asked, "What's up?"

"I'm leaving."

Max blinked at her in surprise. He knew she wasn't happy here but—he didn't think she was happy anywhere. "You signed a contract." Stupid response, not helpful, because of course he couldn't trap her on the island. "The contract stated that if you leave before September and while we still require your services, you lose all the bonus promised at the end, and that is a considerable amount."

Kellen had followed Olympia to the library, but stopped in the doorway.

Olympia stood in the middle of the carpet in the middle of the office, straight and stiff, and he realized she no longer looked like the Olympia Paolergio he'd hired. She was...disheveled. But she sounded like herself—flat, firm and unemotional. "I'm quitting."

Max met his wife's gaze.

She grimaced and gestured at him to continue.

He leaned forward, set his elbows on the table, put a warm understanding in his voice and in his eyes. "Olympia, please sit down."

She crossed her arms over her chest, shutting him out. "I don't want to sit down. I want to leave."

So warmth and understanding weren't going to work. "I did warn you about the isolation and the difficulties in living here. You said you could handle them."

"I'm quitting." When Max would have made another objection, Olympia slashed the air with her hand. "You didn't tell me I'd be receiving my cooking supplies from an alcoholic drug addict. You didn't say there would be winds sweeping across the island that make the house creak, or the walls would sing in languages I don't recognize." She whispered, "The Frog God. All my life, I've heard of the Frog God. The Native Americans talk about him, about his powers. He crushed Kateri Kwinault and brought her back to life, and now—" Olympia's voice rose "—I've heard him in the waves thrashing against the sand."

Kellen put her hand over her eyes. Olympia Paolergio had slipped a gear.

Max almost stammered as he tried to think what to say. "The Frog God is pretty much a Native American icon from the coast up around—"

Olympia focused on him once again. "You didn't say that a woman down the hill hates everyone so much she won't even speak to me except to complain that you're rebuilding a truck. A truck! Like that matters to me!"

So Jamie had complained to Olympia about the F-100. At least she was consistent.

Olympia was almost spitting out her complaints now. "You didn't tell me your family would spend all your time outside, running and biking and—" For a long moment, Olympia appeared to have trouble speaking. Then the words caught up with her. "And leaving me in the house to battle rats who...who steal food from the pantry and scurry away into corners and disappear."

Obviously, Olympia had to go. But Max stalled for time. "Will you give us notice? A week? Two?"

"You didn't tell me ghosts from the old times would dance in the moonlight in the ballroom."

Kellen took her hands away from her eyes and mouthed, *Wow*, to Max.

Olympia's eyes drifted, unfocused. "Do you hear the music at night? Do you find the vinyl records spinning out the old songs and wonder what could have set the needle on them for a last time?"

Max rose. "I have not heard that."

"Underneath I hear the growl of men's voices, soldiers who took the island and then left it—and died. They all came back here, you know. They're alive here." Olympia was rambling. "All those poor boys. Dead and yet tied here. Not gone. Not yet."

Kellen signaled Max with wide eyes and a shake of her head.

Max walked around the desk and took Olympia's arm. "Let me prep the helicopter for flight and tell the Di Lucas in Bella Terra I'll be coming in to their airport. Are you packed?"

Olympia snapped back into her usual brisk mode. "I am packed. Your lunch has been made and is in the refrigerator—sandwiches, a vegetable plate with appropriate dips and a refrigerator cake. I made bread. It's in the freezer. The ham is sliced, separated, vacuum-sealed and frozen in servings appropriate for the three of you. Each container of soup is marked and holds four servings—Rae is eating like a stevedore. I have not left you to go hungry!"

Kellen stepped forward. "Olympia, that's wonderful. Thank you so much for your service, and I hope when you reach the mainland, you'll no longer be haunted by the ghosts of the past."

"Puleaze. I'm not haunted, I just…" Olympia lifted her chin. "I don't like living in an old house where unhappiness walks the halls." She said it as if that made total sense.

Kellen nodded as if she understood.

Max said, "Then we can go."

"Right now," Olympia answered.

WHEN MAX AND Olympia were out of the house, Rae sneaked around from the corner where she'd been hiding and grabbed Kellen in a tight hug. "Mommy, are we going to starve to death?"

Kellen chuckled. "No, dear, it sounds as if Olympia left us with plenty of food prepared."

"But I'm eating like a stevedore."

"Do you know what a stevedore is?"

"No. What?"

Kellen didn't say anything.

Rae sighed in disgust. "I'll look it up. In the dictionary." She made it sound like a dirty word. "But when the food runs out, then what? Daddy can barely make a PB and J and you can't cook."

Stung, Kellen said, "I can. I can Army cook. I can open cans."

"I hate tuna fish."

Kellen smoothed Rae's bangs off her forehead and thought she needed them trimmed, and knew she couldn't do it. She would never trust herself with scissors so close to Rae's eyes. "I know."

"And your hand is better, but you can't use a knife. That's final."

The kid could be bossy. "This probably changes our plans, but not right away. We'll talk when Daddy gets back, figure out our next move."

"Maybe go home?"

"To Yearning Sands? Do you want to?"

Rae squirmed. "Yes. No. I don't know. I like it here."

"I like it here, too."

"But I miss it there."

"I miss it, too."

They heard the helicopter hum, and walked to the window to watch the R44 rise off the ground and zoom toward the mainland.

Rae slipped her hand into Kellen's. "It's scarier out here without Daddy."

"Yes. But even with a bad hand, I can protect you," Kellen promised. "I'm a heck of a fighter."

"I'm learning, too!" Although Rae hated boxing lessons as much as Kellen hated piano lessons. "I didn't mean we'd have to fight anyone. I just meant it felt lonelier." Rae hesitated, looked at Kellen, looked out the window, looked at Kellen. "There's something I wish I could…"

Kellen waited, wanting her to confide whatever was bothering her.

But Rae sighed and looked around as if lost.

"You can tell me anything," Kellen encouraged.

"I know. Maybe. I shouldn't because I…" Rae visibly struggled again with some issue, then brightened. "While Daddy's gone, let's read more of Ruby's diary."

Kellen understood, Ruby's youth and life spoke to Rae, and her resilience taught good life lessons. "Let's do that."

"Up in the attic!"

"You like it up there, don't you?"

"It's safe up there. Away from…all the problems."

"Do you have so many?" What was Rae keeping from them?

"No… No." Rae headed for the stairs. "Let's go. You read first."

## CHAPTER TWENTY-TWO

Father did it. He did it. He demanded General Tempe transfer Patrick, and the general did it. I didn't know until Patrick was gone. I went to the general and demanded to know why, and he said he had daughters and he understood my father's love and concern. General Tempe seemed surprised when I laughed in scorn. I demanded to know where Patrick was. The general said he couldn't tell me, but I was very young and Patrick was only my first love. There would be many more. I wanted to curse at him, and with great dignity, I declared I would never love another. I asked, rather cruelly, if he had found another to replace his beloved wife. He stirred uncomfortably then, said Patrick will probably survive the war and if it's meant to be, we'll be together. I wanted to pound him with my fists, to spit at him for his smug assurances. I didn't, but my emotions, now released by love, hover close to the surface. As I turned away, he asked me if I spoke Japanese. I said yes, and that was the end of our conversation. I hope to never see the wretched villain again.

*Patrick and I made promises to each other, promises we will always keep. But we never even got to say goodbye.*

---

"IT's IMPORTANT TO keep your promises, isn't it?" Rae sat in the window seat, Luna's head on her knee. She petted her dog and stared intently at Kellen.

Kellen picked her words carefully. "It is, as long as the promise was made freely and you know what you promised won't harm anyone."

Rae nodded. "Okay. I agree." She leaned forward. "What happened to Ruby next?"

---

*Today I got a letter! From Patrick! He writes me that he loves me, and that the transfer caught him completely by surprise and he begs my pardon for his abrupt departure. As if he was at fault! He says he can't tell me where he is, but rather than fighting, the military has him writing dispatches from the front to be read by the public to reinforce civilian morale. He is allowed no byline, but it doesn't matter— I hear his voice in his writing! I scoured the newspapers and found a story (in Father's own paper!) and I knew it was his. He's in Hawaii about to board a ship to the South Pacific. His descriptions of the port and the military roar and bustle raised hope in my heart that America will quickly win this war. Then he'll be home and* we'll be together. What an inspiration my darling has become, to me and to others!

---

Father came home to announce I would marry a man named Alfred Herbert. I met him years ago; he is a crony of my father's, an old newspaperman who tried to run his lewd hands over me when I was twelve. When Father announced I would marry Alfred, I told Father about the disgusting incident, and that Bessie said he did the same thing to her. Father said if I was willing to let a filthy Irish Catholic grope me without the benefit of matrimony, it should be a refreshing change to have a husband handle the goods.

That was so crude and so cruel, I ran to throw up. I told Hermione to pack, we were leaving, but Hermione told me we couldn't go. We have no money, she said, and she said I didn't understand what that meant. I'm clearly half-Japanese; I would be hunted down and interned in a camp, and the camps are dreadful places. With no family, I would be hurt, raped. She was very blunt, and she frightened me very much.

We spoke through the night, and at some point we resolved to appeal to Bessie to take me in. In the meantime, I must stay out of Father's clutches. Mad as it seems, we moved my belongings up to the attic. It's a bedroom tower, fanciful in its way, with a bathroom and door that locks. Because we know my father, we also transported many foodstuffs up the stairs. We did all this before dawn. Hermione went

back down to her room, and I locked myself in.
Now I wait to see what Father will do when
he receives my letter. Rage, I imagine.

---

"Ruby's tough, isn't she?" Rae's eyes were wide
and her voice held awe.

"She is." Kellen patted the couch cushion beside
her.

Rae hopped off the window seat, came to sit with
her mother, and leaned her head against Kellen's shoulder. "Ruby's going to make it, isn't she? She's going
to be okay?"

"I hope so, but I don't know. We could keep reading—" Kellen heard the chopping sound of a helicopter. "No, we couldn't. Your daddy's home. He's going
to be mad that we read Ruby's diary without him."

"No. Yes. You're right." Rae was all despair.

"Your daddy's back, safe and sound. Let's talk to
him first, see what he has to tell us, then we can tell
him about Ruby."

"Okay. He'll understand."

"Probably." Kellen stood and hauled Rae to her feet.
"He's a pretty great guy."

# CHAPTER TWENTY-THREE

MAX ARRIVED CARRYING an extra-large chicken and pesto pizza, ready for the oven, a six-pack of beer and a six-pack of Coke, and an assortment of gelato in a freeze pack. He stashed the gelato in the freezer, distributed the drinks and turned on the oven.

He knew how to make himself welcome. "The great thing is," he said, "with Olympia gone we can eat at the kitchen table." Instead of the large, echoing dining room.

Max also brought a flashlight headband, an LED mat light, a telescoping lighted inspection mirror, an LED floodlight...

Kellen looked up from the bag he had placed on the table and raised her eyebrows.

"The carburetor kit is full of really small parts, and I need light in that garage."

She removed a new roll of electrical tape, a big box of knuckle bandages, a solar crank emergency radio and a multimeter to check for hot wires. "What did you do? Stop at an auto parts store and go through it like a whirlwind?"

Without a bit of irony, he said, "I was like a kid in a candy store."

Rae pulled out an electric screwdriver and turned

it on. Eyes shining, she said, "Daddy, we're going to get that truck running."

"Yes, we are." He grinned blissfully. "Check out the coffee maker I bought."

Kellen pulled it out. "It's pretty small, but I suppose it'll work for the garage."

Max started cutting lettuce to make a salad. "Um, I thought we'd take the big coffee maker from in here and—"

Kellen started laughing.

He waited until she finished before saying with dignity, "I need caffeine way worse out there. You shouldn't snicker, because I brought you a present, too." Leaning over, he reached into the bottom of the bag and pulled out a pair of pink padded hand wraps to protect Kellen's knuckles while she pounded the mattress.

She pounced on them. "Thank you! You really know how to make a woman happy."

"I'll do that later," he promised.

Rae sighed loudly and rolled her eyes. "I hate when you use that warm gushy voice to Mommy. It's gross."

While the pizza baked, Rae set the table. Kellen fed Luna, and Max told them he'd contacted his cousin and explained the situation with Olympia. When they landed, Rafe had been waiting for them. He offered Olympia a cruise across the Northern Atlantic that would keep her occupied.

In dire tones, she had said, "I knew something suspicious was going on," and accepted.

At that point in the story, Rae slapped a fork by Kellen's plate and asked, "You saw Cousin Rafe? What about my grandma? Did you see her?"

Max looked alarmed, as if he'd realized he'd put his foot in it. "You know she's in Italy."

"We were supposed to be in Italy, too," Rae retorted. "We aren't!"

"I promise you, she really is," Max assured her.

"Did she send me a message by Cousin Rafe?" Rae begged.

"No, honey, she didn't."

"Why didn't you *call* Grandma?"

"It would have been the middle of the night."

The frustration Rae had expressed in the first days at Isla Paraíso made a whopping return. "Am I dead here? Has everyone forgotten me? Why can't I talk to anyone? I want to go home. I want to go home!"

"Where's home?" Max asked.

Kellen clenched her fists. *No, Max.*

Frustrated, Rae huffed like a steam train. "Where I can talk to my friends! And my grandma!"

Kellen brought the balsamic vinegar and olive oil out of the pantry and handed them to Max. Gripping his wrist, she looked into his eyes. "Did you hear about Verona? Is she—" *safe* was the wrong word to use "— having a good time?"

"She is."

Kellen released him.

"She's with Irene and Annabella, in the old family village where everybody knows everybody and all strangers are kept under careful observation." Max made the dressing and tossed it with the salad. "Don't worry, Rae, I'm sure Grandma is fine, and missing you, too."

Before Rae could react to that platitude, Kellen said, "That pizza smells done." She mouthed to Max, *Never let Rae get hungry.*

"Right." He opened the oven, and the wonderful smell of basil and garlic, fresh crust and bubbling cheese wafted out.

*Great* way to change the subject.

Max cut them each a hearty piece, turned off the oven and slid the pizza inside to stay warm.

As they seated themselves, Kellen looked around the little table and thought that they had become a family. Not a perfect family, not a family with no problems, but a bonded family that in a crisis supported each other.

Max must have been thinking the same thing, because as he served the salad, he said, "This is nice."

Rae nodded, her mouth full of pizza.

Kellen picked up her fork and dug into the salad. "What are we going to do tonight?"

"The same thing we do every night." Max did a great imitation of The Brain. "Try to take over the world."

Rae, who didn't have a clue what he was talking about, said, "Daddy, you are so weird."

Kellen asked, "Are we going to read? Play cards? Play a board game?" All activities they'd enjoyed in the past. "Watch a movie?" They had a stack of DVDs that the old caretaker, Olof Humphreys, had owned: war movies, mostly, and some really gruesome horror.

"We could read more of Ruby's journal." Max sounded eager.

Kellen and Rae exchanged guilty glances.

"Really? You read it without me?" Clearly, Max was hooked on the story.

"It's okay," Kellen said soothingly. "Rae and I don't mind. We can read it again."

"And more!" Rae polished off her first piece of pizza. "I'll get it. Come on, Luna!" She bounded out the door.

Max took advantage of their alone time to kiss Kellen, and when they heard Rae coming back down the stairs, they separated and smiled a promise to each other.

Rae returned with Ruby's journal in one hand and in the other, a broad red leather-bound book. "Mommy, look what I found. It's blank. It's a journal. Nobody's written in it. Can I have it?"

Kellen took it and leafed through. "Where did you find it?"

"In the attic on the desk."

Kellen looked Rae up and down. "I don't remember this." She really didn't, but why would Rae lie? "Has it always been there?"

Rae shrugged. "I guess. Can I use it?"

"I don't see why not." Kellen handed it back. "Writing in a journal is a great idea. I did when I was your age."

"I'll be like Ruby!"

Max said, "I sincerely hope your story is a little more upbeat."

Rae sat in her chair, pulled the salad close and ate

all the tomatoes and cucumbers. "Can I have another slice of pizza?"

They *all* had a second slice of pizza.

With a sigh of satisfaction, Max leaned back in his chair, took a sip of his beer, and said, "That storm. The typhoon. It's one helluva big storm, and it's aimed right at the California coast."

"Will we be in trouble?" Kellen asked.

"Maybe." Max lifted his hands to show his doubt. "Depends. On everything. Whether it stays on the same track and whether it maintains intensity. We've got the solar panels that feed the generators. If the storm lasts too long, we'll lose power. Which is okay except—no water, no sewer."

"Do we have to go back?" Rae had been fed and sounded less eager to leave.

Max said, "We'll see."

## CHAPTER TWENTY-FOUR

"MY WIFE..." Dylan Conkle sat in front of the fire pit on the beach at sunset and threw driftwood into the flames. "My wife doesn't respect me."

"I saw that." Mara watched him through eyes narrowed to evil slits. Not that he noticed, or was sober enough to recognize her intentions if he did. "What's her name again?"

He pushed his glasses up on his nose. "Jamie."

"Right. Jamie doesn't appreciate you as she should. You're her man. You provide for her. You handle the folks up at the big house for her."

"She hates them," Dylan mumbled.

"She doesn't appreciate how you make her life easier." Mara lit a joint and passed it to Dylan.

"Where'd you get this?" He examined the weed with great interest.

"At the university." *At the prison.* "It's dusted with something special. It'll make you *crazy*." She drew out the word to make *crazy* sound like fun.

"Really?" Dylan took a long drag. "What kind of crazy?"

"Killin' crazy." She dug around in her bag and found the Chivas Regal Owen had been so impressed he could afford. "Wash it down with this."

Dylan lifted the bottle and swallowed, then coughed up a lung, then took another swallow and sighed. "That's good stuff."

Every man was at heart a measly peasant boy. "I thought you'd like it. Only the best for you, Dylan. Too bad Jamie doesn't believe that." Mara tossed a few twigs in the fire and watched the orange flames eat them. The night was warm; they didn't need the fire, but she needed the atmosphere to work her magic. Respect seemed to be a thing for Dylan, so she repeated, "Jamie's got no respect for you."

Dylan took another long drag. "No respect. But you do." He flopped toward her, all loose muscles and stupid hopes. "You could be my real wife."

"I'd like that, but I couldn't. Not while she's alive." Mara watched him process that. His mind had slowed to a crawl, making him so easy to read she wanted to laugh. But she didn't. This was a delicate process, sending out a killer, and she needed all her concentration to make it work. "I would never come between a man and his wife."

The dumbshit bought it, tail, hooves and hide. "You're a good girl."

"Yeah. That's me."

"You like me, don't you?"

She smiled at him, flushed from the drugs and sweaty from the fire. "Of course. Everyone likes you. Maybe I like you more than I should." She reached into her bag again, into the side pocket, and found the bottle of pills the prison psychiatrist had prescribed for her. These pills were supposed to alter her moods, make the voices stop and the rage dissipate, be a frontal lobotomy so she could function in society without wanting to gruesomely murder everyone and cut off their hands.

She never took these pills. She liked herself as she was. She offered one on the tip of her finger. "This is a good one."

He took it, stared at it, mouth dropped open, in the flickering light of the fire. "What does it do?"

"It makes you think you're a king." With all the other shit in his system, this little white mood-alterer would turn sloppy, wimpy, worthless Dylan into death incarnate.

"I dropped it!" Dylan scrambled around, patting his loose shorts, his skinny calves, the sand beneath his feet.

Mara sighed, but softly, and brought out another pill. Putting it on the tip of her finger, she said, "Open wide!" and shoved it into his mouth, far enough that he couldn't lose it.

He gagged a little.

She handed him the bottle of scotch again. "Swallow it! That's a boy." She stood up. "You need to go explain to Jamie that she needs to honor and obey you, like your marriage vows said."

He mumbled, "We didn't do those—"

"It doesn't matter what you really vowed. That's what marriage is, right? The man is in charge. You're the head of the family. You shouldn't have to do anything."

"She's not all bad. Tonight she's making me apple cake. I like apple cake."

"Is she making it for you? Or for the folks up at the big house?"

Abruptly sullen, he said, "She'll give them some of my cake, won't she?"

"You bet she will. She should do all the work and whenever you want, she should go down on you and suck you until you come in her mouth, and she should like it." Mara leaned down and put her face near his. "That's what I would do if you were my husband."

As Dylan stared at her, she saw him changing. The booze and the weed and the drugs took effect. The promise of sex created a spark, and the flames kindled in his eyes. Easygoing Dylan Conkle changed into a self-important man on a mission.

"Go." Mara gave him a push in the direction of his cottage. "It's time to make a change."

Dylan walked a straight line, all the way up from the beach to the grasslands and along the path toward the cottage he shared with Jamie.

Backpack in hand, Mara followed.

The drugs worked exactly as they should. He never faltered. He never lost his way. He pushed his way into the well-lit cottage, and almost at once, Jamie screamed.

Mara stayed on the hill overlooking the cottage for a long time, until the crying stopped, and thought how much she enjoyed setting scenes in motion.

When Dylan appeared, carrying a limp Jamie over his shoulder, she wondered briefly what he'd do with the body, then went in to scope out the scene.

Wow. That was a lot of blood and that gray matter... Yes, he'd finished the job.

She breathed deeply. The house smelled like brutality and spices: broken bones, cinnamon and cloves.

*Oh, look. Cupcakes on a cooling rack. Must be Dylan's apple cake.*

She picked one up. A little bloody. But the oven was still on. She opened it, rescued a dozen slightly over-baked cupcakes, and turned them out. She picked one up, tossed it from hand to hand until it had cooled, and bit into it. Apples, nuts and spices. *Good choice, Dylan.* She ate that one, then tossed the rest into a paper bag, then into her backpack—all except the ones with a bloody frosting. She left those.

Jamie had begun assembling tomorrow's basket to be delivered to the big house. No reason to leave it for the Di Lucas to find. Once they stepped inside here, they would never eat this stuff. Mara flung the produce in with the cupcakes.

She turned off the lights and shut the door behind her, knowing the satisfaction of a job well done.

# *CHAPTER TWENTY-FIVE*

THAT EVENING, KELLEN, Max and Rae lovingly stashed the leftover pizza in the refrigerator, then cleaned the kitchen. The cleaning took longer than they thought it should. They might not have liked Olympia, but they missed her.

Then they hustled into the library and took their places, Kellen in a small overstuffed chair with an ottoman that weighed a ton, Max in the large over-stuffed chair.

Rae sat down at the desk, picked up a pen, opened her brand-new journal—and stared at the blank page. And stared. And stared.

To give her privacy, Kellen opened Ruby's diary and started reading aloud what they'd read this afternoon.

After a few moments, Max interrupted her. "What's wrong, Rae?"

Rae looked up, vaguely alarmed. "What should I write?"

"I never kept a journal, but my sister did," Max said.

"Aunt Irene has a journal?" Rae asked.

"She *begged* for a journal. She got it for Christmas, then she wrote in it for about a week and that was that." Max rolled his eyes, all disgusted older brother.

Kellen cleared her throat.

Max changed his tone. "But look at Ruby! She wrote in hers for years, and she wrote about whatever was happening to her at that moment."

"Nothing's happening to me!" Rae retorted.

Kellen decided to step in. "You could write about what you did today and yesterday, what you read, what you ate."

"That's boring." Rae was looking desperate.

"How you feel?" Max suggested.

"I feel fine."

"We mean, what are your feelings are about being here on Isla Paraíso? You were pretty angry at first." Kellen hoped the gentle reminder would not trigger any grand drama. "How do you feel now?"

"Okay," Rae muttered.

"I'm asking. I'm not prying!" Maybe Kellen should stop trying to help. "That's what the journal is for. You tell it your real feelings and thoughts, your hope and dreams. Like Ruby did."

"Like I tell Chloe?"

"Right," Max said.

"Maybe I could pretend to write Chloe a letter?"

"Or Grandma," Kellen said.

"It's your journal. You can do whatever you like," Max assured her.

Rae began to write slowly, then with greater speed.

To catch Max up, Kellen opened Ruby's journal and read aloud the passages she and Rae had read earlier. When she got to the line, "'I locked myself in. Now I wait to see what Father will do when he receives my letter. Rage, I imagine,'" Rae put down her pen, moved to the center of the room and reclined on the rug. Staring at the ceiling, she listened.

---

Indeed, I was right. Father raged and pounded on the door. He cursed me and denounced me. He forbade anybody in the household from communicating with me or helping me, and in the afternoon, men barricaded me in. Father shouted that when I was ready to surrender and marry the beast he had obtained for me, I should wave a white flag out the window like the rest of the Japanese cowards would soon do.

I told him, in a proud voice, that I am not Japanese, I'm American. He sneered and left.

Am I really the enemy because my skin isn't white and eyes are not perfectly round? I don't think so. It is what's in my mind and heart that matters.

Now it's evening, the light is dying, and I'm alone and frightened. Oh Patrick! How did it come to this?

---

The funniest thing happened. Mother appeared in the attic, holding a tray with a hot meal from the kitchen. She didn't say much, she never does, only that Father didn't remember the secret passages the architect installed.

Mother smiled as she watched me eat, and when I was finished and I asked her why she had done this, she said I shouldn't marry a man like Father. Which made me think about her life

and how dreadful it must have been. I looked at
her and realized she's 42. She looks much older,
too thin and sad, and she was younger than me
when she had Larry. I thanked her and asked
if she was coping with the loss of her sons. She
stood. She bowed. In Japanese, she thanked me
for my concern.

She showed no emotion, but I knew—she
isn't coping at all. Her grief is eating her alive.

My poor mother.

---

Now that the way is open, Hermione is regularly
bringing me meals and letters. I am almost merry
up here, except for one thing.

I'm going to have a baby.

---

"That's not good," Max muttered.

Rae sat up and looked at Kellen for a clue of how
she should react. "Having a baby is a happy time, isn't
it?"

"I think this is going to make Ruby's life even more
difficult," Kellen said.

"I don't want her life to be more difficult." Rae
pushed her hair off her forehead.

Her concern made Kellen's heart ache. "I don't,
either."

"I wish we knew what happened to her," Rae said.

Max came to his feet. "When I was on the mainland, I should have looked her up."

Rae caught her breath. "I wish you had!"

"It never occurred to me," Max sounded exasperated with himself. "I'm out of the online habit."

"Rae, just think, someday someone might be reading your journal and be fascinated about your life." Kellen smiled at her daughter.

Rae looked down at the book in her hand, and in a small voice, she asked, "Are *you* going to read it?"

"Read what? Your diary?" When Kellen understood what Rae meant, what she feared, she flushed with anger. "I am not! Do you think I'm like Gerard Morgade? A sneak and a bully?"

"Kellen!" Max put out a warning hand.

But he didn't need to. Rae came to her feet and stood in front of her mother. "I'm sorry. I didn't mean... I just, sometimes..." Her voice trembled with the onset of tears.

That made Kellen calm down as nothing else could. She took a few breaths—this was no time for her voice to freeze in her throat—and in a softer tone, she said, "Sometimes you think bad things about me and Daddy. I know. Sometimes I don't like you, either. But I like you really hard the rest of the time, and I always, always love you." She watched while Rae thought that over, and when her frown cleared, she said, "I promise I will never read your journal."

Rae looked down at the journal, then up at Kellen, then left and right, and her expression was worried again. "A person should always keep a promise, right?"

Again with the promise thing. Had Rae had made a promise she regretted? To Chloe? Or to Maverick?

"Right," Max said. "That's why before you make a promise, you think very hard about what it means, whether it's a good thing, because what if the time comes when you want to break the promise? Or worse, you really *should* break the promise? You're stuck."

"I know." Rae sat back on the floor with her pen and her journal. "Sometimes I wish I could make time go backwards."

"Me, too," Kellen agreed. "I wish that, too. Everybody does at some point."

Max met her gaze.

She knew why. He blamed himself for not being fast enough to stop that killer, Ettore Fontana, from shooting her.

And she wanted back all the years she'd missed of being with Max and Rae. Yet she couldn't regret her time in the Army. It had made her a woman like the real Kellen, tough enough to survive and yet caring. She leaned forward and spoke to Max. "We have each other now, and always will, and that's all that matters." She picked up Ruby's diary. "Do we want to read some more?"

"Not that." Max obviously thought they'd trod on enough precarious ground. He thrust a book into Kellen's hand. "Read more *Wonder*. Auggie is brave like Ruby, but in a whole different way."

# CHAPTER TWENTY-SIX

STILL RESTLESS, MARA wandered up toward the big house and stood in the shadows on the porch. The open window let in the summer air, and she stared through the screen at the family inside.

For so many years, Mara had had to loathe Kellen Adams from afar. Once Mara had been in charge of the smuggling on the Yearning Sands coast. Then Kellen had betrayed her, tried to kill her, sent her to prison.

Years of plotting and planning, then—escape!

Mara had gone to great lengths to attend Kellen's wedding, and that moment when Kellen had seen her, recognized her, knew what was coming—that moment had been a triumph.

But Kellen had slipped out of consciousness and Mara's control, and disappeared into the morass of medical care.

Mara had had to disappear, too. And wait. And wait.

Because Mara aimed all her spite and censure at Kellen, at the sister of her heart, at the competitor of her physical self, and it would not make her happy to unload on anyone else.

Kellen would be sorry. The longer Mara waited, the more ways she thought to torment Kellen Adams. Kellen and her whole wonderful, happy family.

*Look at them. How sweet. It looks like a scene from that goddamn BBC historical series set in a castle.*

Kellen sat in a brocade easy chair, reading something that looked like a fairy tale.

Max sat nearby, all noble and strong, and watched his wife as if she embodied his every dream.

Rae reclined on the rug, one knee crossed, the other leg resting on it and swinging restlessly. She held a red leather-bound book in one hand and a pen in the other, and she stared at the ceiling.

Poor kid. She was bored, listening to someone read out loud. Listening to *Kellen Adams* read out loud.

Kellen had changed. Her hair was longer, as if she'd let it grow to cover the brain surgery scars, and white, as if it had been bleached by the island's sun. That surgery had left its marks in her face, which was more mature, and on her hand. Mara had done her research; she knew Kellen battled atrophy.

Now, as Kellen read, she squeezed a stress ball to build strength. Once she stopped, shook her hand and grimaced, and Mara saw the way the fingers curled toward the palm.

She wanted to tell her not to bother with the stress ball. In another twenty-four hours, that hand wouldn't be attached to her body.

Then Mara frowned and wondered—was a damaged hand even worth harvesting? What a dreadful thought, that the hand of her dearest enemy was imperfect and trifling.

Kellen looked up from that book and right at the window.

Mara shrank back. Had she seen her? They had

been best friends once, like twins who could speak across long distances. Had Kellen heard her thoughts?

But no. Kellen said, "Rae, it's getting a breezy. Would you shut the window?"

Mara hated that voice, fond, warm, a little raspy, as if she'd been reading too long. She hated the knowledge that Kellen had refused the psychic connection between them. Why would she pretend not to know they had been sisters in a previous life?

Rae hopped up and ran to the window where Mara stood. "Are you going to read more, Mommy? Tonight, will you read more?" Without looking outside, Rae shut that window right in Mara's face.

Mara hadn't seen it before, but that kid...looked like Kellen. Her rage swelled. She wanted to break the window, leap in like Dracula, crush them, drink their blood, cut off their hands.

*But no! Not now, Mara. Not yet. You couldn't win against the three of them.*

She fingered her pistol.

*I could if I shot them.*

*Too swift. That's not what you want. You want to take your time, create their fear, enjoy their pain.*

Her hand fell away from her sidearm.

*You're so close. Not long now. Go finish your preparations.*

*Okay. You're right. I will.*

Mara backed away from the window and down the steps.

Kellen had betrayed her. And for that, Max and Rae and most of all, Kellen—they were all going to die.

## CHAPTER TWENTY-SEVEN

THE NEXT MORNING, Daddy installed lights all over the garage, plugged in the big old kitchen coffee maker, arranged all their new tools, turned to Rae and said, "Isn't this great? We can see what we're doing. This will help. We can get the truck running!"

Rae agreed. It was great, and it did help.

But even with the carburetor put together, the F-100 still didn't start.

After long moments of frustration where Daddy tried not to swear the really bad words, he slid under the truck on his wheeled mechanics' creeper and Rae leaned into the engine compartment from the top, and they discussed where the holdup could be. Rae was willing to throw in the towel, but when she suggested that, Daddy slid around and glared up at her. So she didn't suggest they ask Mommy, which would have made all kinds of sense since Mommy was in charge of transportation and stuff in the Army. But Rae already knew sometimes her father was not logical or sensible, and she guessed with what she'd done yesterday—riding off, meeting Miranda, promising not to tell—she was in no position to lecture him.

Mommy came in. That cut and bruise on her jaw looked worse today, and painful, and she was sort of yelling, which was not usual for her, so Rae knew she must be frustrated. "We agreed that between the food in the freezer and the Conkles' morning basket o' food, we could survive without Olympia." She knelt down so she could look under the truck. "Dylan's done it again. There's no basket."

Daddy shot out from under the truck. He stood and wiped his hands on the grease rag. "He's drunk somewhere. Worthless!" Then he said something Rae didn't completely understand. "We don't need this now."

That got her mom's attention, made her calm down right away. She walked to him, slid her arms around his waist, and her voice got softer and calmer. "Max, it's okay."

"No, it's not." Daddy's jaw was squared, his brown eyes flat and almost black, the way they were when he was really angry. "We weren't supposed to deal with this kind of challenge. This was supposed to be us taking it easy while everyone else dealt with the details of—"

Mommy cleared her throat and hugged him very hard. "Max. Stop. Stop."

Rae got it. Her mom didn't want her dad scaring her. Rae couldn't imagine what worse could happen than starving to death, but her parents had been acting weird for weeks. Maybe…maybe something was going on she didn't understand. Her parents looked worried, and she felt guilty about talking to Miranda Phillips and not telling her parents, so she shouted, "I'll go. I'll find our basket!" Before her mom could object, get all weird like yesterday, she said, "I can do it. Really, let me."

The garage was quiet.

Rae remembered that time Jamie had chased her out of the greenhouse, and felt a twinge of fear.

Then Mommy said, "I know you can. Thank you, Rae."

Rae stiffened her spine. Mommy trusted her, so she would stand her ground, no matter what Jamie said. She yelled, "C'mon, Luna!"

Dog and child bounded out the door and toward the bicycle resting on its side on the lawn.

Kellen followed, concerned, preoccupied with all her niggling fears.

"It's okay, she'll be safe." Max followed and pulled her back into his arms. "Luna is with her."

Kellen watched the dog gallop after Rae. "Poor Luna and her paws."

"Hopefully they'll meet Dylan or probably Jamie coming up the path."

"Yes, but—" Kellen struggled for a reason to explain her fears. "Olympia had a nervous breakdown."

"Which has nothing to do with Rae."

"Rae has her nightmares."

"You've told me that's part of *becoming a woman*." He sounded like the announcer on a tampon commercial.

She punched him in the gut. "Oh, shut up."

"Did you hurt your hand?" he asked with fake concern.

"No!"

"Must be all that clobbering of the mattress. Listen, nobody made Olympia have a nervous breakdown. When Olympia got here, she must have been hovering on the edge. My mistake." He took responsibility without complaint. "When I picked out a cook, I should have been more careful."

"How?" Kellen was logical and sensible—when she wasn't worrying about Mara. "Like you said, you didn't have a lot of time to get someone, and Olympia seemed… I mean, she's mean, but I never thought she was going to see ghosts."

"The dead dancing in the ballroom to old records? That was about as weird as it gets." Max drifted over to the truck. "I know you're worried, but we've seen no sign of Mara. Even the devil needs some kind of shelter. The island's basically flat. There's a few trees."

"The redwoods!"

"Not a lot of those. A few rocks. I can't see Jamie Conkle letting Mara move in."

"I can't see that, either. You're right."

He leaned into the engine compartment.

She'd lost his attention. He was back making love to the truck. With a sigh, she poured herself a cup of coffee. "As soon as we get that basket, we'll have vegetables and fruits and maybe some fish. You did well with the fish the other night."

"I didn't do much of a job of fileting." He sounded absentminded.

"You'll learn." She sipped the coffee out of a mug with a cracked glaze. "You could praise the way I got the bread out of the freezer."

"You did do a good job." Max straightened up and got stern again. "But Dylan damn well better have a good excuse for this, or Jamie won't save him. I'll throw him off the island." He stood quietly, then glanced sideways at her.

Guilty. He was feeling guilty about something.

"What?"

"Before I come down on Dylan like a ton of bricks, do you mind if I stay here to work on the pickup?" He ran his hand lovingly over the hood. "Today I'm pretty sure I can get it running."

God, he was cute. "You think so?"

"I know. I know. I've said it every day this week. But today—"

He wanted this so badly. "Go for it. I'll wait here in hopes Rae returns with Dylan, or the basket, or both."

"Or Jamie?"

"No, I can't hope for Jamie. She's just so—"

"She is, isn't she?" Max pulled on his headband with the mag light, reclined on the mechanics creeper and slid under the truck.

# CHAPTER TWENTY-EIGHT

RAE PEDDLED DOWN the trail toward the Conkles'. Luna loped beside her, smiling, her tongue hanging out.

Things were good. Today everybody was normal.

Well. Daddy was always normal.

But Mommy hadn't tried to stop Rae from riding for the daily basket. She trusted Rae to find Dylan, pick up their food and bring it home. Maybe Rae would find Dylan quickly. Then she could run by Paradise Cove and visit with Miranda. Overnight, she had figured it out. Miranda needed to come to dinner. Inviting her was the hospitable thing to do. In the past, Mommy and Miranda had had a fight, but they were both nice. Her mother had returned to being this awesome woman, who ran and fought and spoke and... well, she didn't cook, and that was okay. Mommy and Miranda would meet and make up. They'd have a good meal. Best of all, Miranda wouldn't be a secret anymore, and Rae's promise wouldn't count.

But for Rae's plan would work, they had to have vegetables and a chicken or something. And they would have vegetables. Rae would make sure of it. In the distance, she could see Dylan Conkle walking toward her.

Yay! She didn't have to ride all the way to their cottage.

But when he got closer, she saw he didn't have the basket.

No basket. Stupid Dylan. Why was he such a loser?

He was staggering. He was wearing a black suit...

Even closer...

He wasn't wearing anything.

Dylan Conkle was naked.

Rae hit the brakes and skidded to a stop about twenty feet away.

Luna planted herself between Rae and Dylan and growled.

Dylan slowly focused, and stopped, too. "You. Kid. What's your name?"

Impatient, she said, "I'm Rae. Remember?"

"No."

"Rae Di Luca."

He hit his head with his hand as if trying to knock something out of his brain. "I can't find Jamie. Do you know where she is? I can't find her. I don't know what happened last night, but I can't find her."

Naked. He was naked. Even from this far away, he smelled. He smelled funny, like copper pennies.

Blood. He was covered in dried blood. His hair was spiky with blood. His mouth was smeared with blood. His hands, his belly, his legs, his—

Something clicked in Rae's brain. This was the moment her daddy and mommy warned her about, when she realized she was in danger and needed to stop being polite and save herself from harm.

Adrenaline flooded her system. She didn't know

how, but she got her feet back on the bike's pedals, turned herself around and blasted back up the path toward the house, calling Luna as she went.

Luna ran beside her, no longer smiling, a low growl rumbling from her chest like a jackhammer.

Rae didn't dare glance behind her. What if Dylan was chasing her? What if he was fast? What if he caught her? And did to her what he'd done to Jamie.

*What had he done to Jamie?*

As soon as Rae saw the garage on the horizon, a new terror seized her. What if something had happened to her parents? What if Dylan had got there ahead of her? She shouted, "Daddy! Mommy! Daddy! Mommy!"

Her mother ran out first. Then her father. Because he had to get out from under the pickup. But he outstripped her mother running toward Rae.

Rae skidded to a halt. Dropped her bike. Looked behind her.

Dylan was nowhere in sight.

Luna was panting, looking back the way they came and growling.

Rae knelt beside her dog and hugged her hard.

Luna rubbed her head against Rae's, giving comfort and protection.

Daddy arrived first, and helped Rae to her feet. "What happened?"

Rae couldn't speak.

Mommy grabbed her by the shoulders, gave her a little shake. "Rae. What happened?"

For the first time, Rae allowed the meaning of what she saw to hit her. She swayed. She swallowed. She trembled. She whispered, "He's crazy. He's bloody. He's done something to Jamie."

"Dylan? Is bloody? Dylan? Did something to Jamie?" Daddy sounded frantic, maybe scared.

That frightened Rae even more. She flung herself at them. "Please, no, it's horrible. It's horrible."

# CHAPTER TWENTY-NINE

IN THE LIBRARY, Kellen picked a thorn out of Luna's foot and listened to Max quietly explain what he'd done with Dylan. "I washed him off with the hose, gave him coveralls and told him to get dressed."

"How bad was it?" *How much blood?* she meant. *Should we search for Jamie?*

Max shook his head, his eyes both sorrowful and angry.

"There's no way?" Kellen asked.

"It wasn't just blood," he muttered.

Jamie was dead, then. Kellen shook her head, too.

"When Dylan was dressed," Max said, "I tied him up and left him in the garage. He's quite docile; he didn't seem to have any fight in him."

"I never thought he had any in the first place."

"No. He was so apathetic, I thought he would someday melt away and leave no mark on the world." Max glanced at their daughter.

Since Rae had returned home from her Dylan encounter, she hadn't let her parents out of her sight. The way she sat, close to Luna, and huddled over an encyclopedia, leafing through the pages… The child was in shock.

In a lower voice, Max said, "He says he doesn't remember anything about last night."

"Do you think that's true?" Kellen lowered her voice to match his. It wasn't as if they were trying to keep secrets from Rae; more that they felt as if they were at a sickbed, and didn't want to disturb the patient.

"If he remembers anything," Max said, "he's not about to admit it. Maybe he doesn't—he keeps blacking out, then coming back to consciousness. And vomiting while he's conscious."

"Moonshine. Probably lead poisoning."

"Or he ate something or smoked something that sent him mad. I have to take him to the mainland, to a hospital."

Rae shivered, a sudden violent shudder.

Max took a throw off the couch and wrapped it around her shoulders.

Kellen was sorry about Jamie, sorry for the violence and the waste, but underneath her compassion, she blazed with anger. Dylan and Jamie had created their own icy hell, and Rae didn't deserve to be devoured by the cold. "Call the Coast Guard. Let them come and get him."

"I tried. There was a collision between two excursion boats in San Francisco Bay, and they've got a team on a drug-smuggling operation. They're overwhelmed. As long as we're not feeling threatened, they say keep him confined and they'll get him as soon as they can." Max glanced at Rae. "But he's not staying here."

Right now, Kellen could herself have pushed Dylan into the ocean and dusted her hands afterward. "Then go as soon as you can. But…" She moved a few steps away from Rae. "I think it's time to bring out one of the pistols from the gun safe."

Max picked up her right hand. The stress of the day had intensified the curl of her fingers. "Do you think you can shoot?" His question was about the effect of the atrophy, not about her skill level; she'd learned to shoot in the Army and sharpened her skills in combat.

"I can." She met his eyes. "A pistol is a good deterrent when pointed at *anybody*." At Mara, she meant, if she put in an appearance.

Max's grim face lightened. "That would make me feel better about leaving you alone. Let me get the key. I'll bring you the Ruger?"

"Yes. The Ruger would be good."

He headed for Gerard Morgade's study.

Kellen sat beside Rae and put her arm around her. A firearm would give them security during Max's absence. She only hoped she wouldn't have to use it; she hoped Mara was nowhere around. Surely Dylan had poisoned himself with one of his homemade brews. That made sense, didn't it?

She smoothed Rae's hair. But no matter what, a pistol would make her feel as if she could protect her daughter from harm.

Before Kellen expected him, Max had returned, pale and empty-handed. He gestured Kellen toward the door.

Kellen came to her feet and met him. "What's wrong?" she asked softly.

Just as softly, he said, "The gun safe is empty."

"What do you mean, it's empty?" Stupid question, and too loud, but...*what*?

"The safe was unlocked. The door was slightly open. The guns are gone. The rifles. The pistols. Gone." Spacing his words, he said, "The safe is empty."

They stared at each other, trying to understand the import.

"Olympia?" Kellen asked.

"I guess. Who else? Not the Conkles. Jamie might not have approved of firearms, but she mostly avoided the house—"

"I caught her inside once. She was defensive when I confronted her about it."

"She was always defensive, but she wasn't a thief." Already Max spoke of Jamie in the past tense. "Dylan might have taken them, but even if he had access to the household keys, and I don't believe that, when he was drunk, he could find the key or fit it into the lock."

"Right. Olympia had keys, so I suppose she could have had a key to the gun safe." Kellen rubbed her forehead. "But why?"

"I didn't inspect her luggage, so she might have gotten away with the pistols, but she wasn't carrying a bag long enough for the rifles."

The library looked so normal, so safe, except for the small, shivering figure of her daughter. And now she had no way to protect Rae in case of trouble? *More* trouble? "Max, we have to consider this could be Mara. Remember how she manipulates men? How violence always followed in her wake? Add Dylan together with the missing firearms, and we have to consider that Mara is here. Somewhere. Somehow."

"I know. I agree. But then I ask how she got here and why she hasn't openly revealed herself—"

"Because she's crazy!"

Max lightly placed his fingers on Kellen's lips. "Shh. Yes, true. But so was Olympia. She was afraid to be here, and it stands to reason she might have taken the firearms to protect herself."

"So don't jump to conclusions."

"We can jump, but cautiously, and we've got to look at every possibility. I did a fast search of the study and of Olympia's bedroom." He moved closer. "But, Kellen, think. If Olympia hid the guns in this house, with all the rooms, the drawers, the cupboards... How can we ever find them?"

Hopeless. It was hopeless. "What was she thinking?"

"The isolation of this island makes people lose their minds."

"I'm just fine, thank you!"

"You really are." Smiling faintly, he put his arm around her and together they walked over to Rae. He spoke to his daughter. "Are you two going to be okay here alone?"

"Of course we will," Kellen said. "Right, Rae?"

Rae looked up. "What?" She looked into Max's face as if just now noticing he was there. "What?"

Kellen said, "We'll be okay alone on the island while Daddy takes Dylan in, right?"

"Sure." Rae swallowed. "But we're not alone on the island."

"We aren't?" Kellen mentally jumped to her imminent fear. *Mara.* "Who else is here?" *Mara?*

"Jamie! Just Jamie." Rae glanced away, off to the side, out the window as if expecting to see a face there.

Kellen knelt on the other side of Rae. Between her and Max, they would surround their daughter with love. They would push away the darkness.

Rae looked up at her mother, then at her father. "Jamie's here somewhere, and we've got to find her. She might still be alive."

"No," Max said.

"Daddy, she might be hurt!"

"Sweetheart…" Max faltered.

Kellen intervened. "Your father is convinced Jamie is dead, but if she has somehow survived, I'll find her."

"We have to search. Just in case." Rae pulled the throw around herself like a shawl. "Mommy, I need to help you search."

Kellen gazed into Rae's eyes, afraid, distressed, yet clear and concerned. "You are the best kid I ever met."

"Does that mean I can come with you rather than sneak after you?"

Kellen didn't think it was possible given the circumstances, but she smiled. "Mostly a good kid. Sometimes you're sort of snotty."

"Runs in the family." Rae's spirit shone through her anguish.

"I guess it does."

Max began, "I don't think that Rae—"

Kellen interrupted him. "Rae is right. A search needs to be done."

"And Mommy needs my help."

Max looked between his wife and his daughter, and Kellen could see it; he badly wanted to say they couldn't go.

She put her hand over his mouth to stop any unwise exclamations. "I don't want to leave Rae here by herself to fret and worry. We'll stick together, and for protection, we'll keep Luna with us."

"Luna's paws—" he said.

"I'm going to put socks on her feet." Kellen was determined. "She isn't going to like it, but we need her with us."

For the first time since the morning, Rae giggled. "Poor Luna." She hugged her dog, then sobered. "Poor Jamie. I'm so afraid of what we're going to find."

Sometimes, the child was ten years old going on a hundred.

"Me, too," Kellen told her. "Me, too."

## CHAPTER THIRTY

KELLEN AND RAE—and Luna, clad in four of Rae's socks—stood in the yard and watched the helicopter rise off the ground. It hovered for a moment.

They waved.

Max waved back.

Then he flew a low zigzag pattern over the island and around the coast.

"What's Daddy doing?" Rae sounded far too anxious.

"He's searching."

In a small voice, Rae said, "Oh. For Jamie."

"Right. For Jamie." Kellen stroked Rae's head.

*And for Mara. Before he left them alone on the island, he wanted to be sure Mara was nowhere to be found.*

At last, after making a complete circuit, he roared toward the mainland.

"I guess he didn't see her," Rae said.

"No." Not Jamie, and most definitely not the cold-hearted bitch who haunted their nightmares. He wouldn't have left if he'd seen evidence of Mara. The tight knot in Kellen's stomach eased ever so slightly. "Let's go."

They started for the garage and Kellen's bike.

Luna ran clumsily, stopping to shake a foot occasionally, trying to get the socks off. But in the chest of drawers in Mrs. Morgade's room, Kellen had found the garters early-twentieth-century women had used to secure their silk stockings. She secured Rae's socks with those garters, and now, despite the trauma Rae had suffered, she had to laugh at her puzzled, overdressed dog. She pushed her bike, and stopped occasionally to pet and comfort Luna.

Poor dog. But this was the price she paid for sensitive paws, and for wanting to come with them which she did. Now, especially, after the encounter with Dylan, Luna took her job as their protector very seriously.

"I thought we'd start at the Conkles' home. That seems the likeliest place to find Jamie." Kellen glanced at Rae.

The sunshine and fresh air worked to revive her; she had color in her cheeks, but she stayed uncharacteristically quiet.

"After that, if we're unsuccessful, we'll check the beaches on the south end of the island." Kellen didn't believe there would be an *after that*, but she wanted to speak, to keep Rae distracted from sorrow.

Rae proved she was listening. "Yes. He might have put her there for the waves to wash away." Her voice contained a sharp, bitter note. "What made him do that?"

Kellen reminded herself that Dylan's problems started long before they arrived, and said, "Daddy and I think he poisoned himself with his homemade liquors. Maybe he ate a poisonous mushroom, or smoked bad weed."

"What is it about some people? Why do they hurt the ones they should love?"

Great. The big interrogation, and of course Max was gone. Wouldn't you know when the questions got tough, he'd be flying in the opposite direction? Kellen tried to dig down to the basics, and didn't try to pretend she knew the answers. "Some say people are all the same. But they're not. There's a big fight called, 'Nature versus nurture,' and that means, 'Are we born the way we are, or does the way we're raised form us?'"

"And?" Rae had crossed from torment into belligerence.

That was fair; Kellen was pretty peeved herself. "There's no answer, but I know what I think."

Rae trudged along, pushing her bicycle. "What?"

"I think it's a little of both." Kellen stopped outside the garage door. "'The flame that melts the butter, tempers the steel.' Can you figure out what that means?"

"No!"

"If you want to melt butter, you put it over a fire. If you want to temper iron, make it hard, like the steel on the body of that pickup—" Kellen gestured into the garage "—you put it over a fire. It's the same fire, but completely different reactions because the material you start with is different."

"So everything depends on how we are when we're born?"

"And how we're treated as we grow and live. Some people have an easy life. Some people walk through hellfire to get where they're going. None of us ever knows what goes on in another person's head and heart and life." Kellen went inside, got her bike, came back out into the sun and found Rae standing mulishly still.

"Mommy, you didn't answer my question."

No, she supposed she hadn't. "I guess I don't know the answer."

Rae shouted, "That's not funny!"

Overwhelmed with a surge of love and empathy, Kellen caught Rae in a sudden fierce hug.

Rae resisted, then hugged her back, her face pushed hard into Kellen's chest. "I don't want to see it anymore—Dylan and all that blood." Her voice was muffled. "Every time I let my mind drift, it's there. I don't want to see it. I want to know why it happened. I want Jamie to be alive. I want to be safe."

Kellen understood that, all right. "You want it to be last year."

"Yes!"

She stroked her daughter's tangled hair. "Yes. Things were simpler last year. Except they weren't. I was in rehab and I used to wonder if I could ever fight enough to get better. Your dad was working too hard and being too good, acting as both parents to you and providing all the support you needed. You were being brave for me; you never allowed yourself to have problems because I had so many. Even with all the challenges we have now, I still like today better, where I can be your mother and you can be the child. Right?" She shook Rae a little. "Right?"

Rae took three deep breaths and lifted her head. "If this is what growing up is, I don't like it!"

Almost comical—but so not. "Growing up isn't always bad. Sometimes it's finding a good man like your father. Sometimes it's seeing your little girl be brave and kind even though she's scared."

"I *am* scared." Admitting it seemed to help her. "What if we find Jamie and she is dead?"

"Then we'll treat her remains with respect and when your daddy returns, we'll take her to the mainland to be buried."

"If she's dead, she should be buried on the island. She loved it here."

This smart girl was Kellen's reward for years of trouble and pain. "You're right. There's the Morgade family cemetery. We'll see that she's placed there." Kellen took Rae by the shoulders and stepped away. "Let's go look for her."

# CHAPTER THIRTY-ONE

THE CONKLES' HOUSE looked small, neat, surrounded by herbs, yet closed up, an enigma. In other words, exactly as it always had.

Kellen leaned her bike against the oak in the yard. She pressed her hand on Rae's shoulder. "Let me go in first."

"Take Luna," Rae instructed. "She'll protect you."

"I don't think there's anything in there that will hurt me," Kellen said.

"Have you never seen *Dead Like Me*?" Rae asked in exasperation.

Kellen hadn't, so she whistled for Luna.

Luna came, nose to the ground, a low growl rumbling through her chest. She was no longer concerned with her socks and garters. She cared only about the smells that to her meant pain and trouble.

Kellen went to the door, latched firmly and with no indication of tampering. Somehow, she felt as if she should knock. So she did.

No answer.

She turned the knob and with the flat of her palm, she pressed open the door.

It didn't creak.

The smell of heat, blood and pain rolled out.

Kellen's head swam. She caught the side of the casement.

Rae noticed. "Mommy? Are you okay?"

"I will be. In a minute." In battle and war, Kellen had smelled death. She hadn't missed it, but she knew one thing—Jamie was not alive.

The curtains were open. The sun shone in. Even from the doorway she could see blood in spatters on the wall, trails across the floor, and a pool under the table.

As a contrast, the living room and kitchen were almost untouched. The living room was tidy, and only a little bit of blood had made it to the kitchen, splattered across the floor and three cupcakes on a cooling rack. And...and Kellen had to walk across that floor to check the bedroom and bathroom.

The years of being in the military, of seeing death, hadn't hardened her to the dread she felt now. With each step, she took care where she placed her shoe. She breathed carefully, through her nose, not wanting to taste the odors that pervaded the house. She peeked into the bedroom first.

It was empty of people and of blood.

Nevertheless, she found herself stepping with care as she made her way to the bathroom.

No blood. No Jamie. Thank God.

She retraced her footsteps to the main room, and jumped when she saw Rae by the stove. "What are you doing?"

Calm and prosaic, Rae said, "Jamie forgot to turn off the oven."

"I suppose she did." Kellen held out her hand,

needing Rae's touch as much as Rae might need hers. "She's not here." Nor had the missing firearms been anywhere in sight. "We'll have to look over more of the island."

They left the house together and shut the door.

"We should feed Jamie's chickens," Rae said, so they did, and changed their water.

Then they rode west, checking every beach and overlook as they went. Birds of prey and carrion birds wheeled overhead, carefree and uninterested, congregating in the trees and sailing on the winds. Luna barked at them, but on the beaches, the waves roared and crashed, and Kellen and Rae saw nothing, not a trace of blood or the stain of a body.

Kellen and Rae rode through the redwood grove. As always before, the silence was deep and old, filled with secret rustles of branches and the sudden flutter of birds' wings. But where it had been peaceful before, now the shadows seemed sinister, threatening. Their mission had them spooked, justifiably so, and they rode quickly, eyes straight ahead into the bright sunshine.

The cemetery rested at the high end of the island. Although it wasn't visible from the house, it wasn't far, a half mile over a knoll. It had been placed on the incline so the graves overlooked the ocean and caught the breeze. A short rusty iron fence surrounded the consecrated ground. A single California blue oak, forty feet tall, wide-branched and tormented by the prevailing winds, stood at the far end. Between them and the oak were a dozen headstones, grass that needed to be trimmed, and a massive mausoleum engraved MORGADE.

"Should we go in?" Rae looked around as if unsure. "I never have before. It always seemed...impolite."

"Let me. You wait out here."

"No." Rae was most emphatic. "I'm coming with you."

Kellen headed toward the mausoleum, Rae and Luna on her heels. The glass and iron door hung open, swinging and creaking in the breeze. Kellen stopped Rae and the dog a few feet back and murmured, "Let me look first." She peered cautiously inside.

A great, tall marble slab stood in the middle of the space, waiting for the arrival of a coffin. That was all.

"She's not here. Jamie's not here." Kellen had truly thought she must be in here. But no. It was empty. So empty.

Jamie had disappeared from the island.

Rae joined her and looked inside. "This room, what's it for?"

"I would think Mr. Morgade intended to be interred here."

Rae stated the obvious. "He's not. Where do you suppose he is?"

"Isn't that a good question." Such a splendid resting place that he had designed for himself, and yet— he wasn't here.

A dozen headstones were placed as far away as possible from the splendid edifice. The two oldest were inscribed with Jones, Asa and Sarah, married. Both died in 1918.

"The Spanish flu probably did them in." Kellen

looked around at the isolated, windswept island. "I didn't know anyone lived here so long ago."

Two more graves: Alice Blacker and Doris Comden, "Served faithfully and well." One died 1938, another 1946.

"Maids who worked at Morgade Hall," Kellen explained to Rae.

"Here's Ruby's mother!" Kellen had found a plain headstone inscribed with her name, Reika Morgade, and the dates 1901 to 1948.

Kellen did the math. "She was young, only forty-seven. I wonder what happened to her?"

"Here are Ruby's brothers!" Rae's voice rose in excitement.

The tombstones were side by side, well cared for, with the names clearly etched.

> *Alexander Joseph Morgade*
> *Son, brother, hero*

> *Lawrence Elmer Morgade*
> *Duty above all*

"It's like seeing the story made real," Rae said.

*A very sad part of the story.*

A few more stones were scattered throughout the cemetery, but Kellen couldn't keep her mind on who else rested here. Instead, she looked back at that mausoleum, desolate and empty. Why wasn't Mr. Morgade interred here on his island? Where was he was interred? And why? Why wasn't Jamie here?

Why everything?

In a flurry, the wind picked up. Clouds from the southeast began to sweep over the island in thin, tattered streams. The surf surged against the island, battering against the rocks. Shadows raced across the land; in a few hours, this world seemed to have changed from isolated and still and wild to menacing.

Rae's small, frightened voice said, "Mommy?"

At once Kellen leaped to attention, looked around for a threat, for the remains of Jamie, for Mara, for anything.

But Rae stood, with Luna at her side, over the top of a tombstone and pointed. "I don't understand."

Kellen walked over.

This tombstone looked newer than the others.

It was well tended. Recently tended.

The headstone read:

*Hermione Jasper*
*Friend of the heart.*

The date of her death was…three years ago.

Now, for a different reason altogether, Kellen looked around at the rippling grasses, the headstones, the fence, the oak and that absurdly fancy mausoleum.

"Is this Ruby's Hermione?" Rae asked.

"I think… Yes. Before Harry Potter, it was not a common name in the US. Too hard to spell. Too hard to pronounce. How many Hermiones could have lived on this one little island?"

"Did she live here her whole life?"

"I don't know. Maybe she came here to die. We don't actually know what happened to Ruby, either."

Although Kellen was starting to have a few thoughts. "Isla Paraíso is so plain. A few trees, a lot of grasses, cliffs and beaches and ocean and rare birds. One massive house, and many mysteries. When we get back to civilization, I intend to look up Ruby Morgade and her whole life and her whole family."

"Yes." Rae, suddenly mature, folded her hands in front of her in an attitude of prayer. "I want to solve all the riddles. I need to know." She stared at her mother. "We haven't found Jamie, and I don't know where else to look. I'm hungry and I'm tired. Let's go home. Let's read the rest of Ruby's story."

## CHAPTER THIRTY-TWO

THE ATTIC WAS BRIGHT, then dim, as clouds raced across the sky. The wind rattled the old house, whistled through the cracks of the windows. The storm was making itself felt.

As if she were cold, Rae huddled into the window seat, the throw wrapped around her shoulders.

Luna, minus her socks and garters and tired from the day's exertions, lay stretched out flat on her side beside Rae, asleep except for the occasional moments when she lifted her head to look around. Luna was uneasy.

Kellen, as tired as Luna, stretched out on the couch, and read aloud from Ruby's diary.

It took Hermione to tell me why I was ill. I had no idea that if I was expecting a child, I would throw up every morning, feel terrible all day, and lose weight until my hands look skeletal and my hair breaks off. How can making a baby be such a terrible toil? Hermione assures me it's not so for every woman. She's only twenty-two, but she has younger brothers and sisters and nieces and nephews, so she does know. She tells me soon I'll be fine, but I can see every day she grows more worried. When Mother realized what was wrong, she fled for most of a week. Then she crept back, cowering, as if Father would miraculously appear and punish her. Now she comes up every day and holds my hand and strokes my hair. I'm going to have a baby, and it's no coincidence that nothing feels so good as my own mother's touch on my forehead.

---

It's been three weeks since Patrick's last letter. I know I shouldn't be impatient, for I found a story by him in the Atlantic Monthly, and his ship has sailed from Hawaii. He may write me, but how can he mail the letters? He can't, of course. Nor can my letters reach him. I wish I could tell him about the baby, but that would be cruel, for him to realize that the beautiful moments we shared has resulted in so much illness and trouble for me.

Should I think like that? No! It's a baby! Patrick's child. But I feel so desperately ill, I can't drink even water and I have no tears to cry.

If only I could take a bath, but although Hermione dragged a small tub up the secret passage, I can't sit up long enough. I really think I will die. I, or the child, or both of us.

---

Dear diary, you will not believe the good news! The child is moving in my belly. Kicking at me as if demanding release. I can see a small bump. Despite my constant sickness, the baby is growing, and I am happy. Perhaps we'll live through this, baby and me.

Father has arrived. He came to the attic door and pounded and shouted at me to stop my silly megrims and obey him. I must marry Alfred. I must do it now, or he'll break the door down and beat me until I do his bidding. I listened to him, and wondered why he was so frantic. I think I know. I still read his newspapers. He's losing control. The government gives him war stories, and he has to print them. He doesn't get to interfere in politics and business as he used to. He can't ruin people's lives with a single slash of his pen. He's lost influence and power. He wants to join with Alfred and become the mogul he was before. For that, he needs me.

He gave me three days to come to my senses.

The three days are up. Father had his men tear down the barricades outside the door. He strode in, his belly thrust out in that bullying way that he has. I was sitting in the chair waiting, and when he stopped and really looked at me, at my gaunt face and lank hair, he said, "You look old. You've done this to yourself. Come down, stupid girl, eat from my table and marry the man I've picked for you."

I stood up and let the blanket fall from my lap. I will never forget his expression, or his words. "You'll have to get an abortion."

In my worst nightmares, I never imagined that. He delivered his line so coolly, as if killing his own grandchild, his only grandchild, meant nothing to him.

I staggered back. Hermione caught me and guided me to my chair. Father pointed a finger at her and said to me, "If you don't do as I say, I'll throw her off Morgade Island without a reference."

I never expected what happened next. Never imagined it could happen. Neither did Father, by the look on his face. Mother charged from her hiding place at the top of the secret passage, shouting in Japanese. I understood her, because she taught me the language, but I was the only one in the room. Yet everyone caught the gist. She told Father *No*. Not just a little *No!* It was such an emphatic *No* to everything he had said. He retreated like a giant flounder before a small, vicious shark. Now, two hours later, I think it's funny. Wildly, inappropriately, weirdly funny. Mother, attacking Father, making him run away. He didn't even know what she was saying to him. It was lovely. If I hadn't been so astonished, I would have cheered.

As an aside, I don't think anyone has to bring my dinner up the secret passage anymore.

As another aside, I'm not leaving the attic. I don't trust Father. He'll recover from his shock, and if I'm anywhere within reach, he'll grab me and I'll be hurt in ugly ways. My baby will be torn from my body, and I'll be given to Alfred. No. I'm safe here.

If only I could receive a letter from Patrick. Do you suppose Father is intercepting his letters? Or General Tempe is? Or...or that Patrick has forgotten me and our love?

———————————————

Something is not right. My belly is cramping. The baby's not big enough to be born. Not now. I know this isn't right. I know when this baby was conceived, right to the very hour. Oh, please. Not yet. I've suffered so much, and it's all I have of Patrick. Please, God.

———————————————

Dear diary, my little Aileen was born, and she died on the same day. I held her while she breathed her first breath and her last. I named her for Patrick's mother, who may never know about her darling granddaughter. Mother and Hermione are with me, but I'm empty, and I'm bereft. Please, dear diary, explain to me how it's possible to be so rich with love seven months ago, and to be so alone now.

———————————————

Kellen turned the page. It was empty. So was the next. And the next. She rifled through the rest of the diary.

Empty.

"What's next?" Rae asked belligerently.

Kellen cleared her throat. "Ruby stopped there."

"Stopped? There?" Rae stood up on the window seat, her stocking-clad feet curled around the edge of the cushion. She lifted her arms straight over her head.

239

She shook her fists in rage. "No. No! After all this, Ruby can't have a baby who dies, and Patrick who goes away and doesn't come back. Ruby has to have *something*. Some crumb of happiness. She has to. Please, Mommy. This can't be all there is."

Luna was on her feet, watching Rae in alarm, whining softly.

Kellen wanted to say stuff about, *Life's not fair*, which was true, but right now, after Olympia, and Dylan and Jamie, and being alone on the island—that wasn't what was *needed*. "Rae, you're right. Um..." Kellen looked at the diary, then shut it with a finger in the last page. "There are pages that are torn out at the end. It's the stuff Ruby didn't dare to leave on paper." A lie, but a lie told for good reason.

"What?" Rae demanded.

"Well... Well..." Kellen thought hard and fast, making up stories. "She had lost her baby. So terrible. Such a heartache. She thinks Patrick left her. Her mother is a broken woman. Her father is a bully. She doesn't have anywhere to turn. She talks to her friend, to Hermione, and asks if she'll take a message to General Tempe, begging an interview."

"Ruby is begging General Tempe for an interview? Why?"

Luna stared at Kellen as if she, too, wanted to know.

"Well. Well." Kellen was doing better, coming up with story ideas. "Remember when the general asked if she spoke Japanese?"

"Yes. So what?"

"The Japanese were the enemies. They had bombed

Pearl Harbor without provocation. And…and the American Army needed spies."

"Ruby became a spy?" Rae sounded suspicious.

"Yes. Yes!" *Sure. Why not?* "Her father still didn't know about the secret passages, so with Hermione and her mother covering for her, he never knew Ruby had disappeared from the house."

"That's prodigious!"

*Prodigious.* The word stopped Kellen for a moment. But Rae had always had an impressive vocabulary, the result of having a teacher for a grandmother. Kellen plunged on with Ruby's story. "The Navy took her across the sea to their prisoner-of-war camps, and asked her to listen in on the important prisoners and report what they said. The information she gave them was so good and so valuable, they made her a real spy."

Rae collapsed back onto the cushions on the window seat and hugged Luna around the neck. "What kind of spy stuff did she do?"

"The World War II US secret spy organization—" so secret Kellen didn't have a clue what to call it "—managed to smuggle her into Japan, where she penetrated the depths of their war planning operation!" Her brain was flinging up nonsense so fast Kellen wanted to pat the poor probed and picked-on organ. *Kellen's Brain,* indeed! "When one of her contacts betrayed her, she barely escaped with her life!"

"Whoa." Rae scooted closer. "Is that what really happened?"

"As far as we're concerned, it is."

Rae was good with that. "What about Patrick?"

"The reason why she didn't hear from him was because he had become a spy, too. He was one of the men in charge, and he knew all about her mission. When her transmissions ceased and she vanished, he dressed up like a Japanese fisherman and took a boat to the meeting place. They almost missed each other. At first, she didn't recognize him in his disguise." Kellen was impressed with her own imagination. "Then she ran to his arms. They embraced. They kissed!"

"That is so perfect." Rae leaned forward eagerly. "Then what?"

*Then what? Wasn't that enough?* "They were caught by a Japanese soldier." *Good one, Kellen!*

"No!" Rae covered her mouth in horror.

"Only Ruby's quick thinking and her mastery of the Japanese language saved them. She told the soldier they were newlyweds—and he let them go."

Rae put her hand over her heart as if it was racing. "Then what?"

"They got back to his ship and returned the United States."

Rae sagged in disappointment. "Is that all?"

*Is that all?* "Both of them were so good at their jobs, the US Spy Team didn't want either of them to quit. But in the excitement of the escape, Patrick had been wounded. Fearing for his life, Ruby begged the ship's captain to marry them—" not that shipboard weddings were legal, but this was no time to be reasonable "—and the captain performed the ceremony."

"That's so romantic." Rae sighed.

Luna smiled.

"By the time they got back to the States, she was pregnant again, and the officials realized because of his wounds, Patrick would never be able to return to active duty. So they both retired from military service and lived happily ever after." *Whew.* Kellen had successfully wrapped it up.

Ruby hopped off the window seat and knelt beside Kellen. "What about Ruby's mother?"

Luna came to join them, sat on the carpet and stared at them both.

Kellen had celebrated too soon. "She came to live with them."

"But she died and they buried her here." Rae remembered that tombstone in the cemetery. "What about Ruby's mean ol' father?"

"He died alone somewhere else—" Kellen still wondered where "—and he never returned to Isla Paraíso."

"Good. I did not like that man." Rae scratched Luna's head between the ears. "Did Ruby and Patrick have a boy or a girl?"

"Twins, one of each."

Rae's eyes shone. "Did you make all that up?"

"What do you think?"

"I think you did. But I like it."

Kellen hugged her. "I like it, too. And it could have happened."

"That's the best part." Rae went to the window seat and snuggled into the pillows.

Luna joined her.

Kellen picked up one of the books on the shelves, stretched out on the couch, and read, while Rae watched out the window and daydreamed of a happy ending.

# CHAPTER THIRTY-THREE

IT WAS LATE afternoon when Rae said, "I hear the helicopter!"

They looked out the window, saw Max make another circuit of the island, and when he landed, Kellen and Rae were waiting, fighting against the surges of wind. The air smelled like salt; Kellen could taste it on her lips, and she wondered what news Max would bring about the storm—and everything else.

He acted as if he'd been away for days: he hugged them both hard, took their hands and walked with them toward the house. He had looked the island over. He'd seen no trace of Jamie. He shot a significant glance at Kellen, which told her he'd also seen no trace of Mara. He told them the oncoming storm had gathered strength, and he asked them what they'd done while he was gone. The search of the Conkles' cottage made him look solemn, and he seemed taken aback when Rae reported they'd entered the cemetery and found Hermione's grave, and he stared up at the house as if stricken by the same suspicion Kellen entertained. But he kept walking up the stairs, through the front door and into the library. There he sank wearily into the overstuffed chair. "Sweetheart, would you get Daddy a glass of water?"

Rae ran toward the kitchen.

"Did he remember where he put...where Jamie is?" Kellen kept her voice low.

Max was quiet, too. "No. He's under the influence of something powerful. Not...what we thought."

"Not moonshine?" They'd spoken of it. She'd assumed...

Max gave a quick shake of the head. "I didn't stick around to find out what the EMTs had learned, but I got the impression that wasn't it. Maybe he smoked the wrong weed. Mother Nature's got some powerful hallucinogenics, and Dylan would be the one to try them."

Rae came back with the water.

Max drank it in big gulps, as if he had been running rather than flying. "Dylan kept talking about Jamie and the birds. He said she loved the birds."

"She's dead, isn't she?" Rae asked in a small voice. "She's got to be. There was so much blood." She broke down and for the first time, she wept. "Why didn't we know? Why didn't we help her?"

Kellen sat on the floor with her, pulled her into her arms, and looked helplessly up at Max.

"We didn't know because we didn't know, and we didn't help her because she didn't want to be helped." Max made his voice matter-of-fact. "I don't think Jamie Conkle would have known how to ask for help."

"She didn't deserve to be hurt!" Rae shouted.

"No one deserves that." Not true. Kellen could think of one person. But she wouldn't discuss Mara with Rae. "Bad things happen. Sometimes they happen to people who don't deserve it. Wondering why them, why in this place, why at this time—that doesn't accomplish a thing except make you feel wretched, and we're already wretched enough."

That didn't help. Rae cried harder.

Kellen thought about the men and women she'd served with who had died in a senseless war, about her own first marriage and the gunshot to her brain. She thought about Rae's early years without a mother, and Max's loneliness while she was gone. None of that was fair, either, and truthfully, when life was so uncertain and unjust, she felt like crying herself. So she let Rae cry it out.

Max kept them supplied with tissues, and when most of the emotion had been exhausted, he said, "If this storm is as bad as they say, we'll have problems. The generators and wiring are old. If we lose electricity, our water and sewage won't work."

Rae looked up sharply. "It would be scary to be on this island all by yourself in a storm, wouldn't it?"

"Yes, it would," Max said. "The Coast Guard wants us to come in."

Rae got up, went to the desk, got another tissue and blew her nose with great volume and intensity.

Max continued, "So we need to pack up."

"I've gotta go to the bathroom." Rae sidled out of the room.

Kellen watched her leave. "Poor kid. She gets so she likes it here, and we're leaving."

The front screen door slammed.

Luna barked wildly, a wild canine objection.

"What the hell?" Max strode to the window and lifted it.

Kellen followed to see Rae picking her bike up and

heading down the yard and into the grasses. "Rae!" she called. "Where are you going?"

"To ride my bike one last time," Rae yelled.

Luna barked, ran into the library, and ran back toward the entry.

"Be back in thirty minutes!" Max bellowed.

God bless the Di Lucas, the loudest family in the world.

Rae waved in acknowledgment.

As she always did, Luna barked her objections at being left behind.

Kellen went to the door and called her back into the library, knelt down and scratched her head.

But Luna was desolate. She went under the coffee table and rolled onto her side, and if a dog could be said to cry, she did.

Kellen wasn't any too happy, either. "Max, why are you letting Rae go? If Mara—"

"I looked. No sign of Mara. Or Jamie. And thirty minutes won't take Rae far." His voice, already worried, grew stern. "I need to talk to you."

Kellen hugged her waist and stood. She faced Max and asked, "What? Has Mara found us?"

"Not yet." He corrected himself. "We don't think."

"We? Who's we?"

"Coast Guard. FBI. Nils Brooks. The Di Lucas who keep an eye on this stuff." He took Kellen's arm and led her to the couch. "In the past two days, more than a dozen times, Mara has been spotted in post offices around the country, posing with her wanted poster."

Kellen's knees gave way, and she sat. "She's…showing off that she hasn't been caught?"

"She has been caught. Twice."

Kellen finally understood. "Neither of the women were Mara Philippi."

"Exactly." Max seated himself beside her. "Both looked incredibly like Mara. One was homeless. One was a housewife whose husband had left her with three young children and a house payment. Both admitted they'd taken money to play a hoax. What they did wasn't strictly illegal."

"Wasn't it?" Kellen was hostile and angry.

"The homeless woman has a very limited IQ, it's doubtful she had any idea what kind of fraud she was perpetuating, and the housewife was desperate for cash. They've both been released on their own recognizance, and with a warning."

"Mara's back in the States," Kellen breathed.

"Exactly. But with these multiple sightings, the agencies have no idea where. What *is* clear is that she still has some kind of network she controls—"

"Of course she does. Until she's dead, she'll never be helpless."

"And law enforcement believes she's trying to smoke us out of hiding."

"*Could* she be here on the island?" Kellen gestured toward the window where they'd watched Rae ride away.

"Why would she be trying to smoke us out if she knows where we are?"

Kellen nodded in acknowledgment.

"If she does know—how would she get here? We're out a long way. She'd have to have a seaworthy vessel to get close, there's no harbor, we're surrounded by submerged rocks, and those waves are rough. An aircraft? We'd hear a helicopter, and it's not like she could have parachuted in—the winds are too erratic, the best probability is she'd land in the ocean."

"And drown."

His glance acknowledged Kellen's hopeful tone. "Then—where could she hide? It's a sparse island with not much cover, only Paradise Cove where the intern would typically be camping, and the redwoods, and she'd be roughing it if she was out there. The Conkles' house?" He stood and looked out the window as if rethinking his decision to let Rae go.

"Max." Kellen didn't know how to say what she'd seen. "So much blood. On the walls, on the furniture. Mara is crazy, but she likes her creature comforts." Kellen remembered the exacting standards with which Mara had run the spa at Yearning Sands resort. "She would never stay there."

"So it comes down to this—the FBI wants us to stay put. They think we're safe here."

"I thought we were packing up."

"We are. The Coast Guard wants us to come in. They say the storm's a monster, and we'll be in trouble."

"In danger?"

"In this broken-down old house? Yes." He took Kellen's fragile, still recalcitrant hand, and massaged the palm and the fingers. "But what it all comes down to is—where's Mara Philippi? *Is* she trying to flush us out? We don't want to run into her arms."

"We also don't want to stay and be sitting ducks."

"Exactly. So it's up to us whether to go or stay, but

either way, we should be ready to make the jump." He watched her face. "What's wrong?"

Wretched, she said, "I'm sorry I brought this on our family."

"It's not your fault." He was fierce in his defense. "It's hers."

"I do know that, but I look back at that winter at Yearning Sands Resort when I was assistant manager and Mara was the spa manager, and I try to think— what clues did I miss? She always seemed perky, shallow, competitive, but I thought she wanted to be friends. Instead, she was picking out her prime competitor." Again Kellen heard the echo of Mara's voice, *I chose you as my opponent because I thought we were alike, that you were worthy.* "She considered us sisters under the skin."

"You're not like her."

"No, but I wish I could get into her head right now."

"Me, too," he said with heartfelt sincerity. "It would add much needed sanity to her brain."

Kellen laughed in a sudden, unexpected (by her) gust. "There is that."

"Since you can't read Mara's mind, what do you think—go or stay?"

*The FBI said to stay.*

*The Coast Guard said to leave.*

She looked around the old house. Even with its quirks and its spooks, she loved this place. But Max was right, it had weathered without upkeep. "I think in view of what happened to Dylan and Jamie, and the spooky disappearance of the firearms, and this house and the storm…we'd better go while we can, and trust law enforcement and our own good sense to protect us from Mara, if she's waiting."

"Okay. That's what we'll do." Max trusted her judgment without question, and for someone who'd had brain surgery, that meant a lot. "As soon as Rae gets back, we'll pack up and leave."

## CHAPTER THIRTY-FOUR

"MIRANDA! MIRANDA!" Rae skidded down the path toward the south beach, knocking pebbles into the sand, yelling her head off.

Mara looked up, annoyed. She had been counting the number of anemones in the designated tide pool. Now she'd have to start all over again. "What?" she asked sharply.

Rae stood astride the rocks, trying to get her breath. "Dylan Conkle…did something to Jamie. He was covered in blood."

Mara narrowed her eyes at Rae. *Shut the window in my face, will you?* "Sounds like Jamie's problem."

"There's blood in the house." Rae gasped as if she'd raced all the way from the house. "We think she's dead. You've never seen anything like it."

*Want to bet?*

"Miranda, it's horrible."

*Or wonderful. Depends on your point of view.*

"And there's a big storm coming in."

"I can't do anything about that, either."

"No—" Rae held her side as if she had a stitch "—but I came to warn you."

"Warn me?"

"Daddy and Mommy said Dylan drank moonshine,

or smoked bad weed. You need to be careful. And you need to take shelter before the storm hits."

Mara blinked at Rae, once, twice, three times. "Wait. Why'd you come down?"

"To warn you!"

"You ran down here to warn me?"

"Rode down. Yes. I don't want you to get hurt." Rae swooped in suddenly, right next to where Mara knelt, and hugged her around the waist. "I like you!"

"You like me?" Mara felt funny. Not so angry.

"Yes." Rae scrambled to her feet again. "I gotta go. I have to be home in thirty minutes—"

That reminded Mara again about her visit last night to the big house, seeing Rae with her parents, having Rae shut the window in her face.

Rae was still talking. "—because we have to get off the island."

"What?" Mara suddenly was back in the present with Rae. "What? Why do you have to get off of the island?"

"Because of the storm. Because Dylan Conkle did something horrible, we think to Jamie. Who would hurt Jamie? She was pretty weird. But she had a thing about the environment. She wants to save it. There's nothing wrong with that. Everybody should want to save the planet. But they don't. They're not like you." Rae took a breath. "I want to be like you."

Rae had distracted Mara again with her...her niceness. "Like me? What do you mean like me?"

"I mean coming here, camping all the time, counting bird eggs and slimy seaweed in the tide pools."

Rae was bursting with admiration and enthusiasm. "You're great!"

Rae admired her. Admired Mara. Or rather, who Mara was pretending to be.

*Never mind that.*

The Di Lucas were leaving.

*Rae likes me.*

They were going to the mainland.

*I have run out of time.*

Rae said, "There's room in the helicopter. I'll ask my parents to take you with us. You can't stay here by yourself. Daddy says the storm's going to be horrible!"

"You still call him Daddy?" Mara crowed with laughter, with mockery. "Daddy. Like you're three years old."

"What?" Rae looked bewildered. Hurt.

*Shut up, Mara. She likes me.*

I'm out of time.

*I don't want to hurt her.*

I've got to.

*She looks so much like Kellen. She's Kellen's daughter.*

"If we can't take you, can I tell my daddy—" Rae stumbled over the word "—my father about you."

"You haven't told them? Really?"

Rae looked shocked. "No. I promised I wouldn't."

"You must have thought about it."

Rae's gaze dropped. "Yes," she said faintly. "I don't like to keep secrets."

"That's really honorable of you." Sarcasm oozed from Mara's tones.

Tears welled in Rae's eyes.

*Don't frighten her. Don't upset her. Not now, Mara.*

Rae took a few steps back. "I've got to go. If I don't, I won't get back in time."

Mara had to do this. She regretted it, but she'd make it up to the kid later. She hoped. "Listen, I want to give you something." Opening her backpack, she dug through, found the bottle of pills and shook one out in her palm. "Here. Take this. It'll make you feel good."

Rae froze and stared at the pill. "I don't take drugs."

"What?" Mara hadn't imagined that twist. Everybody she knew took drugs. Guys she slept with, girls she slept with, prisoners, smugglers, antiquity experts, museum directors, rich assholes with illegal collections, street people. They liked drugs. Everyone except her. She didn't like them. They made her sane. And rational.

Now Rae didn't like drugs, either.

That made the kid seem even more like…like her own kid.

"It's not a drug. It's a pill so you won't be worried about telling your folks that I'm here." Mara was making it up on the fly.

"So I can tell them?" Rae asked eagerly.

"After you take the pill."

"No, thank you. I don't take drugs."

The kid was polite, Mara had that to say about her.

"How about you take half and I take half?" Mara simply wouldn't swallow her half. "That way you know it's safe."

"No, thank you." Rae edged toward the path that led up the cliffs. She didn't look so trusting now.

Mara didn't want to jump her and shove it down

her throat. She would, but she didn't want to. "There has to be something of mine you'd like before you go."

"You don't have to give me anything. I... I like you anyway."

Mara thought hard. "I know. I'll go up the cliff with you. At my campsite, I've got this cupcake I've been saving. It's special. Would you like that?"

Rae surrendered. "Okay, but hurry. I'm late!" Now she ran up the path, all gangly legs and arms.

Mara ran after her, not awkward like the kid but not as fit, either. She was panting when she hit the top of the cliff. That irked her, returned her to her initial surly reaction to Rae's appearance. "Come on." She grabbed Rae's arm and dragged her toward the rocky overhang where she kept her equipment. "The cupcake is here." Mara found the paper bag with the cupcakes she'd rescued from the Conkles' cottage. "It's really good, and there's candy on top." Quickly, Mara smashed the pill between two stones, scooped up the shards and sprinkled them on the cinnamon sugar cupcake top. She thrust the cupcake at Rae. "Here. It's good. Eat it!"

Rae looked at the cupcake as if she'd seen it before, looked at Mara, looked at the cupcake, looked at Mara. "I'll take it with me."

"Eat it now." Mara stepped closer to Rae, making Rae feel the difference in their heights, subtly threatening the kid.

"Does it have blood on it?" Rae blurted.

"No. It was in the oven." Mara answered before she thought—*hey, the kid has been in the Conkles' house. She has seen the cupcakes before!*

"I'll take a bite." Rae tore off a piece of cupcake,

crammed it into her mouth, chewed, then ran for her bike. "Come to the house if you want to go in the helicopter," she said with her mouth full. "I've got to go. I'm late!" She crumpled the remains of the cupcake as she ran, and as she rode away, Mara thought she spit out the rest.

But that pill was powerful, and Rae was a child. Whatever Rae had ingested…would have an effect.

Rae rode like a maniac, and Mara didn't even try to chase her. She simply gathered her weapons: the rifle she'd confiscated from the yacht, her sidearm and her hunting knife in their holsters. She screwed her silencer on her automatic handgun. She contemplated the Taser she'd brought along in the hopes she'd get to use it on someone. Not Rae, because those bastards really hurt, but man, how she'd like to dig it into Max's ribs and watch him fall!

She grinned at the thought, and strapped it on, too. Then followed Rae's path through the grass, followed until the bike tracks started wobbling. They straightened up again, then once again they staggered, went in circles—and Mara stumbled over Rae's bike, sideways in the grass.

Right. Good. Really good.

Mara tracked Rae north toward the big house. The kid was going the right way. She hoped Rae made it. She really did.

Abruptly she abandoned the trail. She didn't want to encounter Max or Kellen. Not yet.

Plus—she needed to take care of the helicopter.

The Di Lucas were not leaving tonight.

# CHAPTER THIRTY-FIVE

"WHERE'S RAE? It's been thirty minutes. This is no time to make us stew." Max was irate, irrationally so, the way a father is when he's worried and hovering on the verge of panic.

Kellen tried to soothe him. "She doesn't *want* to make us worry. She probably went too far and is headed back right now." But her mind leaped to Rae as she had been once before, hurt from the jump, limp ing toward the house and crying.

They went out on the front porch and looked for her.

Luna went with them, sat beside Kellen, thumped her tail hard on the boards and growled softly.

Kellen smoothed Luna's head. "You can't go out there. You'll hurt your paws."

The dog strained, looking out as if she knew something they did not.

Kellen had to ask. "Do you think Rae found Jamie?"

Max swiveled to face Kellen. "What a horrible thought."

"That would scar her for life. I was surprised she wanted to leave the house. Do you think she went looking for her?" Kellen ran through all her concerns, her fears. "Is there a chance Jamie is alive?"

Max shook his head. "Dylan is too frightened."

Max and Kellen waited thirty-five minutes, then forty. At forty-five, Luna launched herself off the porch. As she raced across the lawn, nose to the ground, she ignored their calls, and in moments she had disappeared into the tall grasses.

"She's following Rae's scent," Kellen said.

"Right. You follow her, I'll circle wide."

They set out in opposite directions, riding their bikes, searching, shouting. They were united in their task, but alone in their searches.

After two hours, the wind had increased in strength and volume. The grasses rolled and tossed seeds into the air. The oaks moaned. Sea gulls screamed. Foxes and falcons huddled close to their dens and nests. The first tendrils of rain clouds sent brief gray curtains of rain across the ocean and across the island, drenching Kellen.

She had been riding without fear, without considering the speed she used to race down the island paths. Now she stopped, straddled her bike, and wished she and Max had some form of communication with each other. Tin cans, walkie-talkies—anything.

At last, she heard it—a dog's wild barking carried on the wind. She fought her way toward the source of the commotion, and found Rae staggering around in ever decreasing circles, muttering to herself.

She caught Rae and placed her on the ground, looked into her eyes and saw the wide pupils and the manic terror.

Rae seemed unaware of Kellen, of her surroundings. Over and over again, she said, "I liked her. I wanted her to know. Why would she hurt me? I don't take drugs. This isn't right. I need to get home." Her voice rose to a shriek. *"Don't stop me."* Then again, and softer, "Why would she hurt me?"

Kellen knew then. She knew for sure.

*Mara is back. Mara is here. Mara has tried to kill my child.*

Kellen left her bike in the middle of the waving grasses and the ever increasing wind. She coaxed Rae up and with her arm around her, helped her walk toward the mansion.

Luna limped along beside them, whining softly, her eyes wide with doggy fear.

Desperately Kellen prayed, *Come on, Max. Come and find us.*

As if he'd heard her call, he arrived when they reached the lawn. He took one look at his daughter and swept her into his arms. He carried her toward the house…and suddenly switched directions and ran toward the helicopter.

Kellen followed on his heels, so desperately afraid they would be too late to save her baby—and when Max stopped, she stopped, too. Stopped and gaped at the helicopter.

The windshield had been shot out, the door had been sabotaged, one of the propellers had been riddled with bullets. The radio was destroyed.

The helicopter, their lifeline to the mainland, was useless.

# CHAPTER THIRTY-SIX

KELLEN STEPPED UP next to Max. "I will find Mara, I swear, kill her and save Rae."

She turned away.

But Rae grabbed a lock of Kellen's hair with abnormal strength. "No. Mommy, no! Help me. I need you. Why did she hurt me? I liked her..." Her eyes rolled back, her head fell like a flower on a broken stem.

After that, how could Kellen leave?

Max carried Rae to her bedroom and placed her on the bed.

Luna followed, and curled up beside her child, desperate to offer comfort.

"We have ipecac," Max said. "Let me find it."

Kellen caught his sleeve. "It's been too long. The drugs are in her system. We need to flush them through. Bring a sports drink, something with electrolytes."

"Have we got that?"

"Your mother sent it ahead in case someone got a stomach bug."

He nodded and headed downstairs to the pantry.

All the time they spoke, Rae was mumbling, "I liked her. I thought she was nice. I knew I shouldn't not tell you, but I thought she was nice. Why would she hurt me? I liked her. I thought she was nice."

Kellen wet a washcloth in warm water and slid it across Rae's forehead. "Who? Who did you like?"

Kellen's warm, coaxing voice caught Rae's attention, yet she stared at her mother as if she didn't know her. "Miranda. Miranda Phillips."

"Of course." Mara had barely bothered to change her name.

Luna curled into the curve formed by Rae's knees, and whimpered, begging Kellen to make things right.

Kellen passed her fingers over the dog's forehead.

Rae caught Kellen's wrist in a small, fierce hand. "I warned her."

Kellen returned her attention to her daughter. "What did you warn her of?"

"I warned her about the storm. I warned her about Dylan. I told her... Jamie is missing." Tears leaked from the corners of Rae's eyes. "Poor Jamie. Where is she?"

Max returned at a run, a sports drink in his hand. Together Kellen and Max lifted Rae and poured the bottle down her throat.

Rae drank thirstily. Her body knew what it needed—but had they been quick enough?

They could only wait.

The sun set in a violent gasp of red, pink and purple as deep as a bruise.

Night descended. The storm began its true assault. The wind howled. Rain slammed at the mansion. Max and Kellen took turns lifting Rae to her feet and walking her, back and forth.

Kellen put her into the shower and got in with her. She washed her hair and helped her bathe.

When they came out, Max was sitting on the floor with Luna, picking the grass seeds and thorns out of her paws, covering them with cortisone and wrapping them in gauze. "Luna's nails need to be trimmed," he said. "When this is over, we need to take her to the groomer."

Rae dropped on the floor beside her dog and placed her head on Luna's back, and for long, wrenching moments, she sobbed her apologies to them all.

Luna put her paws on Rae's shoulders, licked her face, cried with her if a dog could be said to cry.

Max and Kellen returned to walking Rae back and forth, to pouring sports drinks down her throat, to talking to her in the hopes of bringing her out of her madness and back to normalcy.

Finally Rae begged to be allowed to rest, and Max and Kellen couldn't stand to torment her anymore. They let her recline on her bed.

For one moment, Rae's gaze cleared, and she said to Max, "Daddy, I'm sorry. I was wrong."

Then she was gone, unconscious.

Max checked her pulse in her neck. Kellen checked it in her wrist.

"She's asleep. Maybe that's what she needs." Max sounded more hopeful than sure.

Kellen grasped his hand. "What are we going to do?"

He looked out at the black shiny glass window, streaked with rain. "The storm should lessen…soon.

As soon as it's light, we'll take the boat. We'll take Rae to the mainland."

"*You'll* take the boat. *You'll* take her to the mainland."

"Kellen, I can't leave you here with *her*. With Mara."

"You've got to get Rae to a hospital, and you can't do that if I'm along. Even if the storm gets better, the seas are going to be massive. To get Rae to the California coast, you'll need the motor and the sail." Kellen was calm, matter-of-fact. "You can't have both if I'm with you, weighing down the boat."

Kellen could see Max struggling; he wanted to change this, fix this, make it different.

"I wonder how long she's been on the island? I wonder if the Conkles knew?"

"Dylan knew."

Kellen thought about how damaged Dylan had been. "Yes. Mara got her claws into him. She gave him something that drove him mad and to murder."

Max's gaze shifted to Rae, circled into a fetal position on her bed, so still she might be dead. Luna was curled into her, holding her with a paw across her hips. Max put his hand over his damp eyes. "We can't let the drugs take her."

"You're right, we can't." She hugged him, felt his frustration. "Max, I'm healthy. I'm strong. I'm angry. I can take on Mara and make her sorry."

His chest rose and fell. Abruptly, he loosened her arms. "Wait here." He left with purpose.

Compulsively, she leaned over Rae, checked for her

breathing, smoothed her hair off her forehead. "We're going to take care of you, baby," she whispered.

Max returned with a Smith and Wesson M&P Bodyguard pistol held lightly in his right hand, a nylon holster hanging on his arm. "When I took Dylan in, I radioed ahead to Rafe Di Luca. He brought it for me." He checked the safety, then offered her the butt of the weapon. "You won't be completely without defense."

Kellen wrapped the fingers of her right hand around it. She had been a soldier. She had carried a pistol, aimed a pistol, shot a pistol. The weight, the cool metal, the scent of gun oil settled into her memories, familiar and necessary.

Max said, "As you always point out, a pistol is only good for a short distance. It's loaded."

She looked up and smiled. "My fingers aren't one hundred percent. But even so, I'm more in control of a weapon than most people could ever be."

He nodded. "That's what I figured." As he helped her strap on the holster, he said, "Before dawn, we'll carry Rae down to the dock."

"To the SkinnySail?"

"Yes. To the SkinnySail."

"What if Mara sabotaged it?"

"Then we'll think of another way." Max didn't sound worried. "But Mara doesn't think small. She wants to make the big statement. Shoot up the helicopter. Terrify us."

Max knew Mara better than Kellen did.

"Rae and I will leave on the SkinnySail. We'll avoid Mara. Then you're on your own. You can fight. You can beat her."

She slid the pistol into the holster.

He took her not quite one hundred percent hand in both of his and looked into her eyes. "She'll cheat."

"All's fair in love and war, Max. This is a battle." She allowed her fingers to curl as if they were still far gone into atrophy. "Mara doesn't need to know how well this hand can work."

# CHAPTER THIRTY-SEVEN

KELLEN STOOD ON the beach, her toes curled in the cold, wet sand. She was soaked by the windblown rain and her efforts to help Max launch the SkinnySail into the depths of the roiling surf. There was no way—*no way*—Max could guide the vessel bearing Rae through the storm to the mainland, to the coast of California.

Yet Kellen trusted that somehow he would. He had to. Rae was their daughter, their hope, the proof of their love.

Max struggled against the storm, using brute strength and motorized power. Waves swamped the small vessel; Max and Rae disappeared from view, and Kellen found herself on her toes, straining and screaming at them to come back, come out. As if her shouts lifted the SkinnySail, the boat rose, wobbled at the top of the wave, and finally thrust itself out of the surf and into the rough, gray seas beyond.

Max was frantically bailing water from the tiny vessel.

"My God," Kellen whispered. She observed until they had disappeared behind a curtain of rain.

They were gone. Gone from sight, gone from assistance, gone beyond all the help she could give them—except prayer. She could pray, and she did, as she seated herself on a driftwood log, rubbed the worst of the sand off her feet, and donned her soaking wet socks and worn running shoes. She prayed fervently and constantly as she fought the wind on the steep and twisted path up the cliff. And she wept.

As she climbed, she kept touching the pistol in the holster at her side. Mara was up there somewhere. She wasn't going to make her revenge easy and shoot Kellen; if she had intended to end things that quickly, she could have done that at Yearning Sands from a safe distance. No, that demented bitch had some other crazy plan.

Kellen had her own crazy plan: shoot Mara between the eyes, shoot her in the back, shoot her anywhere and anytime.

The wind continued from the south, pushing her up the trail, and at the same time, rain made the gritty rocks slick and dangerous. More than once, as the wind shifted a few degrees to the east or west, she could have bounced all the way down to the beach. When she reached the top, the sand swirled in her face. She slid backward, grabbed a handful of the rough beach grass, and stopped herself. Struggling erect, she wiped the rain and tears off her face, took that last big step onto the top of the cliff, and heard that familiar female voice.

"I gave her only a half dose, because she loved me."

Kellen used her sleeve to clear her eyes. She looked up at—

**MARA PHILIPPI:**
FEMALE. DARK HAIR CHOPPED SHORT, FAIR SKIN, BLUE EYES.

5'6". 130LBS. AGGRESSIVELY PHYSICALLY FIT. UNCLEAR ON
DIFFERENCE BETWEEN WAR ZONE AND GYMNASIUM. SMUG-
GLER. LIAR. ACTRESS. SERIAL KILLER. MURDERER OF KEL-
LEN'S OWN CHILD.

Mara Philippi: dressed in a rain poncho, standing beside the golf cart, pointing her pistol at Kellen and smiling as if she'd done something kind.

Kellen didn't think, didn't hesitate. She ducked and attacked, head first, driving herself into Mara's belly.

Above her head, the pistol blasted.

Both women stumbled, thrown off balance by the recoil.

Kellen slammed the top of her head into Mara's elbow.

The pistol went flying into the tall, wet grass.

Now Kellen could kill her.

But when she went for her pistol, Mara slammed a fist into Kellen's wrist.

Outraged by the pain, the nerves in Kellen's arm went numb. Her hand, her right hand, curled into the useless ball it had been after the brain surgery.

She stared at it, at the poor thing at the end of her arm, and all the helplessness of the past rushed at her.

But she wasn't helpless. She could use this wrecked limb. She had learned how, in the garage, punching at a mattress Max had pressed against the wall.

She looked up at Mara. At Mara, who stared at her hand, lips curled in disgust. "What's wrong?"

Kellen flung that arm, that hand, at Mara's face. With all the power of her body behind her, she punched her right in the nose. She felt the crunch, felt the satisfaction of knowing she'd hurt the woman who had drugged her baby.

Mara shrieked, fell backward, floundering under the ferocity of Kellen's attack. She whimpered. She moaned. She tried to speak, but Kellen didn't care, didn't listen. She wanted to beat Mara into the ground, make her unconscious, hurt her until she died.

Punch left. Right. A kick. Left. Right.

Mara spun, caught herself, did a flip so athletic Kellen remembered their former rivalry. When Mara landed on her feet, she had a black and yellow weapon in her hand. She stabbed it at Kellen. Kellen parried with her hand and arm and—

*A blast of pain. A shriek of nerve burn. The brain shut down.*

Kellen knew nothing. Nothing. Not even the gray.

## CHAPTER THIRTY-EIGHT

KELLEN SWAM TO the surface of consciousness. She lay on her belly, face turned to the side. The surface beneath her cheek was rough. She ached all over, as if she had the flu. She didn't know where she was, or why she hurt.

She did know who she was, and counted that as a plus.

She listened to the ticking of a clock, to rain and wind rattling the windows, and to an odd, rhythmic clicking. Twice the clicking stopped for a few seconds, then started again.

She opened her eyes. They felt swollen, and when she looked, she saw things from an angle she had never before experienced: shelves lined with books, the legs of a coffee table, a heavy, ornate wool rug that scratched at her cheek. As she looked farther, she saw lamps on the tables that tossed golden light toward the ceiling. On the desk, the gilded edge of a book: Ruby's diary. That meant something, but she could not recall what.

After long moments of orientation, she realized she was at Morgade Hall on the floor in the library. She was wet and cold, and when she shivered, every muscle painfully spasmed. Something had happened. Something momentous.

Slowly she turned her head, and as she did, she heard a woman say, "You're awake. Jesus fucking Christ, you scared me. I thought you were dead."

*Mara Philippi.* For sure. Nothing was never her fault. Whatever happened, she was the only one affected.

Following the source of the voice, she saw Mara's shoes—waterproof hiking shoes, she thought inconsequentially. She followed the length of Mara's legs up to her torso, to her face, that beautiful, hated face, alive with indignation that Kellen had caused her worry. She had a towel around her shoulders, and she held Max's pistol.

Like the queen of all evil, she lolled in the big overstuffed chair, the one Max sat in when he was here, and the sound Kellen had heard was Mara clicking the safety on and off, on and off.

She had stolen the pistol off Kellen's body.

Kellen's memory flooded back. Rae had been drugged. Rae was dying. Max had taken her in that tiny boat in the hope of getting her to a hospital. Kellen had seen them off into the teeth of the storm, climbed the cliff—and Mara was there. They had fought.

Kellen took another look at Mara.

She wore tough clothes meant for the outdoors: waterproof tights, long-sleeve tee, insulated vest. A rifle with a scope leaned against the chair's arm. She had prepared for whatever torment she intended to inflict on Kellen—but her nose was swelling, and one eye had a bruise forming beneath it.

She was the queen of *nothing*.

Kellen had beat the snot out of Mara until… Until what? She worked her lips, her tongue, making sure they were under her command, then asked, "What did you do to me?"

"I Tased you." Mara touched the black-and-yellow weapon at her side. "Why did you pass out? It was just a Taser." She sounded serious—and scornful.

Kellen had nothing to lose. Her daughter and her husband had set out to sea in a violent storm, with little chance of survival. Even if they made it to the mainland, Rae had been drugged. She might never recover. She might never smile, she might never speak, she might never be Rae again.

Grief swelled in Kellen, followed swiftly by rage. She lifted her head off the carpet. "Really? You Tased someone who two years ago had a brain surgery? And it didn't turn out well? I'm so sorry to hear that. What kind of idiot wouldn't know that that would blow all my neurons to hell?"

In a motion so swift Kellen's dazed eyes could barely follow, Mara came to her feet, lifted and pointed the pistol. "I'm not an idiot!"

Kellen had hit a nerve.

"I'm not stupid. Say it. Say it!" Mara's feet, clad in those hiking boots, stomped forward, aiming for Kellen's right hand.

Kellen may have imagined she had nothing to lose, but she'd protected, cherished, worked that hand for too long to have Mara break all the bones. She pulled it close to her body, rolled to her side and onto her feet— and one knee gave way. It hit the rug hard enough to bruise her, jar her spine. Her head spun and with her hand still tucked close, she leaned over the coffee table and retched.

"Yuck!" Mara backed up. "Don't barf!"

Kellen fought for control of her stomach, her body, her mind. She practiced her breathing, in and out, and when she could, she pressed her good hand onto the table and used it to support her as she stood. She swayed and, head down, stared through her lashes at Mara. "You're not stupid," she acknowledged. "You were illiterate, yet still you ran the largest antiquities smuggling operation in this country, from Yearning Sands, and no one knew. No, not stupid. A psychopath. A serial killer. But never stupid."

That was good enough for Mara. "Good. You're not stupid, either, so you understand what I'm doing here."

"No. I don't. You were in prison."

"I got out."

"You escaped!"

Mara smiled with patently false modesty. "Did you imagine I was going to stay there? In that cell? When all I needed was to persuade a few people I should be elsewhere?"

Kellen lifted her right hand to gesture and—

"Look at that. Look at your hand. You were getting better. Now you're not." Mara was irritated. "What's *wrong* with you?"

Kellen lifted her atrophied hand before her eyes and like an infant, stared as if seeing it for the first time. The Taser blast had fried her nerves. She tried to straighten her fingers, but they were white and cold, without feeling, curled into the tight, terrible *C* shape they had been after surgery.

Why did Mara know Kellen's hand had been getting better? Why did she know anything about Kellen's hand at all?

Because she'd been stalking them. Watching them. Worse—Kellen had lost the advantage of pretending to be disabled. She *was* disabled.

Mara holstered the pistol—yes, she had lifted the holster off Kellen's body and strapped it on her own—wandered to the desk, opened Ruby's diary and fluttered through the pages.

Kellen measured the distance between them, took stock of her own uncertain strength and saw the way Mara kept her hand close to the black-and-yellow Taser.

Kellen wasn't helpless. She used her words to give herself time to recover. She used her words to dig at Mara, undermine her, make her snap. "Why me? Why out of all the people in this world have you gone to such dramatic lengths to hunt me down?"

"You know."

"I know? Why would I know?"

"When we were at Yearning Sands Resort together, we were one mind. One heart. We ate together. We trained together. You pushed me hard so I could participate in the International Ninja contest. I could have won!" Mara held up one hand, as if grasping the trophy, and gave her best beauty pageant smile. Then the smile faded. "You stole the opportunity from me."

"How did I do that?"

"By trying to kill me."

"To stop you! You killed people. A lot of people." Kellen found herself wildly waving her hands. As if that was going to help. "You almost killed me!"

"We were like sisters." Mara crossed her fingers to show how entwined they had been. "We understood each other."

"I didn't understand you." How could Kellen find the words to explain madness to a madwoman? "You were pretending to be someone you weren't."

"How could you say that? I was the Yearning Sands spa manager."

"And you were running an international antiquities smuggling operation!"

Mara burbled on. "I finally figured out *why* you were so jealous. I was always the leader. What I said, we did. You resented that."

Four years ago, when Kellen had taken the job at Yearning Sands as assistant manager, she had been newly discharged from the Army. She had been a captain, in charge of transportation in a war zone, a leader who brought the friends she trusted to Yearning Sands to give them jobs. She was the kind of leader who never worried about looking back to see if people were following her. They just always were. There was no explaining that to Mara, though. For all that Mara comprehended, Kellen might as well be speaking Klingon. "You're…delusional."

Mara didn't react.

Kellen realized Mara was trying to read her mind. No—she thought she *was* reading Kellen's mind. *That* was the delusional part. But in a way, Mara was right. They had been friends…of a sort. Four years ago, at

Yearning Sands, Kellen had had no suspicion of Mara's criminal activity, and never had she suspected Mara happily murdered to maintain power.

How had Kellen been so wrong about her? How had she failed to see the thin coil of insanity that wound through Mara's character and strangled all the good in it? Enunciating every word, Kellen said, "I do not understand you. You're a serial killer."

"I'm not, either!" Mara shoved the diary aside, and her eyes snapped with indignation. "I only kill people who deserve it."

"I don't deserve to die, and you don't deserve to mete out justice."

"I deserve every bit of power I can take." Mara didn't doubt herself.

"You tried to kill my daughter. She was delirious. Then unconscious. Fighting for her life!"

"If I had tried to kill her, she would be dead." Mara took a breath that hitched in the middle. "I was going to finish her off. Because she is your daughter."

Kellen's heart missed a beat.

"But she…she came to warn me."

"Warn you about what?"

"About Dylan. She told me he was dangerous. She warned me the storm was coming in. She said we had to evacuate, and invited me into your helicopter. She was *nice* to me." Mara sounded as if such a thing had never happened before.

Kellen supposed it hadn't. So Rae had saved her own life by being Rae, kind and interested. "You had met Rae a few days before, and—" oh, she understood now "—you made her promise not to tell us. You didn't threaten her, because she liked you."

"She did, didn't she?" Mara sounded sloppily sentimental.

Which made Kellen want to slap her. "After you gave her that drug, she rambled. She said she liked you. She said she was worried about you. So who did you tell her you were?"

"The intern from UC San Diego." As if bored, Mara wandered back to the overstuffed chair and reseated herself.

"The biologist."

"Botanist. Multitasker. Whatever science was required. Don't worry. I've been doing the work!" Mara assured her.

"You've been doing the work," Kellen repeated. "Like that matters!"

"It does matter!" Mara's eyes narrowed. "Was Jamie right? Don't you care about the environment?"

Kellen had fallen down the rabbit hole, and soon Mara would be shouting, *Off with her head!* "I deeply care about the environment—" not right now, but in general "—and so does Rae, so of course she admired you, and came to warn you. You gave her drugs—"

"Only a half dose."

Kellen lost her temper and shouted, "What difference does it make, half dose or full dose? If my husband and my child are lost at sea, it's because you sent them out."

"They won't be lost." Mara was blithely certain, like a three-year-old who was playing with fire. "Two days ago, I watched them from the cliff edge, sailing away, laughing. They love to sail."

"In good weather." Kellen flung her arm toward the window where the wind slid its sly fingers under the aged sill and rain slashed at the glass. "Have you even looked beyond the tip of your conceited little nose at what's happening out there? This storm is the remnant of a typhoon. No intelligent person sails in this weather! What did you think, that you, the mighty Mara, could command the elements to let Max handle a tiny vessel in seventy-mile-an-hour winds? In seas so violent the boat disappeared three times beneath the surf and the last sight I had of them, Max was bailing? Not managing the boat, the motor, the rudder—but bailing?" Kellen closed her eyes and took a few deep breaths, realized she was dizzy, ready to fall over. She opened her eyes, swayed, fought to stay on her feet— and noticed her rain gear was gone. Mara had stripped away her plastic poncho, and Kellen was damp. Damp all over, damp all the way down to her underwear.

Damn Mara Philippi.

Kellen plucked a hair off her long-sleeved T-shirt. And another. And another. And realized—all down the front of her clothes, she had a fine coating of red-and-blond dog hair.

*Luna.* Since Olympia had left, no one vacuumed, and Luna's hair was everywhere, on every floor, every surface. Now Kellen wore it… When Max and Kellen took Rae to the beach, they had locked the dog in the house.

Where was Luna? Had Mara killed their dog?

*What did you do with her?* The question hovered on the tip of Kellen's tongue.

At that moment, from the depths of the house, Luna barked.

Kellen jumped.

Mara jumped harder. She got to her feet, looked around fearfully. "Did you hear that?"

Was she kidding? Acting? If she was, she was doing a good job of it—she was *sweating*.

Mara's questions gave Kellen time to think, to consider her accusation. Was Luna in hiding?

The dog barked again.

"You heard that, didn't you?" Mara took a step closer to Kellen, not as a threat, but as if seeking protection.

"I didn't hear anything," Kellen said glibly.

"It was a dog. There's a dog in the house."

"I didn't hear anything," Kellen insisted. "Anyway, what difference does it make? You aren't afraid of dogs, are you?"

"The prison dogs…" Mara's breathing deepened. "They were vicious. They didn't care who I was. If I didn't do what they wanted, they attacked." She pressed her hand to her thigh as if remembering an old wound.

"You couldn't bribe them?"

Mara's head snapped around. "Are you laughing at me?"

Kellen was, but she pretended not to understand. "Most dogs you can bribe with treats."

"You… You're playing games, aren't you? Are you thinking you can distract me with a fake dog barking?

You could disarm me?" Mara's eyes glowed with para-
noia and the pistol steadied on Kellen's face.

Kellen shoved her right hand, with its cold, still
fingers, between them. "How could *I* disarm you?"

"You have two hands!"

Kellen showed Mara her left hand. "This one is
better. A little."

It *was* better. As in, better than ten minutes ago.
Better than five minutes ago. The fingertips on both
hands were tingling painfully, like nerves recovering
from frostbite.

The effects of the Taser were fading.

"We're off track." Mara backed off a few steps. "I
want to tell you the game."

Kellen braced herself. "What game?"

"The game we're going to play. It's called, 'Kill
Kellen the Fun Way.'"

# CHAPTER THIRTY-NINE

KELLEN NEEDED TO buy herself *time*.

Besides, she was hungry.

She started for the kitchen. "Look, Queen of Hearts. Before you start announcing your freaky plot... I need something to eat." She could play her own game, buy time her own way.

"What?" Mara didn't move. Then she did, running after Kellen. "What?"

"I'm hungry. I haven't eaten since yesterday." Since before she'd found Rae wandering through the grasses, crying and hallucinating. "You can talk while I prep."

"You...aren't..." Mara adored being the object of fear; she didn't react well to Kellen's offhanded dismissal.

"I'm not what? I'm not hungry? I assure you, I am." The impulse, Kellen realized, that sent her to the kitchen was a good one. She really did need sustenance and hydration. Irritating Mara was a bonus. "I can't do much cooking with this claw of a hand—" she twitched her fingers to demonstrate her disability "—but I can heat something up in the microwave."

Mara halted, pulled the pistol and took a shooting stance. "Stop. Right now. Or I'm going to shoot you!"

Kellen faced her and opened her arms wide. "Go ahead. Make it easy on me. Shoot me."

Mara stood, still pointing.

"In the leg, so you can watch me bleed out? Or through the heart, and end it all right now? Either way, you're alone on an island in a storm in the middle of the Pacific, with no way to leave. Have you thought this through?" Having put that into Mara's mind, Kellen turned back toward the kitchen, then faced Mara again. Pressing her hand to her aching ribs, she lifted her shirt and looked. Bruises laddered her skin. "What did you do to me? Kick me while I was unconscious?"

Mara lowered the pistol. "I had to load you onto the golf cart, then drag you into the house. It wasn't easy."

"You didn't care if I hit every step on the way in."

"I thought you might be faking it, and figured you'd come awake if you were injured enough." Mara seemed even now surprised. "You didn't."

"No kidding I didn't!" Kellen winced and touched her cheek. "Rug burn."

"Sorry! You were a dead weight."

With Mara's half-assed apology, Kellen judged the immediate danger was over, and walked toward the kitchen again. Once there, she went to the refrigerator, removed the leftover pizza, and placed it on the counter. "Want a slice?"

Mara wandered over, pistol held at ready. "Sure. But I'll use the oven. The microwave makes the crust tough."

Such a domestic scene. Kellen wanted to laugh. Two mortal enemies discussing the best way to heat up a slice of pizza! But if she did laugh, she was pretty sure it would sound like hysteria.

She found a cookie sheet, handed it to Mara, and let her deal with the oven and the pizza while Kellen poured milk and water into the glasses. More and more, her hands tingled, the tips of her fingers hurt; the pain was a promise of better times. She put a bowl of fresh apricots and a bowl of cherry tomatoes on the table, and set two places.

All the time she was thinking—what could she do with a fork? Could she break a glass and slice Mara's throat? Knock her out with a cast iron skillet? None of those would work. She needed skill and speed, and as sensation gradually returned to her fingers, they twitched uncontrollably.

Mara leaned against the counter and smiled, and negligently pointed Max's pistol at her. "I can see you casting around for a way out. There isn't one."

"There isn't one for you, either."

"When this is over and I've killed you, law enforcement will arrive and take me away. They'll return me to prison and put me in solitary confinement. I'll spend a couple of years learning something that will help me escape. Or I'll escape the good old-fashioned way, using sex, intimidation and bribes. Once again, I'll be out in the world, doing what I want. I'll bet you a hundred dollars."

Kellen seated herself at the table and took an apricot from the bowl. "If I'm dead, how are you going to collect?"

"Oh. I didn't think of that." Mara frowned. The timer went off. She removed the pizza, used a long, sharp knife to cut slices, and put them on a platter in the middle of the table. "Are you a fan of Lewis Carroll?"

Pausing in the act of sliding pizza onto her plate, Kellen asked, "What?"

"You called me the Queen of Hearts. Have you read *Alice in Wonderland*? *'Off with her head!'*" Mara snapped the napkin loose and placed it in her lap. "As a child, *Alice in Wonderland* was one of my favorites."

"That figures." Kellen took a bite, chewed, swallowed and put down her pizza. "Wait. You couldn't read."

"Before I started school, my father read to me."

"You had a father who read to you? Sounds like a nice guy." Which made Mara's idiosyncrasies all the more bizarre.

"My father taught English composition at an elite school, Heatherwood Academy outside of Leeds, England. To him, the only thing that mattered was *literature*." Mara rolled out the word like a royal red carpet over castle steps. "He taught me the importance of proper behavior, of making the right friends, and to appreciate the grandeur of the English language."

"But not to read." That didn't add up.

*"Shut up."*

Mara's voice was so vicious, Kellen took another bite of the pizza, chewed carefully and changed the subject. "You drugged Dylan."

Mara shrugged.

"You sent him to kill Jamie."

"Someone needed to. That woman was annoying."

"So are you. No one's managed to off you yet, although God knows you deserve it." Kellen ladled out justice, and waited to see how Mara would respond.

"I deserve nothing except what I work for. You, too. You know that."

That was fair. "Where's her body?"

Mara seemed genuinely confused. "Whose?"

"Jamie's!"

"Why would I know? I didn't *help* Dylan kill her. I didn't *watch* to see what he did with her. I merely *set* events in motion."

"She deserves a resting place." Surely that woman who worshipped the natural world should be interred in the good earth.

"Not my problem. Listen, we're off subject. Here's the way today is going to play out."

No more talking. No more gathering her strength. Kellen ate pizza, and listened.

"You'll take off running, and after thirty minutes, I'll follow. I'll chase you like a dog that deserves to be put down, and I'll kill you."

Kellen had been expecting something like this. How could she not? Rational people who wanted to rid themselves of a pest…would have just killed it. But Mara wanted to prolong the agony.

Calmly, Kellen drank her milk—she needed the calcium—and her water—for hydration—and took another slice of pizza. "This chasing me down thing. That's a cliché. Didn't your father teach you the importance of creativity?"

"Yes, he did." Mara stabbed a tomato with her fork. "He gave me personal lessons in the creativity of suffering."

Uh-oh. So there was more to the father story than Kellen first thought.

Mara stared as red oozed down the tines of her fork. "A cliché is if I shoot you right now."

"What made you think of killing Rae? She's a child. She's never done anything in her whole life that could make her deserve death."

Mara's leaned across the table and shouted into Kellen's face. *"I didn't kill her!"*

"Maybe. Maybe not. Maybe she'll never recover from that drug you gave her."

"Why do you keep harping on about Rae? If she dies, it's not because I tried to kill her. It's not my fault if she can't take meds."

Suddenly, Kellen saw Mara through a veil of livid red. This woman hurt Rae, forced Max to take Rae into the greatest of danger to save her life, and then Mara blithely shrugged aside responsibility. In a calm voice that came from a place deep inside, Kellen said, "You said you would chase me around the island until you caught me and I died."

"That's right."

"All right. That's what we'll do *today*. Because I have no choice. When I get back to the house, alive, I'll have beaten you at your game. Right?"

Mara laughed, a deep indulgent laugh. "Sure. That's how it's going to turn out."

"You've made up the rules. The house is a haven. You can't hurt me here."

Mara wavered.

Kellen dug deep into Mara's insecurities. "You know I'm better than you. You're afraid to make the promise because you're afraid I'm going to win the game."

"If you get back here *after sunset*, you can live another day. In the morning, we'll start again." Mara chortled as if the idea was impossible.

"I'll come back here after sunset, and live *uninjured* until tomorrow."

"Sure." Mara made the promise easily. "You know, I'm doing you a favor. If you're so fond of your husband and your daughter, and so sure they're going to die, you're better off when I kill you."

Kellen could see it. Mara was working it out in her mind, making herself blameless, telling herself that with Kellen's death, she'd done her a favor, and in a fury, she leaped at Mara, shouted in her face. "If Max and Rae die, I'll kill their murderer, then I'll spend my life hunting down every crazy, stupid killer like you."

When Mara's pistol touched Kellen's chin, she realized what she'd done. In her rage, she'd lost her advantage.

She stepped back.

No more mistakes. Before this game was over, Mara would die.

All Kellen had to do was figure out how.

## CHAPTER FORTY

KELLEN RAN OUT of the kitchen door and jumped down all the steps in one bound, into the tempest. The wind slapped rain into her face and blasted more rain through her still-damp clothing. As she raced around to the front of the house, she formulated her goals:

1. Live through this day.
2. Figure out a way to kill Mara.
3. Until that point, annoy the hell out of Mara.

Really, at the moment, all she had to do was stay out of reach. On an island like this, large and wild, thrashed by the storm, that wasn't such a big challenge—if she handled a few things now.

Mara had parked the golf cart by the front door, apparently to make it less work for her to drag Kellen up the steps, and still bruising for Kellen.

Kellen leaned into the cab.

The key wasn't in the ignition.

Of course not. That would be too easy.

Mara had said it. She held all the advantages, and she intended to employ them. Cheating meant winning.

So. Kellen opened the battery compartment and removed the battery. It was compact and heavy, and she used it to smash the spokes of Max's bicycle.

Mara didn't require access to easy transportation.

Kellen, battery in tow, sprinted across the lawn and into the tall wild grasses. She was searching for the two bikes, hers and Rae's, that they'd abandoned yesterday. If she could find them, disable Rae's and ride hers, Mara could never catch her. Easy peasy. Except for that damned rifle in Mara's hands. How well did she shoot?

The rain weighed down the grass. The wind thrashed the stalks. Kellen ran and tripped, ran and tripped, and finally settled into a steady, slogging pace.

She didn't have a hat; her hair was long and wet, and constantly flopping in her face. Her jeans were sopping, weighing her down. Her shoes filled with water. She zigzagged back and forth, searching, seeking, worried and not admitting it to herself. If Mara caught a glimpse of her in the sights of her rifle…

She couldn't. Surely she couldn't. The rain kept rolling across the land in cool gray squall lines, obliterating the landscape, and twice, blasts of wind knocked her off her feet. If not for her fear, Kellen would have felt alone in the world. But she knew Mara was out there, on the hunt.

Kellen had almost given up when she stumbled on the bikes, farther away from the house than she had ever imagined. An ill-starred sentiment caught at her throat. Her little girl had loved that bike, had ridden that bike to try to get home to Max and to Kellen.

Kellen choked. Cried a single tear. But—

No! No emotion. This was about survival.

She smashed the spokes, then threw the battery into the grasses and mounted her bike. She shouted into the roaring wind, "Max, I'm still alive. You be alive, too! You and Rae, be alive!"

No reply, but another explosion of wind. She wanted to believe that somehow, they heard her. That somehow, they had been rescued, or they'd made it to land. That even now, Rae was healing.

Kellen tried to ride through the tall, wild grasses. Yet a challenge in good times was impossible in this storm. She was forced to take to the paths. She stayed low on the bike to avoid detection.

But where to go?

She smiled unpleasantly. She knew where she wanted to be, where she might find a weapon to beat Mara at her own game.

She arrived at Paradise Cove, and Mara's camp, hidden under one of the few rocky overhangs on the island. She combed through the backpack and the tent, the sleeping bag, through containers and papers and all the paraphernalia of a working botanist. She hoped for a weapon. She needed a weapon.

But no. No weapon. No firearms, no knives. Nothing Kellen could use to attack and defeat Mara.

No hope.

She picked up the clipboard. It had been carefully placed in a large plastic bag and sealed to preserve the contents. From what Kellen could see, Mara had been telling the truth; she'd been doing the work an intern should do.

But as to the rest of this stuff—Kellen smashed it. She flung it off the cliff into the roaring ocean. She destroyed the campsite, not from spite, but because she hoped Mara would come here and understand the message; Kellen would destroy Mara and everything she was.

She mounted her bicycle and rode again, toward the Conkles'. Going this way, she fought the wind, and every half mile a gust took the wheels out from under her. The fourth time, she remained on the ground for too long. She'd landed right on those bruised ribs. It took long moments to regain her breath, and that Taser had undermined her strength.

But so what? She had to keep moving. She had to survive.

*She needed a weapon.* There had to be something in the cottage. Jamie didn't approve of firearms, and God forbid Dylan had access to one, but surely somewhere the old caretaker had had a rifle hidden in the attic or in a box in the closet.

As she got closer to the Conkles' tiny house, she used the rain and the wind to hide her approach. As she came around the corner, she kept low, watched for someone's recent footprints. Glancing up at the house, she saw greenery draped across the roof. A branch had blown off one of the wide and ancient live oaks.

No, more than a branch. My God.

She put her feet down, stopped herself, and stared.

The whole tree had toppled. The impact split the cottage in two. The house Kellen intended to search had disintegrated into a mass of dried and splintered boards, rusted nails and shreds of insulation. Wind had ripped open the attic, dismantled cupboards and furniture, left everything inside open to the elements.

Whatever weapons Kellen might have been able to glean had sunk into the mud.

Stunned, she rode toward Jamie's greenhouse. There, one of the oak branches had smashed through the glass, taking out the growing tables, leaving the plants exposed to each blustering squall. The deluge had destroyed the carefully composted soil, and the plants had been uprooted.

It was as if Jamie's spirit had claimed the house and the greenhouse as hers, and only hers, and broken them apart.

Kellen hid her bike and headed into the greenhouse. There she rescued a few cucumbers, some green beans and some baby carrots. She let the rain wash them clean and ate with eager appetite. The water barrel was intact and overflowing, and she scooped up the stream of water in her palms and drank until she couldn't drink anymore. She concealed herself in the wreck of the oak tree and relieved herself. When she was done, she thanked God Mara hadn't found her at that moment; Kellen didn't want to die with her pants around her ankles.

Her trip so far today had yielded nothing. She had hoped for a weapon at Mara's camp. She had hoped for a weapon at the Conkles' home. She was still alive, but so far, she had survived, yet not advanced her cause at all.

Where now? What was the plan?

She set off for the grove of redwoods. As she rode, abruptly, the winds stopped shrieking, and the downpour became a mere rainstorm. The ride became comparatively pleasant, if Kellen could forget the fact Mara was out there somewhere.

Or maybe she wasn't. Maybe Mara had sent Kellen

out to exhaust her while Mara stayed in the house and survived the storm in comfort.

Kellen straightened and grinned.

No way. Not Mara. She'd never allow Kellen to run a race that Mara didn't run, too. Mara's competitive spirit allowed no rival.

Kellen heard a rumble in the distance. She looked up; the return of the storm turned the afternoon skies to black. Lightning flashed, temporarily blinding her. She wobbled.

Then the wind snatched up the bike's rear wheel and blasted it to pieces.

Kellen found herself on the ground, stunned and sure she'd been hit by a lightning bolt. She lifted herself onto her elbows and looked at her bike—and realized that damage wasn't caused by lightning, but by a gunshot.

In those moments of lessening storm, Mara had caught sight of her, used her rifle and proved she could shoot.

Kellen whispered, "Max and Rae… I'm sorry, darlings." She had failed them.

The pain in her ribs was different now. She looked down and saw a long, thin sliver of the bike's spoke had penetrated her clothing and pierced her just below her right breast. She scooted into the relative cover of the grass, and with every movement, the spoke jiggled, tearing skin and muscle. She stopped, took a few deep, deliberate breaths, pulled it out and pressed her hand over the wound.

The puncture was small, she assured herself. Painful, but no big deal. She could survive this.

Within five minutes, she saw Mara running toward the bike, crowing with so much laughter, Kellen knew she thought she'd killed her. Before Mara realized she hadn't, Kellen crawled deeper into the sodden grass. Then, keeping low, she raced toward the redwoods.

She was close. Closer. Almost there…

She heard Mara scream with fury.

Kellen broke cover and dove for the depths of the trees.

A shot blasted past her.

That damned rifle. If Kellen had any firearm, she could even the odds, but to have nothing…

The mighty trees had taken the typhoon and created a haven, a grove made up of whirling redwood needles and spirits groaning with the effort of resisting the storm.

Kellen ran, no plan but to survive. She knew where she needed to be. One mighty tree had in its death fallen into another, providing a pathway up into the protective branches. She found it; a broad old tree at a steep angle. She climbed like a monkey, using hands and feet, and made it into the security of the living tree. She crouched there on a massive branch next to the massive trunk, and waited.

It was always dim in here.

Now, with the towering clouds above, it felt like midnight.

She couldn't see Mara. Mara wouldn't see her.

Directly below her, Mara flipped on a flashlight.

Kellen was a fool. But she watched Mara, sat very still, and concentrated on being one with the tree.

Mara was walking slowly, waving her flashlight

from side to side, and occasionally, she paused as if she had found something interesting. She walked past Kellen's tree, then backtracked, and without looking up, she said, "You're bleeding, Kellen. I'm following your blood tracks."

Kellen looked down at herself. She could see nothing in the dark, but she could feel the warm wet seeping through her fingers. Yes. The puncture from the bicycle spoke must have been deep, because she was dribbling blood.

Mara shone her flashlight into the branches, waved it back and forth, focused on Kellen. "There you are," she crooned. She lifted her rifle onto her shoulder and aimed.

Kellen stood and leaped for a branch above her head—and caught it! For one exuberant moment, she thought she could swing herself up and on to the next level. But the branch gave way. In fact, it wasn't a branch at all, for it was hooked with one end on this tree and one on the other, and with this end loose, Kellen swung like Tarzan across through the air.

A hammock. She was holding the end of a hammock. Pieces of something rained down onto the forest floor.

Hanging on with both hands, she slammed into the trunk of the other tree.

A human-shaped object catapulted out of the mesh bed.

At the moment Mara screamed in horror, Kellen understood.

They had found Jamie Conkle.

## CHAPTER FORTY-ONE

KELLEN BURST INTO Morgade Hall, ran to the kitchen, turned on the water and leaned into the sink. She was wet, soaked to the skin from the rain, yet still she scrubbed at her face and hands, and tried not to think about what she'd seen, about the sickened sounds Mara had made.

But in Kellen's mind, it all made sense. Dylan had killed Jamie, but he had also given Jamie the funeral he thought she would want. She loved the island above all things, the deer, the foxes, especially the predacious birds. So like some Native American tribes, he had taken the body, placed it in a hammock and hung it high, and allowed the birds to feast.

For all that Kellen had found tradition in the Morgade cemetery, she had to admit she found comfort with the idea of Jamie traveling the skies with the peregrine, the hawk, the eagle.

Using a swathe of kitchen towels, she dried herself, and thought encouragingly that the storm had washed her as nothing else could.

She had run and ridden all day. She was famished and dehydrated. She knew Mara was coming behind her, delayed only by whatever harm had occurred from the weight of a dead body hitting her.

She didn't honestly think Mara would keep her promise and allow Kellen to remain unharmed tonight. But in a house of this size, how easy to hide in one of the rooms! Kellen pressed her hand on the wound on her side. As long as this time as she didn't leave a trail of blood.

Desperate for more water, she returned to the faucet, leaned down and drank.

Desperate for a weapon, she rummaged in the knife drawer. An eight-inch butcher's knife. A short, sharp paring knife. She stowed them on her person. Mara would try to finish her—but not without a fight.

Needing food, she headed into the pantry. She didn't trust Mara and her drugs, and everything she chose was sealed in the proper packaging. Canned tuna and crackers. Dried fruit. A sealed sports drink.

Leaving the pantry, she blinked at the canned tuna and sealed package of crackers already on the counter.

Who had placed them there? Was Mara here?

She looked around the kitchen. She didn't see Mara, but the table was growing, stretching from a circle into an oval, and the light over the top had developed a smile, like the Cheshire Cat, only brighter.

"This isn't right," she muttered. "The table can't stretch and the Cheshire Cat is in Wonderland. This isn't Wonderland. I haven't drunk anything to make myself larger." She looked down at her legs and up at the ceiling. "Nope. I'm not taller. I haven't eaten a mushroom to make myself smaller."

The light over the tables smiled brighter and nodded. "Then what happened?" it asked.

"She drugged me." Kellen was sure.

"How could she do that?" the light asked.

"I don't know. I didn't drink or eat anything that she could have touched."

The light developed eyes, and swiveled toward the sink.

Kellen looked at the chrome faucet where she'd poured herself water, at the mini-filtration system that protruded off the faucet's arm. She staggered over there and peered into the chrome, and a Cheshire Kitten smiled with wicked delight. "She put drugs in the filter!" Kellen announced. She pulled herself fully erect, as if holding herself with a straight spine would counter the effects of the drug, and staggered across the kitchen toward the entry. "I've got to get to my hiding place and lock myself in," she announced.

But first—she was *starving*. Opening a package of crackers, she shoved a handful in her mouth. She followed that with another handful.

She really wanted the tuna, but how could she open it? It was in a can. She didn't remember how to open a can. "In the Army, I opened lots of cans," she reminded herself, and stuck the tuna into her shirt.

Again she started toward the stairs, then circled back to the canned tuna. She didn't know how to open a can. "Look! It's a pull top!" she announced, put it in her shirt, then returned to her quest for the stairs.

Dimly she was aware she was behaving as Rae had behaved, moving in dizzy circles, unable to get where she wanted to go.

But Kellen wasn't a child. She could fight the drug and…wow. She found herself standing with her hand on the newel post. Look at the stairs. They never ended. If she climbed them, she could reach the stars. She put one foot up. And another foot up. She ran up three steps.

Something dropped on her foot.

She yelped in surprise, and watched the tuna can roll down the stairs. She laughed, because it was funny, and because she wore waterproof athletic shoes and the can didn't hurt her toes. She ran a few more steps, and something else fell onto her foot. It was a tuna can. She waited for it to roll down the stairs, but it sat there like a guardian tuna, tail twitching in menace.

She backed away, skidded a few steps down, clutched the handrail, and tried to remember where she was going.

Upstairs to her room. She had to hurry, because… She didn't know why.

Yes, she did. Because Mara was coming.

"I'm here." Mara took her arm. "I see you got into the water."

Kellen stared at her, wide-eyed. "You did something to the filter."

"Full points to you." Mara led Kellen up the stairs. "The thing about this drug is when I take it, it makes my brain normal." She smiled, and her face turned into a cat's.

Kellen gasped.

"But when you or any person with a normal brain takes it," the Cheshire Cat said, "it changes your world in terrible ways. Or so they tell me. I do hope you can hear the air quotes when I say, 'Normal.'"

"I don't like talking cats."

"I don't like barking dogs, either."

They reached the top of the stairs, and they weren't in the stars. They were in the corridor headed for Kellen and Max's bedroom.

"I need to go to the bedroom," Kellen confided, "so I can lock the door."

"Why would you do that?"

"Because Mara is coming. Shhhh."

"I'm Mara."

Kellen looked. The cat rearranged its features and became Mara. "You'll have to wait out here." She frowned. "You've got a bump on your head. It's a big bump."

Mara steered her through the bedroom door and over to the dressing table. "That's what happens when a corpse falls on you."

"Nooo. That sounds awful." Kellen sat, because Mara pushed her onto the dressing stool. "How did that happen?"

"You bitch. You know. You did it."

"Did not." But some vague memory pressed against Kellen's skull, wanting out. "Jamie is flying with the birds," she blurted.

Mara trembled with some great emotion. Or maybe that was another illusion. Then she smiled, pressed Kellen's left hand onto the polished wood of the dresser top and spread her fingers wide. "I was hoping it would come to this." Her eyes gleamed with maniacal plea-sure—and she drove a five-inch-long needle through Kellen's left hand.

# CHAPTER FORTY-TWO

KELLEN SCREAMED: SHORT, surprised, agonized. Tried to yank her hand away, and as muscles and tendons tore, she screamed again. She shook in the effort to stay very still, and stared at her hand, pinned to the dressing table, a silver needle protruding from the back. Blood oozed up, bright red and flowing easily as if pleased to be released. She gripped the needle with the fingers of her right hand and pulled.

Torture. Torment.

"How does it feel to be a failure?" Mara asked. "A nobody?"

"Oh, God." Kellen sobbed. "Why? Why would you do this?"

"Your other hand is ruined." Mara leaned against the dressing table and observed her. "Unworthy of my taking. I might as well mutilate this one, too, and teach you a lesson at the same time."

"What lesson does this teach?"

"Don't betray me, unfaithful friend."

Now Kellen understood how completely and cleverly Mara had trapped her. "You're furious because I made it back to the house alive."

"You dumped a dead body on me." Mara waved

a hand toward the window, where demons shrieked and roared.

For one moment, the window stretched sideways. A flash of light, and Kellen saw evil faces pressed against the wavering glass. They laughed, mouths wide open, spitting joy at the sight of human torment.

Pain brought Kellen back to reality.

No. Not demons. The storm. Lightning. Thunder. The old house was shaking under the assault.

"I was trying to avoid your bullet. I didn't know Jamie was there." Kellen closed her eyes, picturing the scene. "There's justice in what happened, and somewhere, Jamie's laughing."

"No, she's not. She's dead!" Mara leaned in and squeezed the sides of Kellen's hand.

Agony streaked up Kellen's nerves. She screamed—and struck out with her free hand.

Mara leaped back.

Kellen twisted sideways. The needle wiggled like the swivel point on a compass. Kellen screamed again.

"Don't be such a baby." Mara moved close and thrust her own right palm in front of Kellen's eyes. "See that?"

Kellen blinked, trying to clear the moisture from her eyes.

"See the scars?" Mara pointed at the center of her palm. "See this one?"

Kellen nodded, in too much pain to speak—or to see.

"That was the first one. I was five years old. I brought home a notice that I needed help with my reading. My father, I told you, taught English composition. In our house, only English composition mattered. Anything else was insignificant." Mara was breathing quickly, staring and remembering. "I didn't need help with my reading, he said. I needed to stop pretending to be stupid, he said."

Pain. Confusion. Kellen couldn't comprehend. "Who?" She blinked again and focused on Mara's palm, dotted with hard blue scars. What was she looking at?

"My father." Mara pointed at another hard blue scar on her palm. "That was the second one. I won a medal for a story I wrote. I was so proud. I thought he would be proud."

"He wasn't?"

"The teacher sent a note with it saying I needed help with spelling and comprehension. She said I got my words mixed up. My father called me Moron. He used the word like it was my first name."

"Your father called you Moron." Kellen didn't understand. Or didn't want to understand. "He... What did he do?"

Patiently, Mara explained, "Every time I brought home a note saying I couldn't read, every time a teacher called to tell my father I needed to be tutored, he took my mother's beading needle and stabbed me through the palm."

"Like you did to me." The pain in Kellen's hand made her queasy.

This story made her sick.

"He nailed me to the kitchen table. I didn't need tutoring, he said. I was his daughter, he said. I should stop being stubborn and perform the work I pretended

I couldn't do." Mara paced to the window and stared out at the night so black it pressed on the glass and howled with the were-wind. "In the morning, every time he released me, he made me kiss his hand and thank him."

Kellen fought through the drug-induced disorientation to certain deduction. "So it's nature and nurture."

Mara turned in a slow swivel away from the window. "What are you babbling about?"

"Rae and I were discussing nature versus nurture, and you—you're the daughter of a madman. You're the daughter of an abuser. You might have been less deadly if you'd had a loving childhood, but he abused you."

"I don't understand what you mean."

Had Kellen said it wrong? Was she back to the time after the surgery when her words were the wrong words? Had the drug destroyed all the work she'd done? She sobbed once, loudly, then control returned with a snap. "Your crazy father tormented you your whole crazy childhood and created a monster."

Mara put her palm on the window and with her nails, she scratched the glass. "He didn't torment me. He wanted me to be better."

Kellen worked her way through the labyrinth of her own words. She'd said that Mara's father was crazy and that Mara was crazy. Mara's reply denied neither of those facts. She said… She said… "You're defending him? His actions?"

"He required the best from me." Mara sounded proud.

The world swelled and diminished, swelled and diminished, driven by the madness rife in this room.

"Classic abused child defending the abusive parent. You are dyslexic. You couldn't read. He refused any help for you. He preferred to hurt you instead."

Mara shouted, "I can read now. I demanded they teach me in prison. They brought in the best, and I learned. I learned!"

"To make your father proud?"

"No. I don't care what he thought." But Mara's voice faltered.

"When you were a child—didn't anyone report him? Try to help you?"

"One teacher." Mara smiled faintly. "Father was a powerful man in the community. I defended my father. She left town in disgrace."

Kellen looked into Mara's manic blue eyes. Damaged. Too damaged. The madness went clear to the bone. Nothing could have saved Mara. Nothing.

"Once when I brought home an award for mathematics, I was so smug. At last he would see I wasn't stupid. Instead he stabbed three needles into me. Mathematics was destroying the natural world, and I should be ashamed of myself for being competent in an inferior subject."

Kellen didn't feel pity for the Mara that stood before her. But she pitied the child, sitting alone all night at a table, in the agony Kellen felt at this moment. "You poor little girl."

"I'm not a poor little girl."

Kellen looked around. Mara had disappeared. Was that a puff of smoke? "Come back," she called. She didn't want Mara with her, but more important, she didn't want to be alone. And always, she harbored the impossible hope Mara would remove the needle.

Suddenly, Mara was back.

Suddenly, a glass of water balanced at the far edge of the dressing table.

Water. Kellen was so thirsty. "Water," she whispered.

It was too far away. If Kellen reached for it, she'd hurt herself. And…and the drugs. Mara would give her more drugs. Kellen turned her face away—and shrieked in terror.

Mara leaned close, so close her face was wild and distorted. Here was the demon Kellen feared. She stroked Kellen's shoulders, dodged into one side of her face, then the other side.

Kellen shrieked again.

Mara whispered, "See how the needle gets broader and thicker where the eye awaits its thread? It's such a tiny bit of width, yet try to raise your hand and slide it off, and free yourself. Come on. Do it!"

That sounded reasonable; Kellen should be able to end the agony with a simple motion. She tried, and one inch of rise equaled a burst of agony. She dropped her head in defeat. Tears rose and leaked from her eyes.

"See? It's not so easy. For you…you're weak." Mara was triumphant. "For me… I endured it for seven years, from the time I entered school until I was twelve. At last, one night I wasn't afraid anymore. I pulled my hand off the needle, and I ended my torment…forever."

"How?" Kellen knew. She knew. But she had to hear the details.

"It was the dark before dawn. So apt! So perfect. I freed myself, pulled my hand off the table. The blood had pooled there. It was sticky, and the wood contained stains from all the other times. Father liked a record of what he'd done."

"A monster." Kellen wasn't sure if she was speaking of Mara or her father.

"I pulled the tip of the bloody needle out of the table. I waited, huddled in Father's easy chair by the fire. He rose, as he always did, at 5:00 a.m.—he believed a disciplined life created a man of character. I heard the water running for his shower—cold, of course. I imagined him dressing, and I heard him come down the stairs and walk toward the kitchen." Mara told the story with animation, creating an atmosphere of dread. "He rounded the corner and looked surprised that I wasn't in my place—and I launched myself at him, and stabbed the needle through his eye."

Kellen didn't know what was worse, hearing about the abuse Mara's father had doled out, or how Mara got her bloody revenge.

"He screamed the way he always admonished me not to do. He tried to knock me aside, but I clung to him. He was my father!"

"You loved him."

"Yes. I loved him." Mara breathed hard. The Cheshire Cat was back, with its cruel smile. "He didn't die all at once, so I knelt on his left arm and plunged the needle through his hand, eight times to commemorate each time he made me pay for my failure, and one time for his failure to anticipate my attack. You see, he had to pay for his failure, too." Mara grabbed Kellen's hair, jerked her head back, and stared into her eyes. "Everyone has to pay for their mistakes."

"Is that what he told you?"

"That's what he taught me. He was right. He paid. He died. I removed his hands, his soft, scholar's hands, and kissed each one."

Kellen could see the ghosts of Mara's prey, floating behind her. "Did you kiss their hands?"

Mara looked wide-eyed at Kellen as if she'd pulled her back from a precipice of memory. "Who?"

"When you took the hands of your other victims, did you kiss them, too?"

"No. They weren't worthy."

The ghosts shrank back and blew away with the wind.

"How did they catch you?" Kellen asked. "The authorities?"

"My mother…she wouldn't stop screaming, and she had never loved me like my father did. She'd tell him not to hurt me. She never wanted me to be better." Now Mara's voice was indifferent. "So I killed her, too."

Kellen couldn't remove her gaze from her hand, pinned to the table, writhing, then still, seeking a way to escape the pain. Yet although agony buzzed along her nerves and the world stretched and rolled, she heard every word of Mara's story. The horror sank into her bones, and she feared the craziness and the cruelty would infect her, too. She feared the drugs would take her to the edge of psychosis and beyond. "You murdered both your parents, and you went to juvenile prison."

"Of course. The authorities released me when I was

eighteen. They said I was fixed." Mara chuckled. "All I had to do was stay on my medication. I didn't. I found a man to pay for my ticket to the US, and I came here with him. He died."

"All your men must die."

Mara shrugged. "Eventually. Eventually, they all try to betray me."

Kellen was thirsty. So thirsty. She reached for the water, but her fingertips couldn't quite reach.

Mara chuckled. "Frustrating, isn't it? I'll free you in the morning. Let you have food and water. Let you run—and shoot the legs out from under you. It's not going to be another day like today. You won't survive."

"I don't care if I survive. I only care if Rae survives."

"She will. She will." In one of those sudden moves that made Mara so spooky, she knelt beside Kellen and took her free hand, her atrophied hand, and held it. "You don't understand. I've decided I'm going to make it my life's mission to care for Rae."

What did she mean? "Max will care for Rae."

"No. He's going to die, too. He was supposed to die first, to make you suffer more, but he got off the island. Broke my heart, that did."

Kellen's heart, too, for she feared for him...and she needed him.

"But Rae—she'll need someone to take care of her, to show her how to control people, make them love her, want to do things for her. How to build a network of sycophants—"

"You want to make Rae into a copy of yourself!" The drug Mara had given Kellen swam in her blood, muddling her thinking and making her afraid of… everything. She'd been afraid Mara would kill Rae. But this was worse, and the horror of imagining Rae, helpless at the hands of this fiend, vanquished every other terror.

Before Kellen could move, Mara patted her shoulder, and with casual cruelty, tweaked the needle in her hand.

Through the explosion of pain, Kellen heard her say, "I realized—it's not you who is my soul mate. It's your daughter. I promise I won't ever let her be alone."

# CHAPTER FORTY-THREE

MARA WENT TO the door and turned off the lights. "Sweet dreams, former best friend of mine. Don't hurt yourself trying to reach that water."

Kellen sank back in the chair and cried. Cried tears of agony, tears of love, tears of failure, tears of hunger and thirst. The moon streamed in the window, white light that made stark and clear her dilemma. Suddenly, the light was extinguished. She looked out.

Clouds from the storm streamed past, darkened the moon.

The moon came out. The rain came down, drops of silver.

More clouds. More rain. More moon.

Somehow, she had to somehow free herself, nourish herself, find Mara and kill her.

Her mind tried to sort through the possibilities. How could she kill Mara? Only with Mara's death could she save Rae.

At the thought of Rae, more tears rained down Kellen's cheeks. She tried to shake them away, but she wasn't in charge of her emotions, they had charge of her. She sobbed aloud, broken with the thought of her daughter and her husband, lost in the fathomless ocean…

*No.* No, they weren't lost. She had faith in Max. He could handle every challenge.

Abruptly the tears dried, and she could think again.

She was pinned to the table. Again, with her atrophied hand, she grasped the protruding end of the needle. Her fingers were shaking. The metal was slick with blood. Mara had driven the point deep into the wood. Kellen couldn't draw it out, yet every time she tried, every time the needle wiggled, the agony that couldn't get worse—got worse.

She stopped, panting with effort and pain.

What had Mara said? That she had pulled the needle through her palm, like a stitch through a cloth.

If Mara could do it, so could Kellen.

Bracing herself, Kellen lifted her hand.

She screamed and passed out…

She lifted her head from the dresser.

Mara. The drug. Her hand. Max. Rae. They all mixed in her confused brain.

Mara had placed water on the edge of the dresser.

Water. Drugged water. But she desperately needed water. If she could reach it, that would give her the strength. She reached and strained. She touched the glass with her fingertips—and knocked it off the dresser.

She cried. Again.

She was a failure. She was a nobody. Less than a nobody. She was a woman who let a madwoman claim Rae as her own.

Consciousness vanished.

Consciousness returned.

With every fade and every return, she was aware the drug's effect was finally, finally weakening. Which didn't help, because what good was cognizance when she hadn't the fortitude to pull her hand free? Yet she tried. And tried.

How long had she been here? The clock said one. 1:00 a.m.? Only that?

Yes, for night still pressed against the window and the storm whistled in derision. How many more hours of suffering before Mara released her?

She couldn't wait for Mara. She had to save herself.

As she braced herself for another attempt, a shuffling noise and a faint light focused her attention at a crack in the wall.

Kellen blinked, trying to clear the hallucination. But the crack grew wider, became a door. In the door, an angel appeared, dressed in loose white robes with white hair swept back from her soft, wrinkled face.

Had Kellen died?

Her attention fixed on the light the angel carried. A flashlight, not a candle or an eternal flame.

What kind of heavenly battery ran an angel's flashlight?

Kellen felt a soft snuffling at her free hand, a paw on her leg. She looked down, and there she was: Luna, alive and well and whining anxiously, nudging at Kellen, wanting to comfort her. An angel dog.

Luna's nose was not spiritual, but wet and cold. Her tongue was slobbery. Her nails scratched at the wood floor; they needed to be trimmed.

Again Kellen cried, tears of joy, and over and over she whispered, "Luna, you're alive. Luna, my darling dog." She rubbed Luna's head, and took comfort from the hard warmth and warm, soft ears.

The angel leaned over them both, and in a voice marked by a delicate tremor, she murmured, "You poor dear," and in an angrier tone, "That woman is a monster." She placed the flashlight on the dresser, went to the door and locked it. "We don't want any unexpected visitors, do we?"

"Please. Water." Kellen's voice held the same tremor. "Fresh water she never touched."

"Trust me, dear. I brought everything." This was an old angel; slowly she went into the heavenly light and slowly she returned with an old-fashioned thermos. She unscrewed the lid, poured water with a shaking hand into the cup, and held it to Kellen's lips.

Kellen steadied her, and the two of them gave Kellen a sip. The first taste was clean and wet, and Kellen couldn't wait. She took the cup and drank it all the way down.

Luna sat and thumped her tail in approval.

"Good for you, dear," the angel said. "More?"

"Please." Kellen drank. This was what she'd needed. Her mind really was clearing now, yet she was aware of a vast exhaustion, sorrow, anger. "Now. Can you remove the needle?"

"I can try." Old Angel reached out a hand, crooked and spotted, and tugged.

The needle twisted.

Kellen sobbed.

Luna whined.

Old Angel pulled away in distress. "I'm sorry! I haven't any strength, and I never imagined this. This I didn't come prepared for. I wish I had my scissors. I think we could cut the needle."

"Yes! Scissors." Hope blossomed in Kellen. "In the bathroom!"

"Perfect." Old Angel made her slow, unsteady way toward the bathroom door.

Luna left Kellen's side and accompanied her, and once when the angel staggered, Luna was there to steady her.

They returned together, and the angel wore an angelic smile. "I have the scissors, but even better—look what I found under the sink!" She showed Kellen a pair of pliers.

"Thank God. Thank you. Hurry."

Old Angel manipulated the pliers as she did everything—slowly. "Your darling husband does scatter his tools around, doesn't he? There's a Phillips head screwdriver in there, too. But I don't think we have a use for that, do we?"

"I tell him—every tool in its place. But he doesn't listen."

"Of course not, dear." Old Angel wrapped the pliers around the head of the needle. "Can you help?"

Kellen wrapped her free hand around the angel's and counted, "One. Two. Three."

They yanked.

The needle stuck, then released so suddenly Old Angel staggered back.

Kellen groaned in pain and relief.

Luna barked.

They all stilled, fearing Mara's knock at the door.

Old Angel sighed. "I don't think she heard us."

"She's afraid of dogs," Kellen told her.

"Is she?" Old Angel sounded satisfied, and not quite so angelic now.

Kellen lifted her hand from the dresser. Blood smeared the surface from the hole in her palm. Dark purple bruising radiated out toward her swollen fingers. "First aid. In the bathroom."

"I was afraid you'd be hurt, so I brought my own first aid kit." Old Angel made her slow way back to the door. "It's very extensive. It has to be, you know, out here."

*Out here.* Did she mean on the island? Or where she lived, between heaven and earth?

"Come, Luna, help me," Old Angel said.

Luna left Kellen's side and returned dragging a small suitcase with her teeth.

Old Angel followed, holding a basket. She gave Luna a chin scratch and a word of praise, picked up the suitcase and placed it on the dresser. The basket she lowered in small increments onto the floor. She rummaged inside, brought out a second thermos and opened it. "Soup," she told Kellen, and handed her a spoon. "Drink it while it's hot."

Kellen recognized the soup; Olympia's chicken and wild rice. It smelled divine and the taste...thyme, garlic, carrots, celery, all fresh from Jamie's garden, and a free-range chicken Jamie had raised. Maybe Jamie wished extra nourishment into her husbandry so Kellen could take revenge on her murderer.

When Kellen looked up, the soup was gone, the accompanying bread was gone, and Old Angel had the contents of her first aid kit organized and waiting.

"This will hurt," Old Angel warned.

She was right, of course. Kellen writhed as Old

Angel cleaned and bandaged the wound in her hand, but when she was done, for the first time tonight, Kellen felt hope that she might survive.

"I have antibiotics." Old Angel rummaged among her bottles. "Are you allergic to anything?"

Kellen shook her head.

"Penicillin then. I remember when it came out." Old Angel trembled as she shook out two white pills. "A miracle drug."

Kellen took them with more water, then placed her right hand on the dresser and braced herself, prepared to rise.

Old Angel read her mind. "I'm sure you need to use the facilities. I'm not very steady on my own, but between Luna and me, we can get you there."

They guided Kellen across the bedroom and into the bathroom, and stepped out to allow her privacy.

The toilet. The hair brush. The mirror and—Kellen shrieked.

Old Angel opened the door at once. "Have you fallen?"

"Look at me!" Kellen shuddered. "I have to shower."

She knew how bad she must smell and look when Old Angel said only, "We need to protect your hand."

They used the plastic trash bags from under the sink, taped around Kellen's wrist, and in a half hour Kellen was clean, dressed in her clothes for the following day, and falling into bed. Old Angel tucked her in and smoothed her damp hair off her forehead. "You're intelligent. You're strong. You can defeat her. Sleep, and while you sleep, the way will be made clear."

An angel's promise of guidance.

Kellen slept.

# CHAPTER FORTY-FOUR

KELLEN WOKE TO the blast of a shotgun, and at the sound, went instantly from prone and asleep to on her feet and battle ready. She stared toward her door, smoking and shattered, and at Mara standing holding a sawed-off single barrel weapon.

Mara's eyes were molten, her mouth was twisted, her color high. She was seething about *something*. Which something it was, Kellen didn't know. Mara seethed a lot.

Kellen's eyes were so wide they hurt. "Hi."

"How did you do it? How did you free yourself?" Mara shoved the door all the way open with her foot and stalked into the room, pointing the shotgun at Kellen's belly. "Where did you put my rifle? Where did you put my Taser? Where did you put my pistol?"

"Um…" The sun shone in the window as if the storm had never been. Kellen shaded her eyes with her bandaged hand, then slowly removed it and squinted into the light. "Actually, it was Max's pistol."

Mara steadied the barrel at her.

*Careful.* This morning, Mara's mental screw had twisted itself almost loose. "I don't know anything about where it is, or about your rifle and Taser."

"Liar!"

"An angel helped me get free." That last part was not true... Was it?

Kellen looked toward the place in the wall where the angel had appeared. It looked like the rest of the walls, paneled and painted. But in the spinning merry-go-round of her memory, she remembered a light. She remembered Luna and an old woman dressed in white. That had been real... Or perhaps not. She also remembered a talking Cheshire Cat in the kitchen light and one grinning in the faucet. And Mara with a cat's head.

"Maybe the angel took the weapons," she said.

"You are so full of shit." Mara was breathing hard. "You did this!"

"Ridiculous!" Kellen said heatedly. "If I had done this, *you* wouldn't be holding a shotgun."

"You didn't know I had it! It's sawed off, so it fit in the bag I stowed at the top of the closet."

Kellen remembered Old Angel, how very human she had seemed, how tiny and frail she had been. If she had taken the rifle, the pistol and the Taser—and how else had they disappeared?—but hadn't been able to reach the bag to check it out...

Kellen lifted her bandaged hand and showed Mara the blood that had seeped through the gauze. "Fine. I freed myself the same way you did—I pulled my hand off the top of the needle. After all, if you did it, it can't be that hard."

Mara bounded forward and pressed the end of the weapon to Kellen's belly.

Kellen recognized the opportunity.

Mara was close.

Kellen was fast, a trained soldier with warrior skills,

and a match for Mara in motive and determination. She could shove the shotgun aside, slam her fist into Mara's face, fight with her, maybe win. *Maybe*.

But kill her? With her bare hands? Even if both her hands were well and whole, Kellen knew herself. Killing someone while looking into their eyes, while seeing desperation and life and soul slipping away... that was the task of a heartless killer. A serial killer.

Yet a memory prodded at Kellen, a memory from last night. Mara's voice, saying, *"It's not you who is my soul mate. It's your daughter. I promise I won't ever let her be alone."*

Rae. Even if Max had brought her through the storm, she was doomed. If Mara lived, she would take Rae, hurt her, warp her, make her into a twisted and damaged version of herself. Mara's soul mate. If Rae fought back, if Mara didn't succeed, Rae would die.

No. *Mara* needed to meet her final, bloody end. For Rae, Mara had be to stopped, and it had to stop here.

Kellen stood very still, looked into Mara's eyes, and through her tumult of emotions and fears, tried to project a Zen-like tranquility. "About today—aren't we going to play 'Kill Kellen the Fun Way'?"

Mara still breathed as if she'd been running.

"If you shoot me, the game is over."

"*When* I shoot you."

"When you shoot me," Kellen conceded, "the game is over."

"The game ends today anyway."

"I imagine it does." Kellen glanced out the window. "You stabbed me."

"In the hand," Mara said scornfully. "A tiny wound."

"You shot at me. Killed my bike. Knocked me flat." Kellen placed her palm on the spot over her ribs where the bicycle spoke had pierced her. "I lost a lot of blood."

"Poor you."

"I spent the day on the run."

"Like I didn't?" Mara spoke through clenched teeth.

"You're the one who made the rules!"

"I intended to drive the golf cart!"

"If you'd told me, I would have left the battery in it." Kellen tried to play it straight, to keep mockery out of her voice.

Mara's hands tightened on the shotgun, so apparently she wasn't successful.

"What? Your father was a professor of English composition and you don't appreciate sarcasm?" Kellen frowned. How did she know Mara's father was a professor of English composition?

Last night, in a nightmare, Mara had told her.

Poor Mara. A childhood of misery followed by an adult life of creating misery. Kellen had to warn her. "You're a human being who has made her choices, dreadful, miserable choices. You're responsible for your life, and for what happens next."

"What does that mean?"

Kellen had to, in all conscience, make the offer. "It means you should quit now, and pay the price for the crimes and the murders."

"To hell with you!" But Mara wasn't steady, almost as if she comprehended the warning, even agreed with it.

"All right. We'll do it your way." In a reasonable

tone, Kellen said, "You slept well last night, longer and better and in more comfort than I did. I'm the one with all the handicaps. Even if you didn't hold the shotgun, you'd win."

"Damned straight." Mara nodded. Her grip loosened. Kellen had talked her down.

"What time is it?"

"Ten."

"In the morning? Tsk. You let me sleep in."

A bloody red climbed up Mara's neck, her cheeks, her forehead. "I didn't let you do anything." She waved a hand at Kellen's door. "Didn't you hear me pounding?"

"I didn't hear a thing." Kellen told the truth.

Mara did not, could not, like that Kellen had slept through her assault.

"Hold on. I've got to hit the john and have some breakfast. Then we'll get started."

Incredulous, Mara said, "You think I'm going to let you—"

Kellen had spent six years in the Army in the toughest environment surrounded by soldiers, men and women, who daily faced fear, death, and bodily functions. She looked at Mara straight on. "You want to fight about whether I get to pee? Because you're likely to get wet."

"Ew." Mara took a step back.

Mara had lived in prison, in that rough environment where women lived, worked and fought without privacy or kindness. But she had a streak of delicacy about her, probably the result of her elite childhood.

Kellen put her hand to her back and limped toward

the bathroom, groaning as various aches and pains hit her. Sadly, she wasn't exaggerating.

But Old Angel had told her to sleep and the solution to her struggle with Mara would present itself—and it had. It was a very final solution…if it worked. *I know one sure way to finish Mara, and I have to do it today.*

She used the toilet, washed her face and hands, drank water straight from the tap—there was no filter, and no glass, either—and wandered out, elaborately casual. "What a difference a day makes. Can you believe this weather?"

Mara scrutinized her, the damp hair around her face, her offhand air, and kept her shotgun pointed right at Kellen. "You make me want to change my mind."

"Then let's hurry and start the game." Kellen headed out the door. She listened for footsteps that followed. She listened for the blast of the shotgun. Foolish, for if Mara shot, she wouldn't hear anything ever again. But nonetheless, the hair rose on the back of her neck.

She heard footsteps behind her, and Mara said spitefully, "You carry on and on about Rae, about how you love her and that's the reason you want to kill me. You never mention the real reason you want to win."

Kellen stopped on her way out the door. "What's that?"

"You're afraid to die."

"I'm afraid to die?"

"Everybody's afraid to die. Except me." Mara sounded so certain. "I'm not afraid to die."

Kellen started down the corridor toward the stairs,

and she thought hard about Mara's comment. "You don't believe it's possible for you to die. You're a child who's never had to live with the consequences of your actions. That's not the same." Without drawing breath to allow Mara to speak, she said, "I *am* afraid to die. But I almost died when I was married to my first husband, and almost died again when I was shot in the head, and was blown up while I was in the Army. I almost died after brain surgery, and the life I have now is precious to me." At the top of the stairs, she turned to face Mara. "It's precious to me because of the people who are in my life. Max and Rae." She ran down the stairs and into the kitchen. She marched into the pantry and grabbed five nutrition bars.

She inspected the seals on each one. None had been tampered with.

When she came out, Mara was handling the shotgun with the loving care of a Chicago gangster. "I'm not feeling as lenient as I was yesterday, so try to stay conscious or I'll be forced to kill you while you stare, eyes wide and your mind vacant."

"You can't use a Taser on me, so I should be fine." Kellen peeled back the packaging of a nutrition bar and took a big bite. "Even if you could, and did, there would be no one to watch how cleverly you've destroyed me." She chewed thoroughly. "It always seems to be that way for you, doesn't it?"

"I work in the shadows," Mara said softly.

"No one appreciates you or gives you credit. Why, if I lost consciousness, not even me, your best friend, would know that you killed me."

Mara's blue eyes blazed in fanatical fury. "Stay conscious, then."

Kellen had thought this out. Thought it through carefully. She had to keep Mara simmering with anger, make sure she was on the edge of mania, and at the same time keep her from prematurely killing Kellen in a last, murderous act of vengeance. "You know, Mara, you think you know me. You think we were once best friends. But you don't even know my real name."

"You're Kellen Adams. Kellen *Rae* Adams." Mara was obviously proud of herself that she knew Kellen's middle name.

"Kellen Rae Adams was my cousin." Kellen finished up the nutrition bar and threw the wrapper on the floor. "I'm Cecilia Adams."

The wrapper rolled toward the cabinet and under the toe kick.

Mara watched the motion, mesmerized, then returned her gaze to Kellen. For the first time today, she seemed more bewildered than lethal. "Why are you telling such an outrageous lie?"

"You know me so well. You know I wouldn't tell you a lie." Kellen made her voice warm and persuasive. "I'm not who you think I am. When my first husband killed my cousin Kellen Rae, I took her identity. I've been homeless, served in the military, had a baby, married Max, survived brain surgery—and all the while I've been lying about who I am. I'm Cecilia. Trust me, Mara. I'm Cecilia."

"No," Mara breathed.

"Everything you've told yourself all these years about you and me, and what friends we are, and how we know each other—none of it is true. I lied to you. I've lied to the whole world." Kellen leaned her palms on the kitchen table, leaned toward Mara, and said, "I'm telling you the truth now, so you know—you can never kill Kellen Rae Adams. She was brave. She was strong. She was your worthy opponent—and she's already dead." Kellen's voice caught on a shard of familiar sorrow.

That, more than anything, helped the information sink into Mara's brain. The manic blue eyes lost their heat, grew cool and deadly.

Kellen allowed her old grief and guilt, and the love she had felt for her cousin, to drive the point home. "I'm Cecilia. Killing me means nothing."

"Killing you will make me happy." Mara pointed the shotgun at Kellen. "I'll give you a ten-minute start."

"Last time, it was thirty minutes."

Mara cocked the shotgun. "Run."

# CHAPTER FORTY-FIVE

Kellen raced out the door onto the front porch.

The wind blew lingering clouds across the island and fed Kellen a much-needed boost of clean, glorious oxygen.

She jumped off the steps onto the lawn.

Shadows chased across the land.

Kellen knew Mara couldn't—wouldn't— keep her word. Any minute, she expected Mara to walk out of the door, shotgun in hand and ready. The problem was… Kellen needed every last minute to complete her absurd and desperate scheme. She hoped everything went exactly as planned, and her hand, her slowly-getting-better hand, would perform as her slowly-getting-better brain required. But in the Army, she had learned the true meaning of SNAFU—situation normal, all fouled up.

Except no one in the military used the word *fouled*.

Mara had to know that with every moment of clear sky, the chance of rescue increased. She didn't want that.

Nor did Kellen. If Max had survived, he would send law enforcement. Law enforcement would save Kellen's life. But they would also try to save Mara.

Mara had to die today.

Kellen ran across the green lawn toward the biggest oak. As soon as the yard dipped, she cut left, toward the garage.

Behind her, at the house, she heard a bark.

*Luna. Please God, not Luna!*

A scream. Mara's scream.

Kellen half turned to see Luna barking and lunging at Mara to keep her from following Kellen too closely.

Mara backed toward the door, screaming obscenities. She lifted her shotgun.

Kellen shouted, "Luna, run!"

Luna turned, leaped the railing and raced toward the corner of the house.

The shotgun blasted.

The dog fell.

The shotgun blasted again.

Kellen stumbled, sobbed, righted herself. She sprinted through the tall, wet grass that slapped at her knees and gave Mara a trail to follow.

Luna. Rae's darling dog. Old Angel's assistant. Kellen's staunch defender.

*All dogs go to heaven*, Kellen told herself.

But she cried as she ran.

The air smelled freshly washed, as if the breeze had wiped away the blood and horror of the last days.

An illusion, of course. *Luna was dead.* Yet more blood would spill. More horror would follow. The question remained—whose blood, and what horror?

Kellen's route took her to the garage in three-point-eight minutes. She hit the back door hard, pushing it open, going into the musty, grease-scented garage, then shoving the door closed...

Almost closed.

It wouldn't pay to be too obvious. Mara was an exceptionally clever killer.

Kellen had this planned down to the second.

First, she shoved the battery charger close to the F-100, opened the hood and clipped the cables to the battery.

Next she opened the old refrigerator door and the creaky freezer compartment, grabbed an illumination star cluster flare and tucked it in her belt.

She pulled out a stick of dynamite, then retrieved a blasting cap and a coil of fuse wire from the vegetable crisper.

Was there an expiration date? Max had asked her.

She sure as hell hoped not.

She should test the fuse, see how long it took to burn down.

No time. She'd have to take her chances.

She placed the stick of dynamite on the work table. To attach the blasting cap to it, she needed both hands. She could do nothing about her right hand; it was clumsy, but uninjured, back to the same normal it had been before Mara had Tased her. The bruised and swollen fingers on her left hand were trapped in gauze. She hated to do it, but she had to remove that bandage.

Last night's angel had tied a firm knot, impossible to free with one hand. Kellen scrabbled through the drawers, found gardening shears, and worked them under the knot.

Rust had dulled the shears.

The wound throbbed as she tugged and sawed at the gauze.

Tears ran down her cheeks.

Finally the gauze gave way, tearing rather than cutting, and she was free. She unwrapped her hand and glanced at the red, jagged wound where the needle had pierced her palm.

*Awful. Awful.*

So what? No time to mourn the loss of her good hand.

She set to work as best as she could, depending on her right hand to do what she asked of it and her left to hold and brace.

She uncoiled the wire and used the shears to cut an eight-foot length. That way, if it burned quickly, Mara would have plenty of time to get in here and Kellen would have plenty of time to get out.

Taking her time, the time she didn't have, she attached it to the blasting cap.

The swollen fingers on her pierced left hand felt as if they'd been dipped in concrete, and served only to hold the dynamite. Her right hand…by God, it did the work her mind required of it. The wire was attached to the blasting cap, and the blasting cap was attached to the dynamite. She had a complete explosive device.

She wanted to laugh, to rejoice. But no amount of dexterity could compensate for the countdown of the timer.

*No time.*

She looked out the grubby window, expecting to see Mara smiling and skipping toward the garage, coming too soon for Kellen to complete her plan.

The horizon was empty.

Where was she? Sneaking up on the other side?

Kellen glanced out each window, searching for movement. But except for the flight of a sea gull screaming into the wind, she saw and heard nothing.

She didn't relax. Mara was cruel and sly, and the pressure to succeed did not ease.

Kellen would win this battle for Rae, for Max, for their family and their peace.

Taking the dynamite, she used one moment of precious time to hesitate, to think. What more could she do to ensure success?

The blue can against the wall called her to attention. Kerosene.

Highly flammable.

*Yes! Exactly what she needed.*

She placed an empty six-fluid-ounce Coke bottle on the workbench. The blue can had a spout; she removed the cap and poured a thin stream of kerosene into the bottle. Pungent, oily fumes filled the garage; she leaned over and shoved the window open. No need to advertise her intentions to Mara. Kellen used electrical tape to cover the neck of the Coke bottle, then united the bottle and the dynamite with the same tape.

The perfect incendiary device. Not bad for a beginner—if it worked.

She ran to the truck. As if she was sliding into home base, she slipped under the driver's side door and taped the dynamite, and the bottle, to the gas-tank-filler tube.

The tank was located under the truck's cab.

She knew the tank was about half full.

She knew fumes rose off the surface of the gas and saturated the empty space in the tank *and* in the tube.

When the dynamite ignited, those fumes would roar to life, ignite the liquid gas and…

As she taped, and taped, and taped, she smiled unpleasantly. She had one chance to kill Mara—

*One. Chance.*

—and she wanted that explosive to finish Mara in an ugly, final way.

Next, she crawled toward the tailgate, looping the fuse wire around the frame on the driver's side, using tiny slices of tape to hold it in place. Two feet from the tailgate, she placed her final piece of tape.

She wanted to light the fuse *right now*…but where was Mara? Had Kellen somehow lost her?

"Don't be stupid now," she muttered at Mara, and crawled out from underneath the truck and looked out the grubby window again.

Mara had crested the rise and was headed for the garage.

# CHAPTER FORTY-SIX

MARA WAS LIMPING.

Kellen wiped at the window for a clearer view. No need to be subtle. After all, she wanted Mara to know she was in here. She needed her to come in, sit in the truck, try to start it while the fuse burned down, ignited the dynamite, set the kerosene ablaze and the gas in the fuel line and the gas tank...and the blast would wipe Mara off the face of the earth.

She needed Mara to take the bait.

She squinted out the window; Mara's jeans were stained below the left knee. That looked like blood. Must be blood.

Luna had done it. Dear, sweet, loving, protective Luna.

She would get revenge for Luna, Kellen told herself.

Lighter in hand, she slid back under the wheel well.

The safety release required one hand. To light the flame took another. And coordination—they had to be done at the same time. She had a wounded hand, and a balky hand, and a brain that screamed, *Hurry! Hurry! Hurry! Light the fuse. Light it. Light it!*

She couldn't. She couldn't make both hands perform at the same time. She was holding her breath. If she didn't take control, she would pass out.

No time.

No choice.

She had to breathe.

She stopped. Closed her eyes. Concentrated on regulating the inhale…slowly. Exhale. Slowly. Inhale…

Three times. She allowed herself three deep, controlled breaths.

She opened her eyes. With one hand, she clicked the safety release. With the other, she clicked the ignition.

At last! Her hands performed as she required. The spark sang. The flame ignited. "Yes!" Before it could extinguish, Kellen pointed the lighter at the end of the fuse.

The spark leaped.

With a hiss, the spark inched toward the front of the truck.

Kellen threw the lighter low and hard toward the workbench, hoping to send it under.

But she didn't watch to make sure.

It didn't matter now.

She crawled out and ran to the emergency radio. She cranked it up, turned it on, twisted the knob. Static blared from the speakers, static that would mask the fuse's sizzling.

Kellen glanced out the window again.

Mara was limping faster, her gaze fixed on the garage.

Kellen smiled, and for the briefest moment contemplated jumping Mara and beating her into the ground. Physically obliterating her cruelty held an appeal that sang like a siren's song.

But Kellen had to be practical. Mara might be injured, but Kellen was hurt far worse and she had no guarantee she would win such a confrontation.

*No.* The kerosene and dynamite were set.

The fuse was lit.

The only thing left was to convince Mara Kellen had tried to start the truck and failed.

Mara would comprehend the advantage of having a moving vehicle, but more important—she would always believe that where Kellen failed, she would succeed. It was Mara's automatic response to Kellen's failure that Kellen knew she could depend on.

Uh-oh. Maybe she did understand Mara's mind a little too well…

Kellen ripped the charger cables off the car battery. Leaping into the driver's seat, she turned the key and pushed the ignition button.

The engine gave that desperate *I want to start* sound. Once. Twice. Three times.

It sputtered. It coughed. For one moment, Kellen thought Max had actually fixed that engine and got it running.

Another fruitless attempt to start. "Come on," she whispered to the truck. "You can do it." If she could drive Mara into the ground…

Sense returned in a rush.

If she drove that truck over Mara, she'd die in the blast she herself had engineered.

Kellen gave it one last fruitless try, knowing Mara would snap at the challenge she had set.

From outside the back door, she heard a mocking laugh.

She leaped out of the driver's seat, leaving the door

open, the key swinging. She shoved open one of the wide carriage doors and fled outside. She ran. God, she ran, and as she did, her mind built the scene in her mind.

Mara entered the garage. She saw the truck, the lights on, the driver's door open. She jumped inside, tried the key, heard the engine almost turn over. Maybe she saw the starter button, maybe she didn't. Maybe she knew what it was for, maybe she didn't. Who cared? She sat in that truck. That was all that mattered.

At a safe distance, Kellen stopped and turned, anticipating that moment when the lit fuse hit the blasting cap, the dynamite ignited, and the garage, and Max's beloved truck, and Mara vanished in a fiery blast.

"Come on," she whispered. "Blow!" How long until the fuse burned down?

Max had never succeeded in making the truck run... He was going to have a hard time with this loss, and the loss of all his beloved equipment... But he was a sensible man and valued her life more than a truck... She was pretty sure...

She narrowed her eyes at the garage. Maybe, when this was over, she would go looking for a truck for him to repair. A goldenrod-yellow F-100. That would ease whatever heartbreak he felt from—

From inside the garage, she heard the roar of an engine.

*What the hell?*

The truck came blasting through the garage doors, driven with maniacal fervor by a grinning killer.

# CHAPTER FORTY-SEVEN

*No!*

What the hell?

*No!*

How was this possible?

Max hadn't managed to get the truck running. He hadn't...

Wait. She remembered. When Rae had come home, horrified by her encounter with the blood-soaked Dylan, Max had been under the truck. That day, he had been sure he would get it running.

Well, he had. "Oh, Max," she moaned. Of course, once his baby girl had been stricken, he never thought of the damned truck again.

Did he even know?

Mara raced forward, gaining speed through the wet grass, toward Kellen.

Great. The woman could drive a stick shift.

As the sun lit the interior of the truck's cab, Kellen could see her, Mara Philippi, maniacal and vengeful, with black hair that stood up like a *Bride of Frankenstein* parody.

Kellen ran.

She ran harder than she had ever run in her life. Because if Mara got close before the dynamite blew,

Kellen would be blasted to kingdom come accompanied by her worst enemy. They might not both be going to the same eventual destination, but by God, Kellen didn't want to make the journey with Mara.

Kellen dashed.

She sprinted.

Only one thing saved her: that low tire gave the truck a terrifying shimmy. The front bumper dragged through the grass.

Behind her, the engine roared, closer and closer.

*Come on. Come on. Dynamite, explode!*

She had placed tape across the eight feet of fuse wire several times. Was it still alight? Or, slapped by wet grass and spattered with mud, had it sputtered out, leaving Kellen to die at Mara's hands?

No. No! In less than a half mile, the cliffs dropped straight into the ocean. Kellen would jump to her death before she let Mara kill her. Before she would let Mara win.

*Why doesn't the truck explode?*

And, she knew, Mara would follow her over.

Behind her, the engine revved.

Kellen glanced back.

The truck, goldenrod yellow with a black roof, spun tires as it headed toward her. Faster, faster— Mara mashed on the accelerator, ripping through the damp grasses.

Closer and closer…

There! That oak! Kellen changed course, dove around the massive trunk.

Mara twisted the wheel. The back wheels fishtailed, turning the truck ninety degrees to face Kellen—and then around too far, leaving Mara stopped and facing the wrong direction.

Gasping, Kellen pulled the flare from her belt, peeled back the seal and, with shaking hands, uncapped it.

Mara looked around, spotted Kellen, rolled down her window and shouted, "Sucks to be you, *Cecilia!*"

Just like that, Kellen's hands stopped shaking. Moving smoothly, she placed the cap on the bottom of the flare, pointed the metal tube at Mara and thumped it on the tree trunk. The flare roared to life, slammed into the driver's door post—too bad it hadn't gone inside—then skittered across the windshield, detonating in a shower of white, red and green stars.

Mara dove sideways on the seat, away from the burst.

Kellen held her aching side and laughed loudly enough for Mara to hear… Or rather, she would have heard if she hadn't been deafened by the explosion. Which Kellen knew she was.

Stupid for Kellen to allow herself this moment of triumph. Maybe she'd screwed up the dynamite, maybe she would die, but at least she'd made Mara sit in a wet seat.

Mara sat up, blinking, blinded.

Kellen saw a large shadow pass over the ocean onto the land, heard a familiar chopping sound—

*Helicopter.*

Another trick of Mara's?

*Or Max?*

For a split second, she glanced up. Orange and white.

*Coast Guard!*

The truck engine roared to life again.

Kellen turned and sprinted toward the cliffs.

The sound of the truck's engine grew fainter.

She peeked behind her.

Mara was on the move, but not as fast, and she wove as if the flare had robbed her of sight.

*The dynamite should explode!*

Maybe the fuse wire was defective.

*Explode!*

Maybe Kellen had screwed up the blasting cap.

*Explode!*

She no longer cared why the dynamite hadn't blown, or even if she was in range when it went, only that Mara should die. To save Rae. And Max.

Less than a quarter mile to the top of the cliff. Maybe Kellen could lure her over the edge...

Mara's gaze found Kellen, fixed on her. She smiled, revved the engine, and sped toward her.

Kellen sprinted a few steps.

The helicopter's shadow passed over them again, lower this time, bending the grasses.

Kellen heard a shotgun blast. She clutched at her heart. But she wasn't hurt. She spun to see the truck half lift off the ground. The headlights grew dim.

Mara slammed on the brakes, skidded sideways. The windshield was shattered, the paint was pitted, and Mara wiped a trickle of blood off her face. She looked up, craning her neck to see the circling helicopter.

For the first time Kellen allowed herself to look up, really look up.

Yes. Coast Guard. Someone inside held a shotgun pointed at the truck.

Without the windshield between them, Kellen could see Mara clearly. Her gaze met Kellen's. Her blue eyes blazed with that hellish flame. In their depths, Kellen read her doom. This time, Mara would kill her.

Unless the dynamite ignited.

The truck took off, moving toward Kellen so fast, she didn't know if she would make it to the top of the cliff. The bumper slashed through the grasses, the engine's heat breathed like a dragon in pursuit.

Another shot, close overhead.

Kellen spun to look.

More blood on Mara's face. She wiped at it with a frantic hand. She had to know—nothing could save her now. But she kept coming.

Kellen ran backward for two steps. So she saw it.

With a *boom*, a ball of flame enveloped the F-100.

The earth shook. The explosion lifted the truck, then spat it out. The blazing F-100 slammed sideways onto the ground.

Kellen lifted her fists.

*Victory!*

# CHAPTER FORTY-EIGHT

THE FIREBALL ROLLED toward Kellen.

*Stupid premature celebration.*

She dove sideways. Heat charred her, rolled over and around. She rolled in the damp grass. As she spun, she caught glimpses of the blazing debris, of the truck's body twisting, flipping after her. The triumphant flames roared.

Kellen rolled down the slope, trying to get away, so terrified of the fire she didn't dare stop.

Someone in the helicopter had shot the F-100. The dynamite had ignited, *finally* ignited, blowing body parts, Mara's and the truck's, all over this part of the island.

And Kellen was alive. She was alive! She was rolling toward the edge of the cliff.

*She couldn't stop.*

She tore at the grasses, trying to turn herself.

The truck barreled past her and over the brink onto the rocks below.

The incline grew steeper and steeper.

Kellen couldn't slow her descent. She was going over—

Something slammed into her, stopped her, dragged her back and away from the precipice.

She gasped, robbed of breath by the familiar weight and warmth of—

"Damn you, Kellen, are you trying to get yourself killed?"

Max. It was Max, his brown eyes furious, his deep voice snapping, his shaking hands holding her close against his body.

He had survived. His weary face was battered, but he was alive.

She clung to him, his warmth, his vitality. "Max. Max. Thank you. You saved me." He was here, so he had to have saved Rae, too. "You did it. You saved Rae! What about Rae? How's Rae?"

"She's alive. She'll be fine. She is fine. In the hospital. She sent me back for you." He patted her, brushed at her back. "You're still smoldering. Literally. My God, you women have turned me gray."

"I'm sorry." She smoothed his hair back from his forehead, then anxiety caught her by the throat. "Is Mara for sure dead?"

"She's obliterated," Max assured her, "and every piece of her and the truck that wasn't blown all over the island went off the cliff and into the ocean."

They were prone and tangled in the grass. Kellen couldn't see anything. "Are you sure?" She clasped his collar in her right hand. "Really? Are you sure?"

"Come on." He crawled forward a few feet and parted the grass.

The ground disappeared, a sheer drop onto the rocks, the beach, the ocean.

The F-100 lay shattered, burning in pieces and

clumps and bits, and out on the sand a headless human shape burned.

Mara.

"She's not coming back," Max said.

"You'll make sure. You'll check her DNA."

"I will. But Kellen—you killed her."

# CHAPTER FORTY-NINE

MAX PULLED KELLEN closer, kissed her face, looked into her eyes, and in a tone of absolute exasperation asked, "Damn it to hell, if you got the F-100 running, why didn't *you* drive Mara into the ground?"

"I didn't get the truck running." She shoved at his shoulder with her right hand. "You did."

"No." He sounded sure. "I never got it started."

"That last time, you did fix it, and if you'd had time to try, you would have been driving it all over the island."

He thought about the past few days, reconstructing them in his mind. "I was working on it when Rae came up screaming that Dylan was covered in blood."

"Right."

"I put it together right at last." Max's voice rang out with incredulous pride.

"Yes! But you didn't know and I didn't know. What I *did* know was that if Mara thought she could chase me into the ground, she would try, for the pure joy of it. So I set a trap. I taped the dynamite, the blasting cap, and a long fuse onto the gas tank and frame."

"Of course you did."

"To lure her into the garage, I tried to start the truck, to make enough engine noise that she would think I'd failed to get it running."

"It didn't start when you tried it because it didn't have gas in the line."

"That has to be it. While trying to start it, I brought gas up to the motor. All Mara had to do was push the starter button, and the motor was running and so was I." Kellen sighed in exhaustion.

"Really? I got the truck running? It was fixed?" Max laughed. He laughed! "I fixed the F-100."

She smiled at him. He was so cute. "You did. Congratulations."

He stopped laughing. "And you blew it up."

*Oops.* "Yes. I was hoping you wouldn't give me any trouble about that."

"I won't." He waited a beat. "Not right now."

Kellen looked around at the sky, so blue the storm might have been their imagination, at the wide green oaks, the damp grasses already regaining their green—and the smoldering trail of ruin where the truck had driven. "Someone shot Mara. From the helicopter."

"I shot at the truck, trying to kill her, or ignite the gas tank. That wasn't what took her out. It was you."

"You, too. You hit her. In the face. You got her. I saw."

"If you insist on giving me credit, okay, I helped. But you made sure she wouldn't go back to prison and pull another amazing escape."

"All right, then. All right." Kellen leaned back on the grass. "Rae's safe. Really now. Forever and ever."

"We would have protected her from Mara, no matter what."

"No." The adrenaline rush was fading. "Mara said... Mara said Rae was her best friend. She would have come after her forever."

Max grew pale.

"It's okay now." She leaned against him, wanting comfort, giving comfort. "Is my hair all burned off? Is it?" She lifted her hands to feel her head. This was a small thing, and stupid, but no hair? Again? "The scars from my surgery will show again. I'm so tired of not having hair."

No answer.

She looked at him.

He was staring at her left hand, at her poor, tortured hand.

Hastily, she lowered it

Gently, Max took it between both of his and examined it.

Stars swam as she stared at the wound, puckered red and oozing.

In a low, furious voice, Max asked, "What happened?"

"What you said would happen. Mara didn't fight fair." All the pains grabbed Kellen at once. She winced and moaned.

"Your arm. Your back. Blisters are coming up now. We've got to get you to a hospital." Max wrapped his arm around Kellen's waist, and lifted her to her feet. He started her toward the helicopter.

"No." Her knees collapsed.

He held her, kept her from hitting the ground.

"Not yet. I have to go to the house. I have to tell her…" The world spun.

He picked Kellen up and ran with her to the Coast Guard helicopter. "Stay with me. Hang in there."

"Not the helicopter. We've got to go back to the house and tell her..." Pain took Kellen's breath away.

The helicopter had come prepped for medical emergencies.

As gently as he could, Max placed her on the stretcher the Coastie had pulled out.

She gave a small moan, caught her breath and said, "Sorry. Sorry. I didn't mean to. So melodramatic. I couldn't help it. We need to go to the house and—"

"Lady, we've got to get you to the hospital *now*." As the Coastie stuck a needle in her arm, he introduced himself, "I'm Bill Stevens, medic."

"No." Kellen had to convince them. "We've got to tell her—"

"She's hallucinating," Bill said.

Max and the Coastie lifted her in.

They shut the doors.

The drugs took effect. The pain receded and so did the world, until all of a sudden they were in a hospital emergency room and doctors and nurses were working on her hand and her burns at the same time. She came to complete consciousness, hovering on the edge of agony.

"Give her more pain relief," someone said.

"Not yet. Max. I have to speak to Max."

Right away, he was there, leaning close to her face. "She's still there," Kellen told him.

His brown eyes were anxious. "Relax, honey. You killed her. Remember? Mara is dead."

"Ruby Morgade is not." Kellen respected Max's intelligence above all things, and she trusted him to put the pieces together, but before she could say another word, the darkness took her under.

## CHAPTER FIFTY

"As soon as Kellen told me Ruby Morgade was living here, alone, I sent a medical team to assess her. I also sent a cook and a housekeeping team, and a team to assess the damage to the house." Max piloted the helicopter, the recently repaired Di Luca Robinson R44 Raven II, off the coast of California, across the Pacific and toward Isla Paraíso.

From the back seat, Rae asked, "How did you know, Mommy?"

"That Ruby was alive?" Kellen turned to Rae and Verona in the back seat. "She saved my life."

"I knew it." Rae sounded fiercely proud, as if Ruby was her own personal champion to exalt. "So I was right. Someone did come into my room and stroke my forehead. Luna knew her!"

"That's right. That's why Luna didn't bark." Kellen's voice broke a little.

It had been only four days since Kellen had arrived at the mainland hospital, and those days had been busy, filled with doctors, medications and her reunion with Rae, and in that time, they hadn't told Rae about Luna's death. Kellen knew the time was rapidly approaching. But how to tell a child that her beloved dog had died a hero?

Max gave Kellen a sideways look, and continued, "The nurse is Tichi Barlow. She's impressed with Ruby's mental and physical health. Ruby's appetite is good, and she's been speaking to the construction team about what needs to be done to the house."

"She sounds like a remarkable woman." As soon as Max sent word, Verona had returned from Italy, and she said, "If Miss Morgade's in such good shape, why did we have to come so quickly? Kellen's barely healed."

Max glanced back at his mother, then at Kellen.

"I had a gut feeling we should come as soon as possible." Kellen wasn't trying to be dramatic, just truthful.

"All right. Yes. That's a good reason," Verona acknowledged.

Kellen inclined her head, and glanced down at her hands, one wrapped and taped, the other in need of physical therapy. She sighed. As soon as she got back to Yearning Sands Resort, she would be practicing the piano again…but without Luna and her complaints.

Her eyes filled with tears, but she forced them back and swallowed.

As Max made his first pass over the island, Rae chatted at Verona. "This is it, Grandma. Isla Paraíso. Isn't it neat? Don't you love it?"

"It's very pretty. So isolated. Who could imagine such a thing off the California coast?" Verona craned her neck to see what was below.

As did Kellen. She strained to get a sense of the violence that had occurred here. Instead she saw the serene beauty of the island: the sandy beaches and crashing waves, the mighty oaks and grazing deer. The evidence of the truck's explosion had been obliterated by the grasses that, with the rain, had turned a brilliant green and grown gloriously tall. "Mara Philippi left no mark," she muttered.

"None on the island," Max answered. He meant that *she*, Kellen, had been marked.

Yes, she had, marked by the fight, marked by the torture, marked by Luna's loss. Her hand had required extensive repair, she'd needed minor surgery to remove a piece of the bicycle's spoke and, once again, she had lost most of her hair, singed away from the fire that had blasted out of the F-100.

But she didn't care. She was healing, Max and Rae had survived their harrowing trip across the storm-tossed ocean, Rae had recovered—and Mara was dead. Completely, DNA tested and certified dead.

"Mother, there." Max pointed. "There's the house."

"It's a mansion. Out here," Verona marveled.

Seeing it with her fresh eyes made Kellen reassess it, and marvel, too. That ostentatious French chateau sat alone in the middle of the Isla Paraíso wilderness, out of place with its painted tones of blue and brown and scarlet accents.

"Grandma, wait until you meet Ruby!" Rae said. "She's so cool."

"I think you should call her Miss Morgade," Verona said.

"Why? She's not old," Rae protested. "She's Ruby!"

Kellen turned back to look at Rae. Of course, Rae had met Ruby Morgade through her journal, and to

Rae, she was a young woman who had won her admiration.

"Sweetheart," Verona said gently, "she has to be almost one hundred."

Rae blinked at her grandmother. "That's right. She's like your age!"

"Oops," Max said softly.

Verona glared at the back of his head. "I'm not quite one hundred years old yet."

"But Daddy said—"

Max put the helicopter down on the lawn a little too quickly. "Here we are!" he opened the door and leaped out. "Come on, girls!"

Rae jumped into his arms. "I can't wait until I meet Ruby!"

Verona followed more slowly. "I know she must be anxious to properly meet you, too." She put her hand on Rae's arm. "But remember, she's not the young lady you read about, so you've got be gentle."

"I know, Grandma. I will, Grandma." Rae was stiff, proud and angry. "I'm not stupid!" She took off running across the lawn, up onto the porch, past the waiting nurse and into the house.

Verona sighed. "Do you think that drug permanently harmed her?"

"The medical staff assured us there would be no lingering effects. We have to believe that." Max offered his hands to Kellen.

She put her hands on his shoulders and let him lift her out. He was gentle; she had bruises and burns and bandages everywhere, and she winced at the twinge that went through her ribs where the stitches had been placed. He held her for a minute, his cheek resting on the top of her head. He frequently liked to reassure himself that she was still with him.

She frequently liked to let him.

Finally he let her go, and she planted her feet firmly under her. She looked around. She'd been gone four days. She had changed. Max had changed. Rae had changed.

Morgade Hall hadn't changed. It was still tall, eccentric, and crumbling. The storm had wreaked havoc on the aging structure.

They started toward the house.

"Rae's a little…testy," Verona said.

"I think," Kellen said, "it's a combination of Rae knowing she did a foolish thing that caused much harm, and the ongoing crisis of adolescence. I did try to talk to her, but she would have nothing of it."

"Mothers and daughters. They're either best angel friends or hell's demons incarnate, and there's nothing in between." Max repeated Kellen's maxim back to her.

"Rae's never been one to let something fester," Verona said. "She'll come to you sooner or later, Kellen."

Max reached for Kellen's uninjured hand and squeezed it.

Kellen understood why. Verona had been a stand-in mother for Rae; now she was gracefully stepping aside.

On the porch, a middle-aged woman stood waiting.

"That's Ruby's home nurse, Tichi Barlow," Max said.

Tichi waved them toward her, and when they were close enough, she called, "Come in. Miss Morgade is waiting."

They joined her, entered the house...

It was so weird, coming in to silence. Everything was exactly as it had been. So much had happened here, yet they'd left no mark.

Tichi said, "Miss Morgade was so excited you were coming today, she got up early, bathed and got dressed, came down to the porch to wait—and collapsed. We carried her upstairs to her bedroom. She's waiting for you there."

Kellen ran toward the stairs, paused and turned back to Verona and Max. Max waved her on—he was grinning, which confused her—and she took the steps two at a time, all the way to the top.

The attic room looked as it had before: window seat, desk, paintings, bookshelves. But the door between it and the inner attic was open.

Kellen paused before she entered, to catch her breath, to prepare to meet her angel, and heard—

*A bark.*

She took two running steps inside.

A bed.

Rae.

An old woman.

And Luna, standing on the mattress, her backside wrapped in gauze, her tail wagging wildly, while Rae and Ruby restrained her from jumping at Kellen.

"Mommy, Ruby says Luna's not supposed to jump off the bed. Did you know she got hurt?" Rae sounded bewildered and aggrieved.

"I knew. Yes, I did. I was so afraid..." Kellen rushed to the bed, knelt beside it, put her arms around the ecstatic Luna—and burst into tears.

## CHAPTER FIFTY-ONE

WHILE KELLEN SOBBED, Luna kissed her, cuddled with her, whined in worry and nudged her bandaged hand.

Rae protested, "Don't cry!" and wrapped her arms around Kellen and Luna.

In her soft, creaky voice, Ruby said, "I know, dear. I know."

It was a soft, sentimental, mushy pile of feminine distress.

Kellen looked up, her eyes blurred with tears.

**RUBY MORGADE:**
FEMALE, 97YO. ONCE TALLER, NOW LESS THAN 5', 100 LBS? THIN, WHITE HAIR TWISTED INTO A BUN. OSTEOPOROSIS. ARTHRITIC HANDS. HER EYES, ONCE BEAUTIFULLY ALERT, DROOPED WITH AGE, BUT HER SKIN REMAINED A GOLDEN BROWN HUNDRED WITH THE CREASES BESTOWED BY GREAT AGE. HAD BEEN, AND REMAINED, A BEAUTIFUL WOMAN.

Ruby continued, "When I heard the gunshot and Luna didn't come back, I was terrified. I went out to look for her—if I'd come on that awful woman then, I would have done her a damage—and found our dear doggie huddled against the foundation at the back of the house. She was bleeding in so many places and panting with the pain."

"What did you do?" Rae's eyes were wide in horror.

"I called her. Dear Luna struggled after me, up the steps and into the house. She collapsed in the kitchen. I didn't know what to do, so I gave her water, found a blanket in the library and spread it on the floor. She dragged herself onto it. I got towels, wet them, sat down on a chair and cleaned her. She cried when I touched her, and I cried, too." Ruby extended one shaking hand to pet Luna's head, and one to smooth Rae's hair.

Kellen understood what Ruby didn't say—that the emotion and the effort had exhausted her almost beyond the reserves of her strength. Kellen pressed Ruby's hand between Luna's head and her own hand. "Thank you. Thank you. We all thank you."

"I didn't do anything. I didn't do enough. Simply sat with her, and wondered if we were going to die there. Then I heard the helicopter that your dear husband sent." Ruby glanced toward the door.

Max and Verona stood there, listening.

"Kellen wouldn't rest until I understood you were here and needed help." Max gave credit where credit was due.

Kellen gave a watery laugh. "Max, you jerk. Why didn't you tell me Luna was alive?"

"I didn't know until this morning when I spoke to Tichi. The medical team didn't realize we thought Luna was dead. At that point I thought you should really see our dog." Translation: Max didn't want Kellen bursting into tears when he was alone with her.

Ruby watched them fondly. "What a lovely couple you are." She extended her hand to Verona. "You must be Rae's beloved grandma."

Verona carefully shook the twisted, arthritic hand.

"All I've heard about since I returned is the brave and strong Ruby Morgade."

Introductions were made, Max set chairs around the bed, and he and Verona seated themselves. Rae remained close to Ruby, and Kellen stayed where she was, crouched beside the bed to pet Luna.

"Please, Miss Morgade, tell us what happened next," Verona said.

"Dear Tichi found us first. She came through the kitchen door, saw me and Luna, and in no time she had the whole medical team working on Luna."

Tichi popped in from the outer room. "She insisted we help Luna first." Seeing how Ruby sat up to talk, how she gestured, Tichi came in, fluffed the bed pillows, pressed Ruby back and urged her to relax.

Ruby smiled tremulously. "Tichi is fierce."

"You're supposed to be resting." Tichi pointed to Luna and to the mattress. "So are you, Miss Luna."

Luna subsided at Ruby's feet, head on paws, watching them fondly.

Tichi took up the story. "The team removed seven shotgun pellets from Luna's hind quarters, then we carried Miss Morgade and Luna upstairs to bed. Luna is recovering well, although we are worried about nerve damage in her spine."

"I blame myself," Ruby said. "I took that woman's guns away, but I didn't find that wicked shotgun."

"If I'd had access to Mara's other weapons, or our own—" Kellen now knew who had removed the guns from the gun safe "—my battle would have been much briefer." Reminded of her aches and pains, Kellen shifted uncomfortably.

Ruby shook her head. "I couldn't... I *couldn't* give

them to you. I feared for you, darling girl, but I had faith in your ingenuity, a faith which you justified."

"I'm grateful for everything you did for me. You saved me." Appreciation and resentment mixed until Kellen couldn't tell where one left off and the other started. "I'm just saying it could have been easier."

"I'm glad you beat that awful woman. If I had witnessed nothing of Mara Philippi and her cruelty, I would still have been on your side because of your interest in my story and your kindness in giving me a happy ending."

"What I did, with the explosives, was so much more difficult and risky than pointing a gun at her would have been." When Kellen remembered how she had plotted and struggled and sweated, her heart thumped an uneasy, fearful beat.

With sad certainty, Ruby said, "She would never have yielded, and you would have had to kill her."

Hmm. Yes. That was probably the truth. "But I killed her anyway."

"Not face-to-face. You didn't see the blast of blood and bone, and the light of life flee from the poor, shattered body. You didn't face your own inevitable guilt, and have to turn your mind away before you went mad."

Rae proved she'd been listening. "None of this would have happened if my parents had told me the truth about why we came to the island." She spoke in a clear, cold voice, and she stared at Max and Kellen with clear, cold eyes.

Kellen stared back, stunned by the blunt attack.

Tichi made a sudden retreat and shut the door after her.

Rae transferred all her attention to Max. "Daddy, why didn't you tell me the truth?"

Kellen glanced at him.

Max fumbled for words. "Your mother and I—we wanted to protect you."

"You treated me like a child—"

"We didn't want you to be afraid," Kellen said.

Rae glared at Kellen. "I am sorry I was a sucker about Mara Philippi. I'm really sorry I made a promise not to tell you about her. That was a stupid thing to do because I was mad at you." She looked back and forth between Max and Kellen. "But it's your fault, too, because you didn't trust me."

Kellen's hackles were up at being so plainly criticized for what she had thought was the right thing to do.

But look at her daughter, sitting straight, speaking up for herself, and not, as Verona had said, letting her grievances fester. When had Rae become so clear-sighted, so mature? When had she become a young woman?

"I've never been a parent," Ruby said softly, "but it seems to me she does have a point."

Verona leaned back in her chair, crossed her arms, and made a concurring, humming sound.

Max and Kellen exchanged looks.

Kellen nodded at him.

"Look, kid, we're parents. Your parents." Max reached for Kellen's hand and pulled her onto the chair next to him. When they faced Rae, they did so as a united front. "We're going to make mistakes. And this time, you're right, we did. You were hurt because of it."

"And Mom was hurt!" Rae rose up on her knees.

"And Daddy almost died getting you to a hospital," Kellen reminded her.

"None of that would have happened if you'd told me the truth!" Rae was mad—and offended.

"Maybe," Kellen said. "Mara Philippi got to the island through guile and deceit. Her goal was to kill me and all who were dear to me. Even if we'd told you, she would have come after us. It would have been different, but one or all of us would have somehow been injured. Daddy's right. We made a mistake. As you become an adult, we'll try not to make any more—but we will. So will you. That's why God made love—so when things go wrong, we'll always come back to each other."

Rae stayed on her knees, unwilling to let go of the moment. Finally she dropped back on her heels and sighed. "Yeah."

Ruby slid old, slow hands through Rae's hair. "Your mother seems like a very smart woman. Don't you agree?"

"Yeah." Rae leaned into the caress as if she craved the comfort—and knew that Ruby craved human contact.

Ruby said to Max and Kellen, "You two have a daughter who is smart and dear, and it's lovely that you've taught her so well."

"I'm proud of them," Verona said. "They're a family."

"That's rarer than one might think." Ruby smiled, but her lips trembled.

"Miss Ruby, what horrible thing happened?" Rae asked. "Guns don't shoot themselves. Why didn't you allow my mommy to have her guns? What were you afraid of?"

## *CHAPTER FIFTY-TWO*

RUBY SIGHED. "It's another sad story. Do you really want to hear it?"

Verona said, "I want to hear it. I want to understand."

"These children—they read my journal." Ruby spoke to Verona. "They told you about it?"

"Rae told me every word," Verona assured her.

"Then you know about my father, what he was. He worshipped power, he lived to create fear, and as the war proceeded, he lost more and more control of his newspaper. It wasn't merely that he was diminished in the eyes of the world; everyone he had crushed and hurt and bullied took the opportunity to laugh in his face." Ruby smiled as if that pleased her. "After the war ended, he had only one chance to retrieve his power. He had to force me to wed Alfred, that disgusting old man. Alfred still had influence, and he wanted me."

"That's atrocious!" Rae's color was high, her face burned with fury.

"My father was atrocious, a man without honor, and Alfred was unfit for Patrick to wipe his boots on." Ruby ran a trembling hand across her forehead. "It was so long ago, but I remember..." She looked around the room as if she saw the people as they lived through the scene. "Mother was here with me, and Hermione, when Father brought Alfred up to the attic, this attic, where I still lived."

At Ruby's words, images of angry words, of gunfire, of two powerful, elderly men and three women on the defensive filled Kellen's mind. Max, Verona, Kellen and Rae leaned forward, transfixed by Ruby's fierce retelling of the story.

"Father said I was of no use to him if I refused to do his bidding. He pointed a pistol at me. He threatened to shoot me. I refused—and he did shoot." Ruby's voice wavered. "My mother leaped between us."

Kellen remembered the headstone in the cemetery; Reika Morgade, died 1948.

"He killed her," Rae whispered.

"Yes. He killed her. My mother, who had suffered to protect me." Ruby accepted a tissue from Verona and wiped her eyes. "He murdered her. His wife. His slave. The mother of his children."

Silence fell as everyone tried to comprehend the terrible act that had taken place so long ago. Yet the repercussions echoed down the years.

Rae snapped to attention, and snapped out the question. "Was he sorry?"

"Perhaps in his way, he was. The blood. Our tears. My outcry." Ruby leaned against her pillows, closed her eyes, and was silent for so long Kellen wondered if they should leave her to rest. When Ruby spoke again, her voice was weary. "I had no way to report the crime, so I told my father to get out. He blustered. He said it was his house, and he was still in charge.

Then he noticed Alfred had gone. Marriage to me, the daughter of a murderer, had lost its luster. My father's dreams of power ended that day, and for five years he sat downstairs in his chair in his study, brooding, eating, growing fat—fatter—and bitter. When he died of a heart attack, I had the chair burned. I had his body removed to the mainland, and buried under a simple stone with nothing more than his name and the dates. I've never visited him. No one has. No one cares about Gerard Morgade. He made sure of that."

Max leaned his elbows on his knees. "I guess there was no happy ending, no eventual marriage to Patrick?"

"I never heard from Patrick again. My mother died—"

"Was murdered!" Rae said fiercely.

"Yes. She was murdered in 1948. My father died in 1953. As soon as the vile man passed on, the servants let me know. I came down from the attic to search for Patrick. I had heard nothing from him since '43, and I had to know…" Ruby rested her hands, palms up, on her lap, and stared out her window at the horizon. "I knew his hometown, you see, and I hoped to go there, to find him settled with a wife and children."

"You wanted that?" Rae asked incredulously.

Ruby switched her attention to the girl who had rooted for the young couple who had lived long ago. "I loved him. Wasn't that better than the alternative?"

Rae gave a short jerk of a nod.

"By then, I hadn't been out of the attic for years. But I had money, so I made my way to Butte, Montana. Butte was a mining town, and the Irish moved there to work in those dangerous mines. Patrick had told me about his father, how he supported his family going down in the hole every day for years. His last name was Sullivan, his father's name was John. Patrick had told me he lived on Franklin Avenue. When I got to town, I went to the library, and looked up John Sullivan on Franklin Avenue in the yellow pages. There were three John Sullivans." She laughed. "I went to the first house, but that family of John Sullivan said no, they had no son named Patrick. Same at the second house. By the time I got to the third house, the whole Sullivan family stood in the yard, four sons, five daughters, countless grandchildren, and John and Aileen Sullivan."

Max came to his feet and started pacing. "Patrick's family?"

Ruby nodded. "Patrick's family. I saw them, watching me in silence, and I knew. I opened the fence gate, and faced them. Some of them were angry, I could see it, and I knew that at least two of Patrick's brothers had fought in the Pacific theater and might very well hate the Japanese. Hate me."

Kellen felt her blood pressure rise as she pictured the scene. A peaceful working-class neighborhood, a white picket fence, a hostile family facing one lone Japanese-American woman.

"Mrs. Sullivan stepped forward, and she said, 'Ye're looking for Patrick, are ye, Ruby Morgade?' I said yes, and she said, 'Ye've come to the wrong place. He's in the graveyard at the edge of town with a white cross planted at his head.'"

Kellen was aghast. "That was no way to tell you!"

"It was a test. I dropped to my knees and wept bitter tears." Ruby's voice choked.

Kellen teared up, too.

Verona sat with her hand over her heart.

"Aileen came to me, wrapped her arms around me, yelled at her sons to help me. I ended up on a lounge on the porch. The test was over, and they took me into their hearts." Ruby sat quietly, gazing at a grave she'd seen long ago and far away. "Patrick had died in 1943, and why should anyone tell me?"

"The Sullivans should have told you!" Rae burned with outrage.

"He'd written them, said I no longer corresponded with him, and his heart was broken."

"Your bastard of a father—" Rae said.

"Rae!" Verona said.

Rae subsided. "Well, he was," she muttered.

Ruby fought a smile. "Yes, my father confiscated my letters, and Patrick's. But Patrick also told his family he suspected foul play, and he feared for me and my fate. So the Sullivans were inclined to believe the best of me. They took me to Patrick's grave, let me weep and place my flowers. They took me to their church and had another memorial service for him, so I could participate. When I told his mother about the baby—" Ruby developed a hitch in her voice "—she cried for me and wished we had that bit of Patrick in this world, and she prayed for the baby's soul. I had never done that. I had cried, but never prayed. I had no surety of God or belief in another world. Turns out, I didn't need it. Aileen Sullivan had enough for the two of us." Ruby smiled with the remnants of lost hope.

"All of her sons had gone to war. Patrick was the one who didn't return. When I left, I had found a comfort of sorts, and a family. I corresponded with Mrs. Sullivan until her death in 1981. Then the Sullivans forgot me. As they should. That was a long time ago."

That broke Rae's heart, and Rae knew that Ruby, while putting on a brave face, was hurt, too. She hugged Ruby and looked into her eyes. "I'm sorry about your baby."

"Thank you, darling girl." Ruby pushed Rae's bangs out of her eyes. "When you read about Patrick and Father and how I lost Aileen…it brought it all back. That's good, to remember what the events of my life have been, the pains and the joys." She looked up at Kellen, and her lips trembled as she smiled. "I look at you girls and think that Aileen would have grown up as brave and strong as you."

"So none of it was true? The stuff my mom said? About you being a spy, and Patrick coming for you, and getting married on the ship, and the twins…?" Rae knew Kellen had made it up, but she clung to the happy ending she had demanded for Ruby.

"I'm afraid none of it is true." Ruby allowed herself a dramatic pause. "Except for the part about being a spy."

# CHAPTER FIFTY-THREE

YOU KNOW, it was funny. Afterward I thought Ruby's words were like a hair dryer dropped into a full-of-water bathtub. We all jerked as if we'd been electrified.

The questions started, and everyone was asking.

"You were a spy?"

"You went to Japan?"

"You spied for the US?"

Ruby relaxed against her pillows and beamed at the fervor she'd caused, and for one moment, I caught a glimpse of the determined young woman she had been. "Yes. Yes. And yes. If you'll recall, General Tempe did ask if I spoke Japanese."

"He had a job for you." Rae spread her arms wide. "Tell us everything."

"If I told you, I'd have to kill you."

Rae collapsed on the bed in despair.

Ruby laughed aloud and patted Rae's ankle. "The information has been declassified, and I have a journal that I wrote about my adventures. When I've passed, the journal will be yours."

That was all we could get out of her, and by that time, she was worn out.

We left her to rest, stayed overnight and returned to the attic the next day. Ruby filled in some of the gaps.

After Ruby's father died and she had returned from her search for Patrick, she realized she couldn't care for the house and the island, and she needed to sell them. But she'd been confined to her attic for so long, she wouldn't, or couldn't, leave. She found a buyer in Elia Di Luca and worked out an agreement that she could remain on the island in her attic for as long as she lived. "Of course," she said with a smile, "I don't think he believed I would live so long."

Inevitably, servants became impossible to find. Hermione had left to get married and returned after her children were grown, to be Ruby's dear friend and companion. The island caretakers were instructed to care for them. First Olof, then Jamie Conkle, provided them with meals and services.

And that was why I saw Jamie in the mansion. Even after we arrived, she continued to try to care for Ruby.

When Hermione died, her family gave Ruby permission to bury her in the Morgade family plot, and Ruby's life went on as before, albeit lonelier. It was only when Olympia arrived that the system got fouled up.

"So the Di Lucas knew you were here?" Max asked.

Ruby hesitated. "Perhaps one or two of them. The older ones. I think, for the most part, I was forgotten."

Max shot a look at Kellen that promised trouble for *someone*.

After Ruby finished her story, Max left to talk to the construction crew. They told him they had been speaking with Ruby. On her death, she wanted the house torn down and all trace of the past erased. She said the ghosts needed to be laid to rest...which made us wonder if Olympia had been crazy after all.

We flew out the next afternoon. Rae offered to leave Luna behind as Ruby's companion and assistance dog, and Ruby gratefully accepted. She promised not to keep Luna too long; only as much time as it took Luna to heal from her injuries. Ruby said a girl and her dog should be together, and we left them resting on the bed.

After we were away from the island, I asked Rae what Ruby had whispered in her ear. Rae said, "She told me when I wanted to confront you with a grievance, I should do it without an audience, and she told me to think about how I'd feel if you yelled at me in front of my friends."

Ruby made it so easy for Max and me to be parents to Rae.

The Di Luca family gave Isla Paraíso to the state of California to be used as a wildlife refuge and funded all future research conducted there by UC San Diego. I knew we wouldn't be visiting again, yet Max, Rae and I would never forget our time there, the bad and the good, the horrors and the glories. There we had become a family.

Back at Yearning Sands Resort, Rae rejoined her friends, went to her camps, got a new phone, declared her life was complete, and on being told in September that Max and I were going to Italy on our honeymoon, threw a massive adolescent tantrum which ended with her being grounded from her friends, her camp and her phone.

As Max said, "I hardly feel like a grown-up. I've got this kid, and I don't know the right way to parent."

*Me, too, sweetheart. Me, too.*

"But we are going on our honeymoon!"

*Most definitely.*

Three weeks after we left Isla Paraíso, Luna returned home with a package addressed to Rae. Rae opened it and cried.

Ruby's journal was inside, and told of operations in the Philippines and Japan, dangerous operations that Ruby survived through guile, cleverness and luck. She had saved many US troops with the intelligence she provided.

We—the Di Luca family—remember and honor Ruby Morgade.

# CHAPTER FIFTY-FOUR

*Washington's Pacific Coast*
*Yearning Sands Resort*
*October of This Year*

KELLEN CAME OUT of the bathroom in her nightgown. She looked at Max, naked and sprawled on the bed pillows, doing his sexy beckoning smile. "Close your eyes and put out your hand," she told him.

Max grinned—he obviously thought she had been swept away by his sexiness and they were galloping off on some fabulous bedtime adventure—and stuck out his hand.

She dropped the small plastic piece into his palm.

He opened his eyes, glanced at it, and dropped it on the sheets. "What is that?"

"Something I just peed on."

He scowled at the plastic strip. "Peed on? But…" He wasn't a stupid man. He knew what she was saying. "But…we never had unprotected sex."

She started to speak, sighed and shook her head in disgust.

He admitted, "Once."

She made the exasperated face at him.

"Only once!" he insisted.

"How many times does it take?"

His voice rose. "You're pregnant?"

"Shh!" Rae was right down the corridor, and yes, sometimes she still had nightmares. "So it would appear."

"Pregnant?" He kept getting louder. "You're going to have a baby? We're going to have a baby?"

Kellen gave up. "That's what pregnant means."

He stood on the bed, bounced on the mattress and crowed, "I am the most potent man in the world."

She leaned against the wall, put her hand on her belly, and laughed at him. "You are such a tool."

"A big, hard, long, potent tool!" Undeterred, he kept jumping.

"Is this as good as your very own F-100 to fix up?"

"Better!" He paused. "An F-100 would be a great Christmas present, though." He leaped onto the floor and hugged her. "You're healthy. I mean, you are healthy now, right? Your hand is healed, and your other hand is improving."

"Because I play the piano every day."

"God help us all, yes."

She pinched him.

"Your brain is completely healed and normal, so you can carry a baby, right?"

"I'll call the doctor in the morning, but yes. I'm fine." She sighed. "I'm nauseated. That's how I knew. I was nauseated with Rae, too. I didn't understand then. But I recognize it now."

"A baby. A baby." She didn't have a pregnant glow, but he did. "We're going to have a baby together."

His excitement began to percolate in her bloodstream. "We are!"

"With this baby, you can enjoy every queasy moment." He was sincere.

"You make it sound so appealing."

His smile became sadder, yet more eager. "To do this together, to bear the burdens of pregnancy and childbirth together… I'll help you every step of the way."

"I know you will." She clutched his shoulders. He was so warm, so strong. So potent. "I trust you."

"You're happy?" It was more than a question. It was a concern, a need for reassurance.

"I'm happy."

He kissed her. And kissed her. "From now on, everything is smooth sailing."

TWO HOURS LATER, Kellen woke with a start. Someone was standing over her in the dark. This time, she wasn't afraid. She knew now who it was. "Rae?"

"Mommy…" Rae's voice was only a breath.

"What's wrong, sweetheart? A nightmare?"

"No…"

She sounded so miserable, Kellen came up on one elbow, and beside her, she felt Max tense. "Are you sick?"

"No," Rae's voice was barely a breath. "I think I've started my period."

*  *  *  *  *

*Read on for a sneak peek at* New York Times
*bestselling author Christina Dodd's next thrilling
novel,* Wrong Alibi, *about a young woman
who escapes into the Alaskan wilderness after
being wrongfully convicted of a brutal crime
and fights to prove her innocence.*

*Midnight Sun Fishing Camp*
*Katchabiggie Lodge, Alaska*
*Eight Years Ago*

JANUARY.

Five and a half hours a day when the sun rose above the horizon.

Storm clouds so thick, daylight never penetrated, and night reigned eternal.

Thirty below zero Fahrenheit.

The hurricane-force wind wrapped frigid temperatures around the lodge, driving through the log cabin construction and the steel roof, ignoring the insulation, creeping inch by inch into the great room where twenty-year-old Petie huddled on a love seat, dressed in a former guest's flannel pajamas and bundled in a Pendleton Northern Lights wool blanket. A wind like this pushed snow through the roof vents, and she knew as soon as the storm stopped, she'd be up in the frigid attic shoveling it out.

Or not. Maybe first the ceiling would fall in on top of her.

Who would know? Who would care?

The storm of the century, online news called it,

before online disappeared in a blast that blew out the
cable like a candle.

For a second long, dark winter, she was the only
living being tending the Midnight Sun cabins and the
lodge, making sure the dark, relentless Alaskan winter didn't do too much damage and in the spring the
camp could open to enthusiastic fishermen, corporate
team building and rugged individualists.

Alone for eight months of the year. No Christmas.
No New Year's. No Valentine's Day. No any day, nothing interesting, just dark dark dark isolation and fear
that she would die out here.

With the internet gone, she waited for the next inevitable event.

The lights went out.

On each of the four walls, a small light-charged
night-light came on to battle feebly against the darkness. Outside, the storm roared. Inside, cold swallowed
the heat with greedy appetite.

Petie sat and stared into a dark so black it hurt her
eyes. And remembered...

*There, against the far back wall of the basement,
in the darkest corner, white plastic covered...some-
thing. Slowly, Petie approached, driven by a terrible
fear. She stopped three feet away, leaned forward and
reached out, far out, to grasp the corner of the plastic,
pull it back and see—*

With a gasp, Petie leaped to her feet.

No. Just no. She couldn't—wouldn't—replay those
memories again.

She tossed the blanket onto the floor and groped for
the flashlights on the table beside her: the big metal
one with a hefty weight and the smaller plastic head-

lamp she could strap to her forehead. She turned on the big one and shined it around the lodge, reassuring herself no one and nothing was here. No ghosts, no zombies, no cruel people making ruthless judgments about the gullible young woman she had been.

Armed with both lights, she moved purposefully out of the great room, through the massive kitchen and toward the utility room.

The door between the kitchen and the utility room was insulated, the first barrier between the lodge and the bitter rattling winds. She opened that door, took a breath of the even more chilly air, stepped into the utility room and shut herself in. There she donned socks, boots, ski pants, an insulated shirt, a cold-weather blanket cut with arm holes, a knit hat and an ancient full-length sealskin Aleut coat with hood. She checked the outside temperature.

Colder now—forty below and with the wind howling, the windchill would be sixty below, seventy below...who knew? Who cared? Exposed flesh froze at twenty-eight degrees, and it froze quicker the colder it got. Frozen was frozen, so she wrapped a scarf around her face and the back of her neck. Then unwrapped it to secure the headlamp low on her forehead. Then wrapped herself up again, trying to cover as much skin as she could before she faced the punishing weather.

She pointed her big flashlight at the generator checklist posted on the wall and read.

*Hawley's reasons why the generator will fail to start.*
*The generator is new and well tested, so the problem is:*

*1. Loose battery cable*
*Solution: Tighten*
*2. Corroded battery connection*
*Solution: Use metal terminal battery brush to*
*clean connections and reattach.*
*3. Dead battery*
*Solution: Change battery in the autumn to avoid*
*ever having to change it in the middle of a major*
*fucking winter storm.*

If she wasn't standing here alone in the dark in the bitter cold, she would have grinned. The owner of the fishing camp, Hawley Foggo, taught all his employees "Hawley's Rules." He applied them to every occurrence of the fishing camp, and that last sounded exactly like him.

The generator used a car battery, and as instructed, in the autumn she had changed it. This was her second year dealing with the battery—it had been easier than the first time, and she felt secure about her work.

So probably this failure was a loose connection or corrosion. Either way, she could fix it and save the lodge from turning into a solid ice cube that wouldn't thaw until spring.

That was, after all, her job.

She shivered.

So much better than her last job, the one that had led to her conviction for a gruesome double murder.

"Okay, Petie, let's grab that metal battery cleaner thingie and get the job done." Which sounded pretty easy when she talked to herself about it, but when she pulled on the insulated ski gloves, they greatly limited her dexterity.

Out of the corner of her eye, a light blinked out.

She looked back into the lodge great room. The night-lights were failing, and soon she really would be alone in the absolute darkness, facing the memories of that long-ago day in the basement.

*Good incentive to hurry.*

She grabbed the wire battery connection cleaner thingie and moved to the outer door.

There she paused and pictured the outdoor layout.

A loosely built lean-to protected the generator from the worst of the weather while allowing the exhaust to escape. That meant she wasn't stepping out into the full force of the storm; she would be as protected as the generator itself. Which was apparently not well enough since the damned thing wasn't working.

She gathered her fortitude and eased the outer door open.

The wind caught it, yanked it wide, and dragged her outside and down the steps. She hung on to the door handle, flailed around on the frozen ground and when she regained her footing, she used all her strength to shove the door closed again.

Then she was alone, outside, in a killer storm, in the massive bleak wilderness that was Alaska.

*Don't miss* Wrong Alibi
*by* New York Times *bestselling author*
*Christina Dodd!*

Copyright © 2020 by Christina Dodd

# BEVERLY LONG

**continues her A.L. McKittridge series with the second book in the series, *No One Saw*.**

**Nobody saw a thing. Or so they say...**

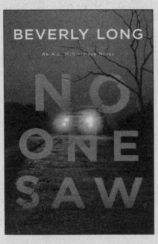

Baywood Police Department detective A.L. McKittridge is no stranger to tough cases, but when five-year-old Emma Whitman disappears from her day care, there isn't a single shred of evidence to go on. Neither the grandmother who dropped her off nor the teacher whose care she was supposed to be in can account for the missing child. There are no witnesses. No trace of where she might have gone. There's only one thing A.L. and his partner, Rena Morgan, are sure of—somebody is lying.

With the clock ticking, A.L. and Rena are under extreme pressure as they discover their instincts are correct: all is not as it seems. The Whitmans are a family with many secrets, and A.L. and Rena will have to race to untangle a growing web of lies if they're going to find the thread that leads them to Emma... before it's too late.

**Coming soon, wherever MIRA Books are sold!**